# MILLTOWN

Best wishes and happy reading,
Rosie.

Regards

Jimmy Higgins x.

# MILLTOWN

Jimmy Higgins

www.jimmyhigginsauthor.co.uk

Matador
9 Priory Business Park
Kibworth Beauchamp
Leicestershire LE8 0RX, UK
Tel: (+44) 116 279 2299
Fax: (+44) 116 279 2277
Email: books@troubador.co.uk
Web: www.troubador.co.uk/matador


ISBN 978 1780885 193

British Library Cataloguing in Publication Data.
A catalogue record for this book is available from the British Library.

Printed and bound in the UK by TJ International, Padstow, Cornwall
Typeset in 11pt Aldine401 BT Roman by Troubador Publishing Ltd, Leicester, UK

Matador is an imprint of Troubador Publishing Ltd

## Dedication

*To my beautiful late wife, Anne Frances,*
*and our three wonderful children Ciaran, Roisin and Mhairi.*

## In Memorium

Most readers will be able to imagine their own 'Milltown'. As the cradle of the industrial revolution, the United Kingdom in general - and the West of Scotland in particular- is full of such towns whose transition from an agricultural community to a commercial/ industrial centre came about with the expansion of such mills across the land during the late eighteenth and nineteenth centuries.

However, my own particular Milltown is Neilston, in East Renfrewshire, Scotland.

What makes this novel particularly pertinent to Neilston is that, unlike almost every other parish in Scotland, at the time of going to press this town currently boasts no public monument recording, or honouring, the dead from the village whose lives were sacrificed in either of the world wars.

In the First World War alone there were at least ninety six men from this small village who joined up, or were conscripted, and who lost their lives in the conflict.

This book is also dedicated, therefore, to those young men named below from Neilston whose lives were wasted in the futile carnage of the 1914-1918 war.

S. Agnew
J.T Eslick
A.J. Campbell
W.M. Honeycombe
H. McArtney
J. Murdoch
W. M. Anderson
R. Ferguson
D. Clark
T.A. Hughes
D. McReady
J. Orr
F.D. Andrew
W.W. Fulton
A. Craig
R. Inglis
D. McCue
D. Paterson
T. Bennett
J. Gillespie
I. Davidson
H.B. Johnston
P. McCusker
W.P.G. Paterson

W. Black
W.M. Gray
G. Docherty
J. Laird
R. McDade
I. Paterson
M. Brophy
A. Hay
F. Donelly
J. Lawns
W.J. McDonald
J. Paton
J. Cairnduff
J. Higgins
T. Dorby
P. Leckie
P. McGuffock
A. Pollock
E. Clannachan
W. Hopkinson
C. Elliot
D. Leitch
D. McKendry
A.M.G. Pollock
R. Cosh

A. Allan
A.R. Ferguson
T. Love
F. McKinlay
J. Porter
A.A. Craig
W. Andrew
T. Fox
K. MacDonald
R. McLintock
T.E. Shemwell
R. Dickson
D. Barr
A. Gebbie
A. Martin DCM
J. McMurdo
J. Smith
P. Donaldson
D. Black
A.C. Graham
S. Maxwell
M. McMahon
A. Stewart
H. Donnelly
J. Blakely

J. Harrigan
R. McArthur
N. McNicol
R. Walker
A.N. Dunlop
J. Brown
J. Hay
H. McAnley
M. Milligan
R. Watson
D. McVean
M.K. McVean
M. Montgomery
P. Munley
T. Munley
B.S. Watt
J. Wilson
A.R. Winning
J. Wood
R. McMaster
W. Munley
T. Murray

Those wishing to support/contribute to the campaign for a war memorial in Neilston to these 96 men from the village whose lives were sacrificed in the First World War should contact:
www.facebook.com/neilstonwarmemorialassociation

*"I don't order you to attack, I order you to die."*

Lieutenant Colonel Mustafa Kemal, (1881-1938) 19th Division at Gallipoli, 1915.
(Later, 'Ataturk', the first president of the Turkish Republic, 1923.)

*"War is organised murder and nothing else."*

Harry Patch, (1898-2009) 7th Duke of Cornwall's Light Infantry and the last survivor of the trench warfare of the First World War.

# The Graves of War

## Thiepval, the Somme, August 4, 2012

… he had a story to tell.

This cataract cripple. This hirpling bag of bones. This bent and trembling bundle of smelly rags.

Miss O'Neil introduced her Primary Seven class to 'Private' Tam Carlton, a local survivor of the Great War, the fiftieth anniversary of which we were apparently 'celebrating'. She called him a "hero".

What was he – or that – to us? We were too impatient to embrace the lingering death of his disfigured memories; too distracted by the moment to pay tribute to his pain, his sacrifice; too attracted by the vibrant promise of Tomorrow to dwell on the decay of this man's past.

For this was 1964, the Swinging Sixties. The world of the Beatles; of Rock and Rolling Stones; of space rockets and fast cars; of Pele and Cassius Clay; of mini-skirts and Carnaby Street; of Top of the Pops and Radio Caroline.

Of Youth.

Through his bronchial rasps he tried to solder the imprint of the horrors he had experienced in his trench at Kruseik Ridge onto our mocking, restless souls. The gap was too wide. Unbridgeable.

His broken gait shuffled this shell-hole of a man's crumbling spirit out of the classroom and into the cold blast of indifference. Rejected by those whom he had once cited as justification for pursuing his own role in the madness and the murder: "For our children's children."

Sometime in the next millennium these anguished voices were silenced forever.

Harry Patch no more. Their nightmares all quietened now, surrendered to a deep serenity.

Standing here in the mist shrouding the Somme, I shiver and gaze on their fields of battle, on their graves of war. Wondering what it must have been like, here and at home. Imagining what *they* must have been like. Asking myself what in God's Name it was all for: these piles of dreams broken by bad faith; these heaps of squandered outrageous courage and blind, blind loyalty, never to be repaid.

The mist begins to lift…

# CHAPTER ONE

# Schiller's Delicatessen

"Es ist nichts. Es ist nichts."

The blood frothed and spilled out of Franz Ferdinand's mouth. It gushed over his uniform and down over his wife, dying at his feet.

Count Harrach struggled to free the Archduke from his tunic.

"I can't get it open! Someone...scissors...a knife...anything!"

"Es ist nichts" proved to be the greatest understatement ever uttered. For this was a 'nothing' which was to kill its author and his wife. A 'nothing' which was to lead to Austro-Hungary declaring war on Serbia; prompt Russia to mobilise against Austro-Hungary; provoke Germany to declare war on France and Russia, immediately prior to invading Belgium and, for this latter transgression, commit Britain to declaring war on Germany.

It was a "nothing" which would lead to the Marne, Passchendaele and the Somme; Vimy Ridge, Tannenberg and Gallipoli.

A "nothing" which would, given time, lead to the Russian Revolution and the Cold War, the rise of Nazi Germany and the Second World War, the Treaty of Versailles and Srebrenica.

And all over a sandwich and a slipped gear!

To Gavrilo Princip of the Serbian Black Hand it certainly wasn't "nothing".

He was one of the six men placed along the Appel Quay in Sarajevo mingling with the crowds – those there for the horses and the hats, the pomp and the parade, the music and the majesty.

Not that Gavrilo and his friends were there to appreciate any of those things. He, like them, was there for one reason and one reason only: to assassinate Archduke Franz Ferdinand, heir to the Austro-Hungarian Empire.

By the time he had seen the Royal motorcade whizz by him, one of his accomplices had already stalled in the act of throwing his bomb – frozen to the spot, eyes wide open like a choked chicken, mouth gaping darkly like a disused tunnel, arms straight down by his side. It was a pose that he would be fated to repeat on a cold morning in February 1915 at the end of a judicial rope.

Next up the line, another accomplice had managed to throw his home-made bomb at the Royal car. However, he had miscalculated the timing of the delay fuse and it bounced harmlessly off the roof, exploding instead under the car two behind in the entourage.

At once Loyka, the Archduke's chauffeur, sped out of his stately crawl and away from the adulating crowd to make good his escape to the town hall, where a no less warm but altogether more courteous reception lay in wait.

After giving a tongue-lashing to the Mayor, who – as Countess Sophie gently reminded her husband – hadn't actually flung any bombs in anger so far, Ferdinand calmed down and resolved to change his itinerary in order to pay a visit to those who were now in hospital due to injuries sustained in the attack.

Gavrilo Princip, meanwhile, was fuming.

To be fair he had been out of sorts all day. His girlfriend had refused the virginal Princip sex on the eve of what may very well have been his last day on earth. He confessed to one of his fellow assailants that he was "So angry" that he could "shoot God himself."

The sight of the Royal pristine plumage driving past disconcertingly unruffled did nothing to assuage his humour.

Nor did the cries of the stunned crowd offer much encouragement: "Bomb…! Explosion…! Safe…!"

Safe?

After all the risks? All the sacrifices? Safe?!

The drama over, cold reality began to reassert itself.

The reality of another failure. The reality of the tuberculosis which would kill him within the next few years. The very pressing reality of his immediate hunger.

His aimless meanderings over the past few hours since the botched attempt had randomly brought his feet to the Latin Bridge. Princip used them now to walk purposefully across from there to the dead end opposite in Franz Josef Street. He quickly found what he was looking for: Schiller's Delicatessen.

He entered and ordered a sandwich, just as the wheels of the Royal car drew to a stop outside. It presented the Archduke and the rest of the Royal cast to Princip, like the offering of a pod of beached whales to a Faroese fisherman.

He rushed out, forgoing his sandwich.

Loyka saw him coming. Saw him reach for his Browning from under his coat. He tried to reverse at high speed. His foot slipped off the clutch. The car stalled.

A hapless pedestrian strayed in the way of the advancing Princip only to be pistol-whipped to the ground.

Loyka frantically attempted to restart the engine.

A mere five feet away now, Princip fired into the car. A bullet tore through the Archduke's jugular. His second bullet missed his intended target, General Potiorek, and entered Sophie's abdomen instead.

Blood from the Archduke splattered over Count Harrach, who was standing on the running board.

"What happened to you?" asked a bemused Countess just before slumping unconscious onto Franz Ferdinand's lap.

"Don't die Sophie! Don't die! Live for our children!" implored the Archduke.

"Is your Highness seriously hurt?" Count Harrach enquired impotently.

"Es ist nichts. Es ist nichts!"

The war to end all wars had begun.

CHAPTER TWO

# A Kick in the Gorbals

The girls lined up on the opposite side of the hall, talking animatedly to one another as if no one else was there. Certainly not the fifty or so testosteroned young men staring longingly across at them, petrified and pitiful.

As the band struck up the Al Jolson hit of the day, 'You Made Me Love You', one little braveheart timidly crossed the great divide to ask the girl at the top of the line for a dance. She refused. And the next. And the next after that. Until, eventually, he was right at the bottom of the line facing bonnie Elspeth Farmer who also refused, in spite of herself, out of the pressure of expectation created by the sheer mass weight of all the preceding refusals.

Just as he was slouching away from his forlorn quest, big Lachie McMillan stepped forward.

"Thanks fur askin', Wullie," Lachie chortled gleefully as he picked his 'partner' up from under the arms and whisked him through space and across the floor in a mock dance.

"Lachie, whit ur ye daein'? Pit me doon! Pit me doon!" Wullie cried helplessly, as he struggled in vain against fresh air and Lachie's superior strength.

The boys cheered and wolf-whistled. The girls looked on disdainfully at this boisterous behaviour, with the exception of Marilyn Heron, who laughed too heartily and with forced affectation all the way to the toilet, occasioned by the mood of the moment.

Lachie, having enjoyed *his* moment in the spotlight, dutifully put Wullie down.

"See you Lachie, ye're a big eejit," spat Wullie bitterly. "And for by, ye're an eejit wi' a big mooth an' an even bigger erse."

4

"Aye, an' big fermer's haunds tae," Lachie retorted as he grabbed Wullie by the throat and pretended to strangle him with extras.

"Right, Lachie, ye've hud yer fun. Leave him alane noo."

Lachie turned to see the still, dark, menacing figure of Archie Ferguson.

Archie's eyes bore straight through to the back of Lachie's head. His chiselled face set, he proceeded grimly to the task.

The atmosphere in the hall changed. The band stopped playing. Young men crushed forward. Young women shrank into the wall.

"Fight…! Fight…! Fight…!" the audience at ringside cried.

A panic entered Lachie's eyes. Confused. Not quite sure how to respond. He grabbed hold of Wullie from behind.

"Whit, Archie? Surely ye widnae fight me ower a wee runt like this?"

Archie's face lightened.

"Ach, yer right Lachie. Whit wis Ah thinkin'?" he said, extending a hand of friendship and reconciliation.

A relieved Lachie let Wullie go and stretched out his hand in return.

"Ah thought as much…"

The words flew back down Lachie's throat as Archie's fist crashed into his mouth. Red blood sprayed across the hall.

Lachie hurtled back.

"Archie, Ah didnae mean him ony herm, so Ah didnae." Turning to Wullie pleadingly he cried, "Sure Ah didnae, Wullie? Ah wis just huvin' a bit o' fun…Ye're no' hurt ur ye, Wullie? Sure ye're no' hurt?"

"Doon oan yer knees, Lachie, and apologise tae ma wee freen' here fur embarrassin' him in front o' aw these lassies."

Lachie thought about this for a split second, but Archie's fist remained threateningly poised. Slowly, reluctantly, Lachie went down on his knees.

"Look, Archie, there's nae need…" Wullie tried to intervene.

"Apologise!" Archie barked.

"Ah'm sorry, so Ah um Wullie," Lachie whined pathetically.

"Well, look at that, wid ye? It looks like ye managed tae huv a dance wi' a lassie efter aw', Wullie," Archie sneered callously over Lachie's cowed and quivering hulk.

★ ★ ★ ★ ★

Micky sat by the grate, aimlessly stirring the coals with a poker. Contorted faces looked back, melted away and re-formed. Animal shapes played there too. And then there was Britain, or was it Italy? Witches and wizards, goblins and fairies…

"Should ye no be aboot yersel' lookin' fur work instead o' tryin' tae get hauf wey up the lum?"

"Aye, Maw," Micky groaned.

Officially, 19-year-old Micky McGoldrick had left school at 14, although in truth he actually left at least two years before that. He could read, write and count well enough to get by. He knew his Bible, even if he didn't know what to think about it.

And he knew his Marx.

"Property is theft" was a maxim that he was fond of quoting to the men at Pigs' Square, a local meeting place where the men of the village caught short of the price of a pint could escape the constraints of the hearth and meet to express their opinions – or, as Raymond Patterson put it, "Bum their load" – on anything and everything.

If property was indeed theft, however, then neither Micky nor any of his family, friends or neighbours could be accused of anything more than petty larceny, given that they owned virtually nothing – the clothes they stood up in, some miserable bits of furniture and, exceptionally, a hand-me-down fiddle.

'Plod' McCarthy once owned a horse, right enough, that he swore had just turned up at his door one day. He kept it in the drying green at the back of the tenement, tethered to a pole set in cement. However, it disappeared just as quickly, leaving Plod with a black eye in the process.

Finding employment locally was difficult for Micky. The biggest employer for miles around, the local textile mill which employed well over a thousand workers, was out of the question due to Micky's support there in 1910 of one of the country's first all-female strikes.

It was this event which introduced Micky to socialism, as many of the Red Clydesiders – Maxton, McShane and even John Maclean himself (who dreamt of turning Glasgow into a Petrograd) – all descended on Milltown "tae organise the lassies." The lassies had ideas of their own, though, which included marching the ten miles from Milltown to the mill manager's home in the affluent Pollokshields area of Glasgow. Once there they besieged the poor mannie and his wife and weans with stirring songs, defiant chants and abuse of a somewhat personal nature.

It worked. Their terms were met after 17 days, but Micky the bosses remembered well enough to make sure that he was never offered a position at the mill.

Seasonal work on the farms and odd labouring jobs here and there peppered Micky's occupational history.

He stepped away from the fire.

"God it moves!" gasped his mother.

"By God's grace," Micky replied routinely.

"Father O'Keefe was just sayin' the other day that they're lookin' fur another man tae work in St Conval's cemetery, doon in Arthur Lea. Wid ye no' fancy tryin' yer hand at that, at least fur a while. It's a good line o' work wi' steady business. Ah mean, there's folk dyin' noo that never died afore."

"Aye, maybe Ah wull, Maw. Wull Ah go up and see him then?"

"Naw, son, why don't ye just coorie roon by yer wee fire there an' wait till it comes intae the good Faither's heid tae come doon an' offer you the job afore ony o' the other unemployed men in the village!"

"OK, Maw, Ah'll call up the day."

"Where ur ye aff tae onywey?"

"Ah'm awa' tae jine the Salvation Army, Maw, whit else?"

"Dinnae build yer hopes up, son. Ye'll probably fail the medical."

★ ★ ★ ★ ★

"And Ah just said tae him, so Ah did, Ah said, 'Whit dae *you* know aboot fishin', Tommy? You don't even like fish. Plus, fur by, ye've never caught a fish that wisnae already deid, aw covered in chips and wrapped in yesterday's news.'"

"You said that tae big Tommy Finnegan?" questioned an impressed guest of the Bottom Shop – a local pub, so called as it was situated downhill from the 'Top Shop', a rival drinking establishment also known as the Traveller's Rest.

Social drinking featured very heavily in Milltown, as elsewhere in West Central Scotland. In the nineteenth century, before licensing laws came into being, there were reputed to be over forty drinking establishments to serve the needs of a village of just over a few thousand inhabitants.

"So whit did Tommy say tae that?" asked another of the Bottom Shop's customers.

"He tried tae say that he learned everythin' there wis tae know aboot fishin' frae books. And Ah just said, 'How did ye manage that Tommy when ye cannae even read?' "

A ripple of laughter went round the pub.

"Ah mean, Ah'm no' sayin' that Tommy disnae huv ony books in his hoose, but Ah know fur a fact he husnae managed tae colour them aw in yet?"

More laughter.

"Shite!" cried a customer sitting at the bar as some beer spilled onto his shirt. "Look whit ye made me dae wi' aw this laughin'."

"Well, if ye wahnt tae stoap laughin' just read the papers. They're aw goin' on aboot this Austrian bloke that's been shot in the Balkans."

"Shot in the Balkans, eh? That sounds as painful as gettin' a kick in the Gorbals," piped up a local wit.

"Aye, that wid be painful right enough," a squirming customer mused.

"So, whit's aw this got tae dae wi' us onywey?" queried a Glasgow Irishman, injecting a serious note into the proceedings.

"The square root tae the power plus o' absolutely fuck all!" pronounced the barman. And the matter was closed.

★ ★ ★ ★ ★

Lachie's mother was a huge wee woman. Every morning around nine o'clock the window was flung open to be followed by an enormous bosom resting on the sill. This provided a foundation for two fat elbows which served as supporting pillars for the all-seeing, all-knowing orb that was her head.

When she was not taking in washing for the monied people of the village, she was the carrier of local gossip. Nothing was missed, everything analysed from a visceral perspective, to be commented upon viciously. She hovered above the street, from her tenement set back on a small hill, like a raptor, swooping down and over all tasty items of gossip.

From the age when he could dress himself (which admittedly wasn't until he was about fourteen) Lachie had virtually brought himself up. A piece and jam often sufficed as his tea and a skelp round the ear was what routinely passed for maternal bonding.

That day her son's swollen lip was hardly noticed on account of the stranger in the street. Tall, of indeterminate age, an aquiline nose, piercing blue eyes that had perhaps seen too much, a rash of boils on his head and the voice of a raspy angel which was the key to his fortune, if a miserable fortune at that. A man with no name, he was known to the local children as 'Breezy Breeks' on account of his diaphanous trousers, which were held up precariously by some string.

Now, Breezy would call into the village from some clandestine hideout nearby and walk around the streets, pausing every hundred

9

yards or so to sing the new hot Gospel hit, 'The Old Rugged Cross'. His trick then was to sell the handwritten words of the song round the nearby doors for a halfpenny. At least that was the plan.

Arriving beneath Aggie McMillan's window must have seemed like a Cyrano de Bergerac moment. And so he sang his little black heart out, while Aggie, doubling as Roxane, looked down from on high.

The end of his performance was treated with a "So whit?" silence and a glassy stare.

After an uncomfortable shuffle, Breezy looked directly up at Aggie and, summoning up the courage from somewhere in his leaky boots, asked her if she wanted to buy the words of the song for a halfpenny.

Aggie looked down from her ivory sill with cold, unfeeling eyes and a sharp sense of the denouement about to follow and said, "Naw, mister, Ah widnae gie ye a hae'penny fur 'The Old Rugged Cross' – suppose ye wur nailed tae it!"

★ ★ ★ ★ ★

Johnny Byrne was hungry. A consequence of him having no money and food not being freely available from the shops – well, not legally at any rate.

As a very young man he had been in the Boer War and had seen action at Spion Kop, for which he had received a medal for gallantry or, as he would later refer to it disparagingly, a medal for dysentery.

Life had not been kind since his return. No jobs. No housing the heroes. Only poverty and misery as constant companions. The fruits of the greatest Empire the world had ever seen were too far up the tree to be enjoyed in the Byrne household.

However, Johnny was nothing if not resourceful. He was adept at helping himself to the produce of the land: turnips, cabbages, potatoes and apples, when in season, just seemed to turn up in his shoulder bag after a day's walk in the countryside. And he was a hunter, especially during the hungry gap months – rabbits, fish, deer and even, it was rumoured, squirrels, stoats, pigeons and crows found their way from their natural habitat into Johnny's pot.

"So tell me, Johnny," asked Ian Martin one day at Pigs' Square, "if ye wur huntin' rabbits wi' a dug, why wid ye no use a feckin' greyhound, given it's feckin' speed an' all?"

"Well," started Johnny laconically, " ye see, Ian, rabbits tend tae live in the country and in the country there tend tae be a lot o' hills: big wans, small wans, in between wans…"

"So…?"

"So ye set the feckin' greyhound efter the feckin' rabbit. Oh, it chases it awright, but then, like as not, the feckin' rabbit disappears ower wan o' them feckin' hills. Now tae a feckin' greyhound, bein' so feckin' stupid, oot o' sight is oot o' tiny feckin' mind and it forgets whit the feck it's runnin' fur. Of course then it stops, barks at the trees fur a wee bit, before toddlin' aff back tae his demented feckin' maister."

"You just made that up," sighed an incredulous Ian.

"Ye'll never know, Ian. Ye'll never know."

But Johnny and his family were hungry. So hungry that he walked out into the country to the Harelaw Dam and set an otter – a totally illegal square wooden board designed to float above scores of baited metal hooks attached to its underside – to ensnare a lorry load of fish.

Making his way back across the fields with his catch, he was stopped by the farmer and owner of the dam.

"Whit huv ye goat in the bag, Johnny?" (As if maybe he didn't know.)

"Ah, that wid be fish, Mister Robertson."

"And wid that be fish frae ma dam, Johnny?"

"Aye that wid be where Ah fun' them awright."

"Well then, Johnny, ye're just efter stealin' ma fish."

"*Your* fish, Mister Robertson?"

"Aye, Johnny… *Ma* fish!"

"Well, Mister Robertson, if Ah hud a hat Ah wid need tae take it aff tae ye, 'coz Ah never yet met a man who could make a fish."

And for his wit the gallant (official) Johnny, hero of Spion Kop and defender of His Majesty's illegally acquired territories in the far-flung reaches of the British Empire, was now enjoying free board and lodgings in Glasgow's Barlinnie penitentiary at the pleasure of King George the Fifth.

"Too easily feckin' pleased if ye ask me!" quoth his ungrateful guest.

★ ★ ★ ★ ★

Reverend John McDonald's brain was working overtime. The Church of Scotland Minister of Milltown Parish Church was engaged in his passionate hobby of many years standing: unsolved murders.

Indeed he had already embarked on the writing of a book which was to be entitled, 'They Got Away with Murder'.

It would include many of the celebrated great Whodunnits? Unsolved crimes like the Austin, Texas murders, the Princes in the Tower and Lizzie Borden.

But none more celebrated than the one currently under review: Jack the Ripper. This series of crimes had perplexed and confounded the best minds of his generation. Now Milltown's minister was confronting the problem as well, with an approach which we may today consider to have been the precursor of criminal profiling.

First of all, the victims.

Some people claimed as many as eighteen murders on the Ripper's behalf. Of the eleven outstanding in most people's minds, the minister had already dismissed those of Emma Smith, Martha Tabram, Rose Mylett, Alice McKenzie, Frances Coles and the mysterious, somewhat sinister, 'Unidentified Woman'.

Each of these unfortunate victims had failed the test of subscribing to the Ripper's signature: his stylistic technique. They betrayed too many inconsistencies, unlike the canonical five of Mary Ann Nicholls, Annie Chapman, Elizabeth Stride, Catherine Eddowes and Mary Jane Kelly.

Their murders were all perfectly aligned dramaturgically. All had been prostitutes, all had been murdered within the Whitechapel area of London, all had been found with their throats cut, all had been found with their abdomens ripped open (hence the sobriquet), and all had been found with internal organs removed.

Anything less, thought the Reverend John, was at best a poor copycat version not to be confused with the real thing.

"What are you doing, darling?" asked the minister's wife sweetly.

"Working on my sermon for next Sunday," the good minister lied.

"Now, don't be making it too long dear. Last Sunday's was a marathon. Mrs Spooner's head kept dropping and drooping, much to the amusement of those sitting behind her. Are you going to mention the European crisis?"

"No dear, it'll pass over – unlike the Passover."

"It's what's on people's minds."

"Seven days are a long time in newspaper headlines. Let's see where we are this time next week. I may take it up then."

"OK darling. Toodley 'bye."

The other 'signature' was the timing. They all happened not just within a confined area, but within a confined timescale: from August 31, 1888 to November 9, 1888 – then they stopped. To the minister's mind this implied that the murderer had moved into the area shortly before the murders began and moved away again (or died) almost immediately after eviscerating his last victim.

"It is very unlikely," the minister thought to himself, "that he would have been able to stop just like that and return to polite society after tasting the fruits of his evil trade."

13

On considering the type of person the Ripper was likely to be, the minister had drawn up a list which included:

A misogynist. (Obviously!)

Low self-esteem. (Needed to be in control.)

A particular hatred of prostitutes. ( Religious intolerance? Bad experience?)

Someone who had lacked love as a child. (Abused? Neglected? Orphaned?)

Someone with a history of violence. (Criminal record?)

Probably between the ages of 25 and 35. (Give or take.)

He compared his list with the suspect currently on the Reverend McDonald's radar. He ticked every box. His name was William Henry Bury.

And even more than ticking the boxes, God had given a sign!

★ ★ ★ ★ ★

Pigs' Square was quiet tonight, probably on account of the grey drizzle and the biting cold which was edging towards freezing. The temperature was even lower if you factored in the wind chill, which no one had heard of then but everyone could feel.

"Mrs MacDuff" – Todd always referred to his wife as such – "was frettin' the other day aboot us gaun tae war ower this Archduke that's just been shot. Ah just said tae her, 'Mrs MacDuff, dinnae fash yersel'. There'll be nae war.' "

"How can ye be so sure, Todd?" asked Archie Currie.

"Wars ur a thing o' the past, Archie. Countries noo ur too interdependent economically tae fight each other. There can be nae winners, ergo nae mair wars."

At this his head made a pecking gesture, emphasising the finality of his point, almost like a visual full stop. Todd liked to have the last word on everything.

"Somebody should tell the Germans then," retorted Archie. "Ah'm readin' a book the noo by a guy called Bernhardi. It's called

'*Germany and the Next War*'. He believes that war is part and parcel o' evolution where the fittest survive and the weak disappear. He believes in Darwin and aw that shite. Germany, he says, is the up and coming super race to take ower frae the weak and degenerate British."

"Ah'll tell ye whit Ah think," piped up Bertie Boyle, father of Wullie. "Onywan who says there'll be nae mair wars might as well try and tell us that the Pope wull be the next Moderator o' the Church o' Scotland an' heid o' the Orange Ludge for by, 'cos there's always been wars and Britain's aye been at the heart o' them."

"Ye're right there, Bertie," Archie agreed. "Britain manufactures wars aw ower the wurrld tae reduce unemployment. Ye don't need a job if ye're deid."

"But why noo? Why ower this? Who in Britain gies a fiddler's fuck ower some upper class Austrian twit who apparently isnae even liked by his ain people? How in the name o' Christ does that affect us?" cried an impassioned Todd.

"It won't be aboot ony Austrian Archduke," said Archie Currie. "Germany wahnts a piece o' oor action an' she knows that she's gonnae huv tae fight us fur it. Why else dae ye think she's built the Dreadnought?"

"That wis just posturin'," replied Todd dismissively. "Germany could never compete wi' Britain at sea. Nae country in the world can, never mind a country no' yet fifty years old whose people prance aroon in lederhosen." Peck, peck, peck. Game set and match.

Sleekit Tam spat aimlessly into the air, following the saliva's progress intently, as if somehow its form and substance gave purpose to his presence. "Iceland," he pronounced dourly as his phlegm splattered and settled on the pavement.

Archie Currie looked across at the clock on the kirk tower. "Ah'll huvtae go up by. Ah'll see youse aw later."

"Aye, six o'clock. Time tae fin' oot whit Mrs MacDuff hus made Mr MacDuff fur his tea."

15

"Wur ye at the dance oan Saturday night?" Alice Henderson asked Jeanie Broon as they took their tea break on the fire escape landing outside the mill.

"Naw, but Ah heard there wis a fight."

"No' so much o' a fight, Jeanie. Mair like a slap and tickle."

"Did ye get a lumber then, Alice?"

"Naw, Ah hud tae walk hame aw by masel. Nae airm tae clique, nae mooth tae kiss. Still, Ah'm gaun tae Ronnie Leach's twenty-first party on Friday night. Ah hope tae make up fur it there. Ur ye gaun yersel?"

"Ah wid love tae, but Ah'm gaun tae huv tea wi' Harry's parents oan Friday on account o' Ah've been gaun oot wi their son fur the last three months."

"Aw, that'll be nice!"

"Naw it wullnae. It'll be borin' as fuck. Besides, Ah'm gonnae chuck Harry soon."

"Why?"

"He's as borin' as fuck as well. Nice guy. Very respectable. Teacher's son and aw that. But, well, three months and only a good night kiss at the end of every date tae show for it. Ah'm beginnin' tae wunner aboot him."

"Just pass him ma way, Jeanie. It's been ages since Ah've hud a kiss o' ony description."

"Besides, Ah fancy somewan else."

"Who?"

"Naw, Ah cannae…"

"Aye ye can. Who?"

"Well… if ye promise no' tae tell onywan."

"Cross ma tits and hope tae die."

"Oh, awright then. Archie Ferguson."

"Archie Ferguson! He wis in the fight on Saturday night. He can fair handle himsel', so he can."

"If he wis wi' me, Alice, he widnae need tae handle himsel'."

Their raucous laughter reached a crescendo just as Paddy Moran came through the door, fag in hand already lit. Paddy was an older man who wandered round the floors of number two mill lifting, fetching, cleaning and clearing. Many people suspected Paddy, with his roving commission, of being a spy for the bosses. They certainly seemed to have been particularly well informed of the workers' intentions in number two mill during the strike of 1910. Consequently, he wasn't very popular among the girls.

"Can onywan join the party?" asked Paddy.

"Well noo, that depends," spat Alice, belligerently.

"Depends on whit?" Paddy asked, failing to catch the implication in Alice's tone.

"Well, Paddy, let's go through the list, wull we?"

"Whit list?"

"Can ye sing? Naw!

"Can ye dance? Naw!" (Jeanie, by this time, was joining in the response with gusto.)

"Can ye tell jokes? Naw!

"Can ye juggle yer balls? Naw!

"But Ah'll tell ye whit ye can dae, Paddy."

"Whit wid that be?" Paddy asked with rising optimism.

"Ye can fuck off!"

In the face of such withering mockery, Paddy flicked his cigarette dout over the bannister, shook his head and said pathetically, "Ah wis only tryin' tae be friendly lassies, that's aw."

As his hinnermost disappeared back through the door, Jeanie said, "He gies me the creeps. They say he spies fur the bosses."

"They can fuck off as well."

"Listen, Alice, Ah've got somethin' tae tell ye…"

"Whit, ye're no' ur ye?!"

"Naw, it's nothin' like that. It's just that ma brother Craig's jined the army."

"Does he like fightin' or does he just like the thought o' walkin' aboot in a uniform."

"Naw, he's just sick o' no' huvin' a job. But they say there's gonnae be a war, an' a big war at that. It's terrifyin' ma maw and da'. Me tae."

"Aye, Jeanie, they say that the moon's made o' cheese, but Ah bet ye it isnae. Dinnae worry Jeanie, there'll be nae war – unless Paddy Moran comes back through that door wi' wan o they bosses."

★ ★ ★ ★ ★

Father John O'Keefe, Father Dannfald's curate at St Thomas' Roman Catholic church in Milltown, was getting on in years. Probably late sixties. A Dublin man, he had been born around the time of the Irish famine. To Father O'Keefe that tragedy – which resulted in one million of the population dying of starvation and a further one million forced into exile in overcrowded, disease-ridden ships across the Atlantic – was not an act of God but an act of ethnic cleansing by the English of which Cromwell would have been proud. The cost of Trevelyn's corn was the price of English wickedness towards the Irish. Here be devils.

"For how could God inflict such misery on the Irish and Him an Irishman Himself?" he would say. Father O'Keefe believed that the Irish were the Lost Tribe of Israel. "It says it in the very *Leabar Gabala* itself," he ranted from the pulpit, "which to those of you who have lost the special gift of your Irish tongue, or even your sense of Irish history, means 'The Book of Invasions' – the true and authenticated ancient written account of how God's chosen people ended up in the land that God had reserved for them, that being Ireland."

Indeed, the parishioners of St Thomas' were treated to stories of the Children of Lir alongside the Children of Abraham, Bricriu's Feast alongside The Wedding Feast at Cana, and Deirdre and the Sorrows alongside The Sorrowful Mysteries. Father O'Keefe intermixed the two traditions so completely that it was often impossible to tell which had come from the Bible and which from the Ulster Cycle.

He was a priest renowned for somnolent sermons which could last an interminable forty-five minutes without taking time for breath or thought.

The signal that the faithful were about to be indulged in a rambling tour of the good priest's moral entrails was given in the form of a pause just after the Gospel Acclamations and immediately before the Nicene Creed.

If, on the other hand, he launched directly from the Acclamations into "Credo in unum Deum, Patrem Omnipotentum..." (I believe in One God, the Father the Almighty) then they were off the hook. However, the merest hint of a delay and the day, never mind the mass, just got a whole lot longer.

And so it came to pass on this scorcher of a summer's day, with the small church packed with sweaty, unwashed bodies (and each one of them praying that the inspiration of the Holy Spirit would be on holiday this fine morning) that he halted just before the Creed.

The shuffle of uncomfortable souls getting ready to suffer the oppressive heat for an extended duration seemed to register a collective "Oh, fuck!"

Father O'Keefe surveyed his discomfited congregation severely, allowing the crushing disappointment to settle into a sense of resignation, before proclaiming: "So yez t'ink it's hot? Well, yez better be good!

"Credo in unum Deum, Patrem Omnipotentum..."

★ ★ ★ ★ ★

"Ye see, Calum, in this life it's just as important tae know whit ye urnae as much as whit ye ur. And whit ur ye no', Calum?"

"A Kafflic, Daddy."

"Ye're right there, Calum. Nae son o' Eddie Millar's gonnae talk tae lumps o' porcelain or kiss a Bishop's ring."

"Daddy, whit is a Kafflik?"

"Just somethin' ye're no' an' that's aw ye need tae know. Tell the boy, Sandra."

"Ye're no' a Catholic son. Ye're a wee Protestant."

"Whit's a Prodesunt, Mammy?"

"Somebody that's no' a Catholic."

"Is Gerry Collins a Prodesunt or a Kafflik, Mammy?"

"Whit school does he go tae Calum?"

"St Thomas' Primary."

"He's a Catholic then."

"Is that good…?"

"Is that good!" exclaimed an exasperated Eddie in disgust. "Is that good?! Tell him Sandra, tell him!"

"Naw, son, it's no' good. Catholics ur traitors."

"Whit's a traitor, Mammy."

"A traitor's a person who disnae like oor King George and likes the Pope in Rome instead."

"When did Gerry Collins meet King George?"

"Naw, Ah'm no' sayin' he ever met him…"

"So how can he no' like him if he disnae know him?"

" 'Cos he's a Catholic," Eddie intervened, "and they're aw stupid and full o' superstitions, that's why. They dae whit they're tellt by an auld man who thinks he's God."

"Is the auld man God, Daddy?"

"Calum, Ah'm beginnin' tae wonder if you ur ma son. Of course he's no' God. Only God's God," Eddie explained. "Catholics believe in leprechauns and the little people and rubbish like that."

"Do leprechauns and the little people exist, Daddy?"

"Of course no', Calum. Tell him Sandra, tell him!"

"Naw of course they don't, son," Sandra confirmed.

"How dae ye know they don't exist, daddy?"

" 'Cos ye cannae see them, can ye!" Eddie answered with a triumphal finality.

Calum quietened at this response and reflected on the bigger question which lay behind it, before piping up, "Daddy, do you believe in God?"

"Of course Ah believe in God, son."

"So you can see God then!"

★ ★ ★ ★ ★

Mr Anthony O'Neil was a teacher in St Thomas' school, Milltown. He was a kindly man who very rarely used the belt, and even then it was usually to punish a miscreant from one of his female colleagues' classes who felt the need for her pupil to be punished by a man. As the only male teacher in the school he was uniquely placed to fulfil that role.

One of his passions was Modern Studies, before the subject was ever on the curriculum or even had a name. He felt that it was important for his pupils to know what was actually happening in the world and to feel a living connection with it. Especially given that he taught the Advanced Division, those pupils who were not going to continue with their education beyond the age of fourteen and who had not yet passed their leaving certificate. These were the ones who were due to leave school and join the 'real world' within the next few years.

His pedagogy ran counter to the philosophy prevalent at the time that, "A child should be seen and not heard." Instead, he was more of the St Augustine school of thought which proclaimed, "I learned not from those who taught me, but from those who talked with me."

Today he was attempting to share his interest-cum-concern, over the recent troubling headlines involving events in Europe. It wasn't an easy task.

21

"OK Patrick, you're Austria. You can hold this flag. Your country's here on the map. See, next to Germany and Italy."

"Sir, can Ah be Italy. Ma granny's Italian."

"Sorry, Maria, I'm afraid I left the Italian flag I made back at home. We'll need to carry on without it."

"Aw, sir," sighed a disappointed Maria.

"Is war like a game o' fitba, wi' winners and losers and can sometimes end up in a draw?" Charlie asked.

"To that extent, yes, Charlie. But that's where the comparison ends. In war people get killed and property gets destroyed, so it's not really a game."

"We're the best at wars, aren't we, sir?" John said proudly.

"Yes, John, we are the strongest nation in the world, but that's not necessarily something to boast about."

"So who ur we gonnae fight then?" asked Thomas. "Ma daddy says that we're gonnae huv tae fight France and Germany someday, so we might as weel fight baith o' them noo and get it ower wi'."

"That, Thomas, is precisely the point of this exercise – to see who might end up at war with whom and why. So let's get on with it, shall we? Right, Matthew you're Serbia. Serbia is here on the map over by Hungary, Rumania and Bulgaria. Here, take its flag, Matthew."

"Serbia!" cried Matthew with distaste, "Can Ah no' get a real country?"

"Serbia is a real country, Matthew," Mr O'Neil explained. "It's just that it used to be ruled by another country."

"Ah've changed ma mind," Maria announced, "Ah wahnt tae be Scotland."

"I'm sorry, Maria. I don't have a Scottish flag either."

"Aw, sir! Thon's a scunner! Ah'm no' playin' then!"

"So we won't be in the war?" asked Marilyn.

"We might be, Marilyn, but as Britain, not Scotland."

"Are we ruled by another country?" asked Matthew.

"Yes...er, no...er, not exactly. Our government is in England, so to that extent yes. But Scotland is still Scotland."

"Will we get tae fight England in this game?" Alex asked with enthusiasm.

"No, Alex. Why would we want to fight England?"

" 'Cos we hate the English and they hate us," Alex replied assertively.

"And we've hud loads o' wars against them," John added.

"We could go to war wi' Ireland against England and then everywan wid be happy," suggested Frank.

"Ah bags tae be Robert The Bruce," shouted Gerry who had just woken up.

"He's deid…Ah think…Isn't he no', sir?" queried Marilyn.

"Only for about six hundred years or so," Mr O'Neil replied. "Now, let's get on with this. Mary, you're Mother Russia. See, here it is on the map and this is its flag"

"You're really big!" observed Frank.

"You callin' me fat, ya wee plook ye?!" Mary retorted angrily.

"Now, Mary, that's enough. Frank was just pointing out that *Russia* is really big and he's right. It's the largest country in Europe and one of the biggest in the world."

"Are we big, sir?" asked Helen.

"No, Helen. Compared to countries like Russia and China and India we're very small, but we're probably the most important country in the world because of our Empire," Mr O'Neil answered. "Right, John, you can be Britain. Here's a Union Jack for you. Can anyone show me Britain on the map? Not quite, Gerry, that's Australia on the other side of the world. It's up here. You can see that we're an island because we are surrounded by water."

"Is the whole world an island then, because the whole world is surrounded by water?" Brian asked.

"Whit's that smell?" erupted Jane.

"It wisnae me. It must huv been you," said a flushed Michael defensively.

"Oh Gawd, open they windaes afore we aw get gassed," pleaded Margaret.

Mr O'Neil duly obliged.

"Now, whose flag is this?" asked the teacher, holding up the red, white and blue tricolour.

"It's no' mine onywey," a concerned Gerry answered.

"No, Gerry, I mean which country has this flag."

"Is it Norway?" Brian suggested.

"No, Brian. Gerry, again?"

"Africa?"

"No, that's a continent, Gerry. It doesn't have a flag."

"Gie in," submitted Patrick.

"Well then, Patrick, it's France. Thomas, you can be France. Here it is on the map next to Germany and Belgium."

"Whit language dae they speak in France, sir?" asked George.

"French."

"Can they no' speak English?" asked Marilyn.

"No, why should they, Marilyn? They've got their own language."

"Whit's the point o' that if naebody can unnerstaun them?" Marilyn wondered out loud.

"But...but..." the teacher stammered.

"A big bee's just came in the windae," screeched Maria.

The commotion and the distraction that this caused gave Mary the opportunity to stab Frank's backside with a safety pin. His howl of pain was drowned out by the shouts and screams of those boys and girls being 'chased' around the class by the bee. Eventually Mr O'Neil, with one good shot, squashed the offending member of the apoidea superfamily with a dictionary.

"Do you think I'm entitled to a refund on this book?" Mr O'Neil asked no one in particular.

"Why?" no one in particular answered.

"Because there's no 'bee' in this dictionary," Mr O'Neil joked.

No one in particular laughed. A few groaned.

"Anyway," the teacher continued, "we need a Germany. That'll be you, Jim. Germany is this big country here, next to Holland, France and Belgium. Here, Jim, take this flag."

"Sir, Mary stabbed Frank in the bum wi' a safety pin!" a few pupils shouted out in high indignation.

"Well, he shoodnae huv said Ah wis really big."

"Stay behind at play time, Mary. I need to speak to you about that. Finally, we need a Belgium...Are you OK by the way, Frank? Yes? Good...Belgium is this little country here."

"Is it bigger than the Shillford?" asked Gerry – the Shillford being a tiny hamlet of about a dozen houses between Ouplaymoor and Milltown .

"Of course it's bigger than the Shillford, Gerry. It's even bigger than Scotland. Helen, here, you can be Belgium and this is your Belgian flag."

"Right, all the countries come out here onto the floor. Now imagine that you are in the playground and that the playground is Europe. Patrick with your Austrian flag and Jim with your German flag, stand as a small group over here. Good. Matthew as Serbia, Thomas as France and Mary as Russia, stand as another group over here. Good, good. Helen with your Belgian flag and John with your Union Jack, you can be the final group and stand over here. Good, good, good. Now you are all friends in your various groups," Mr O'Neil explained.

Matthew's hand shot up. "Sir, Ah'm no' friends wi' Jim. We've never been fr..."

"No, I don't mean friends as people. I mean friends as countries. Austria and Germany are friends. Russia, Serbia and France are friends. Britain and Belgium are friends. Understand? Good. Now if Patrick wants to fight with Matthew what do you think might happen?"

"Matthew's big brother, Paul, would batter Patrick," Maria suggested.

"No, Maria, think of them as countries, not as people. But Mary – or should I say Russia – you've already told Serbia that if anybody hits her you will hit them. So what are you going to do if Austria attacks Serbia?"

"Ah'm gonnae get stuck right in tae Austria, so Ah um. Austria, you're claimed!"

"Precisely, but then Germany, you've also told Austria that you will support her if she's attacked. So Jim, or Germany, what are you going to do if Russia declares war on Austria?"

"Ah'll gie handers tae Patrick, Ah mean Austria, against Mary, Ah mean Russia."

"However France, you've assured Russia that you will defend her if she's attacked by Germany. So what are you going to do if that actually happens?"

"Go to war against Germany."

"Exactly. So from an argument between Serbia and Austria – Matthew and Patrick here – suddenly we find ourselves in a situation where all the major countries on the continent of Europe could be at war with one another."

"What aboot Britain? Whose side ur we on?" asked Maria.

"Well actually, Maria, we've only agreed to help Belgium, if she's attacked. So what are you going to do as Britain, John, about all the fighting that's going on all round you?"

"Nothing. Let them get on with it."

"Exactly. Unless Germany or France invades tiny Belgium – and that's hardly going to happen – then Britain won't be in the next war, should it start.

"Now then, does anyone have any questions? Yes, Gerry?"

"Who built Edinburgh Castle?"

## CHAPTER THREE

# *The Darkling Thrush*

The window pulled up. The bosoms made their appearance on the sill to meet the morning sun. The two pillars followed. Now the orb was in place. It sniffed the air. Something was different. What was it?

When it came to local gossip, Aggie McMillan operated on a 'need to know' basis: if there was something to know she needed to know it!

She had a highly sensitive in-built antennae for scandal.

She was the one who read that wee lassie Moira Henderson's terrified face and knew, just knew, that she was pregnant. She was the one who noticed that different spring in Alice Craig's step and knew, just knew, that she was having an affair. She was the one who watched Joe Fox slouch up the street in the middle of the afternoon and knew, just knew, that he had been given the sack.

But this was different. Of a different order altogether. Something was happening that was bigger than the street, bigger than the village. Perhaps even bigger than the country.

The day just had a different taste to it. The air smelled different. The trees had a different sway to them. The birdsong sounded different. The way everything seems different on Christmas Day. Except it wasn't.

"Gie me a clue!" she asked the sky.

"Gie me a clue!" she asked a passing dog.

"Gie me a clue!" she asked God.

And then it came. The sky opened, the dog barked and God pointed the way. How could she have missed it?

At the far end of the street, down in the McKinnon's garden, she saw the Union Jack fluttering in the breeze tied to the top of a tree.

Mental check: "Naw, we've hud the Orange Walk last month. It's no' that."

Then she remembered that the last time there had been a Union Jack in the street, other than for the annual Prodfest on July the twelfth, had been for the relief of the siege of Mafeking during the Boer War.

"War! That's it!"

Aggie was nearly sure that we hadn't been at war yesterday, so it must have happened today.

"Wonder who we're at war wi'?" she asked herself now that she knew she knew. "Maybe it's somethin' tae dae wi' Ireland. There's always trouble ower there. Maybe France is getting' too big fur their wellington boots. They could aye be daein' wi' a kick up the boney parts.

"Nae doot Ah'll fin' oot soon. Ah'll no' go fur ma mid-mornin' break until Ah've managed tae catch Maggie McKinnon passin' by on her wey tae the shops, which should be right aboot…ah, here she comes,

"Mornin', Maggie."

"Mornin', Aggie."

"Ah see we're bein' treated tae some patriotic flag wavin' this mornin', Maggie."

"Whit, ye mean the Union Jack? Aye Aggie, huv ye no' heard?"

Now this was a serious challenge to Aggie's credibility. The thought of admitting that there was something, anything, happening that she was late to hear about was anathema to her.

"Of course Ah've heard, Maggie…Ah wis just…"

Maggie didn't like Aggie. Not after she told the whole street about her having to borrow money from Mrs Ellingham ("How did she know?") after her man drank the wages in the Bottom Shop one Friday night. Her instinct was telling her that Aggie was on a fishing expedition here and hadn't a clue, but was gagging to find out.

"Oh well then, Aggie, ye'll know it aw," she replied curtly and walked primly on.

"Will yer man be gaun aff tae the war then, Maggie?"

This, Aggie knew, was a desperate hand to play which risked making her sound ridiculous and could completely ruin her hard earned reputation. That sudden, almost imperceptible, tightness in the shoulders told Aggie all she needed to know. She had thrown a dart backwards and blindfold and had landed plum centre of the bull.

"Eh, Ah don't know, Aggie. He's got a very responsible job. Ah don't know if they'll let him gie it up tae go tae Germany."

(Germany! Double Tops! Game over!)

"Aye, right enough, Maggie, it's no' everywan that could dae a tram conductor's job. Ah mean, ye've got tae be ower eighteen fur a start."

"But your Lachie disnae even huv a job, does he, Aggie?" Maggie bristled. "Ah'm sure they'll be comin' fur the likes o' him first."

"How much does it pay, Maggie, dae ye know?" Aggie asked, undeterred.

"A single man? Probably aboot a shilling a day."

Seven shillings a week! Better than a poke in the eye wi' a big blunt stick, as her mother used to say.

"So tell me, Maggie, how did we get intae this war in the first place?"

Now that she had convinced Maggie that she had known the headlines all along, she had no qualms about plumbing her for the details.

"Apparently the Kaiser invaded Belgium. We tellt him tae get oot, but he says he's no' gaun, so the King says he's gonnae fling him oot."

"That Kaiser again, eh, Maggie. There's a man who really puts the 'turd' in 'basturd'!"

"Aye, ye're right there, Aggie. Anyway, Ah'll need tae go. It's ma turn fur the steamie."

"Right Micky, so ye've come about the job in St Conval's cemetery, have ye?" asked Father O'Keefe in his rich Dublin accent. (Cue The Commitments.)

"That's right Father, my Maw wis…"

"Ye mean yer 'Mother', do ye not Micky? Always show respect fer the woman who bore the pains o' ye on the day ye were born and whose heart has bate in time to yer every need since. Ye widn't refer to Our Lady as 'Jaysus' Maw' wid ye?"

"No, sorry Father. My Mother was tellin' me that you could do with another hand in the graveyard down in Arthur Lea."

"Well, sure we could rightly, but wait till Ah tell ye – it's got to be the right man, Micky? Are you the right man?"

"I'm sure that I could do the job, Father."

"I'm sure you could too, Micky. Ye're young enough and strong enough. But sure, Ah didn't ask you that. Ah asked if ye were the *right* man."

"I…I don't know what ye mean, Father."

"Don't ye now? Perhaps ye're not the right man after all then. Ye see Micky, here at St Conval's we bury souls, Catholic souls, on their way to heaven," Father O'Keefe pronounced while solemnly making the sign of the cross. "It's important that they are surrounded by Catholic worshippers," he continued, "on the final stage of their journey to eternal rest. So let me ask ye again Micky McGoldrick: are ye the right man fer the job?"

"Do you mean do I go to mass?"

"Aye, amongst other t'ings."

"Such as, Father?"

"Well, ye've a grand name on ye, Micky McGoldrick. Where do you t'ink it came from?"

"My father?"

"Aye, and him coming from Rasharkin in County Antrim."

"Yes, Father."

"And yer lovely mother, what wid she have been to her own name now?"

"Phee, Father."

"Sure another fine Irish name. Daughter of a Draperstown man she wis telling me.

"In St Conval's cemetery, Micky, the majority o' the names are fine Irish names. Some Scottish, to be sure, that came down from the Western Isles after their own famine and Highland clearances. Some Italian here and there. A small sprinkling o' Polish. But mainly Irish.

"Now we widn't want to be disrepectin' their names by having their graves tended to by a man who didn't respect the country o' their birth. The country that gave them their music, their dance and their humour. The country that gave them a twinkle in their eye in this life and their religion to see them through to the next.

"So I'll ask ye again, Micky McGoldrick, son o' a Rasharkin man that ye are: are ye the right man fer this job?"

"Well my da – sorry, my father, Father – always says that if Irishmen were purple with pink dots then I'd be purple with pink dots."

"But wid ye be proud o' it Micky, that's the point. Wid ye be proud o' it?"

"I would never deny or apologise for who or what I am, Father."

"Good man, Micky, good man. When can ye start?"

"Would next Monday be alright, Father?"

"Eight o'clock in the morning. Report to Tony Travers. He's the head groundsman. He'll keep ye right."

"Er, sorry to have to ask you this, Father, but what's the rate for the job?"

"The rate? The rate is it? Jesus, Mary and Joseph don't tell me he wahnts paid fer doin' a service fer the Catholic dead of his own parish! Surely not Micky? If the crucified Jaysus on the hill o' Golgotha had asked ye fer a drink o' wahter, wid ye have had him quote ye a rate fer the job afore ye wid have obliged him?"

"No, of course not, Father, but…"

"Eleven shillings and sixpence fer a fifty hour week. You stop at one o'clock on a Saturday. That should give ye time to follow the Celtic on the Saturday and go to mass on the Sunday. Ye do follow the Celtic, I take it?"

"I follow their results, Father, but I don't get the chance to see them very often. I play for Milltown Victoria on a Saturday."

"Good man yerself, Micky. I hear yez won t'ree cups this year, so."

"Yes, Father. I was their top scorer."

"See, it takes the son o' a Rasharkin man to show these Scotsmen how to play the football."

"Well, I'll be on my way, Father. Thanks for the job."

"Micky, wid ye be good enough to close that gate behind ye afore yer hin' end disappears from view.

"By the way, did ye say that ye went to mass?"

"No, I didn't say, Father. God bless."

★ ★ ★ ★ ★

"That was a disaster, Jeanie," lamented Harry Burchill. "Why did you hardly speak to my parents the whole night? I was cringing."

"Well, dae ye wahnt me tae tell you why?"

Jeanie stopped dead in the street and turned to face Harry.

"Oh…!" said Harry, "so there was a reason."

"Aye there wis, Harry. Ah shoodnae huv gaun there in the first place."

"It wasn't that bad."

"Aye it wis. You wurnae the only wan that wis cringin'. Ma buttocks were clenched from the second Ah went in tae the second Ah came oot and ma palms were sweatin' like a tart in the jungle. Ah could hardly look at them, especially yer mother. Ah could tell that she could see right through me."

"What did they do? What did they say to make you feel that way?"

"Nothin', Harry. They wur really nice. That just made it harder. But Harry, Ah didnae wahnt tae like them, an' Ah didnae wahnt them tae like me either."

"Jeanie, that's my parents you're talking about…"

"Aye, Ah know, Harry. That's the point."

"What point? I don't understand."

"The point is Ah went there knowin' that Ah wis gonnae chuck ye afore the night wis ower. Ah felt like a fuckin' fraud."

"You're going to…? Tonight…?!"

"Aye, Harry, you're chucked. Ye're a lovely fella, ye really ur. But we're just no' right fur each other, ur we? Ye know that yersel', dae ye no'?"

"Do you know then?"

"Know? Know whit?"

"Why we're not right for each other."

"Well, Ah like ye, Harry, but Ah'm just no' attracted tae ye anymair an' Ah've been thinkin' for a while that you don't find me attractive anymair either."

"You're right, Jeanie, but do you know why?"

"No, Ah don't, but Ah wid huv expected ye tae huv tried it on by noo. Maist boys dae, but you never did."

"I was scared that you would sense it in my kiss."

"Sense whit? Harry, whit the fuck ur ye talkin' aboot?"

"When you said that we're not right for each other you have no idea how right you were, Jeanie. No girl's right for me."

"Ach, don't pit yersel' doon just because a confused wee lassie chucks ye. There'll be anither pretty lassie aff the next coach, just wait an' see."

"No, I don't want another girl. I don't want any girl."

"Ye're talkin' noo as if ye're gonnae be a priest an' ye're no' even a Catholic… whit!…Jesus Christ, ye're no' ur ye…?"

"Not what?"

33

"Wan o' they hammysexuals."

"Homosexuals. Yes, Jeanie, I am attracted to men, but I'm too scared to tell anyone."

"Fuck, nae wunner!"

"My parents and family would disown me. My friends would shun me or worse. Christ it's even illegal, I could be locked up."

"Harry, Ah don't know whit tae say."

"Can I ask you to say nothing, Jeanie? Absolutely nothing. At least till I'm gone."

"Whit, ye mean deid?"

"No, Jeanie, I'm going to London where there's a lot more people like me and where I've got more chance of being accepted for who and what I am. I'll write to my parents from there and explain everything in a letter."

"When ur ye plannin' tae go?"

"Within the next month or so. I'll probably sign up for the war down there."

"Harry, Ah'll miss ye. Ah know that life's no' gonnae be easy fur ye, but Ah really dae wish ye aw the best."

"It's not going to be easy for anyone if this war takes off."

"Harry, can Ah ask ye somethin'?"

"Of course, Jeanie, unless it's about the mechanical details of men having sex with men, because I don't know either."

"Naw, it's just, why did ye go oot wi me, Harry, if ye knew that ye wur that wey inclined?"

"I was trying to prove to myself that I wasn't that way, Jeanie. I desperately wanted to be normal. I desperately wanted to be attracted to other girls. Life's difficult enough without adding a massive complication right at the outset. You're a really good looking girl, Jeanie. Any normal guy would find you insanely attractive. But all I did was prove to myself that I'm not normal."

"Ye're normal fur you, Harry. Ye cannae help bein' whit ye ur."

"Thanks fur that, Jeanie. Thanks for being so understanding, but it's not you I have to worry about, it's the rest of the world."

34

"Can Ah ask ye wan mair question, Harry, 'cos efter the night Ah doot if we'll ever be able tae talk like this again."

"Sure. What?"

"Ur ye *actually* attracted tae men, Harry?"

"Yes, Jeanie, I am. Just like you. In fact, to the same one as you."

"Whit...? Who...?"

"Archie Ferguson."

★ ★ ★ ★ ★

"Here we go again," said the drooped head in the Bottom Shop. "Another decade, another war."

"The army'll sort oot those bastards in nae time. Britain disnae lose wars," the voice at the top of the bar added emphatically.

"Whit ur we fightin' fur onywey?" asked a quiet voice in the corner.

" 'Cos Germany invaded Belgium," replied the barman.

"Where is Belgium? Zitno in Africa?" asked the wee fat man beneath the dartboard.

"Naw, that's the Belgian Congo ye're thinkin' aboot," the barman pointed out. "Belgium's between Germany and...Denmark, Ah think."

"So why ur *we* fightin' fur it?" queried the one legged man at the door.

"'Cos it's a fight an' we've got tae prove we're still the best," proffered the drooped head at the bar, with a touch of sarcasm.

"Ah think it's tae take oor minds aff Ireland where there's real fightin' tae be done," the high pitched voice at the centre of the bar declared.

"We'll still huv fightin' in Ireland long efter this war's been fought an' won," said the one legged man.

"It's aw right fur you, Hoppy. They won't call you up," the wee fat man commented.

"There wullnae be conscription," the voice at the top of the bar shouted. "We could beat those bastards wi' a handful o' ramblers. Just you wait an' see."

"So, who's aw gaun tae jine up?" asked the barman.

Six or seven voices shouted in unison.

"Where can we dae it?" asked the skinny young man standing by the toilets.

"Ah'm gaun in tae Glesga the morra tae try an' jine the Highland Light Infantry," the tall young man next to him replied. "Ma faither wis in it durin' the Boer War. They suffered badly at Magersfontein. A lot o' his mates didnae make it back, an' they were just fightin' bushmen."

"We've learned a lot since then," the voice at the top of the bar said. "Onywey, we won that war did we no'?"

"Depends how you count the score," said the barman.

"Why wid onywan in their right mind think aboot jinin' up tae fight fur a country that naebody can fin' on a map?" asked the drooped head.

"We need tae fight fur the King," said the skinny man by the toilets.

"Dae we fuck!" said Hoppy.

"You wan o' those traitors, Hoppy,"

"How is the King threatened because a lot o' Germans go aff tae Belgium withoot passports and at government expense. If they turned up in Blackpool then, aye, it might be different," replied Hoppy.

"Aye, but if they get away wi' it in Belgium, wherever it is," said the wee fat man, "they'll just keep gaun an' gaun until they huv tae be stopped. Might as well take them on right away. Nae messin'."

"Well, we've invaded a quarter o' the planet and naebody's stopped us," Droopy pointed out.

"Aye, but we gave civilisation tae the world," said the barman.

"Pity we hud tae kill so many uncivilised people tae help them see the benefits o' oor civilised ways," Droopy replied morosely.

"Heh, you in the corner, you're a Catholic ur ye no'?" asked the wee fat man belligerently.

"Aye, whit of it?" the quiet voice answered.

"Wan o' they priests in your church there, is he no' a German?"

"Aye, but as far as Ah know he didnae invade Belgium."

"Disnae matter, he's the enemy noo."

"Leave the priest oot o' this," the barman intervened. "He coodnae help where he wis born. Ah've spoken tae him a few times. He's a nice man. A very clever man."

"How dae ye know he's no' a German spy?" asked the skinny man by the toilets, menacingly.

"If he wis a German spy in Britain Ah'm pretty sure he widnae be sent tae Milltown, an' he's been here fur sixteen years," said the quiet voice.

"They've been plannin' this war fur decades, Ah bet," said the wee fat man. "How dae we know they don't huv a spy in every toon. He might just be their man in Milltown."

"He's no' a spy, he's a man o' God," the quiet voice protested.

"No ma God he's no'," the skinny man piped up, "and when oor boys start tae come back deid Ah'll be lookin' tae kill ony German Ah can get ma hands on."

"Another decade, another war," said the drooped head beside the bar.

★ ★ ★ ★ ★

"…And for us and for all humanity, God gave His only Son…

"That, dear brothers and sisters in Christ, would normally have been the end of my sermon. However, this has been a dramatic week of cataclysmic proportions right across Europe, which has, I think, particular implications for your parish priest here in St Thomas'," said Father Dannfald, sounding now more avuncular than Sermon on the Mount.

"It is right that I should say a few words concerning these events.

"I came to this country as a young man over twenty years ago. Sixteen years ago my wanderings brought me to this lovely town by the banks of the Levern. From the first day you accepted me as one of your own, as part of the community of worshippers here in Milltown. This, for me, has not just been my Parish, it's been my home.

"But now it seems that your young men may be asked to join the army and go abroad to fight and kill young men from Germany, my native country.

"It is not for me to question the whys and wherefores of how this all came about, least of all because I don't know. But that doesn't stop my heart being weighed down with a profound sadness for the country of my birth and for my adopted country, both of which share the same values, the same high ideals.

"Of course, I can't speak for the leaders of either country or their motives. Although I am forced to ask myself: What would God say? Whose side would He be on? Does He rejoice in the killing of men by men? Did He sacrifice His only Son on a cross so that we could crucify ourselves?

"Well, I happen to know what He would say, because He has told us in four simple words: Thou shalt not kill. *Thou – shalt – not – kill.*

"You can read those words backwards and forwards and I defy you to find any exceptions, qualifications or reservations. The message is clear, simple and unequivocal: Thou shalt not kill.

"Thou shalt not kill if you're young, thou shalt not kill if you're old; thou shalt not kill if you're white, thou shalt not kill if you're black; thou shalt not kill if you're male, if you're female, if you're Catholic, if you're Protestant, if you're British, if you're German. *Thou – shalt – not – kill.*

Now, as your parish priest, I merely offer you spiritual guidance; I am not your conscience. That must be a matter between you and your God. You must decide what you will do when you are asked to offer service to your King or service to your God. You must decide, for doubtless one day, be it near or far, you will have to answer to both of them.

Credo in Unum Deum, Patrem omnipotentum…"

★ ★ ★ ★ ★

Viewed from the fire escape at number two mill, life looked grim and grey. The wind blew the rain and dust across the open yard and over everything with gusto. The mist lay across the Levern Burn at the foot of the Fereneze Braes, shrouding the entire countryside in an ominous, oppressive gloom. The incessant clacking noise of the mill's machines were periodically drowned out by huge steam trains spitting fire on their way to Glasgow, Kilmarnock, Dumfries, Carlisle or London, leaving behind a trail of acrid vapour.

Jeanie Broon stared blankly across this dismal picture, still trying to come to terms with all that had happened over the previous week.

Her brother, Craig, was in uniform and the uniforms were heading to Belgium or France or Germany. Or straight to Hell itself for all she knew.

Britain had declared war against Germany, who had declared war against everyone else. The world had gone mad.

But even more bizarrely, her ex-boyfriend had turned out to be attracted to other boys, despite kissing her these past three months. It was now his intention to take himself off to London to find a boyfriend!

Just as well too, she mused, for otherwise he may have been competing with her for the attention of Archie Ferguson. Perhaps they could share him, she found herself thinking, before immediately dismissing the notion as absurdly perverse.

Her cigarette, which she had hardly puffed, had been burnt away to a stub as she contorted these facts in her very confused mind.

The door opened and Alice Henderson's face emerged through a circle of newly puffed smoke.

"Hi there, Jeanie. Whit's the world like wi' you the day?" she asked innocently.

"Same as yesterday, and the day afore that and the day afore the day afore that," Jeanie replied, trying to keep control of her voice so as not to betray her inner conflict.

"Well, apart from us getting' oorsels intae a war!" said Alice, hoping to turn the conversation in that direction, since no one had anything else on their minds. Apart from Jeanie that is.

"So the moon is made of cheese, Alice?"

"See if we ever get there," Alice rejoined, "we'd better just send wan man up. If we send two they'll huv declared war on each other by the end o' the week. Is Craig away then?"

"Aye, left last Thursday. He's barrackin' at Barassie the noo, but he'll be sent tae somewhere in England soon and frae there ontae Europe. Don't know where. It's a state secret. The War Office wullnae tell us in case the Germans get tae hear an' drop a bomb on Craig Broon's heid."

"Aye, it's a sair fecht right enough, Jeanie. How did he seem when he left?"

"Och, in high spirits. Not a care. It's lifted him from his boredom and he's desperate tae fight fur his King and country and aw his new mates. He thinks it's a fuckin' game."

"It's the same in ma hoose. Billy an' Alex ur rarin' tae go, even though they're four and five years too young tae fight in this war."

"Whit is it aboot young men and fightin', Alice? Is it part o' their make-up or their instincts or whatever? Does it come frae the days when they went oot tae dae the huntin' and the killin' an' hunners o' shaggin'? Are countries run by men just huge tribes that huv tae compete wi' wan another for land, food and breedin' stock?"

"Talkin' aboot breedin' stock, how's the boyfriend?"

"Ex-boyfriend, you mean."

"Naw?"

"Aye."

"When?"

"Friday night. Just efter Ah hud tea at his parents' hoose."

"Did you chuck him?"

"Aye, Ah suppose Ah did, but just afore he got roon tae chuckin' me onywey."

"Really? Whit did he say?"

"Ah cannae tell ye, Alice. Don't ask."

Now Alice Henderson was a first cousin once removed of Aggie McMillan, though family relations had been a bit strained ever since Aggie told the world that her younger sister Moira was pregnant, even before Moira's parents knew. So the scent of the chase in the hunt for gossip was in Alice's blood. To be told that there was something so secretive and so juicy that it just couldn't be revealed only added spice to the quest.

Five minutes later Jeanie had told her. Everything.

"Your boyfriend wis gonnae chuck you fur a boy you wur chuckin' him fur? Jeanie, Ah cannae believe that!"

And she laughed and she laughed and she laughed all the way home.

The next forty eight hours and beyond saw Alice closeted one to one with friends, family and workmates, close, distant and non-existent, with whom she introduced her topic of choice behind cupped hands as she whispered the words, "Noo, ye didnae hear this frae me, but…"

By the time she got round to telling her first cousin once removed, Aggie had already heard, but settled for listening to Alice's finer embellishments of the story anyway.

★ ★ ★ ★ ★

Mr O'Neil looked across his class. He could see the pain and the worry in each of their young faces. Many of them had fathers or brothers getting ready to fall-in and head for the Great War.

Mary had been crying.

There was a brittle stillness throughout the room. It was only two months ago that he had virtually assured them that Scotland wouldn't be in the war. And now it was. He felt as if he had lied to them. As if some invisible thread of trust connecting them had been cut, to be replaced with a keen sense of hurt and betrayal. As he looked at them he wondered how long this conflict would last. In another five years or so these young boys might be old enough to kill. To be killed.

Mr O'Neill loved poetry and was gifted in being able to share his passion with his pupils. In particular he loved the recitation of poetry. He loved the sound of it and the magical effect its rhymes and cadences could produce. He loved the music of it. His ear could pick out its melodies and his voice could give expression to the rich resonance of its rhythms.

While generally providing some sort of context to introduce his performance, Mr O'Neill rarely attempted to have the poem analysed afterwards, preferring instead to allow his 'audience' to savour its aftertaste. He always took a dramatic pause for a second or two to soak in the silent reflection, the calming of the stirring souls in the class rising to the wonder of the words – even ( perhaps especially) when those words were more felt than understood.

When he started, a hush fell upon the class in anticipation of the poem's rapture and sense of mystery.

He (and they) loved Blake ("Tyger, Tyger" being the all-time favourite) and Longfellow (Hiawatha of course) and Burns and his "Wee, sleekit, cowrin' tim'rous beastie". The poetry to which he introduced them provided a rich tapestry of colour and shade and unexpected delights.

He was ready to embark on a new poem.

"Today, ladies and gentlemen, I am going to introduce you to a poet we haven't heard before. His name is Thomas Hardy and he's from England, just like Blake and Wordsworth and many other poets that we've already met.

"The title of the poem is called "*The Darkling Thrush.*" The poem describes the poet out in the winter countryside alone as the light of the day is fading. The landscape appears to be plunged into a deep despair where there seems to be no joy or delight in a frozen world. Everything is bleak and dark and lonely and sad. And then out of the gloom comes the song of a bird, a thrush, which fills the air with beautiful music and with life and joy and a spirit of optimism – a sense that things will get better.

"I know that many of you are feeling unhappy just now. Perhaps you are feeling worried and sad. Perhaps you feel that you can't imagine things in your life getting better. It won't last. They will get better. It only takes one candle to banish the darkness or, as is the case in this poem, the song of one bird to breathe life into the withered soul of a withered land.

And then he began:

"*The Darkling Thrush*, by Thomas Hardy:
*I leant upon a coppice gate*
*When Frost was spectre-gray,*
*And Winter's dregs made desolate*
*The weakening eye of day.*
*The tangled bine-stems scored the sky*
*Like strings of broken lyres,*
*And all mankind that haunted nigh*
*Had sought their household fires.*

*The land's sharp features seemed to be*
*The century's corpse outleant,*
*His crypt the cloudy canopy,*
*The wind his death-lament.*
*The ancient pulse of germ and birth*
*Was shrunken hard and dry,*
*And every spirit upon earth*
*Was fervourless as I.*

*At once a voice arose among*
*The bleak twigs overhead,*

*In full-hearted evensong*
*Of joy illimited.*
*An aged thrush, frail, gaunt and small,*
*In blast-beruffled plume,*
*Had chosen thus to fling his soul*
*Upon the growing gloom.*

*So little cause for carolings*
*Of such ecstatic sound,*
*Was written on terrestrial things*
*Afar or nigh aground,.*
*That I could think there trembled through*
*His happy good-night air,*
*Some blessed Hope whereof he knew*
*And I was unaware."*

Mr O'Neil paused, stared out the window into the great beyond, and repeated quietly and forlornly:
*"Some blessed Hope whereof he knew*
*And I was unaware...."*
Mary lowered her head onto her arms on the desk and sobbed.

★ ★ ★ ★ ★

"Hello, Mrs Ferguson. Is Archie in?"
"Aye, he's in his room, Alan. Away ye go on, on, on in."
Alan Johnston was Archie Ferguson's best friend. They had started Milltown Primary School together, ran about the braes together and got into trouble together. Over the years Archie had become the dominant one, especially after that incident down the Milltown Glen. From then on, Alan was scared of Archie's capacity for raw violence.

Alan opened Archie's bedroom door and entered a dark world of clutter. Clothes were strewn over the floor which was almost entirely filled by a large double-spring bed frame. Plates with half eaten meals lay like landmines under the clothes.

The curtains had been pulled across towards each other leaving space for a head – Archie's head – to look between them and out into the courtyard at the back.

"Sssh!" ordered the head as Alan entered the room, "and shut that fuckin' door quietly."

Alan did as he was commanded.

"Whit ur ye daein', Archie?"

"Waitin'. Noo sit doon and shut yer mooth,"Archie replied.

Once again Alan obeyed.

Three minutes of total silence elapsed before Alan heard the spit of Archie's airgun.

"Missed the bastard!" Archie cursed. "That's the sixth wan Ah've missed the day. Might as well gie it up as a bad job. It's getting' too dark onywey."

"Missed whit?" Alan asked.

"Sparrows. Craws. Burds."

"Ye're shootin' burds?"

"Fishin' fur them. Ah use the same bait – worms. Ah hang them up on the wahshin' line oot the back and shoot the burds as they come doon tae feed. Last week wis the best laugh."

"How?"

"Ah hud just shot a wee speug aff the the line ontae the green, when guess whit Ah saw?"

"Dunno."

"Mrs Collins' cat comin' tae eat the burd, so Ah shot it as well. Ah didnae kill it outright and Ah hud tae go oot the back and finish it aff at close range."

"Whit did Mrs Collins say aboot that?"

"Aye, that wis the problem. Ah didnae wahnt her tae know that Ah hud shot her cat, so Ah put it in ma maw's shoppin' bag and took it doon tae Milltown Low railway line and flung it under a passin' train. It wis pure mince by the end o' it let me tell ye."

"Does Mrs Collins know its deid?"

"Aye, that wis the best bit. Ah tellt her. Ah said Ah wis walkin' doon by Wylie's Loan when Ah saw a ginger cat that looked like Rusty lyin' in bits at the side o' the railway."

"Whit did she dae then?"

"She started tae greet. And then she went in tae her purse and gie'd me twopence fur bein' sae good as tae tell her. Pished masel laughin' efterwards, so Ah did."

"Archie, Ah've got somethin' tae tell ye that ye're no' gonnae believe. Can we go outside fur a walk? Ye're gonnae wahnt tae shout and swear when ye hear whit Ah've got tae say."

"Aye, Ah could be daein' wi' some fresh air onywey."

Archie put on his jacket and hailed through to his mother who was already making her way out to the hall to meet them.

"Right maw, Ah'm away oot. Ah'll be back in a few hours."

"Right ye ur son. How ur ye, Alan?"

"Fine thanks, Mrs Ferguson."

"And how's yer mum and dad?"

"Aye, they're baith great so they ur."

"Good. Tell them Ah wis askin' fur them. Well, Ah'll see you pair o' scoundrels later."

"Right, Alan, whit huv ye got tae tell me? Ah'm burstin' tae fin' oot."

"Ye'll be burstin' somebody else wance Ah've tellt ye, so ye wull."

"Alan, ur ye gonnae get on wi' it? Hurry up fur fuck's sake. It'll be Christmas in four months."

"Awright. Ye know Jeanie Broon and Harry Burchill?"

"Alan, ye know I know them. Sure we sat beside them in the same class in school."

"Aye, right. Ye know they've been walkin' oot thegither?"

"Aye whit a waste. Jeanie Broon's a wee cracker and he's a pure weed."

"Well, they're no' gaun oot thegither noo."

46

"Naw?"

"Naw. They split up last Friday, ower you."

"Ower me?"

"Aye, Apparently Jeanie fancies you."

"Me? Nae kiddin'? Still Ah suppose she's only human."

"But there's mair."

"Just let me take this bit in first. How dae ye know she fancies me?"

"Archie, you're the last tae know. The whole town knows and knows the reason why they split up. It's just that everywan's too scared tae tell ye."

"Why wid onywan be too scared tae tell me that a stunnin' wee lassie like Jeanie Broon wahnts tae step oot wi' me? It's fair made ma day, Ah can tell ye."

"Because Ah've only tellt ye the half o' it."

"Whit's the other half?"

"Ah tellt ye they split up ower you. Ah tellt ye that Jeanie fancies ye. Whit Ah didnae tell ye is that Harry fancies ye as well."

"Harry? But he's a bloke!"

"Aye, a bloke who fancies another bloke: You!"

"Alan if you're huvin' me on, Ah swear Ah'm gonnae kick yer heid in!"

"Archie, Ah'm no' huvin' ye on, but there's worse. Apparently he's tellin' folk that he's kissed Jeanie and he's kissed you and you're much better."

Archie froze. Stunned.

He stared hard at Alan, looking for any sign that he was about to break into a belated 'April Fool'. Eventually the pressure of silence became so great that he took the palm of his hand and struck Alan on the side of the head, knocking him to the ground in the process.

Alan looked up helplessly.

"Whit did ye dae that fur, Archie? Ah'm only tellin' ye whit Ah heard…whit everywan's heard."

Archie grabbed Alan back to his feet by the scruff of his neck and screamed, "Is this true Alan? 'Cos if it is that wee bastard's deid, an' if it's no' you're fuckin' deid."

"Ah swear, Archie, on ma mither's life, it's true."

Archie pushed Alan back on to the ground while viciously kicking the fresh air between them.

More than the slap, the push and the threats, Alan was scared of that look in Archie's eye. The same look he had seen when Archie smashed a hammer into the mouth of one of those boys from Arthur Lea who was camping in Milltown Glen. "If they come up tae Milltown they know whit tae expect!" was Archie's lame justification for an act which deprived its victim of several teeth and which put him in hospital overnight.

When the police tried to investigate no one would talk. They had seen that look in Archie's eyes as well.

"Alan, Ah'm away back doon the road, but sooner rather than later Ah'm gonnae catch up wi' pretty boy, an' efter Ah'm finished wi' him he's no' gonnae be so pretty!"

Alan watched Archie's spiralling bile roundly chastise the moon as he frogmarched his temper home.

# CHAPTER FOUR

# A Call to Arms

Alex McKinnon, husband of Maggie, turned up for work in Coplawhill tram depot at 10.00 a.m. on Sunday, 13th September, 1914.

Not that it had anything to do with being a conductor on a tram. He was answering the call of James Dalrymple, the manager of the Tramways Department in Glasgow, to join the army.

Dalrymple had discovered that Glasgow Municipal Authority had decided to form two new infantry units. At 5.00 p.m. on Thursday, 10th September, he phoned round the depots asking for the names of those willing to join a tramways battalion.

By 9.00 the next morning there was a list of 1,100 men waiting on his desk. It had proven to be the quickest enlistment for the creation of a new battalion in the history of the British army.

One of those names was Alex McKinnon from Milltown.

The crowds were everywhere, jostling under the high girded roof: on the floor, round the walls and seated inside the ranked tramcars.

The mood was generally euphoric and jocular. "Ah hope they've enough change in King's shillings for this lot once they've passed," joked one of the men.

"It'll take hoors tae get us through," moaned another. "They've only goat two doctors and wan attesting officer."

"If that weighin' machine breaks doon we'll aw still be sittin' in this queue this time next week!" cried another.

"The war'll be ower by the time they get tae me at this rate," a tall baldy man quipped.

"Dae ye think we'll get tae travel tae the front-line in oor trams?" mused a wee bachle with a cheeky grin.

"It'll no' be on a number forty-nine onyway. It only goes as far as Shettleston," a voice from the crowd responded. Everybody laughed.

"Who's that man in the collar, tie and bowler hat staunin' up by the table?" Alex asked the wee man standing next to him.

"Apparently he's the Justice o' the Peace," his neighbour replied.

"Justice o' the Peace?" thought Alex. "Tae administer a war? A bit o' a contradiction thon!"

There was a word for it that escaped him. What was it…?

"Ironic, intit?" said his newly adopted mate.

"Ironic! That's the word!"

"Does your wife know ye're here tae sign up?" asked the small man. (Not quite five foot three, Alex thought.)

"Well, *Ah* huvnae tellt her yet, but there's a wummin in oor street that seems tae know everythin' that happens afore it even happens, so *she's* likely goat her tellt already."

"Whit dae ye think she'll say when she finds oot?"

"What can she say? We've goat tae dae oor duty. She might no' like it, but she'd like it even less if her husband wis the only wan walkin' roon the streets in civvies."

"And even less again, Ah suppose," said the wee man, "if the Germans were tae come marchin' up her street on wahshin' day."

"Exactly!" replied Alex, who was by now beginning to feel more certain that he was doing the right thing.

"Ma wife disnae ken either."

"How will she react when ye tell her?"

"First and foremost she'll be really disappointed that Ah'm no' actually workin' the day. She'll huv the Sunday overtime money coontit and spent in her heid already. Beyond that Ah don't think she'll gie a damn. We don't really get on that well."

"How come?"

"She's a good bit taller than me, which didnae appear tae be an issue when we got hitched, but is noo. She's always sayin' tae onybody who'll listen that when she wis a wee lassie she dreamed o' marryin' her Prince Charmin', who wid be tall, dark and handsome – and instead she ended up wi' me who's short, ginger and ugly as fuck!"

"Whit height ur ye?" Alex felt compelled to ask.

"Five foot wan and a quarter inch."

"Dae ye think they'll take ye? The recruitin' adverts say ye've goat tae be at least five foot three."

"They're so overwhelmed tryin' tae get us aw through Ah doot if they'll be askin' us tae remove oor shoes afore they measure us. Ma shoes huv a false heel so that Ah don't look much shorter than ma wife. They make me five foot three and a half inches tall. Actually, Ah'm too auld as well. Ah'm thirty wan, but Ah'm just gonnae lie. Ah'm bankin' on them bein' so desperate fur men that they'll no' be too fussy aboot checkin' their details."

"Ye're probably right," Alex agreed. "Ah heard o' a boy o' seventeen who tried tae enlist. The recruitin' officer confessed to huvin' a shockin' memory and said that if the lad went oot an' walked roon the park fur a couple o' hoors afore comin' back in – huvin' gained two years in the process, of course – he wid be able tae sign him up. Onywey, how desperate ur ye tae join?"

"Some men ur driven by the need tae protect their hame; others by the need tae get away frae it."

Five hours later and the mood had changed as there were still hundreds of men waiting to be attested. Some had already marched off in frustration and disgust. As he stomped out, one man shouted back angrily, "Gie me a call when the Germans reach Paisley – if ye're finished wi' this lot by then!"

Fights were breaking out with queue jumpers. "Save that for the Germans, boys!" growled the policeman on duty.

One man had gone right through the process only to be blocked at the very end when he refused to take the oath (which involved kissing a card) to King George the Fifth.

"Why don't ye join the German army then, ya fuckin' traitor?" angry patriotic voices screamed.

At length it was Alex's turn. At five foot seven, and with a chest of 38 inches, he flew through the medical. Nor did he have any difficulty kissing a card – a test his little friend with shoes in hand wasn't required to take.

So there he was, a member of the 15th Highland Light Infantry and ready to take on the Germans. Once he had faced his wife!

★ ★ ★ ★ ★

The posters were stuck up all over Milltown main street.

---

### Your King and Country
### Needs
### You!
### A Call to Arms

**An addition of 100,000 men to His Majesty's Regular Army is immediately necessary in the present grave National Emergency.**
**Lord Kitchener is confident that this appeal will be at once responded to by all those who have the safety of our Empire at heart.**

### TERMS of SERVICE

**General service for the period of war only.**
**Height 5ft. 3in and upwards. Chest 34 in. at least.**
**Medically fit.**
**Married Men or Widowers with Children will be accepted, and will draw Separation Allowance under Army Conditions.**

---

**MEN ENLISTING FOR THE DURATION OF THE WAR**

**Will be discharged with all convenient speed, if they so desire, the moment the war is over.**

---

## HOW TO JOIN

**Men wishing to join should apply at any Military Barrack or at any Recruiting Office; the address of the latter can be obtained from Post Offices or Labour Exchanges.**

### GOD SAVE THE KING

---

A crowd of men wearing caps gathered round the proclamation stuck on the post box at Milltown Cross.

"They're lookin' fur a hunner thoosan' men immediately," said Tommy Finnegan.

"We heard you coodnae read," John Lochrie quipped.

" 'A grave national emergency!' That disnae sound too good. Ur we losin' this war already?" asked a concerned Peter Black.

"Word is comin' back frae a place called Mons in France," Ian Martin informed the gathering, "that the BEF ran smack intae the middle o' the whole fuckin' German army. Apparently that set the Huns aff like a swarm o' bees an' oor boys were forced ontae the retreat."

"We cannae stay here if oor lads ur getting' pushed aroon by the Germans," Wully Boyle said. "Ah hear that the Glasgow Chamber o' Commerce ur recruitin' fur a new battalion o' the Highland Light Infantry. Ah'm gonnae see aboot joinin' their recruitin' march frae Irvine when it passes by the mill oan its way tae Maryhill Barracks."

"Aye, Alex McKinnon joined it on Sunday, alang wi' his mates oan the trams," Dennis Wright announced.

"Naw, that wis the 15th Highland Light Infantry, which is made up exclusively o' Glasgow Trammies. This'll be a completely new wan – the 17th Ah think," Wully pointed out.

"This toon's gonnae be like a ghost toon within a week. There'll be naebody left tae kiss the lassies," Tommy Finnegan remarked.

"Eh lads, Ah've changed ma mind," Wully Boyle laughed. "Ah'll just stay here tae dae ma duty by the girls while yer aw awa' daein' yer duty by the country."

★ ★ ★ ★ ★

"Right men, Ah wahnt tae talk tae ye aw the day, an' it's goat nuthin' tae dae wi' fitba'," said Dennis Wright, player-manager of Milltown Victoria football club. "You might huv heard that the entire Heart of Midlothian football team has jined thegither tae fight at the front against the Germans. Brave lads every wan o' them…"

"Pity they're such a shite fitba team," laughed Danny Harkins.

"Ah never thought Ah wid hear masel say this, Danny," continued the manager, "but there are some things in this life even mair important than a game o' fitba – no' many, but some – an' this might just be wan o' them.

"Onywey, ye're aw eligible, fit young men an' far too ugly tae be married. If there is conscription – an' if the losses we've apparently suffered at Mons continue, Ah wid say that's gonnae be inevitable – you wid aw be called up. So why dae we no' jist jine up thegither the noo? We'd be fightin' fur each other oan an' aff the pitch.

"As far as fitba's concerned, that's ower fur the season at least. The league committee's meetin' the day efter the morra an' will almost certainly suspend aw organised fitba' until the war is feenished. So the sooner we get ower there an' beat this bunch o'

54

Huns the sooner we can come back tae Milltown and defend oor three cups. Whit dae ye say?"

"Ah think it's a really good idea, boss," enthused Peter Black, the uncompromising centre half and captain of the team.

"Ah wis gonnae jine up onywey," added Chris Slaven, "but Ah'd rather fight alongside you lads than some total stranger wi' a posh accent."

"Brilliant. Let's dae it then," Menzies Campbell shouted.

The din of approval filled the room, giving the manager the confidence he needed to suggest, "Right, let's aw get thegither at wan o' clock on Saturday, as if we wur meetin' up fur a gemme, an' we'll get the train intae Glasgow where we'll sign up for the Highland Light Infantry. Everybody OK wi' that?"

"Naw, no everywan boss," a hesitant voice announced.

Heads turned to identify the source. It was Micky McGoldrick.

"Would you prefer tae jine up another day?" Dennis Wright asked helpfully.

"Naw, Ah'm no' gaun ony day. Ah don't agree wi' this war."

The players groaned.

"There's always fuckin' wan," Harry Miller said.

"Ur ye feart, Micky?" Tommy Doncaster asked, " 'Cos Ah don't mind admittin' it, an' Ah bet Ah'm no the only wan, but Ah'm feart as well. But Micky, it's goat tae be done, so we might as well aw dae it thegither."

"He didnae say that, Tommy. Wur ye no listenin'? He said that he didnae agree wi' the war," the manager pointed out like an interpreter for the daft.

"So why ur ye no' prepared tae fight fur ye'r King and country?" Fergus Smith asked bitterly.

"Because Ah hate violence and Ah've got nae loyalty tae ony king."

"That's treason, Micky!"

"Away back tae Ireland!"

"Shitebag!"

The abuse and shouts of disapproval broke out all around.

Dennis Wright called them to order. "Micky, Ah don't think Ah wahnt tae hear this but, then again, Ah started the discussion, so Ah feel obliged tae gie ye yer say."

"Let him say fuck all!" Fergus spat contemptuously.

"Noo, come on lads, wan singer wan song. Right, Micky, tell us, why will ye no' jine us?"

"OK, Ah'll try," gulped Micky. The silence as he spoke hung in the air like a hangman's noose. "We're aw workin' class in this room," Micky observed, "an' it'll be workin' class men that'll dae the vast bulk o' the fightin' an' the dyin' in this war. And fur why? In order to protect the interests o' the capitalists an' imperialists."

"Shite!" Peter Black protested, unable to contain his anger.

"Ah'm no prepared tae go an' kill another human bein' Ah've never even met just tae keep capitalist bosses an' their class in power. As John Maclean said in Glasgow last night…"

"That rabble rousin bastard!" Fergus interrupted. "Man should be fuckin' shot!"

"As John Maclean said in Glasgow last night," continued Micky undeterred, "a bayonet's just a weapon wi' a workin' man at either end. Well Ah'll no' be at the end o' wan tae kill ma fellow workin' man."

"So we just let big countries run over and bully wee countries then," said Menzies Campbell. It was a statement not a question.

"You mean like Britain's been doin' in Ireland fur centuries. Like it's bein' daein' tae vulnerable country efter vulnerable country across the world fur generations?"

"Ye've goat tae protect yer family, Micky. Surely ye can see that?" pleaded the manager in as reasonable a tone as he could muster.

"Aye, of course, Ah can see that. Ah wahnt tae protect them frae exploitation and discrimination fur bein' poor, but Ah'm no' gonnae dae that by fightin' fur the very people that ur oppressin' them."

"Ah'm sick o' aw this," Fergus Smith exploded. "Ah've hud it right up tae here wi' aw this shite! While we've been listenin' tae this coward, brave men huv been dyin' in France fightin' fur him an' his family. They didnae say 'Ah cannae die fur ye because the world's no' perfect or exactly the way Ah'd like it tae be,' they just lay doon an' fuckin' died."

The room burst into a round of applause at this intervention.

Micky picked up his bag, looked around the dressing room and said, "Ah suppose this is the end fur me in this fitba' team?"

"Ye're too fuckin' right it is," said Peter Black.

"Well, Ah'll awa' then. But afore ye aw go away tae be slaughtered just remember who you'll really be dyin' fur, an' it's no' Micky McGoldrick. It's the mill owners, the mine owners an' the slave drivers of British industry who just wahnt tae exploit workin' people like you an' me an' don't gie a fuck fur oor welfare. They won't be fightin' alongside ye, well neither will Ah."

"Anywan else agree wi' this cowardly bastard 'cos they can go wi' him right noo?" Peter Black barked.

Danny Harkins twitched. His voice stuck in his chest. He looked at Micky with a mixture of pity and awe. Micky was saying what he really believed, but didn't have the guts to stand up for. It was a lack of courage which was to take him to Ypres where he would be bayoneted to death in a bombed out shell hole by a young German lad who had terror screaming from his eyes.

★ ★ ★ ★ ★

Lachie was staring blankly, sitting in the chair beside the fire. His big frame filled the room dwarfing his eight-year-old sister, Maureen, kneeling on the floor beside him.

The window pulled down. Aggie McMillan reversed her backside back into the room.

"That's the Blairs fightin' again. As if there's no' enough fightin' in the wurrld these days," Aggie sighed. "Talkin' o' fightin', Lachie, ur ye no' thinkin' o' jinin' up?"

"Naw, Maw."

"Ur ye just gonnae sit oot the war oan yer big fat erse while aw yer mates ur away fightin' in France?"

"Ah don't wahnt tae fight, Mammy. Ah'm no' good at fightin'. Ah cannae fight. Don't make me, Mammy."

"But the army'll show ye how tae fight son an' they'll gie ye a big shiny new gun."

"Ah'd be scared, Maw."

"Aye, you an' everywan else. But just think how prood ye'd make yer Mammy an' yer wee sister tae think that oor Lachie wis oot in France daein' his wee bit fur his country."

"Ah don't wahnt tae go tae the war, Mammy."

"So ye don't wahnt tae fight fur yer family, Lachie? Fur yer Mammy? Fur wee Maureen there?"

"But ye're no' in ony danger, Mammy."

"Ah heard whit they bad Germans did tae the poor women o' Belgium efter they invaded their country. It wis terrible, Lachie. Thon wisnae nice. Ur ye gonnae wait till they're at the bottom o' the gairden afore ye'll fight fur us?"

Maureen looked up from her Victorian scrapbook, fixed Lachie's gaze with her pleading eyes and pined, "Will ye no fight fur me, Lachie? Will ye no' fight fur me?"

"Of course Ah wid, Maureen", a melting Lachie sobbed.

"That's ma boy. Yer Faither, God rest his soul, wid be awfy prood o' ye. So, when ur ye gaun?"

"Gaun where?"

"Gaun tae jine up fur the army."

"Ah don't know how tae dae it."

"Well, lucky fur you Ah've goat it aw arranged. Yer uncle Jack is gonnae come roon the morra efternoon tae take ye in tae a recruiting centre so ye can jine up."

"Is uncle Jack gonnae jine up as weel, Maw?"

"Naw, he's no' very well wi' his legs an' all, so he cannae. But the least he can dae is tae make sure that wan o' the McMillan's wull be there an' that we'll be daein' oor bit alang wi' everywan else."

"Can Ah see ye in yer uniform, Lachie?" Maureen asked.

"Wull Ah get a uniform, Mammy?"

"Of course ye wull son. Yer mates in the army wull need tae know ye're on their side so as tae know no' tae shoot ye. You'll look very handsome in yer uniform away there in France."

"But, Mammy, Ah cannae speak German. Whit if Ah run intae some o' they German sodgers?"

"Ye'll no' be talkin' tae them, Lachie, ye'll be tryin' tae kill them wi' yer gun an' yer bayonet."

"Wull they be tryin' tae kill me as well, Mammy?"

"Aye, they'll be tryin', but that's no' gonnae happen tae ma boy, 'cos you're big an' strong."

"Mammy…!"

"Aye?"

"Ah don't wahnt tae go to the war, Mammy. Don't make me, Mammy!"

"Of course ye dae, Lachie. Ye'll be fine. Uncle Jack'll be roon the morra tae pick ye up wi' his sair legs."

★ ★ ★ ★ ★

"Naw…!!Naw…! Naw…!" Teresa Boyle screamed. "Don't tell me. Ah don't wahnt tae hear it!"

Her son Wully had just announced that he was going to the front.

"Naw!" Teresa cried again. "No ma wee bairn. They cannae take you. They're no' gonnae take you. No' fur their mad war."

"He's made his mind up, Teresa. He's away in the morn'."

"Oh, that's OK is it, Bertie Boyle?" said Teresa Boyle scathingly. "Just say, 'Fare thee weel, Wully. Ah hope ye huv a nice death.' Stoap him, Bertie! Ye've goat tae stoap him!"

"He cannae stoap me, Maw. Ah'm twenty years old an' Ah'm ma ain man."

"Why ur ye daein' this tae me, Wully? Why?"

"Ah need tae fight fur the King."

"Wully, the King disnae gie a farthing's rub fur ye son. Ye'll just be another pawn in a rich man's game. If the King wahnts tae fight the Kaiser he can dae it himsel'. He disnae need tae sacrifice ma son tae dae his fightin' fur him."

"Teresa…" Bertie tried to explain patiently, "aw his pals ur daein' it. He disnae wahnt tae be back hame while they're aw fightin' at the front fur their country."

"Ah don't wahnt ony o' them tae go, but if they dae that's their folly. Ah'm no' huvin' ma wean marchin' away wi' them just because they wahnt tae play stupid deid heroes."

"Ah've made ma mind up, Maw. A recruitin' march frae Irvine will be walkin' past the mill at the Low Road the morra on its way tae Maryhill Barracks. Ah'm gonnae jine it there and walk wi' them tae Glesga tae sign up wi' the Highland Light Infantry."

"Oh, ye've made yer mind up huve ye, son? An' ye've decided tae leave me here worryin' aboot ye? Worryin' that every footstep will be somewan comin' tae the door tae tell me that ye've been bayoneted tae death. Leavin' me here tae cry masel tae sleep every night wunnerin' if ye're lyin' deid by some God-forsaken French road."

"But Teresa…" Bertie pleaded, "he's goat tae dae his bit. Whit wid happen if the Germans won this war?"

"Whit if they did? Whit ur they gonnae dae? Take away the vote Ah don't even huv? Ah don't care. German bosses, English bosses, Scottish bosses, they're aw the same. Ah wid rather live under the Germans fur the rest o' ma life than spend wan day in it withoot ma son…"

"Ah'm gaun, Maw, an Ah'm gaun by my ain free will. Ah'm no' a wee boy onymair an' Ah'm gonnae jine up tae dae ma duty."

"Right, go then, Wully. But don't kiss me goodbye. If ye walk oot o' ma life an' intae that war ye'll huv turned me tae stone – cold, hard an' unfeelin'."

"Tell her Da'. Ah'm awa oot."

"Teresa, ye've goat tae unnerstaun'…"

"Ah only unnerstaun' that ma son's aboot tae go away tae be butchered an' you seem tae think that *Ah'm* the wan who's bein' unreasonable fur no' wahntin' tae let him."

"Ter…"

"Don't 'Teresa' me, Bertie Boyle. You stood there and encouraged him tae walk oot o' here tae his death just like that sick, bampot Abraham in the Bible, willin' tae sacrifice his only son. An' fur whit? So you can boast at Pigs' Square aboot yer son daein' his bit by bein' blawin' tae bits. Ye're sacrificin' yer son fur the sake o' yer stupid male pride!"

Her heart broke. Her face crumpled. Her soul wailed. She sank to her knees and offered her joined hands in pleading supplication to her God, rocking backwards and forwards inconsolably as tears ran down her cheeks.

Bertie looked down impotently at the pity of it all.

★ ★ ★ ★ ★

"Now ladies, for many, many years we've been fighting against men who have been denying us the right to vote," said Emma Groves of the Renfrewshire Ladies Suffragette movement to a large audience of dedicated followers in Paisley.

"Over the past few of those years we have been taking much more direct action – with, it has to be said, some success – to make sure that our campaign remains a heated household issue throughout this land. Of course, as with our beloved sister Emily Davidson and the King's horse at the Epsom Derby last year, this has not always been without cost, but remains a tribute to the courage and dedication of the women of this country.

"The past few months, however, have seen our circumstances alter dramatically. We are now at war against the most pernicious, vicious and evil country on God's earth. If Britain loses this war and Germany becomes our masters it will set our aspirations back by decades. We will never see our personal freedoms and rights fulfilled in our lifetime.

"You will have heard the horror stories emanating from occupied Belgium as to how the German soldier treats women: raping and butchering them, young and old, in their thousands."

(Loud hisses and boos.)

"While we breathe we must resist the German soldiers and their dastardly Kaiser." (Cheers.)

"But what is the best way to do that? The leadership of our movement under Emmeline Pankhurst – and I have to say here and now ladies that I agree with it one hundred per cent – has decided that our campaign of social disruption and civil disobedience against the government should be halted with immediate effect. Nothing should be allowed to deflect the Government's time or resources away from the war effort."

(Applause.)

"It is also a time to show the Government and the people of this land our true worth to our country. We must be ready to stand in to do the jobs left behind by our heroic men at the front. If we can't fire the bullets, we can, at least, help to make them."

(Rousing applause.)

"By the end of this war many arguments against women's suffrage – that women are frivolous, lack constitutional fortitude, don't contribute to the defence of the nation etcetera – will have been completely debunked. We have this opportunity to show that, no less than the men, we are serious and steadfast in the application of our patriotic duties.

"But there is one equally important task to which we can apply ourselves in our commitment to the successful prosecution of this war: the task of ensuring that our young men go off to do their duty at the front."

(Shrill applause.)

"As women, we have some very direct methods of bending men to do our will. Separate beds night after night being one of them."

(Tittering.)

"Equally, we are in a unique position to flatter or decry something that all members of the male population hold dear: their manhood. It is up to us to constantly remind the shirkers and cowards that failing to do their duty at this critical time marks a failure as a man. Failure to protect their women and children cuts to the very core of what it is to be a man."

(Screams of approval.)

"There are a number of ways we can set about doing this. We should be prepared to publicly harangue young, able-bodied men strolling around our streets in civilian clothes as if the war has nothing to do with them. They should be disabused of the notion that this is acceptable in our eyes."

(Shouts of 'Cowards', 'Traitors', 'Big Jessies' etc.)

"You should refuse to be the sweetheart of any young man until he has taken the King's shilling and donned the khaki. Men who don't think enough of us to fight for us should be shunned by us."

(Prolonged standing ovation!)

"To emphasise the point further, you might wish to consider sending such 'men' a white feather as a mark of their cowardice."

(Earnest nods and murmurs in agreement.)

"Equally, and by contrast, those young men who do put their lives at risk for their country and all the women in it, should receive our unconfined gratitude publicly and, ahem, privately."

(Uproarious laughter.)

"I am confident that the women in this hall tonight, and indeed across the United Kingdom, will apply themselves to this task with the same initiative, imagination and sense of purpose that they have shown over these many years in the cause of Women's Suffrage.

"By the end of this conflict, not only will we have helped to win the war for Great Britain, we will have won over the vast majority of this nation to the belief that the women of this country are critical to its integrity, prosperity and progress and are no less worthy of the vote than our male counterparts.

Thank you."

The applause was rapturous. Emma Groves received a five minute standing ovation from an audience truly fired up by her message.

None more so than the young woman standing some nine seats along on the eighteenth row: Alice Henderson.

## CHAPTER FIVE

# *Close Encounters of the Unkind*

Jeanie Broon was standing at the top of the stair of the fire escape at number two mill waiting for Alice Henderson to come out for her morning break. She was already through her second cigarette, which she dragged on intensely, hand shaking as she did so.

She looked across the yard, across the burn, over the Low Road and up towards the Fereneze Braes. The world looked as it always did: cows chewing the cud monotonously, birds aimlessly circling the infinity of space, a kestrel hovering with ravenous intent. Life's routines went by and by, dripping slowly to some eternal rhythm. But inside, Jeanie was in a raging turmoil, withering with indignation. The word as made flesh by Alice Henderson had travelled full circle, returning to Jeanie complete with bells and whistles. She felt disgusted. She felt humiliated. She felt guilty.

But most of all she felt angry.

"Poor Harry. Poor Mr and Mrs Burchill. Poor me!" she thought. She felt that she had become a spectacle for pity. Worse, a figure to be mocked. Her life had become an open book in which the world was free to write graffiti. How could Alice Henderson have been so wilfully spiteful, so wicked?

At length the door opened and Alice came through.

"Hi, Jeanie," she chirped.

Silence.

Alice was confronted by Jeanie's back, rigid and tense.

"Ah said hi, Jeanie," repeated Alice, this time a bit more cautiously, sensing the volatility in the air.

Jeanie swung round to face her. Her lips were writhing in contempt as she spoke.

"So, whit's wi' the village two-bit gossip? Whit lies and scandal huv ye goat tae spew oot o' yer gub the day?"

"Whit dae ye mean, Jeanie?" an anxious, defensive Alice uttered.

"Ah blame masel," Jeanie continued, "Ah should never huv shared a confidence wi' a low-life guttersnipe like you."

"Who's a guttersnipe…? Whit…?!"

"And tae think ye wheedled it oot o' me wi' promises never tae tell another livin' soul – unless, of course, ye count every livin' soul in Milltown.

"You must huv tellt somebody else, or maybe Harry did. Ah heard it frae other folk, so Ah assumed it wis common knowledge."

"Ah see, Alice. Well, ah must admit that changes everythin'. Ah must apologise fur just callin' ye a gossip."

"It's awright, Jeanie. Don't mention it…"

"Naw, Alice, ye're no' *just* a gossip – ye're a fuckin' liar as well."

With this she stepped forward and slapped Alice across the side of her face.

Alice curled up against the railing defensively.

"Aaagh! That really hurt!"

"Nothin' like as much as the hurt you've caused other people wi' yer lies an' yer gossip. Your pain will disappear in a minute; the hurt you've caused wull last a lifetime."

"Ye're a fuckin' maniac," moaned Alice.

"Just remember that then the next time you go aroon the village spreadin' stories aboot me. Ah'm away back in tae sniff diesel fumes. The stench roon here is absolutely putrid."

Alice felt the bile rise in her stomach. She knew from that moment on that she hated Jeanie Broon, that she would eventually make her pay in full measure for the humiliation that had been inflicted upon her this day.

There would be no hurry. This was a vengeance which could stew for years if necessary.

But someday…

★ ★ ★ ★ ★

Micky McGoldrick arrived at St Conval's cemetery in Arthur Lea at five to eight on the Monday morning.

Next to what was obviously a public reception hut was a wooden bothy. Micky chapped the door. No answer. Then again with more force. Still no answer.

He paused and listened intently. He was almost sure that he could hear hushed voices.

This time he hammered on the door.

The door flew open and a small man with a face made for girning and a cap off-centre, shoved his neck forward whilst managing to keep every other part of his anatomy still.

"Jesus man, whit ur ye daein'? Ur ye tryin' tae wake the dead?"

The laughter from the men sitting behind him was of the, "Not that old joke again!" variety. Micky apologised and said that he was looking for a Mr Travers.

"Dead or alive?" the squinty bunnet asked.

"The live version would be preferable."

"Right, pardner, come in an' meet the only Mr Travers still alive in the cemetery."

Micky had just stepped inside the door when the bunnet turned smartly, straightened itself up to its full height, clicked its heels together military style, saluted itself sharply and announced, "Tony Travers reporting for duty, sir. How can I be of service?"

Micky had by now deduced that Tony was either grade A asylum material or a gross eccentric.

"My name's Micky McGoldrick and I'm also reporting for duty. Father O'Keefe said that you would keep me right."

"Keep you right? He said that did he now?" a thoughtful Tony repeated slowly, rubbing his pointed chin all the while. "Did you know," continued Tony, springing to life, "that giving directions is the most confusing task in the world? And do you know why?"

Micky confessed that he would need to be enlightened on this point of interest.

"Because left can be right and right can be wrong!"

Once again the reaction of the two men in the corner told Micky that they had heard this 'joke' ad nauseum.

"Well, Micky McGoldrick, just sit yourself down there. Have ye brought a can?"

"A can?"

"Aye, a can. A can fur yer tea?"

"No…Ah didn't…".

"Right, this is St Conval's can, but since he's no' been seen aroon here fur thirteen hunner years or so Ah suppose he widnae mind if ye borrowed it fur the day. Just the day, mind ye. Bring yer ain efter this. The morra: no can, no can do.

Noo, let's get the introductions oot o' the way," Tony continued.

Pointing to a red-haired man in his thirties, Tony said flamboyantly, "The gentleman here on my right doesn't exist. However, this reprobate's name's Gerry Sweeney."

"Pleased to meet you, Gerry," said Micky, extending his hand in friendship.

Gerry spat richly into his own hand with a full spittle before clasping Micky's hand tightly.

"That's us brothers noo!" Gerry proudly proclaimed. "In fact we're the spittin' image o' each other."

Micky was beginning to get a feel for the madcap mentality that permeated this workplace. His mind started to work on a parody of a well-known saying: "You don't need tae be mad tae work here, as long as ye don't mind bein' the odd wan oot!" That was about right.

Tony took over again and, in the style of a Victorian Gaiety Theatre Master of Ceremonies, exclaimed, "And this little piece of human excrement on my left would be 'It-wisnae-me-Ah-didnae-mean-it-Ah'm-only-the-choirboy-roon-here'-Master-one-eye-Michael-Crossan!"

"Pleased to meet your boring acquaintance, Micky," Michael said with feeling.

"This is a university for personal insults," Micky thought to himself as he shook the hand of Michael who, on closer inspection, had indeed but one eye.

"Michael gies special help tae the new starts," advised Tony. "Ye can always rely on him tae keep an eye oot fur ye."

"At least it keeps me oot o' the war. Ah shoot wi' this eye."

For the first time Micky felt close to smirking, but managed to resist the feeble urge.

"Ah suppose ye'll wahnt tae know whit yer duties ur, Micky?"

"Would be helpful," Micky agreed.

"Can ye dae This an' That?"

"Well, Ah can dae This, but Ah might need special trainin' tae dae That," Micky quipped, concerned at how easy he found it to fall into the zany humour.

"Well, This an' That's neither Here nor There," said Tony. "Aw we dae aw day is flick oor cigarette douts intae a doused fire. Ye see we're in the ashes tae ashes business!"

"This is getting' too fuckin' bizarre," thought Micky. "Ah feel exhausted an' it's still only ten past eight!"

Reality seemed to be in meltdown, as if he was drifting off in a sea of pink marshmallow.

"No, really…" Tony said in a new, serious, business-like, 'OK jokes over, no messing now' tone. "we are fortunate, Micky, to be employed in a growing industry: there's folk dyin' noo that never died afore."

It was going to be a long shift.

★ ★ ★ ★ ★

*William Henry Bury. Born 1859.* (Tick.) *Sister died in epileptic fit in the same year.* (Tick.) *Father died in freak accident in 1860.* (Tick.) *Mother incarcerated in asylum for Melancholia in 1860 until her death four years later.* (Big tick.) *Moved from Midlands to Bow next to Whitechapel in October 1887.* (Even bigger tick.) *Hurriedly left with new wife for Dundee on a false pretext in January 1889, after trying desperately to emigrate to Brisbane, Australia.* (Huge tick.) *Murdered his wife in February, 1889.* (Mega tick.) *Slit open her abdomen.* (Humungous tick.)

Put all of that alongside the fact that, when in London, he often stayed out till very late the next morning, or disappeared for days on end, without ever offering an explanation. Or that he routinely carried a knife and, indeed, slept with one under his pillow. Or that he contracted venereal disease from a prostitute. Or that his new wife had worked as a lady of the night. Or that two people in London who knew him described him as a "violent drunk". Or that five days after his wedding he was interrupted kneeling on top of his wife with a knife at her throat threatening to kill her. Or that he matched the description of the suspect seen by PC Smith and William Marshall in Berner Street moments after Catherine Eddowes had been murdered there. Or that his wife described him as having "gone berserk" on returning late in to the night of Annie Chapman's murder – the only killing from which a lost murder weapon was found. Or that the police found graffiti chalked on the back door of his Dundee flat which read "Jack Ripper is behind this door," and "Jack Ripper is in this seller," (sic) on the stairwell. Or that the *Dundee Courier* reported that William Bury had confessed to Lieutenant Parr that he was Jack the Ripper. Or that a startled William dropped his paper when an acquaintance, David Walker from Dundee, asked him to look and see if there was any news about Jack the Ripper. Or that his wife, when asked about Jack the Ripper, told people in Dundee that, "Jack the Ripper is quiet now," and, again, that "Jack the Ripper is taking a rest."

Or that his Dundonian hangman felt confident enough to tell people that he had just executed Jack the Ripper in April 1889.

His hangman. That sign from God.

In the 1881 census, William Henry Bury was mistakenly

recorded as being William Henry *Berry:* the same name as his executioner-to-be.

The Reverend McDonald sat back contentedly from his notes. He had found his man. Jack the Ripper was William Henry Bury of Stourbridge, late of an unmarked prison grave in Dundee.

He could now turn his attention to The Servant Girl Annihilator!

★ ★ ★ ★ ★

Todd MacDuff was in Pigs' Square, holding court again.

The world had turned on its axis since last he was there, pontificating that wars were a thing of the past.

"This war'll no' last long," an unabashed Todd opined authoritatively. "The German generals are predicting that it'll be over by the time the leaves are falling from the trees, an' oor generals are tellin' us that it'll aw be ower by Christmas."

"Who do you think wull be right, Todd?" asked Ken Butterworth deferentially.

Sleekit Tam's chin pushed his head up and around, the better to hear Todd's reply.

"Right now the Germans have two armies heading for Paris, wi' the British and French in full retreat. If the Huns reach Paris, which they might do within the next month, then the war wull be ower and the balance o' power in Europe wull huv shifted dramatically in favour o' the Germans. We'll just huv tae – peck, peck, peck – live wi' it."

"Ah think it'll be like an arm-wrestling competition," Archie Currie observed. "There'll be a period o' grunting, bulging eyes and sweaty foreheids afore it becomes apparent who's the stronger. Once that happens the dominant force will push tae victory quickly."

"Who do you think that'll be?" Ken asked again.

"The Germans have the right amount o' men in the right

positions on the ground tae win this war. The French committed suicide against the German guns in the first few weeks. Ah think they thought they hud nothin' tae dae but button up their red troosers an' ride their cavalry straight tae Berlin. Meanwhile the Germans just walked roon the French guns via Belgium as if neither they nor Belgium existed. If the Germans hold their nerve the war is theirs."

"That aw sounds a bit defeatist," Bertie Boyle lamented. "Ma son's in the khaki noo. Ah've goat a wife back hame who's breakin' her hert an' wahnts nothin' tae dae wi' me because she thinks Ah didnae dae enough tae stop him. Is it aw fur nothin'?"

"Naw, Bertie, it's no' fur nothin'," Raymond Patterson piped up. "Yer son's a brave man riskin' his life fur his country. That can never be fur nothin'. The trouble is we're tryin' tae raise an army o' a hunner thoosan' men oan top o' the hunner thoosan' we awready huv, when we're gonnae need tae commit millions o' brave Wully Boyles if we wahnt tae contain the Hun never mind defeat him."

Sleekit Tam kicked a stone aimlessly through and past the group of men as if to remind people that he was there.

"Of course," added Archie, "the mair men that turn up fur this war the mair men that'll get massacred on baith sides. They'll be facin' huge, absolutely huge guns capable of killin' hunners o' people an' destroying buildings wi' wan shell fired frae a single gun sittin' behind a hill miles away frae its target. This war wull produce death on an industrial scale, the likes o' which the world's never seen afore."

"Ah see the entire Milltown Victoria fitba team's away tae the front thegither," said Johnny Byrne.

"You make it sound as if they've just gaun away oan holiday, Johnny," Raymond Patterson remarked reproachfully.

"Ah think some o' them dae think it's gaunnae be a holiday," Johnny sighed.

"Actually," Ken Butterworth pointed out, "it wisnae the whole team that jined up. Micky McGoldrick refused tae go wi' them."

"Did he say why?" asked Archie Currie.

"Apparently he said that he didnae agree wi' the war," Raymond intervened. "He said it's an imperialist war tae decide who's gonnae huv the right tae exploit poor people."

"He's a Socialist, is he no'?" Archie queried.

"Aye, a bit like you," Raymond replied. "Do you think he's right?"

"Ah don't rightly know. All Ah know is that this war is noo a fight tae the death. If we lose the chances ur we'll huv the Kaiser's men ower here tellin' us whit tae dae. Prussians like orderin' people aboot. Ah cannae huv that. If they raise the age o' recruitment Ah'm gonnae fight like your boy, Bertie, Socialist or no'."

Sleekit Tam gobbed on the pavement. "Cyprus," he announced mournfully as the slivers settled on the paving stone.

"It's aw very weel the Micky McGoldricks o' this wurrld sayin' that they're no' gaun tae the war" Todd MacDuff proclaimed. "The thing is, they might no' always huv that luxury. Whit wull they dae – peck, peck, peck, – if the war comes tae them?"

★ ★ ★ ★ ★

Harry Burchill was puzzled and perplexed.

None of his friends had called round over the past week. He had watched them pass the door, sometimes in groups, almost rushing past, hands in pockets, heads down.

He had called in for a few of them without success. On each occasion he was met by the mothers at the door, standing like humourless sentinels, not inviting conversation. Just, "Naw, he's no' in." Door closed.

He was now heading towards Pigs' Square. There were four elderly men standing there, all of whom Harry knew by sight, and Sleekit Tam that Harry knew to ignore by sight.

On reaching the point at which it would have been customary to acknowledge and be acknowledged, the backs seemed to turn against him. "Probably deep in discussion about the war," Harry thought.

Across the street a group of girls were walking past, including Marilyn Heron. They were looking across at him. Staring at him, in fact, before huddling together and laughing.

Was he just imagining this?

He checked his pockets. He had eight pennies. More than enough for a drink. He could certainly do with one.

As he entered through the swing door of the Bottom Shop he noticed Hoppy in his usual corner, the man with the drooped head at the bar and a skinny, aggressive looking man standing by the door at the toilets.

The barman visibly reacted as Harry approached the bar.

"Nice day the day," Harry said, trying to inject an air of bon ami, as well as seeking confirmation that he was actually a real person in the land of the living.

No response. Absolute dead silence.

"A pint of your best beer when you're ready barman, if you please."

Nothing again. The barman continued to stare in stunned silence at Harry, as if he was a kangaroo who had just come up to the bar to complain about being given a dirty glass. His hand remained frozen over a pump.

Harry was becoming intensely irritated by this treatment.

"Hello? Customer here! Is there anybody there? Any sign of intelligent life?"

The barman started out of his trance. His decision was made.

"Look, Harry, can you come through the back fur a minute? Ah need a word wi' ye first."

"Aye, sure. Whit's the problem?" Harry quizzed.

As they walked through, the skinny man said something that Harry didn't catch, but which he guessed was less than complimentary.

Once in the back room the barman turned to face Harry.

"Look, Harry, Ah don't know how tae put this…"

"Why don't you try putting it in English? You do speak English, don't you?"

"Aye, but it's difficult. Ah've never hud tae dae this afore… anyway, the thing is…look, Ah'm no' wan fur judgin' people. In ma line o' work ye cannae afford tae huv too many fixed opinions. But for by the morality o' it, first an' foremost Ah'm a businessman…"

"Sure, and I'm doing my best to give you some business. Why are you making it so difficult for me?"

"The thing is…" he paused and gulped… "…the thing is, if Ah serve you in ma pub other folk'll no' come in, an' there's plenty o' other pubs for them tae choose in this town."

"What are you trying to tell me? Am I barred? What for…?"

"Because men don't like tae be sharin' a drink wi' a man who might be lookin' at them in a certain way."

"A certain…!" Then the penny dropped. Jeanie Broon! She must have blabbed!

"What have you heard exactly," Harry asked coldly.

"Just what everywan else in Milltown hus heard, Harry: that ye find blokes attractive."

"Who did you hear that from?"

"Harry, Ah'm a barman. Ah hear everywan talkin' an' their aw talkin' aboot you. Ye even managed tae knock the war aff the front pages fur a day or two there. Anyway, Harry, ye cannae come back in here again. Ah'm sorry, but business is business.

By the way, ye'd better watch oot fur Archie Ferguson. He's heard ye fancy him an' he's no' happy."

Harry stepped out on to the street. He looked over across to the cemetery and the parish kirk ahead. There had been a religious community on that spot, since at least the twelfth century. The old handsome building was of late eighteenth century design. It seemed to gaze down on him with disapproval. Ages of puritanical proselytising appeared to surface to register its disgust. He was on the road to perdition. Everything seemed to reinforce his dislocation from his own community.

"How many graves were turning over there?" he wondered.

It had taken Harry six years to come to terms with the fact that he had active sexual inclinations that seemed perversely different from everyone else he knew. Now that his guilty secret was no longer a secret he would cease to be a real, multi-faceted person in the community. He would just be Harry Burchill, "the poof!" No shades of being. No redeeming personal qualities. Nothing to enrich his soul – especially now he didn't have one! He would be a figure of fear, prejudice, disgust and hate. A totem of justification for intolerance.

And who could he talk to? The one person he imagined might understand him had betrayed him for a moment of cheap gossip, no doubt mocking him for being a "hammysexual!"

Obviously, Jeanie had told Archie that Harry fancied him. Did she use it as conversational bait to ensnare him? Are they together now, deriding the very thought of Harry and his weird sexual preferences?

Harry had never felt so alone, so rejected, so utterly miserable. He would need to go to London as soon as possible.

But first he would need to talk to his parents.

★ ★ ★ ★ ★

Two men in dark clothing stood outside St Thomas' church waiting for a response to their knock on the door.

Mrs Brophy the housekeeper answered.

"Good evening," the taller of the two men said, "we're here to see Father Dannfald. Is he available?"

"Yes, he's upstairs. Can I say who's calling?"

"It might be better if we tell him that ourselves," replied the shorter of the two.

"I see. Well, I'll let Father Dannfald know that you're here."

As they waited at the door, underneath the statue of the Madonna and Child, Inspector Flannagan and Detective Sergeant

Mulgrew admired this recent extension to the Parish church which Father Dannfald had commissioned to be built.

At length, they were joined by Father Dannfald. He could see immediately – or rather sense – that they were policemen.

"Good evening, gentlemen. How may I help you?"

"Good evening, Father," both men replied.

"My name, Father, is Detective Inspector Flannagan, and this is my colleague Detective Sergeant Mulgrew," said the taller man. "We wonder if we might have a word with you about a couple of matters?"

"Certainly," Father Dannfald answered whilst ushering them into the public room on the left. "Right, gentlemen, make yourself at home. Have a seat. Now what's on your mind?"

"Just a few general questions before we start, Father, if we may…"

"Before we do start though, may I say that there is no need to call me Father, although I appreciate the tone of respect that it carries. The term, in the context of the Roman Catholic Church, is a reference to a 'spiritual Father', which if you're not Catholics, doesn't apply. Just call…"

"We are both Catholics, Father. Probably the reason why we were selected to come and speak to you today."

"Very well. So, I repeat, what's on your mind?"

"As I said," the inspector continued, "if we could begin with a few general questions to confirm that we are authorised to speak with you about these matters by establishing your identity,"

"Of course."

"You are Father Dannfald, yes?"

"Yes, Inspector, that is correct."

"And you are German by birth, are you not?"

"Indeed."

"Can I ask where in Germany you were born?"

"I was born in Freiburg, which is a town in Baden-Wurttemberg in South-west Germany, on the edge of the Black Forest."

"When was that exactly?"

"The twenty seventh of February, eighteen-seventy.".

"Ah, the year of German unification!" quoted the Sergeant.

"I see that you are a student of history," said Father Dannfald.

"Hopeless with dates normally, but for some reason that one has always stuck," the Sergeant replied.

"How long have you been in Britain, Father?" the Inspector continued.

"Twenty two years, eighteen of which have been in Scotland and sixteen of which have been in Milltown."

"Do you often go back to Germany?"

"Very rarely. It's a hectic four-day journey and very expensive. However, I do still have family there and I keep regular contact with them through letters. Or at least I did until this war.

"Now, I don't wish to be rude, but I am due to do my rounds visiting the sick of the parish in half an hour, so I would greatly appreciate it if you could get to the point, as it were."

"Of course, Father, of course. At the outset, could I say that Detective Sergeant Mulgrew will be taking notes. You will be able to read them to check their accuracy at the end of the meeting, if you wish."

"What is the purpose of these notes and who are they for?"

"They are merely to form a record of the meeting so that my bosses can be sure that I have communicated their concerns accurately."

"Concerns? Am I under investigation, Inspector?"

"Absolutely not, Father. When I say concerns I mean concerns *for* you, not *about* you."

"In what way?"

"Your safety, Father."

"I see."

"You don't seem surprised?"

"Well, I am not insensitive to the prevailing atmosphere of hatred here towards my country, gentlemen, which I should imagine will only get worse as the war continues. It is not difficult to foresee a situation where someone might wish to take his anger out on the only German living in their midst."

"Exactly, Father. We would not wish to see you come to harm as a result of an act of violence at the hands of someone who may have just suffered bereavement from the front. But the danger is real – very real."

"Quite."

"Have you thought about, perhaps, moving out of Milltown until the war is over to the relative safety of a Catholic retreat house?"

"Has this already been discussed with the Bishop by any chance?"

"Yes, he has given us permission to say that the decision is entirely yours."

Father Dannfald emitted a short laugh.

"Father?"

"Excuse me, Inspector, Bishop John may well have said that, but he knows perfectly well what my response would be."

"Which is…?"

"Which is that I am here to do God's work. There have been many times in the history of this church when being an evangelist has been fraught with dangers. The church is littered with martyrs."

"You wish to become a martyr?"

"No, I don't wish to become a martyr. But will I be silenced in my proclamation of the Truth as revealed to us by the teachings of Our Lord Jesus Christ? No, I will not."

"Well, could we at least suggest that you take sensible precautions?"

"Such as…?"

"Such as perhaps making yourself less conspicuously available to any would-be assailant. We know, for instance, that it is your practice to walk up and down the garden in front of the church reading your Bible."

"Of course I do. I think that it is important to demonstrate that devotion to God is part of one's everyday life and is not merely to be closeted away in private as if it is something to be embarrassed about. You can't compartmentalise God in your life."

"People would understand, Father. I am sure that your parishioners would prefer that their spiritual leader was safe among them than at risk. God, too, I am sure would understand."

"I don't wish to seem dismissive, Inspector, and I do appreciate your concern for my safety. I will give consideration to the matter. Of that I promise."

"Would it also be possible to restrict the number of occasions when you need to go out and about in Milltown? For example, you've just told us that you are due to go out to visit the sick of the parish. Could your curate not be given that task?"

"He already does. We both do. It is a very important and necessarily time-consuming task. I can see no situation which would prevent me from going out among my flock in the context of their everyday lives. People come to this church to be of the 'Many gathered in His name' and to hear the Word of the Lord as expressed through the Bible. But, equally, the Church must go to its people through its priests and share first hand their everyday experiences.

"As I say, I appreciate your concerns, but I feel sure that God will protect me."

"Unlike your very own Bishop of Freiburg who was stabbed to death by a mad butcher in 1299!" the Detective Sergeant commented caustically.

"As I said, Sergeant, you are quite the student of history, but the very fact that you have to go back to over six hundred years ago surely makes it the exception that proves the rule."

"Well, we're here today to alert you to the risk and to informally request that you assess those risks and to take them seriously. We would strongly advise that, at the very least, you change your routines in a way which would make an attack on you more difficult to plan and to execute."

"Of course, I respect your concerns and your advice gentlemen, I really do.

"However, if I remember correctly, you said that you wished to discuss a *couple* of matters. What is the second matter?"

"Your anti-war sermon last Sunday…"

★ ★ ★ ★ ★

Harry Burchill needed to get out of Milltown. Quickly. Permanently.

But that would need to wait at least a week.

He had resolved to tell his parents tonight what everyone else in the town already knew: that he was a homosexual.

Firstly, he needed a few drinks to fortify the constitution.

He assumed that the attitude he had encountered in the Bottom Shop would be replicated in every drinking establishment in Milltown. Rather than put himself through the humiliation again, he elected instead to walk down to neighbouring Arthur Lea about a mile and a half away.

Milltown was situated to the south of Glasgow on top of a series of hills overlooking the whole of the city and the Clyde basin. As he started his descent down the Kirkhill Brae towards Arthur Lea, he marvelled at the valley twinkling magically below, spreading across the darkness like a bowl of light and filling him with a sense of hope and wonder.

Harry was scarcely known in Arthur Lea, which was just as well, given the circumstances.

The first pub on the road from Milltown was the Arthur Lea Inn, a typical spit and sawdust licensed premises of the time. A working man's pub where all the great and not so great issues of the day were debated fiercely, incoherently and inconsequentially.

It was scarcely busy with only about nine people scattered throughout.

Harry arrived at the bar where a grey-haired man was nursing a half of whisky and a half pint of beer. Harry ordered the same and planted himself next to the silver top.

"Haven't seen your face in here before," said the forty-something well-spoken man.

"That's because it hasn't been in here before," Harry explained.

"Are you from around here?" the pub regular enquired.

"No, I'm from Milltown."

"Oh, a moon man from Hilltown," joked the resident in reference to Milltown's loftier topography. Roses in Arthur Lea were always in bloom before those in Milltown because of the slight temperature differential.

"'Fraid so," Harry admitted.

"You know, just this morning at work in Shanks I heard a cracking story about Milltown…I'm John by the way." He interrupted himself as he shook Harry's hand. "Apparently, there was a couple up there who chucked each other because…wait for it…they both fancied the same bloke! What do you think of that? I bet when they kissed they both thought of Jack Johnson!"

Harry sounded a forced laugh at this reference to the boxing Heavyweight Champion of the World. Inside, however, his heart sank. How far would he need to go to get away from all this? To get away from himself?

"Sorry, I didn't catch your name?" John prompted.

"Andrew," Harry lied, scared in case John had already heard the name of the man involved and might be able to put two and two together.

"Tell you what though," John continued, "it's all very well joking about it when you don't know them personally, but I wouldn't even like to be sitting in the same room as a willie watcher."

"No, you would never know either, John. You could be sitting next to him at a bar and you'd never know," Harry teased.

"I would never share a pint with a uranian," John retorted, with disgust dripping from his voice.

"Cheers!" said Harry, clinking glasses as he did so.

"It's time," thought Harry. "No more delays."

He finished his drink in two gulps, shook hands with John and left the pub to go home to face the ordeal of his life.

The road back up to Milltown was steep and treacherous, especially in the dark. Harry was a reasonably fit young man, but even for him this was quite an effort.

Once he had negotiated the last and steepest of these hills – which awaited the unsuspecting traveller round a bend like a ladder to the sky – he turned down the narrow winding road which led towards Kirkton Field and his great dread.

His mind was racing along with his pulse. How would he start? Should he lead in with a big introduction or should he just blurt it out? Images of how they might react loosened his bowels. His mother would be crushed. Mortified. And his father, would he shout and bawl? At least that would be preferable to crying. He had never seen his father cry before and the very thought of it seemed distinctly odd.

So absorbed was he in this contemplation of his own fears that he was unaware of the footsteps fast approaching from behind.

As the road wound round to the left where it would begin to run parallel to the densely packed trees of Kirkton Wood, Harry felt a firm hand on his shoulder.

"Hello, Harry."

It was Archie Ferguson.

★ ★ ★ ★ ★

Dawn broke over the Western Front.

Out in No Man's Land at Kruseik Ridge in the Ypres salient, a young Scottish soldier lay still in his trench, his rictus mocking his exposed, gouged throat.

Death was all around, contorting this way and that.

Here the soldiers who never more would rouse. There the dismembered bits of human detritus – the eyes fixed within a shattered skull, staring inanely from deep inside the mud bank, the 'comical' corpses buried arse-up, the hands groping blindly up the slope of a shell hole lacking a body to lever to the top.

And, staring blankly down on this first light, out through the trees of Kirkton Wood onto Kirktonfield, the hanged body of Harry Burchill.

Milltown stirred. The horns of its mills sounded a reveille summoning its workers to their posts. Horses snorted impatiently. People shuffled out into the day, eyes still baked in sleep. Janitors stoked the school boilers, awaiting their reluctant arrivals.

Mr Brown arrived at the sorting office to arrange the town's mail, wondering if there might be one from Craig among the piles laid out there.

Mrs Burchill knelt devoutly in front of a cold, empty grate with rolled newspapers, kindle, firelighters and matches to prepare the fire that would welcome in a blaze her waking children.

And ten year old Betty Thomson took her dog Shep for its morning walk into Kirkton Wood.

# *Interlude*

So the war raged on.

The Germans did indeed lose their nerve at the Battle of the Marne, when a gap opened up between the German First and Second Armies. The British Expeditionary Force moved into the gap, thereby exposing the German flanks. The Germans retreated, almost in a rout, chased by the French and British as if they were on a foxhunt.

Once over the river Aisne, however, the fox turned.

The Germans started digging to build solid, defensive positions with massive rear works and deep concrete dugouts.

Then the 'race to the sea' – or, rather, the race to outflank each other before the sea was reached – began.

At length, the line of trenches ran across North Western Europe for some 500 miles from Belgium to the Swiss Alps. Armies faced each other, sometimes only 50 metres apart.

The allied trenches were far flimsier, reflecting their desire to keep on the offensive and push the Bosche back across the Rhine.

Attack, however, in such an attritional environment was extremely costly, especially in the face of bombardment, barbed wire and machine gun enfilade fire.

Losses, consequently, were astronomically high.

The Germans had lost the prize of a quick victory, but they had gained territory across Belgium and deep into Northern France, including most of its iron ore deposits, crucial for the continuation of the war. Moreover, they were very strongly entrenched in such a way as to make their dislodgement seem almost impossible without a commitment to the most appalling scale of casualties imaginable.

By the end of the first Battle of Ypres in November 1914, ninety per cent of the original British Expeditionary Force (the 'Old

Contemptibles') had become a casualty. The regular army of 1914 was now giving way to the largely untrained and untested recruits of Kitchener's New Army.

Delusion, however, was still very much in the air. Generals on all sides still dreamed of scattering the enemy and making the 'breakthrough' with a charge of horse cavalry, or imagined that you could wear down machine guns and gun batteries with sheer human sacrifice.

Elsewhere, more devious, if practical, minds were designing the shock and awe of the tank, or preparing to channel gas for perfidious purposes.

## CHAPTER SIX

# *Kruseik Ridge*

Craig Brown had been passed out as a soldier of the regular army into the 2nd Battalion of the Scots Fusiliers just before the war started. Like most of the lads of his age in August, 1914, in and out of uniform, he couldn't wait to go to Europe and see some action against the Germans.

"It's no' gonnae be a game o' toy soldiers!" his sister Jeanie had warned him. "Lots o' folk ur gonnae get hurt. Some might even get killt."

Not that the thought of that bothered Craig in the slightest. He couldn't wait to get on to that field of play and "get stuck intae them!"

He had heard the stories (some exaggerated or invented) of the German atrocities in Belgium. Well that was fine by him. He didn't want to think of them as decent people being misled by autocratic rulers. He didn't want to think of them as people at all. In his dreams whole Teutonic divisions had surrendered to his Tommy gun. "Just let me at them," he thought. "Just let me at them."

At first Craig imagined that he would be sent to Gibralter where the 2nd Scots Fusiliers were stationed. He was overjoyed to learn, however, that the Regiment was coming home to meet him in Catterick before being transported across the sea to Zeebrugge on October 7th. From there, they were due to travel north to support Antwerp ("the pistol aimed at England's heart"), which was under siege.

Disobligingly, Antwerp fell two days later when he was barely on the march and so the 7th Division, of which the 2nd Royal Scots Fusiliers were part, was re-routed to a place called Ypres in Flanders.

The German army, reformed under General Falkenhayn, was flinging everything at this town a few miles from the Channel ports. It was also at this point at which the Germans hoped to outflank the British Expeditionary Force, make a dash southwards behind them into France and encircle the Allies.

Now, in terms of military strategy, this meant diddly-squat to young Craig, but he reckoned with grim, simplistic logic, that if that's what the Hun wanted to do then it must be bad and it was up to him and his mates to stop him.

He was delighted to find that there were another two Milltown lads in his battalion: Tom Carlton and Paddy Lynch. Both were on the other side of the (religious) fence back home. Well they were all on the same side now. In fact, they were even in the same Company – Company B – under Major Burgoyne.

As they marched to a place called Broodseinde Ridge, Tom told Craig some disconcerting news.

"Craig, wis it your sister that wis gaun oot wi' Harry Burchill?"

"Aye, still is Ah think."

"Well no according tae ma sister, Susan, she's no'. She tellt me aw aboot it in a letter ah goat frae her the other day."

"Oh, really! Whit did she say?"

"Afore Ah tell ye, whit did ye think o' Harry?"

"He's OK. A bit posh fur ma likin', but then Ah'm no' the wan that's gaun oot wi' him."

"The thing is, you could," said Tom, which sent Paddy into guffaws of laughter.

"Whit? Ah could go oot wi' Harry Burchill?!" Craig queried. "Sorry tae disappoint ye lads, Ah think ye've been lookin' at khaki in the jungle fur too long, but Ah'm no' like that."

"Naw, but Harry is," Paddy chipped in.

"Harry…? Harry …that's gaun oot wi' ma sister? Ur we talkin' aboot the same bloke here?"

"Aye," confirmed Tom. "Harry, the teacher's son, who lives doon at Kirkton Field back in Milltown. That's the wan."

Craig stopped for the ten seconds or so you might get out of line before some gorilla with toothache orders you back in.

"You're kiddin' me lads. Tell me you're just kiddin'"

"Well, the way Susan tells it," Tom continued, "they chucked each other two weeks ago because they both fancy Archie Ferguson. Apparently it's aw roon the village."

"And for by," added Paddy, "he told your sister that he's kissed both of them and Archie's better."

"Archie's wan as well?!" gasped an open mouthed Craig.

"Naw, naebody believes Harry, an' Archie says he's gonnae kill him when he gets his hauns oan him."

"How far is it tae Broodseinde Ridge lads? Ah feel like killin' somebody masel!"

★ ★ ★ ★ ★

When Craig Brown disembarked at Zeebrugge on the 6th October, 1914, he had never seen a dead human body.

By the 23rd, he had seen hundreds, many grotesquely mutilated.

On the 6th October, he had never fired a gun directly at another human being. By the 23rd, he had used countless rounds of ammunition against the advancing grey uniforms of the German army.

On the 6th October, he had only plunged a bayonet into a sandbag in a public park in England. On the 23rd, he would, within 24 hours, use his bayonet to kill four German soldiers, one as he pleaded for mercy.

On the 6th October, Craig saw himself as a regular bloke who liked a laugh, a drink and a pretty girl on his arm on a Saturday night. As someone who was just in Flanders to do his duty and go home.

By the 23rd, he didn't recognise himself anymore.

He had watched over 500 of his battalion being slaughtered by gunshot, shrapnel or bayonet. He had become anaesthetised to pain and suffering. He didn't laugh. He didn't cry. He didn't dream. He didn't sigh. Life had become all about killing and not being killed.

He had watched some of his fellow soldiers break down under constant shelling. He didn't care. He could have shot them himself just to shut them up. He obeyed orders. He didn't question. He didn't expect. He was in survivor mode, a form of shock which allowed him to still function as a soldier, but not as a human being.

Tom and Paddy had also changed.

However, Tom, whilst now capable of bending his mind, heart and hand to slaughter, still had an awareness of a life beyond the trench. He still thought about home – past, present and future. He prayed constantly that he and all his mates would survive the fighting and manage to get safely back to their homes in Renfrewshire, Ayrshire, Wigtownshire and the Borders.

Nor had he yet become blasé about the killing and the dying. He was still disturbed by others' suffering, even that of the enemy.

He sometimes shot with his eyes closed while sobbing into the butt of his rifle.

Paddy was in bits.

He spoke obsessively to himself, punctuated by random high pitched yips which betrayed his madness. He was afflicted by a constant trembling and, with a gun in his hands, was a liability to his comrades.

"If he survives this," thought Tom, "he will need to be sent back to Blighty."

Tom needn't have worried. He wouldn't.

Word had come back that A, C and D Companies had fought a great battle the previous day in an effort to clear the houses at Poezelhoek. The more Germans they killed the more that seemed to appear. They were forced back. There was a growing sense of being overcome by a much superior force.

There was also an intense anger when it was reported that Captain Fairlie of A Company had been shot dead by one of the thirty German prisoners whose surrender he was in the process of accepting.

"The only German prisoner Ah'll ever take," growled Sam Aitken from Symington, "wull be a deid wan. Nae fucking mercy." Sam needn't have worried either. He would never get the chance.

To the left of their trench was a battalion of 2nd Yorkshires (The 'Green Howards').

Twice now within the last few days the Germans had penetrated between the two battalions only to be repulsed. But the probing was becoming more intense, the fighting more personal.

And on they came again.

A grenade landed in front of the trench. The blast knocked Paddy backwards. He was stunned, momentarily unconscious. He came to, just in time to hear a rabid spray of guttural German and to witness the blur of a huge man in a grey uniform end his life with a savage, downward thrust from his bayonet.

The Germans were in the trench.

The Scots fought back ferociously with Lieutenant McKenzie leading a bayonet charge which butchered many Germans in a frenzy of killing.

During this carnage, Craig clinically despatched three German soldiers with a bayonet slice under their arms as they raised them in anger towards his comrades.

The Germans turned and ran – or at least those who were able.

Craig heard whimpering on the fire-step. It was a young German soldier of about seventeen. (The Germans were later to refer to this battle as the 'Slaughter of the Innocents' as so many of their companies had been filled with students.) He had been badly injured. He lay defenceless and bleeding, begging for his life.

Craig wasn't angry. He didn't get angry any more. But he killed the boy with his bayonet, slicing his throat with no more thought than a farmer might give to thrawing a chicken's neck.

The Scots had repulsed the Germans once more, but they would be back.

The Second Scots Fusiliers had been in the trenches since the 17th. In the twelve days since, they had lost more than half of their thousand strong operational number, greatly reducing their effectiveness as a functional unit of fighting men.

They were sent to the key point of Kruseik Ridge, two miles east of the town of Gheluvelt.

It was in a horrible position, being exposed on the forward slopes. It suffered from a poor line of fire from very poor trenches which, because of the constant shelling, couldn't be improved upon.

On the 29th, the Germans made their big push against First Corps at Gheluvelt crossroads. From there, severe pressure was put on Kruseik Ridge itself. By evening the battalion had less than 200 men.

Tom was prostrate next to Craig, guns pointing north-eastwards towards the German lines.

"This'll be something tae tell the men back at Pigs' Square, will it no'?" Tom laughed hollowly.

Craig grunted, "You'll never see Pigs' Square again, Tom. This time the morra we'll baith be deid. The only question is how many o' the bastards can we take wi' us first."

Major Burgoyne was deeply worried. Holding the Ridge was now all but untenable. Byngs cavalry protecting his right up at Zandvoorde had been blown away and the 1st Division had now retreated in step, exposing his flank. The troops to the left had been forced back to Zandvoorde itself. He was practically cut off and surrounded.

He knew from a captured German soldier that the Germans had been massively reinforced and now greatly outnumbered the British at that point. He also knew that their forces had been reorganised under General von Fabek's army group, who were now attacking the Gheluvelt-Messines sector.

But, most importantly, he knew that if the Germans took this ridge before the British had time to regroup behind him, nothing could stop the Hun going through Gheluvelt and onto Calais. The British flank would be turned and the Germans would be able to envelope the Allied armies and attack them from the rear.

Meanwhile, his Commander, Brigadier Watts, had seen how futile it was for Major Burgoyne to hold on. He tried to phone to order their withdrawal, but the lines had been cut by the shelling. He sent two runners with the order to retreat. Both were killed before they got there. The order was never received.

The bombardment commenced at daybreak on the morning of the 30th, quickly followed by the attack. Craig didn't flinch. He just waited for it to arrive, knowing that his time had come.

A shell landed at the section where Major Burgoyne was standing. Three soldiers, including Sam Aitken, were vapourised. The Major was knocked unconscious from flying debris.

Now there was no one to give or to receive the order to withdraw, even if it did come. And they were completely surrounded.

Meanwhile, the British artillery started shelling the ridge, assuming that the only British soldiers who could possibly be up there would be dead ones, so completely was it infested with German troops.

"At least we now know that oor gunners ur better than their gunners," Tom said blackly as the Scots were further depleted.

The battalion at this stage was supported by just one light machine gun to face four ways against hundreds of advancing German infantry who had swarmed into the trench.

A veteran German soldier yelled as he plunged his bayonet towards Craig. It missed and stuck in the sandbags behind. Craig cooly shot him in the face, killing him instantly.

Along with the force of recoil, he felt his head being pulled back and to the side, causing him to drop his rifle. He was staring wildly across to Tom Carlton as the German dagger slit his throat in a series of clumsy, jagged, slicing movements.

Craig's discarded carcass fell to the ground. Tom shot his killer in the chest. The German boy lay in the mud, looking up despairingly. Tom approached him with bayonet extended towards the fallen enemy's face.

Through the rich, crimson blood that gurgled from within the boy's lungs and out in rivulets across his mouth, Tom heard him plead in clear English not for his life, but for his death.

"Shoot me. Please shoot me, sir," he asked as if he was making a polite request of his teacher to leave the room.

Once more Tom closed his eyes, sobbed into the butt of his rifle and pulled the trigger.

At a signal, the Germans evacuated the trench, unaware of how close to completely overrunning it they had been.

Night had fallen. B Company had been reduced to less than 20 men, including Tom Carlton and Major Burgoyne, who had now regained consciousness.

It was agreed that they should withdraw under the cover of darkness and attempt to link up with the rest of their Division.

Major Burgoyne was of the 'last man standing' school of army philosophical thought. Kruseik Ridge had been the Major's Thermopylae. His critics would later say that he tried to hold on to an indefensible salient for too long, needlessly costing the lives of hundreds of his men. Others would recognise that this little plug at Kruseik Ridge managed to stem the tide of the German army just long enough for the British army to recover under the 2nd Worcesters and the 2nd Welch Fusiliers, who would spectacularly retake the ridge the next day.

The sacrifice of the 2nd Scots Fusiliers frustrated the German breakthrough that threatened to end the war in their favour.

At home, Major Burgoyne had a sweetheart called Estella. Army life had not been conducive to settling down and having a family. Just another sacrifice on the road of service to his country.

He was resolved, however, that, should he survive this war, they would tie the knot. "Hardly a celebrity wedding," he thought, "but it should at least merit an acknowledgement in 'The Times'.

First though, he had to survive the night.

"Right men, there's no point in staying on here. We could only hold the Germans back for about ten minutes before we would be wiped out to a man. We'll be much more use to our country by trying to get back to our army and living to fight another day."

"So, where to, sir?" asked Sergeant Alex Moffat from Bathgate.

"Well, our headquarters lie about a mile to the west of us. At least they used to. We'll try to make it to there. If it is still being used we should be able to team up with forces protecting it. But remember, we don't know where the Germans are. We'll need to go through Polygon Wood and there are likely to be detachments of their soldiers in there."

"Whit'll we dae if we run intae them, sir?" asked Corporal John Nimmo.

"Take up defensive positions. We want to avoid a fight if possible. If we're confronted by vastly superior forces we'll surrender," the Major replied.

"If they'll let us, efter whit we've been daein' tae them ower the past few weeks," Sergeant Moffat pointed out.

"Hmm, you're right, Sergeant," Major Burgoyne acknowledged. "On my order, every man must drop his weapon and make it abundantly clear that we're surrendering. No heroes please, or we're all likely to end up face down in a ditch."

The forest held many fears. On several occasions they froze as they heard voices approaching and then, thankfully, receding. There were raised voices, gunfire and shelling echoing around from every direction. After the eternity of one whole hour they broke through the bush and out onto the clearing overlooking the farmhouse that hosted divisional headquarters.

Smoke spiralled out of the chimney. Incredibly it was still operational.

The sorry group slouched down the hill into the courtyard. Sergeant Moffat was already permitting himself the tantalising thought of the comforts offered by a warm fire, a cigarette and a hot cup of coffee.

The Major approached the door as the Sergeant was killed outright and three more injured by a burst of machine gunfire from the byre to their left.

"Don't shoot! Don't shoot! We're British!" Major Burgoyne screamed.

"Unfortunately for you, Major, we're not," the German voice on the megaphone bellowed.

The clicking noises of the guns from all round the courtyard betrayed the fact that Major Burgoyne's rump was surrounded and outnumbered.

"Right men, drop guns. Hands up," cried the Major.

From the dark enveloping the courtyard emerged about 40 German soldiers with their cocked guns pointing directly at the British, within a hair-trigger of a massacre.

The remnants of B Company of the 2nd Royal Scots Fusiliers were now prisoners of war destined for Coburg or Stralsund or Berlin.

The rest of the battalion, fragments of A, C and D Companies, would be wiped out the next day south of Main Wood, after which 2nd Lieutenant Thomson and WE Clutterbuck, along with 30 stragglers, would be all that would be left.

The 'Great Immortals' of the 2nd Royal Scots Fusiliers had ceased to exist.

★ ★ ★ ★ ★

General Haig, stern of eye, resplendent in military uniform, sat imperiously on his beautiful black horse, overlooking the scene.

Already the trench warfare, which was to be set from Belgium to Switzerland, was starting to congeal here in Flanders. He reflected how, after the heavy murderous fighting of the past two weeks, the Germans seemed to be more exhausted than the British. He cursed bitterly the incompetence of the officers of the 7th Division who had placed their troops on the forward slopes around Gheluvelt where the enemy could see and so effectively shell them. He thought of the 2nd Royal Scots Fusiliers, part of a regiment stretching back to 1678, all but wiped out. To the names of its honours – Blenheim, Dettigen, Inkerman – would now be added Gheluvelt (Kruseik Ridge).

He stopped awhile to pay tribute to men he had never met, but would never forget.

"It could have been so different," Haig thought.

It was obvious to the General that, had the Germans persevered here at Kruseik Ridge and amassed overwhelming forces in an almighty carnage of self-sacrifice, never turning back, they would have overwhelmed the Scots and would have made the decisive breakthrough which could have ended the war. Instead the German ambitions were checked by their own caution. Consequently, the balance of holding on had moved in favour of the Allies.

"Such great opportunities lost," Haig sighed with a deep sense of professional intolerance. He told himself there and then that, should fate ever place him in the position of inflicting a decisive action against the enemy, he would not be found wanting for a lack of perseverance, regardless of the losses which might be sustained.

With such stirrings in his breast, he turned his horse back to his army in the south as the sun set on Kruseik Ridge.

## CHAPTER SEVEN

# *Tresspass Against Us*

The fire had caught and was spreading with good intent. Mrs Burchill levered herself to her feet.

"Gravity must be getting more powerful around Milltown," she joked to herself. "Either that or I must be getting heavier, 'cos it's getting a lot harder to get up off my knees. Thank God I'm not a Catholic," she thought.

It was nearly half past six. Time to think about waking the house. "Didn't hear Harry come in last night. Wonder what time he made it back?"

As she moved into the kitchen to fill the kettle for a cup of tea, she heard an almighty, frantic battering on the front door. The kind of knocking that makes you rush towards and recoil from in equal measure.

Mr Burchill was already running down the stairs.

"Who in God's name is that?" he was shouting.

He opened the door aggressively.

At first sight he knew that something dreadful had happened. His neighbour, Mrs Thomson, was standing in the rain, still in her nightgown, tears streaming down her cheeks, face deathly white.

"Alice, what's wrong? Come in! Come in!"

"Naw, Fred… You've goat tae come oot. Noo. Right away. It's Harry…he's…"

The mood music changed. Fred Burchill felt a tremor rise up from under his heart. His stomach turned. His bowels weakened.

Behind him stood Agnes, her hands at her throat. Her eyes questioning wildly, scanning Alice's face for the slightest sign that it wasn't that bad. She tried desperately to unsee her. Make her disappear. She wasn't really there at all. She was the shake of a head away from never having existed.

Alice slumped against the frame of the door, sobbing.

"Ah'm so sorry, Fred…Harry's dead."

Those two words suspended time itself.

From now, and for the rest of their lives' narrative, all description of times past would be prefaced in relation to whether they came before or after hearing those two words.

Fred immediately calmed. He needed to assume control even though he was succumbing to shock. At least he now knew the worst. The How of it, the Where of it, the When of it would all emerge in the fullness of time. But right now it was the What of it that really mattered. This was when being man of the house meant more than wearing big braces.

Agnes screamed at Alice. "How dare you come here and frighten us with your lies at this time of the morning, you witch!"

Alice was impervious to Agnes's outrage. Her mind was still enduring the torture of that hellish image… of Harry's broken neck rising out of his stilled body at a forty-five degree angle; of his eyes wide open, staring blankly down and into her own; of his blue lips hollowed into an ellipse, mocking the breath that never came after his last; of his arms lying limply by his side as if on parade.

She spread her own arms out and enfolded Agnes, who accepted her caress in mournful resignation. They burrowed into each other's shoulder and gulped deep sobs together in shock and pain.

Fred slowly and deliberately put on his hat and coat. Not so much to fend off the rain and the wind as to dignify his visit to his son, wherever he was.

The children had scrambled out of their beds, fully awakened by the cacophony.

Harry at 19 had been the oldest, followed by Fred, 15, then Lisa, 13, and, finally, by Agnes, 8.

They looked at the scene in stunned silence. Scared to speak. Not knowing what to say. What was their place in this drama? To whom did their concerns go first? To their mother? To their distraught neighbour – or was she to be blamed? To the 'something' about their brother?

"Right, children," said their father in a voice they scarcely recognised, "could someone make your mother a cup of tea? I'm going away with Mrs Thomson for a wee while. I'll be back in a bit."

He kissed his trembling wife on the top of her head with a tenderness which belied the tumultuous fear that was pulsating through his veins.

"OK, Alice," he said matter of fact, "let's go for a little walk."

Agnes sank to her knees. It would be more than gravity that would make it difficult for her to rise again.

★ ★ ★ ★ ★

Micky arrived at the cemetery on his bike early that same morning. Michael was already there, brewing his tea.

"Morning, Syklo," Micky chirped.

'Syklo' was Micky's version of the word Cyclops – his affectionate nickname for Michael on account of him having only one eye.

"Aye," grunted a slightly hungover Michael.

"Lots of police activity up in Milltown this morning, Syklo. Part of Kirkton Field was sectioned off. Ah wonder whit's gaun' oan?"

"Maybe they've found the Kaiser hidin' in the bins," Michael suggested helpfully.

"If the Kaiser wis in Milltown," said Micky taking up the theme, "they widnae need tae look fur him. He'd willingly surrender rather than be marooned up there."

"Maybe if they put aw o' they wurrld leaders thegither up at Pigs' Square fur a chin wag session they'd be able tae sort oot aw this trouble withoot the need fur young men tae huv tae go and die in France an' fuckin' Flanders."

"Aye, right enough," Micky chuckled, "whit a sight thon wid be! The Kaiser, Asquith, Clemenceau and the Czar aw hingin' roon

Pigs' Square in deep conference wi' Todd MacDuff tae sort oot the wurrld's problems. You know, that might just work, especially if they wur tellt that they hud wan hoor tae come up wi' a solution or they wur gonnae be handed ower tae the Bottom Shop!"

"Morning lads." Tony had breezed in. "Onybudy died the day who hudnae died afore?"

"Aye, that joke," said Michael.

"Ah wid need tae disagree wi' ye there, Syklo," Micky protested, "That joke dies in here a thousand times a day."

"Tony, Jimmy says that there's been a commotion in Milltown."

"Zat right? Did sumbudy miss their turn at wahshin' the stairs?"

"Loads o' police aroon," said Micky. "They're stoapin' folk frae gettin' too close tae whitever it is."

"As if that wid stoap Aggie McMillan frae finin' oot," Tony said. "Still, chances ur we'll aw fin' oot soon enough."

"Probably be buryin' the 'soon enough' by the end o' the week," commented Michael.

Just at that, Gerry turned up.

"Good mournin'," he greeted them solemnly, using an old in-house joke.

"Mournin'," all three replied in the same lugubrious tone.

"Have you heard onythin' aboot the goin's on in Milltown, Gerry?"

"Aye, there wis a big fight up in the Co-op yesterday. Apparently wan o' they eggs wis tryin' tae get fresh," Gerry replied, triggering a collective groan at this, the oldest joke in the book before books were invented.

"Seriously," said Micky, "somethin' big's up. Ma aunt Catherine lives doon in Kirkton Field. Ah just hope she's awright."

At that, the door opened vigorously.

"God bless all here," pronounced Father O'Keefe theatrically.

The atmosphere changed immediately.

"Now wid there be a bit of a brew in this House of God, d'ye t'ink, Tony?"

"Sure, Father. Ah'll make it masel, so Ah wull."

"Good man, Tony. Good man."

Preliminaries over, and ensconced with a can of tea, Father O'Keefe began.

"Now men, wait till I tell yez…I'm here wit some news fur yez, so I am. Some really important…did I say important…no, I wid say it wid be more like devestatin' – devestatin' is it?… no, it's more like cataclysmic – that's what it is – cat-a-clys-mic news fer yez."

"Whit might that be?" asked Micky cautiously.

"Well might ye ask what that might be, Micky McGoldrick, son of a Rasharkin' man that ye are. But before I tell yez, yez must swear by all that's holy an' about yez, at the risk o' the perdition o' yer immortal souls, that what I am about to divulge to yez on this grey, dismal mornin' must not be breathed to another livin' person."

"Don't worry about that, Father. We only talk tae the deid aroon here," Gerry pointed out.

"Aye, an' I'm bettin' that yez get a more intelligent conversation out o' them out there than yez are likely to get in here.

"Anyway, the t'ing is this. How can I put this tactfully? Did I say tactfully? No, sensitively wid be a better word. Sure it's not sensitively either. How can I put it so that yez won't all be runnin' to the same place at the same time fer the same t'ing?"

"Is it serious then, Father?" asked Tony.

"Is it serious? Is it serious the man asks!"

At this point, Father O'Keefe turned his pleading eyes heavenward as if to invite God Himself to take part in the conversation.

"No, not really, Tony, except in so far as ye might consider bubonic plague to be a bit o' an inconvenience."

"Ye've got me worried now, Father," admitted Micky.

"And so ye should be, Micky McGoldrick. So ye should be."

He took a long slurp of his tea and sat with his hand cupped round his can, staring blankly at the wall. After an interminable silence, Tony plucked up the courage to ask, "So, Father, what is this awful news?"

"Och aye, of course. I wiz away there fer a minute, Tony. Well boys, let me tell yez. The t'ing is, to come right out wit' it, to cut a long story shorter than a pigmy's pinky and beat about the burnin' bush no further: a member o' the King o' England's armed forces paid our good Bishop John a visit the other day an' he says to him so he did – as if, mind ye, that he wis a bosom buddy o' the church his very organisation has been tryin' to supress in Ireland these centuries past – he says. "Bishop John, we need men who can dig."

"Dig?" queried Tony.

"Dig?" echoed Michael.

"Oh fuck!" thought Micky.

"Aye lads, dig. Apparently on the front-line just now they're beatin' the bayjesus out o' t'soil from Paris to Palestine an' from Calais all the way to China."

"Whit fur?" asked Michael.

"Ach now, Michael, that wid be because those Germans over there have this nasty habit o' shootin' at those poor English soldiers, and those big, brave English boys wid like to avoid bein' shot, if that might be at all possible, by hidin' in holes in t'ground."

"So whit's that goat tae dae wi' us?" asked Michael, who was not the brightest Smartie in the tube. In another age Michael would probably have thought that Boxcar Willie was a reference to a sexually transmitted disease.

"Well now, hardly at all. Unless of course you t'ink it might be of some pertinence to yez that the English government, in her benign wisdom an' providence, has decided to conscript all the gravediggers in Britain an' Ireland to dig their trenches fer them. Yez are all away to France after ten o'clock mass on Sunday, so."

"But whit aboot aw they people that huv died an' huvnae died afore?" asked Michael in all seriousness.

"Ach sure, they'll no' be goin' anywhere in a hurry. They can wait fer yez to come back. That is, of course, if yez do come back."

"Father, can Ah ask ye a question? Did Ah say question? Naw Ah meant conundrum. A conundrum is it? Naw, it's mair like a theological riddle so it is?"

"Of course, Micky McGoldrick – you bein' the son o' a Rasharkin' man an' all."

"OK Father, when is a lie not a lie?"

"When is a loy not a loy? He asks me his spiritual guardian! Well sure we could be here all day an' me wit' mass to say fer the faithful in Milltown in just over an hour. OK then Micky, when is a loy not a loy?"

"When it's yer priest that's tellin' it. That's the biggest load o' codswallop Ah've heard since ma Da tellt ma Maw that he wis just gaun oot fur the wan pint."

Father O'Keefe laughed heartily. "Sure ye can't fool a Rasharkin' man, 'cos they're all fools already!"

"Whit? Wis aw that just rubbish?" asked a startled Tony, whose head by now was birlin'.

"Well now, it kept me out o' t'rain fer twenty minutes, so it did," acknowledged Father O'Keefe.

"Ah need tae go tae the john," Michael announced.

"So dae Ah," chimed Tony.

"Where's Gerry?" asked Micky.

"Ach didn't himself go five minutes since," bellowed Father O'Keefe, who by now was feeling mightily pleased with himself.

★ ★ ★ ★ ★

"...And then they threatened me with the Defence of the Realm Act. They said that I was undermining the British will to fight."

"And were you?" Bishop John asked Father Albert Dannfald pointedly.

"The Word of the Lord exists beyond the pursuits of men, does it not, Your Grace? The sixth Commandment is the sixth Commandment in times of peace and in times of war. Do you want me to guide people to ignore the Ten Commandments when they are inconvenient to the political establishment?"

"When Jesus said, 'Render unto Caesar what is Caesar's' were those just empty words for ignoring?"

"No, of course not. They were a platform for the next line, which was the whole point of the message, 'Render unto God what is God's.' "

"So, they were empty. Not to be taken at face value. To be interpreted out of existence when they prove to be inconvenient to our own arguments. 'We know what God would say, because He told us,' you said. Yet here He tells us but you appear not to know what to think! Or could military service – as it was in Caesar's time – be viewed as a reasonable expectation on its citizens by the establishment. A legitimate service to be 'rendered'?"

"What about 'Love thy neighbour'?"

"What about 'A tooth for a tooth'? But let's go back to the Ten Commandments, since you brought that up. What was the first thing that Moses did when he came off Mount Sinai, still carrying the Commandments in their tablets of stone?"

"He ordered the Levites to kill those tribes who insisted on worshipping false gods."

"Exactly, not a man, woman or child to be spared. Three thousand put to death. And yet God – this God who is totally against all forms of killing – the God of 'Love thy neighbour', 'Turn the other cheek' and, yes, 'Thou shalt not kill', still favoured him. Tell me, Father Albert, would you kill for God?"

"Of course. Why do you ask?"

"I'm just testing to see if your own commitment to 'Thou shalt not kill' has a limit. It would appear that it does. Do you eat meat? Would you kill a fly?"

"Of course…but…?!"

"But in your sermon you declared the words 'Thou shalt not kill' to be absolute, without any scope for interpretation. Well then, Father, the words do not stipulate who or what is not to be killed.

I invite you to read the words backwards and forwards, as you yourself said. It, as you preached to your parishioners from the altar of St Thomas' last Sunday, forbids *all* killing. We must assume then, do we not, that this is to include all of God's creatures. Mind you, if the Commandment forbids all killing, we might wonder why then God bothered to give us teeth and a stomach instead of letting the air we breathe be our sufficient nourishment.

Unless, of course, the words are indeed capable of being interpreted and sensibly adapted and adopted."

"Your Grace, I tell you in all candour, that the God in my heart forbids me to kill a fellow human being, or to sanction others to do so in my name."

"Very well, Father, I accept that that is your viewpoint, but we've already seen that *your* viewpoint has been moulded somewhat to fit with what you want to believe rather than what may be the absolute Truth. There may be other just as acceptable versions of your God in other men's hearts which permit – nay, even oblige, – them to kill their fellow man in certain circumstances. Especially in circumstances where Good can be seen to be confronting Evil."

"So, what do I tell my parishioners now?"

"Where you left it. That it is a matter for individual conscience, but that, should they choose to take up arms in this cause, God will not abandon them. Just as He did not abandon Abraham when – indeed because – he proved himself capable of murdering his only son in the name of God.

"For those of us who believe that in this war God is on our side – and, Father Albert, I truly believe that He is – it may be seen as a sacrifice in His name."

"I cannot bring myself to even begin to imagine that God would sanction this war; that He could possibly approve of these horrific killings."

"You are trying again, Father Albert, to shape and design a God in your image and likeness rather than the other way around. The

God you would choose to believe to have existed rather than the God who is. The God who railed in the Temple…"

"The God who forbade Peter to strike the Roman soldier with his sword…"

"Yes, but it was in God's plan that the Romans should kill His son. They and their killings were the very instruments through which God chose to show his love for us by conquering death itself through His own persecution.

" 'Thou shalt not kill?!' God had His own Son killed! Do not put yourself above God with your pious platitudes."

"Where is *my* God in this war, Bishop John?"

"Perhaps this is His test for us. A test to see how ready we are to take up the fight in His name against the forces of evil. Do you deny the possibility? Can you gainsay it by your rigid, narrow interpretation of four monosyllabic words?"

"God's four monosyllabic words, Your Grace. God's words."

"Ah, yes. God's words. So infinitely simple. So infinitely enigmatic. So infinitely inscrutable…"

★ ★ ★ ★ ★

Aggie McMillan not only knew when she knew, she also knew when what she was being asked to believe was true wasn't!

And she didn't believe that Harry Burchill killed himself.

The police had arrived some two hours after the body was found and had closed the area off.

But only until the body was removed, after which they moved on without any proper investigation, forensic or otherwise.

A search of Harry's bedroom revealed the only evidence that they required: a half-written letter due to be sent at some unspecified time from London, in which he confessed to his parents that he was a homosexual. He couldn't bear, he said, to bring shame to the family at home, so he would move on to somewhere where he was not known.

107

Too ashamed to live with his guilt. Obvious suicide.

Case closed.

Aggie's nose told her that there was more to it than that. Her professional curiosity as the local gossip, if nothing else, compelled her to investigate the matter further.

The day after the grim discovery, Aggie went for a walk in the wood where Harry's body had been found. She looked at the scene over the gorge. From the end of the rope to the ground, she reckoned, was about 20 feet. Harry was about five foot seven inches, so there would be about fourteen feet or so between Harry and the ground. The thickly entwined rope which someone, somewhere at some time had 'borrowed' from a shipyard in Greenock – and which, unbelievably, had been left hanging on the tree after the removal of the body – had been in use these past two years as a swing. It had been anchored to the banking by a metal peg stuck about 18 inches into the ground. The end of the rope had been knotted compactly to serve as a seat for the person swinging out over the gorge. Now it had been loosened and looped as a noose. From the edge of the banking to the end of the unfurled rope, Aggie guessed, was about five feet. Harry was about eleven stone. That drop, Aggie surmised, would indeed have broken his neck. However, her instinct told her that Harry was dead even before he found himself at the end of that rope.

She started to look – sniff, more like it – around the area. Her attention turned to an apple which had had one bite taken from it, lying by the side of the hanging tree. Not more than a day-old bite, she thought. Still, anyone could have been here.

Never mind, it was still worth bagging, which she did with the use of a poke which she had brought along for the purpose.

She looked again at the point of the jump-off. It had been raining that night. It was raining now. She saw distinctive marks on the soft ground right at the point where the rope would have been used. They were made by an adult – perhaps by more than one – she observed, given the size of the boots and the depth of the marks.

There was a tread of four inverted v's running in rows on the sole of one of the marks. There was a breach on the left side of the pattern on the third row down. She took out her notebook and made a drawing of it.

Further out she found a button. A man's button, forcibly removed from a navy blue jacket. This she knew because it had a ripped sliver of the jacket attached. Had it been removed during an act of passion by one of the couples who used this sylvan spot for a romantic liaison or had it been as an act of violence, Aggie wondered?

The button was placed in the poke alongside the apple. All of this, of course, could be Harry's – Harry's apple, Harry's boot, Harry's button. In which case, who knows, perhaps he did commit suicide. But if they weren't, then almost certainly someone else was with Harry when he died and if that was the case it wasn't suicide: Harry Burchill had been murdered.

Had this happened a month ago the list of suspects would have been so small there wouldn't have been a list. But such was the disgust at the revelation about Harry's sexual orientation, if you weren't at the front (in Aggie's mind at least) then you were at the front – of the queue of possible murderers.

She knew that last week, in the main street, Steve Reynolds had stepped in front of him from out of a crowd of five young men to spit into his face. What made it worse was when Stevie's friend, Boxer McGinty, jumped between them, ostensibly to defend Harry, only to shout, "Stoap it Stevie. That's a dreadful thing tae dae tae a spittle!"

Harry, a good six inches smaller than Stevie – and no match for Boxer who earned his name from winning prize fights at boxing booths – simply had to wipe the spit from his face and walk away with the sound of jeers and catcalls behind him.

But were they capable of murdering him? Probably not, thought Aggie. It had been more a show of bravado in front of their mates, however cruel.

But somebody was capable of it, Aggie knew she knew. And, of course, she had heard the story concerning Archie Ferguson.

The same Archie Ferguson who was watching her now.

★ ★ ★ ★ ★

"Have you seen that poem that Tony gave his Advanced Division?" Nelly Lochery scathingly enquired of her colleague, Moira Caffrey, in the staff room of St Thomas' school. "Listen to this, you'll not believe it." She picked up the book of poetry that Tony O'Neil had left on the staffroom table. "It's called 'The Darkling Thrush' and it's written by a man called Thomas Hardy."

"Never heard of him," said Moira.

"No, neither has anybody else. Honestly, where does he get them from? Anyway, I'll just pick some lines at random:

'*The ancient pulse of germ and birth*
*Was shrunken hard and dry*
*And every spirit upon earth*
*Was fervourless as I.*' "

"What in God's name is that supposed to mean?" asked Moira, incredulously.

"Exactly! You can imagine this drivel going right over the head of Gerry McCue and all the rest of the children up there. I mean, when Gerry left my class two years ago he was struggling to write his own name and Tony's giving them this garbage!"

"Personally, I don't care what Tony thinks he's teaching them. They're too thick to take anything in anyway. If you ask me, keeping people like that on at school beyond the age of ten is just wasting public money on education for eejits.

"No, what I really object to is his chummy, chummy relationship with them. The way he talks to them as if they are on the same level as adults. He even lets them talk to each other and discuss their views. Some of them actually think that they have opinions worth listening to."

"Well, they'll soon find out how much their opinions count when they leave school in June and have to go out into the big, bad world."

"Yes, but the discipline of the Advanced Division sets the standard for the rest of the school, Nelly. If the big set isn't cowed, the other sets see pupils who have no respect for –and worse, no fear of – teachers."

"I've stopped sending my pupils to be belted by him. Not one has ever come back crying. I belt them myself now, and by God do I make it hurt."

"Maybe I should start sending my worst to you, Moira. What a comedown for a man that would be if a woman became the disciplinarian for the school."

"Not that he cares. He's always spouting on about personal development and learning through talking and all that guff."

"Yes, Moira. What's that quote he likes to bore us with. From St Thomas Aquinas or one of those, I think: 'I learned not from those who taught me, but from those who talked at me' – or something like that."

"He doesn't have any saints up in the Advanced Division, that's for sure, Nelly. Children learn best through fear. They always have and they always will."

"Couldn't agree more, Moira. We must show our authority in absolute terms and make a terrible example of anyone who steps out of line."

"It's the same for society at large. How else can we ensure that discipline is maintained at the front and that everyone sticks to their task? The only way is to offer them the choice of perhaps being killed if they do fight with the certainty of being executed if they don't."

"You can imagine troops at the front under Tony asking, 'Why are we doing this?'"

"Or refusing to follow orders because they think they know a better way of doing it."

"Or wanting to discuss it with their friends first."

"No, what these children need is a daily dose of the four R's."

"Do you not mean three R's, Nelly?"

"No, Moira, four R's: Reading, 'Riting, 'Rithmetic and Retribution."

Just then, the door opened and Tony O'Neil walked in. His face was clouded in concern.

"Someone's just told me that a young man has been found hanged in Kirkton Wood this morning."

"Any name?"

"Apparently it's someone called Harry Burchill. Doesn't mean anything to me. What about you?"

"Nor to me. What about you Nelly."

"Well, he didn't go to this school, but the name is familiar. Wait a minute…I know…he's that man who finished with his girlfriend because he's a homosexual!"

"There's the fourth R for you in practice, Nelly: God's retribution against wicked perversion."

"I don't think I like your God then," Tony said acidly as he left the staff room to go to his class.

"Even God's to be questioned now, Nelly" said a clearly ruffled Moira. "No wonder he can't lay down the rules: he's got no rules to lay down!"

★ ★ ★ ★ ★

Jeanie Broon had a lot on her young shoulders. It was over a week since Harry's body had been found. Now that she was beginning to come out of the initial shock, her mind was turning to Harry himself. To a large extent she blamed herself. If only she hadn't blabbed to Alice Henderson, Harry would be alive today.

She was still unable to come to terms with Harry's final act. He was probably the most balanced and stable person she knew. Clever. Dependable. Responsible. All qualities which, when she had been his girlfriend, had seemed boring, but which now seemed wholly admirable – even attractive.

She just couldn't imagine the thought processes Harry must have gone through which would have led him to take his own life.

She walked into the cemetery, passing rows and rows of generations of Milltown names. Eventually she came to Harry's grave. She started to speak.

"Hello, old friend. I'm sorry that it's taken a week for me to come and see you. I thought you might have a lot of visitors and I just wanted to speak to you on my own.

"Harry, I know that you must have known that I was responsible for the village finding out that you were a homosexual. And you were right. It was me… Stupidly…stupidly…stupidly I told Alice Henderson and she told the world! I didn't say anything about you kissing Archie Ferguson. She added that bit herself for effect and I'll never speak to her again. But I'm really, really sorry. I know I let you down badly.

"I wanted so much to apologise to you in person. But I'm a coward, Harry. I did see you in the street one day. I saw your pain. I saw your hurt. I saw your loneliness and sense of rejection. I wanted to come over and speak to you, to beg your forgiveness. But I couldn't, Harry. I just couldn't. Not because of what others might think of me. I just couldn't face what you might think of me. I shrank from the prospect of seeing your disappointment in me.

"I'm not going to stand in front of you, Harry, and say that I loved you. You know me too well to tell that cheap lie. And, anyway, we were always honest with each other, in your case too honest.

"But I meant what I said at the end of our last date when I wished you well. You were a good person, Harry. You were very kind to me and treated me with respect. More than any other boy I ever went out with.

"Do you remember when I asked you to confide in me about your feelings towards other men? I really appreciated that you took me seriously and spoke to me on equal terms as an emotional adult who didn't need to be protected from the real world. So many men think that their role in life is to patronise and protect women and keep them from engaging with life openly and fully.

"I wish you could confide in me again, Harry. I wish you could tell me what drove you to take your own life.

"My uncle Andrew said that his friend at work, John Bannerman, is almost certain that he spoke to you in the Arthur Lea Inn a few hours before you committed suicide. That man said that you were relaxed and friendly – even cheeky when he looked back on it – and that you showed absolutely no sign that you were thinking of taking your own life.

"Still, what do any of us know about the workings of the mind or the weakness of the human spirit?

"I hope he was right. I hope it was you and that you were at peace with yourself.

"I'll need to go, old friend. I will miss you. I will miss your wisdom, your integrity.

"You know Harry, you were never the bonniest beast in the byre – there goes that honesty again – but I'll even miss that dimple on your chin. It gave so much character to your beautiful smile.

"Wherever you are now, Harry, I hope that you are at peace. Goodbye dear pal. Goodbye."

She had already shed her tears. It was time to go. It was time to move on.

In the shadow of her grief, the silence of the graveyard was broken by a voice calling her name. She moved forward from behind a row of gravestones and saw her Uncle Andrew running towards her.

He launched himself, wrapped his arms around her and cried, "Oh Jeanie…Jeanie…it's Craig! There's been a telegram!"

# CHAPTER EIGHT

## *The Lie o' the Land*

The four girls walked up the mill brae after work.

"So how do we dae it?" asked Sadie McKelvie.

"First of all," Alice Henderson growled, "we aw stick thegither. All four o' us."

"Aye," agreed Sharon Stewart, "thegither we'll scare the shit right oot o' them. We'll force they cowards tae jine up oot o' sheer embarrassment."

"We need tae be hard and vicious," said Alice. "nae pleadin' or bargainin' or acceptin' excuses. Nae sympathy. They must go tae the war or face oor fury and contempt."

"But whit can we actually dae?" Sadie asked again.

"There's loads we can dae," Alice pointed out. "We've got oor stock o' white feathers. Tae hell wi' sendin' them through the post. We'll hand them directly to the cowards in public, in a place that will create maximum publicity for us and maximum shame for them. We can send hate letters. We can picket them at their place o' work or, as we did to that auld codger Haugh durin' the strike, harass them at their hame. We can put pressure on their girlfriends, if they huv wan, tae dump him until he jines up."

"Whit aboot mair direct, forceful action, Alice?" asked Sandra Watt.

"Such as?"

"Well, when we were campaignin' fur the Suffragettes afore this truce we resorted tae violence as well as civil disobedience – smashin' windaes, peltin' wi' eggs, daubin' graffiti on their gable ends – that sort o' thing. It wid just make them feel a bit mair uncomfortable remainin' within the community that they ur refusin' tae fight fur."

"Nae point in us landin' oorsels in the jile, Sandra, but if we're sure that we can get away wi' it then we'll consider it," Alice agreed.

"Right, let's get stertit. Who will we target first?" asked an enthused Sadie.

"Ah think Ah know the wan," said Alice.

"Who?" Sandra asked.

"Thon footballer who refused tae jine the rest o' his team at the front because he said he didnae agree wi' the war."

"Aye, that traitor," Sharon shouted in agreement. "His team's getting' ready tae face the guns in France while he's preparin' tae steal their jobs an' their girlfriends."

"What's his name?" asked Sandra.

"Micky McGoldrick. He's a Socialist."

"Ma cousin Mark's a Socialist," Alice pointed out, "but he's away aff tae the front. That's nae excuse. He'll dae fine."

"So, wance again, how'll we go aboot it?" Sandra repeated.

"Ah've goat an idea," said Alice. "Ah've been thinkin' aboot this. On Saturday, Charlie Haggans is getting' buried at St Conval's where Micky works. It's bound tae be a big funeral 'cos Charlie either knew ye or wis related tae ye. We'll attend the graveside, wait respectfully until the service is over and the mourners are beginnin' tae leave, and then we'll approach Micky and pin a white feather on him in full view o' everywan."

"Who'll dae it?" asked Sharon.

"This is oor first outin'. Ah'm willin'tae dae it," Alice offered.

"We need a banner," Sandra suggested.

"Sayin' whit," Alice asked.

"How aboot: 'Our Soldiers Put Women and Children First'."

"It isnae direct enough," objected Sadie. "It disnae attack the cowards and make them come face tae face wi' oor wrath."

"Whit aboot: 'Ye'll never be in oor arms till ye take up arms'," Sandra proposed.

"Clever," Sharon acknowledged.

"A wee bit uncomfortable wi' that," Alice confessed. "It could be taken as a promise Ah might no' be willin' tae keep!"

"Whit aboot huvin' two banners: wan sayin' 'A Coward Lives Here' an' the other sayin' 'A Coward Works Here'?" said Sharon.

"Ah like that!" exclaimed Alice. "It's simple, direct and straight tae the point."

"OK" said Sadie, taking up the theme, "we'll need black and red paint and a couple o' white sheets."

"Whit aboot a chant?"

"Aye, Sandra. Somethin' that attacks their dignity," Sadie suggested.

"Ah've goat it!" Sandra exploded. "Whit aboot: 'Ye're no' a man until ye jine the men!'"

"Brilliant!" agreed Alice. "It will even embarrass his family and his girlfriend. Whit woman wahnts tae think that her son, brother or boyfriend isnae regarded as a real man?"

"OK, let's adopt it," moved Sandra.

"Nae banners or chants at the funeral on Saturday though," cautioned Alice. "We don't wahnt tae turn people against us. Just the white feather – fur noo."

"Right girls, we'll need tae get Saturday aff work. We'll just say we're gaun tae a funeral, which isnae a lie," Sadie suggested.

"Aye, the funeral mass is at ten in St Thomas'. The burial will probably be aboot midday tae gie folk time tae walk tae Arthur Lea. Let's meet at Milltown Cross at eleven an' we'll aw walk doon thegither. Ah'll bring the white feather," said Alice.

"Aye, Micky McGoldrick can become the first coward in Milltown tae jine The White Feather Club," Sandra spat.

★ ★ ★ ★ ★

The Reverend John McDonald was vexed.

The similarities between the Austin, Texas murders and the Whitechapel murders were intriguing, if not disturbing.

Firstly, there was the timing.

Between December 30th, 1884, and December 24th, 1885, seven women, five black and two white, and one hapless man who happened to be in the wrong place at the wrong time, were butchered to death. A further six women and two men (similarly disposed to their dead male counterpart's lack of timing) were seriously injured.

Of course, Reverend McDonald reassured himself, serial killings were nothing new.

In the fourteenth century, Giles de Rais, a French Baron and one time Marshall of France, who fought alongside Joan of Arc against the English, killed at least one hundred and forty peasant children in the most horrific way imaginable. "Here was the devil living in our very midst," thought the minister.

Then, in the late sixteenth century, there was the Hungarian 'blood Countess', Elizabeth Bathory who, it was alleged, murdered at least 80 adolescent girls. Rumour suggested that the Countess bathed in the virgins' blood, believing that it would retain her youthful looks. "The original bloodbathory!" mused Reverend John.

Not to forget Thug Behram, of the Indian Thugee cult, who killed between 125 and 931 unsuspecting travellers by strangulation, a fate visited upon Behram himself at the end of a British gallows in 1840.

But they were the exceptions that proved the rule. Civilian serial killings were a very rare phenomenon indeed. Yet here were two serial murders whose timing almost overlapped, save for a pause for breath.

They also shared some stylistic preferences.

In both cases the primary victims were women. In both cases they were murdered after sex. In both cases the victims were slashed. In both cases the attacks were frenzied and brutal. In both cases the victims were disfigured. In both cases the murders were committed within an intense but short time frame.

And in both cases there was Maurice.

Maurice was a Malay cook who worked in Austin's Pearl Hotel, within the immediate vicinity of the killings, from just before the murders began until just after they stopped.

Of course, that in itself didn't unduly implicate him, given that the area around the Pearl hotel played host to several hundred souls. However, it is unlikely that anyone else living in that vicinity then moved away to London to live adjacent to Whitechapel just before the Ripper murders started until just after they stopped, Maurice having worked his passage there on a merchant ship.

It did not escape the good minister's notice either that, in the years following the Ripper murders, similar murders were reported in Nicaragua, Tunis and Jamaica – all places likely to have been visited by cargo ships.

Of course, there were differences.

The Austin, Texas murderer – or, as O.Henry, the American short story writer christened him, 'The Servant Girl Annihilator' – sought out his somnolent victims by attacking them in their beds in the middle of the night, rendering them unconscious, dragging them outside, raping them, brutalising them (often by inserting a spiked object between the ears) and finally bludgeoning them to death with an axe.

At any rate, there could be no doubt that, as the ship's cook, Maurice would have been a dab hand with a knife by the time he reached London.

"Damn it!" cursed the minister. "Just when I was sure that I had my man, up pops this bloody cook to spoil the broth."

Time to rethink.

Certainly Maurice was the more exotic of the two, given the sketchy details of his life. William Henry Bury, on the other hand, was the more home-grown, the more recognisable, the more identifiable.

To be fair, William H. – the Whitechapel murders notwithstanding (although most of them were!) – was a convicted killer. Maurice, as far as anyone could be sure, may have been guilty of little more than murdering the odd Malay Satay, or murdering the peace by beating wild Asiatic rhythms on his old Malay Gendang.

But then in *"They Got Away with Murder"* Maurice was definitely going to have to assume the title of the Servant Girl Annihilator. How was he to be expected to write the postscript to those evil crimes? He could hardly say, "The Servant Girl Annihilator murdered his last victim on Christmas Eve, 1885, then, overcome with a Dickensian Christmas spirit, he decided to toddle off and make a clean start with a new life in the Whitechapel area of London either side of the Jack the Ripper murders.

No, Reverend McDonald was resolved: Maurice the Malay cook *was* the Servant Girl Annihilator *and* Jack the Ripper.

Poor William Henry Bury was henceforth reduced to the status of a wife beater who went too far – which is what most people think who end up travelling the roads and the miles to Bonnie Dundee.

* * * * *

The hills between Arthur Lea and Milltown presented a challenge which forced you to be continuously upwardly mobile, no matter which route you chose.

Years of cycling round these parts, plus his football, ensured that Micky McGoldrick's level of fitness was very good. Strength and stamina combined in him, which enabled him to pedal the steepest of those climbs with relative ease.

He would regularly try to beat his impressive record of 8 minutes and 20 seconds to cycle the 3 plus miles of very steep hills between St Conval's and his home at the far end of Milltown.

Some days, however, especially if the weather was good, he would opt for the scenic route which led up towards the Arthur Lea dams, across by the picturesque route which led up by the burn at Springhill and on past the rural part of the Glasgow to Milltown railway. This was no route for a time trial, but was rather an opportunity to commune with nature.

This peaceful idyll sat as an incongruous juxtaposition to the thought of the war which was being prosecuted on the Western and Eastern Fronts.

Micky thought of the lads he knew and had grown up with heading for the slaughter and shuddered.

Despite the criticism which he had had to endure, he had never questioned for a second his own stance. It *was* a capitalist war, he reminded himself, and its victims *were* the working-classes of all nations, who were being offered the dubious privilege of fighting for their oppressor's right to further oppress them.

Just as the young men from the Ganges or from the mud huts at the foot of Mount Kilimanjaro had been plucked from their homes to defend their right to be exploited by a country of occupation, so too the working-class men from the sweat shop mills of the Levern valley, with their near starvation wages, were being asked to risk their lives so that the rotten, immoral capitalist system could continue for the benefit of those whose only active participation in the war was to look for ways to profit from it.

At least, that's how Micky saw it.

And as for fighting for a king? Why should he fight for an institution which he regarded as elitist, parasitical, hierarchical, anti-democratic, imperialist and sexist (even if the word hadn't yet been coined).

Even its dirge of a tune, 'God Save the King', was anti-Scottish – 'Rebellious Scots to crush', which of course they did – frequently!

He was baffled by the passionate, often fierce, loyalty evinced on their behalf by people who seemed to have as little as he. Truth be told, he didn't even know what the Royal Family was for, other than as a totem for the ruling class and to rally a nation around in times of war.

These were the well-rehearsed themes in Micky's mind, alongside the Marxist-Socialist doctrine that he was learning from the Red Clydeside Socialists like John McLean, Harry McShane, Willie Gallagher and a local firebrand Jimmy Maxton from Arthur Lea, who all constantly pontificated in open air debates at Glasgow Green on the evils of capitalism and the corrupt nature of the British capitalist state.

These thoughts, however, were quickly set aside as a young woman about Micky's age came in to view beyond Johnny Blue's well: Jeanie Broon.

It had been six months now since her world had fallen apart with her brother being killed at Kruseik Ridge and Harry Burchill committing suicide.

In that time Micky had acknowledged her in the street with a sympathetic nod, but he had yet to have a conversation with her.

He slowed his bike alongside her.

"Hi, Jeanie. How are things?"

"Oh, hi, Micky. Been better, been worse. And you?"

"Fine, fine. Are you just out for a walk?"

"Just trying to keep my mind off things. A stroll in the country on a nice evening like this is a good way to relax."

Micky stepped off his bike and pushed it between them.

"Ah know you must huv a lot on your mind and in your hert Jeanie. Can Ah say how sorry Ah wis tae hear aboot Craig."

"Yes, Ah know. Thanks fur that, Micky. In one sense though Ah don't feel as bad aboot Craig as Ah dae aboot Harry Burchill. At least Ah tried tae stop Craig from goin' tae war. Ah even quoted you as an example o' somewan who could see it fur whit it wis. Ah'll no' repeat whit he said back tae me."

"Aye, Ah can imagine."

"But at least it wis his choice. Not that it wis ony consolation for it still broke ma hert."

"Ah can imagine that as well. But, you know, Craig wis press-ganged by poverty. He jined the army afore the war broke oot because he didnae huv a job."

"He wid probably huve jined up onywey. His heid wis full o'

Boy's Own adventures, fightin' for the flag wi' Kitchener against the Dervishes at Khartoum an' aw that sort o' thing.

"But wi 'Harry, far from tryin' tae stop him frae killin' himsel', Ah felt as if Ah actually pushed him to it."

"You? How?"

"Because Ah betrayed his confidence, Micky, and told somewan that Harry wis a homosexual and she told everywan she ever met an' knew. He couldnae cope wi' that an' it drove him tae commit suicide."

"You didnae drive him tae his death, Jeanie. It wis the intolerance of the community he lived in that drove him to it."

"Ah know you went out wi' Harry. How close were you?"

"Ah really liked him, Micky. By the end Ah hud lost ony sense o' physical attraction fur him – and obviously he was never really attracted tae me. But he wis a good friend Micky and Ah miss him. He wis always somebody Ah could really talk tae an' who wid treat me seriously. Ah don't huv anywan like that onymair."

Just then, Micky realised that he was becoming smitten by Jeanie. He felt that he could listen to her forever just to hear the sound of her voice. They obviously shared a dislike of the war. They both had an empathy for people's suffering and for the vulnerable. They had a shared sense of values.

Jeanie, nevertheless, was a Protestant and Micky a Catholic. Close friendship, never mind marriage, between a Catholic and a Protestant in this part of the world in 1915 was viewed as the product of some kind of exogamous relationship, or worse.

But at least they could be companions.

"Anyway, here Ah um talkin' tae you as if you'd be interested in ma problems. Mind you, Ah suppose it's better than askin' you aboot life an' death in the cemetery."

She laughed and when she laughed her eyes twinkled and her face glowed with a wonderful radiance. Micky McGoldrick had never noticed it before, but Jeanie Broon was a beautiful looking young woman. When she reached her door and said cheerio, Micky felt a pang of loss. It was a pang that was to keep him awake for many a night to come.

As Jeanie turned the handle and crossed the threshold, she was aware that she felt differently about the world. Her pulse was quicker. She was exhilarated. She was already wondering when she might see Micky McGoldrick again.

★ ★ ★ ★ ★

The young man sitting with a crutch at the bar in the Bottom Shop was the first soldier in Milltown to come back from active service at the front.

Strictly speaking, though, he didn't bring all of himself back as he managed to leave a foot in a street in the village of Neuve Chapelle in Northern France.

He was attracting the attention of the entire pub.

"So," the wee fat man started, "we've got those bastards on the run, huv we?"

"Eh, naw. Ah widnae say that," said the soldier solemnly. "We're aw stuck in the trenches oot there right noo."

"How did ye lose yer fit?" the quiet voice enquired.

"Oor ain artillery."

The pub fell silent. Captivated.

"We hud just bombed the shit oot o' the German front-line. When we attacked there was practically nuthin' or naebody left. Just a handful o' dazed, confused and frightened German soldiers who were only too happy to surrender. We then attacked their support line which had also just been shelled. We expected a reception party there, but when we knocked on their door there wis naebody in. It turns oot there hudnae been onybody there since afore Christmas.

"At that point the road wis open tae a village called Niv Shapelle, or sumthin' like that. So doon we traipsed only tae find that the Germans had scampered frae there as well. Unfortunately, oor artillery imagined that we wur still dealing wi' the German supply line and they moved on tae their next objective – which was the place we happened tae be staunin' right in the middle o' when they opened up.

"Ah wis hit by shrapnel above my ankle and said goodbye tae ma left foot. Mind you, there wis a bloke staunin' next tae me whose heid disappeared, so Ah suppose Ah wis lucky."

And from that moment, till the moment he died forty nine years later in 1964, he was known as Lucky.

"Well, Lucky," said the drooped head, "welcome back. At least you survived."

"Aye, that's right, Droopy. As they wur draggin' me back tae the field hospital aw Ah could think o' wis, 'Ah'm gaun hame. Ah wullnae die oot here.' "

"Ah take it you heard," said the loud voice from the domino table, "that Craig Broon wis killed at a place called Wipers."

"Aye," the wee fat man added, "the way we heard it wis that the whole battalion wis slaughtered, sacrificed in a futile stand like the fuckin' Alamo."

"Widnae be surprised," said Lucky. "It happened tae the 2$^{nd}$ Middlesex battalion fightin' wi' us at Niv. They wur attackin' a four hundred yard line of front which hudnae been shelled 'cos the guns hudnae arrived in time tae dae the job. A thoosand o' the poor bastards attacked headlong intae the German guns.

"Visibility wis very poor an' when naebody came back we aw thought it wis because they hud taken their objective. It wisnae till the next day that we realised that naebody came back 'cos deid men cannae walk."

"So, because we were shellin' a place full o' oor ain soldiers and nae Germans, you lost your foot and some other poor bastard lost his heid; and because we didnae shell a place bristlin' wi' German troops an' German guns a thoosand British soldiers walked straight tae their deaths. That disnae make us sound too bright."

"Naw, we're no', Droopy," agreed Lucky. "You know when we went through the German trenches at Niv, we hud actually breached the whole fuckin' German line. The first time it had happened in the entire war. And whit did oor commanders make us dae? Stoap! That's whit! Stoap an' dig in. Simply turn the back o' the captured German trench, the parados, and turn it into a parapet and wait fur the Germans tae regroup. No' that we hud tae wait very long!"

"That's the problem," another loud voice piped up, "too many English public schoolboys in the officer class who are all brains and nae balls."

The barman had been listening to all of this intently and was just about to tell Lucky that his new name was prophetic as he would receive all of his drinks free for a week This spirit of impetuous generosity, however, froze at the thought of this gesture then having to be repeated for all of his customers who might return from the front. The offer would do well to be somewhat reduced.

"Whit ur ye huvin', Lucky? This wan's oan me."

"Pint o' beer thanks."

"Don't mention it," said the barman humbly.

"No, really, that's very generous of you."

"Ah know. That's why Ah don't wahnt ye tae mention it. Ah don't wahnt tae huv tae buy a pint fur every Lucky that walks through that door frae the front."

"Well, onywey, under the circumstances, Ah'm sure you'll appreciate that Ah'm just glad that Ah wullnae huvtae foot the bill!"

★ ★ ★ ★ ★

Although Aggie knew she knew that Harry Burchill had been murdered, she was, when all's said and done, just a local gossip. A good – no, make that a very good – one to be sure. But just a gossip, nevertheless. If 75 per cent of her nosed-out facts proved to be 75 per cent correct then that was a pretty good batting average.

Being human, however, it's always gratifying to receive confirmation that your suspicions are well-founded. Whether it's in the form of the slight stiffening of Maggie McKinnon's back, or whether it comes in the form of the knife which now lay on her bed beside a note written in fresh blood warning, "This is for you if you talk!"

"Wid ye look at that," said Aggie to herself, " ye go oot tae the shops fur a couple o' hoors tae buy a loaf o' breed an' a pint o' milk an' some star-crazed romantic fool breaks intae yer hoose tae leave a love note on yer bed."

She considered calling the police. What would be the point? They would never connect this with Harry Burchill's 'murder'. No, they were more likely to point out that, as the local gossip, it was probably from someone whose name she had traduced. And, to be fair, there were so many of them.

Aggie opened the drawer containing the button and the plaster of Paris impression that she had made of the apple.

They were both still there.

The apple: fruit of Fallen Man! Perhaps this would be the apple to bring about the fall of Harry's killer.

And she already had a prime suspect. Her suspicions were heightened when she heard that Archie Ferguson and his innocuous wee pal Alan Johnston were 'running away' to Belfast to join the 36th Division. She didn't buy Archie's reasons which were, in order: one, that he had cousins there and he wanted to fight alongside them; two, that he wanted to defend Ulster against the Irish rebels who were threatening Ireland's link to Britain; three, that he was born there for all of five minutes before his parents brought him over to Milltown.

One reason might have been more plausible. "Wait long enough an' there'll be another ten tae join them. Every reason under the sun, except the right wan!" Aggie reckoned.

But then, wee Alan was going with him to keep him company – or at least that was the official line.

"Could it have been a two-man job?" she asked herself.

She consulted her guts for guidance: nothing stirred. "Cannae imagine Alan daein' sumthin' like that. Still, who knows whit he wid be capable o' daein' when under orders frae Archie," she speculated.

It occurred to her that her gentle giant son Lachie might, at that precise moment, be killing a complete stranger on the fields of France, spurred on by the barking orders of a rabid commanding officer. "The wurrld's upside doon an' back tae front," Aggie mused. "Budgies ur killin' eagles an' fish ur fixin' bicycles. Who can tell…who can tell!"

Anyway, she had a problem. How does she manage to entice Archie Ferguson to take a bite – just one bite mind you – out of an apple before he disappears away to Belfast and then to the front? "In time he'll wear his jacket an', if it's the same wan, the missin' or repaired button will be obvious. But he's as unlikely tae agree tae me marchin' up tae him in the street an' askin' him tae take wan bite oot o' an apple as he wid be tae agreein' tae pay a request on demand fur the cleanin' o' the blood he left on the bedclothes." Especially now that he knew she was on tae him.

"Whit tae dae?" Aggie moaned in need of another sign.

As far as she knew (and surely she would have heard) she was the only one in the village who suspected foul play.

She had gone to Harry's funeral to pay her respects to the family. Due to Harry's well-publicised homosexuality, there were hardly any young men there.

But Archie Ferguson was.

Aggie scanned his face for a sign, even a flicker, of self-conscious guilt. Nothing. It was studiously inscrutable.

The fact that he was there, though, told her something. Like two posts in a washing green, Harry and Archie had been poles apart socially, culturally and intellectually. They had never been more than passing acquaintances. And yet here he was, attracted either to Jeanie Broon, whom he knew fancied him, or to see first-hand the grim product of his dark work, enjoying his bloody secret in the midst of the public grief it had caused.

However, there had been a fleeting moment – just one – when

Archie's glance in Aggie's direction appeared to focus for that micro-second too long to be casual. Not a stare, but a sure sign that Archie was particularly aware of Aggie's presence there by the graveside. It troubled her slightly at the time without exactly sending a shiver up her spine. She knew it was meaningful, just didn't know what it meant.

Until now.

She now knew that he knew that she knew.

But whether he knew that she knew that he knew that she knew? – that was the question!

★ ★ ★ ★ ★

The Sunday eleven o'clock mass at St Thomas' in Milltown was packed as usual. The overspill had to be catered for up in the choir loft, out at the entrance hall and even in the sacristy next to the altar.

Somewhere in the middle of the congregation were two members of MI5 who had attended all of his Sunday masses since his interview by the police. They didn't even try to disguise their presence.

"Perhaps they will be brought to the Word of God through their weekly attendance here," Father Dannfald thought by way of consolation.

Father Dannfald had already come to a decision that there would be no sermon today. How could there be? If there were it could only be about one topic and that would surely bring him into conflict with the authorities, both within the church and within the land.

After the Gospel Acclamations he tried to move on with the sacrifice of the mass. He turned his back on the congregation to face the Holy Eucharist on the altar.

"Credo in un…" He paused, overcome with emotion. Moved to speak by the inspiration of the Holy Spirit, or by the turmoil that was churning his insides he knew not. He only knew that he felt compelled to say something.

He turned round to once again face his parishioners. He looked across at the sea of faces before him. Trusting. Expectant. Waiting to hear the familiar sounds of the priest and his altar boys talking in a dead language that very few of them could understand.

Like the pupils in the Advanced Division listening to poems being recited by Mr O'Neil, the faithful didn't need (or perhaps didn't even want) to understand the literal meaning of the message, so much as to be transported by the atmosphere induced by the mysterious sounds of that ancient, imperious Latin tongue.

"Forgive me," Father Dannfald begun. "I can't move on without saying a few words that I believe to be pertinent to the gospel and to me.

"This war has now touched Milltown poignantly and tragically. We have all heard, and perhaps know, of people who have been killed and maimed in it. Good people. God's people. All God's people. Created and loved by God.

"From all walks of life have they stepped forward to give their lives: the fisherman and the tax collector, the great and the good, the simple and the devout – they have all answered the call.

"The Caesars have sounded their trumpets of war and their loyal subjects all over the world have come to render what is their due.

"But where is God in all of this? What shall we render unto Him?

" 'In my Father's House there are many rooms' Jesus promised us. 'If it were not so I should have told you.'

"Between us and that salvation, however, lies the devil, tempting us and diverting us from the Way, the Truth and the Light.

"This war is one such manifestation of that fact.

"I have heard all manner of reasons why good, decent people should march to lands hundreds of miles away with hatred in their hearts in order to kill good, decent people whom they have never met and will never know.

"They are wrong. They have been duped by the devil and all his agents to spread chaos, strife, hatred and conflict in order to scatter God's Peace and God's Love. It is Satan who reaches out to us in this war and it is Satan who is dragging good, decent people into hell and to the eternal torture of their souls.

"One such no doubt good and decent, if misguided, person fired a gun three weeks ago at a place called Auber's Ridge in France, which killed a loving, trusting, vulnerable young man. An act which left a family aching with grief at the loss of this child of God. The tragic loss of a life which was just beginning and had so much to offer.

"Misguided maybe, but how could the man who fired that gun – or the people that support him – ever say that twenty-three-year-old Private Erich Dannfald of the 6th Bavarian Corps, my brother, was killed in God's name.

"As I said at the beginning of the sermon, my dear people, forgive me."

The deference and devotion of the congregation had broken. What had started as a rustle was now a rush as people rose from their pews, genuflected in front of the altar and left. One voice was heard to say, "Shame on you, Father!"

Of the three hundred or so community of souls who had joined in worship at the start of the Sacrifice of the Mass, barely one hundred remained.

Two of whom were the MI5 officers.

★ ★ ★ ★ ★

It was the day of Charlie Haggan's funeral.

An Irishman from Cookstown, in County Tyrone, he had come to Milltown 50 years earlier when he was 19 to get a job with the harvesting – and never left.

He shortly met and quickly married Alice Coubrough, a girl from the town. They had nine children, who all married and produced over sixty grandchildren, some of whom had already presented a sprinkling of great grandchildren. Even if no one but family attended it would be a big funeral.

"Did you know him, Micky?" asked Tony.

"Sure, he was a great auld fella aroon the town. Made it his business tae get tae know everywan. A big, warm, welcoming man. Very popular."

"How many people dae ye think will come to the burial?" Gerry asked.

"A couple of hundred, easy. If it had been in Milltown cemetery, I'd have said a lot more."

"Sixty-nine, eh? No' a bad innings," Tony commented."

"Ah think Father O'Keefe's conductin' the service," Michael said. "Ah heard a rumour that Father Dannfald is to be demoted as parish priest."

"Ah heard that masel'," admitted Micky. "Don't know if it's true."

"Must be difficult tae be a German in Scotland right noo, what wi' the war goin' on an' aw'," Gerry acknowledged.

"He's like me," Micky said, "he disnae agree wi' this war."

"Ur there any wars ye wid agree wi'?" Tony asked pointedly, with an edge to his voice that Micky had not heard before.

"Well, maybe a war in which the workin' class had taken control o' the means of production and the dispossessed ruling class was tryin' to take them back by force."

"Is that aw that Socialist stuff?" Tony asked gruffly.

"Aye, it comes frae a man called Karl Marx. He wis a German who's written a book called *Das Kapital*. It shows how political and economic control is exercised and maintained by the capitalists through the exploitation o' the workin' classes."

"So, Micky, when did ye learn tae read German as well as bein' able tae spout aw that political tripe?" Tony continued.

"Ah cannae read German," Micky confessed.

"Ye cannae?! Don't tell me you've never actually read this book, Micky?"

"Not exactly."

"Not exactly? Whit dis that mean exactly? Ye've either read the feckin' thing or ye huvnae. Which is it?" challenged an increasingly exasperated and intolerant Tony.

132

"Naw, but Ah've heard a lot aboot it in debates on Glasgow Green frae the Socialists like John Maclean and Harry McShane."

"An huv they read it?"

"Ah think so."

"Ye think so, but ye don't know so," Tony dismissed contemptuously.

"Whit dae ye mean?" asked Micky defensively.

"Micky, they could aw be talkin' rubbish fur aw ye know, maybe even fur aw they know if they huvnae read it themsels, which Ah doubt. Karl Marx might be a figment of someone's imagination. He might never even huv existed. A sort o' Socialist Santa Claus."

"Well, even if it's a lie, it's a beautiful lie and a lie Ah could live ma life aroon," Micky's ears heard his voice say.

"You're tryin' tae tell me, Micky, that you could knowingly live a lie?!" Tony gasped.

"Don't we all live oor lies o' choice? The lies that all babies ur beautiful; that oor faithers ur invincible; that oor mithers are saints."

"Clerrtae me," Gerry Sweeney gushed, "don't be lettin' Father O'Keefe know that your life is just wan big lie, Micky. Ye'll be tellin' us next that you think God is a lie!"

"Could be the biggest lie of all, Gerry. A lie that we can't live withoot. The 'opium of the masses', as Karl Marx once said."

"Talkin' of Father O'Keefe, Ah think that might be him noo bringin' Charlie Haggans' remains tae their final restin' place," Michael prompted.

The occasion was dignified. Tears, but no hysterics. Alice Haggans was a rock for the rest of the family.

At length, the funeral was over and everyone started to drift off. Micky was standing close to the grave, waiting on everyone to leave before beginning to fill it in.

As he stood leaning on his shovel, his mind went back to the conversation with Tony in the bothy. There had been a different atmosphere which made him feel uncomfortable. Tony had been like a dog with a bone. He had seemed hostile, not just to Micky's views but to Micky himself. Something had changed.

His preoccupation with these thoughts was broken by the sudden appearance of three young women from Milltown whom he knew by sight. All three were beaming big, welcoming smiles at him.

"Micky, have you got a minute," Sharon blurted, "only, we've a friend here that wid love tae meet ye, but she's a bit shy."

Micky was confused at the jocular demeanour of the women at a funeral and at their attempts to fashion an introduction for a friend in such circumstances.

"Well, maybe later girls. Ah'm a bit busy just now," Micky mumbled.

"Ah, but this cannae wait," shouted a loud voice behind and to his left. Loud enough to attract the attention of many of the mourners and make them stop and turn their heads.

It was Alice Henderson who, with one deft movement, had pinned a white feather onto the front of Micky's shirt.

"There's a white feather fur ye, Micky McGoldrick. A badge of dishonour tae show the world whit a coward ye ur, stayin' at hame while aw the real men are oot fightin' an' dyin' fur *your* country."

With that, all four girls moved away, leaving Micky speechless.

The warm, open smiles, which had greeted Micky a moment ago, had now dissolved into sneers of contempt. The mourners looked on shocked, but no one remonstrated against their behaviour or offered Micky a single word of support.

Micky had heard of people receiving white feathers. Now that it had happened to him he felt utterly violated. For the first time he realised that everyone was against, not just him, but his right to hold a different opinion from the established view.

People now seemed to be looking at him with open disdain. Or was it that he had now, for the first time, been forced to see the way people had really felt towards him all along? He looked pleadingly across to Tony who appeared to be neither shocked nor outraged.

He just seemed to be accepting of the situation, as if it was to be expected. Tony's whole air of resignation confirmed for Micky the extent of his alienation.

As he looked through the crowd he could see that some – no, many – were enjoying the theatre of the moment. They were revelling in Micky's humiliation.

He wanted to shout. To rail. To protest. To explain. But at that moment he felt as voiceless as Charlie Haggans.

Tony walked across to where Micky was standing.

Without a hint of sympathy he leant over and said in his ear, "You see, Micky, in their eyes all you need tae dae is tae bury some gey dubious principles; they're facin' the prospect of buryin' their faithers an' sons an' brothers an' sweethearts.

"Think aboot it," he concluded and walked away.

Micky unpinned the white feather. He felt rebuked by it. He felt challenged to the core.

As he started to shovel the dirt over Charlie Haggans' coffin he wondered what Charlie would have said about being buried by a coward.

Gerry, Tony and Michael were in deep conference thirty yards to his right.

He had never felt so lonely, so shunned. For the first time he questioned whether he was nothing but a coward worthy of a white feather.

Was his 'principled stance' against the war merely one of his 'lies of choice'?

# CHAPTER NINE

## *Forbidden Apples*

Cattle Show day was the biggest day of the year in the communal life of the village. Its origins went back to 1825 and to a dispute between two farmers as to who had the finest prize bull. One word borrowed another and, before you could sing the first line of 'The Farmer's Boy', all the local farmers were summoned together to adjudicate in a neutral field.

From that time on, the first Saturday in May became the day when the farmers would meet in a local field to show off their prize cattle, livestock and other produce in an effort to catch the judges' eye and to return home with the coveted prizes.

It developed from there to include games, (tug of war, pillow fights on a log over a burn, etc.) races and feats of strength: the Milltown version of the Highland Games and even – as some clientele from the Bottom Shop, over-bloated with civic pride and too much whisky, might say – the forerunner and inspiration for the Olympic Games themselves.

Later in the century, the showground people started to arrive with all the fun of the fair, which became settled as a permanent accompaniment to the whole event.

It was a lively, exciting occasion for people of all ages, which filled the town with gaiety, laughter and alcohol.

And as for the original farmers' bulls? Do you need to ask? They both won of course!

Aggie McMillan was after another prize.

Every year Aggie ran a stall at which she would invite the public to judge all kinds of vegetables, fruit and flowers entered by the village locals.

She was an excellent MC, with a loud voice and a wonderful turn of phrase to silence any would-be heckler in the crowd not already silenced by the thought that Aggie might just be tempted to reveal some embarrassing aspect of their life which could leave people amused, not just for the moment, but for a lifetime.

In this, the year of Our Lord, 1915, the fair had at first been cancelled because of the war, only to be rescheduled for the first weekend in September. "Nae German's gonnae stoap the Milltown Cattle Show. Whit a boost that wid be fur their morale!" farmer Whiteford announced bombastically.

And, anyway, Aggie McMillan had an extra surprise competition to sit alongside the best marrow or best tattie in show. She had an apple from each of six phantom 'contestants' which would be tasted and tested by a 'randomly selected' member of the audience. After taking but one bite from each apple, he/she would chew and spit before acting out his/her enjoyment of the apple to the audience, who would then register that appreciation by their applause. This applause would be translated into marks by a panel whose decision was final. It was a bit like wine tasting but with apples.

Of course the timing would depend on Archie Ferguson being there.

Archie was due to leave for Belfast on the Monday. He would surely be at the fair. But would he stop by her stall? Aggie reckoned that, given the incident with the knife, he would make a point of being there to intimidate and unsettle her.

And she was right.

"Whit ur we watchin' aw this keech fur, Archie?" complained Alan Johnston impatiently.

"Ah want tae see who wins the best parsnip competition, Alan. We cannae go away tae Belfast withoot knowin' that."

"Ah'm mair interested in findin' a pretty lassie tae admire ma parsnip afore we go tae aff tae war."

"Ah don't think your parsnip wid win best in show, Alan. No' wi' me aroon at ony rate."

"But look at them, Archie. They're just a bunch o' tattie heids themsels."

A shout went up from the crowd when presented with Rosemary Murphy's parsnip. In true auctioneering style Aggie lamented, "Huv yez lost yer voices or huv Ah just lost ma ears? That wiz a pathetic response fur such a fine specimen grown in the rich, dark soil o' Rosemary's ain gairden patch up in Murdoch Muir. We'll just call that pathetic whimper a practice shot. Noo, come oan ladies an' mentalgents, gie it laldey fur Rosie's magnificent specimen."

The shout increased to something approaching a muted roar.

To Aggie's right was the panel of three judges whose job it was to mark the applause (not the parsnip) out of ten.

"A six, a five an' a six," pronounced Aggie. "No' bad, Rosie, but will it be good enough, Liddles an' Griddlepans, tae win the competition? We'll just huv tae wait an' see."

And so it went on.

Archie Ferguson stared fixedly and aggressively at Aggie the whole time, challenging and threatening her with his clear blue eyes.

"A handsome devil!" Aggie was forced to admit. "Pity he's such an evil bastard."

Rosemary Murphy didn't win the prize. Not because of the size or shape or colour or consistency of her parsnip, but simply because her family was considerably smaller than the Finnegans who had turned up en masse to give Bridget and her parsnip a good decisive cheer.

Funnily enough, Bridget Finnegan won every year!

"Right, ladybirds and gentiles, we huv a mystery entry never before on offer at oor Cattle Show. This comes frae the Paisley Growers' Club – yes there is wan! Whit else is there tae dae if ye come frae Paisley? – and they huv asked us tae judge the best apple frae six different contestants. So as no' tae be accused o' influencing the outcome, they've all agreed to stay away an' accept oor verdict. The fools!

"Noo ladles an' jellyspoons, Ah'm no' sayin' that folk frae Paisley ur mean or anythin', but did ye hear the story o' the two Paisley fermers who bet each other sixpence as to who could stay unner wahter the longest? They baith drowned!"

The crowd lapped it up. With the exception of Archie Ferguson who remained disconcertingly stoney-faced.

"Since this competition is essentially based on taste, and since it would be impractical tae ask everywan here tae take a morsel oot o' every apple, Ah'm gaunnae pick wan o' yez tae come oot, take wan bite o' each o' them, spit it intae the bucket and indicate yer satisfaction wi' it tae the crowd by the expression oan yer face.

Now who shall I choose?"

At this point the voluble crowd were lifting names from among themselves, accompanied by the non-too-convincing 'refusals' of the 'shy' would-be appointees.

Aggie began to move among the crowd.

"Somewan wi' a pleasant face tae look at. Someone wi' young, sensitive taste buds. Someone who obviously likes apples. Someone like…YOU!"

Aggie came from behind, grabbed Archie by the sleeve of his jacket and rushed him out in front of the crowd before he had a chance to object.

He immediately sensed that there was something happening that went way beyond the tasting of apples, but in the confusion he couldn't even begin to work out what, never mind find a way to extricate himself from the situation.

"Thank you Flotsams and Jetsams. Archie has just agreed to be our apple taster."

"Whit the fuck…!" thought Archie

"A big hand for Archie if you please, everyone. Thank you. Thank you.

"Right Archie, efter tasting the apple you should first make a face to the crowd which might indicate its taste."

At this point Aggie acted out some facial postures which she thought might indicate bitter, sweet, tasteless etc., much to the amusement of all the people gathered.

"...to be followed by your personal satisfaction of that taste or otherwise." Again Aggie ran through a repertoire of exaggerated contortions that kept the crowd in fits of laughter.

"Oor good panel here wull score each apple based on the applause and then declare a winner.

"Got the idea? Good, good, good.

"Right now, Archie, we mean business here and a good worker never works wi' his jacket on. So, jacket off, sleeves rolled up an' let's get down tae the task in hand."

Again unwillingly, and with a reticence which betrayed his instinct that in some way or other he was being set up, Archie allowed Aggie to remove his jacket. As she did so, Aggie noticed that the colour and material matched that sliver left on the button in the poke. While Archie was going through the motions of apple tasting, Aggie's fingers were searching out the buttons on his jacket from top to bottom.

Button. Space. Button. Space. Button. Space. Space! A missing button!

But was it exactly the same button as the button she had found in Kirkton Wood? As with her sense of smell, Aggie's eyesight was extremely poor. Without holding the button right up to her eyes – which would definitely have aroused suspicion – she just couldn't be sure.

Two seconds later and there were two spaces on the button row of Archie's jacket.

Later inspection would confirm that the button and the bite marks on the apples matched exactly with what had been bagged.

Archie had been there!

Within ten minutes the charade was over. The Man Who Never Was from the Paisley Growers' Club which never existed won first prize. The rest, appropriately enough, were nowhere.

"Easy-peasy" thought Aggie later from the repose of her comfy chair back home. "Now that wis a turnip fur the book!" she chuckled heartily to herself, unaware that the first traces of smoke were already pushing through from under the door.

★ ★ ★ ★ ★

Micky's mind was vexed.

A strange formality had existed between himself and Tony for the rest of that day. Nothing overtly unpleasant. That was the difficult part of it. Their relationship had suddenly become far too precious to be able to cope with the mock slagging that had characterised their easy banter up until now. Their friendship had stepped back into the dark of the unsaid.

After work, his cycle took itself up towards the dams as if it knew that he needed to reflect away from the hustle and bustle of the main route.

The stunning light and shade stretching above and beyond the hills went by unnoticed. Like Time itself. His legs pedalled on automatic pilot, while his troubled thoughts preoccupied themselves with the hurtful images endured that day.

His spirit felt weak, hollow and ashamed.

And there, just beyond Johnny Blue's well, was Jeanie.

"No, not tonight! I can't face her."

He fleetingly wondered if his assumption of her apparent endorsement of his attitude to the war was another of his lies of choice. Was she involved in some cruel deception, along with Alice and her cronies?

He recoiled from himself in her presence, in the presence of her loss. He felt weak. It was a weakness far greater than physical weakness; far greater still than mental weakness. He felt morally weak in the face of the disapproval and shame with which he had been confronted.

"Hi, Micky!" Her voice was light and tender, her smile warm.

An image of the saccharine, fake smiles that had greeted him earlier that day came flooding back.

He dismounted.

"Hi, Jeanie."

So primed was she now to read his every sign that she immediately knew there was something disconnected in the sound of his voice.

"Are you OK?"

"Aye, fine," Micky replied flatly.

"No you're not, Micky. Whit's wrang?"

He told her, terrified that she would find something to be commended in their actions 'under the circumstances'.

She remained unnervingly silent for a few steps.

"Alice Henderson again!" she cried bitterly. "That woman seems determined to destroy any relationship that becomes important in my life."

Never had the word 'important' been so important to Micky's ears.

Her hand reached out to entwine his fingers. She had moved into his private space.

"Don't let that witch destroy your belief in yourself, Micky. You're better than ten thoosan' Alice Hendersons. Believe in yourself, Micky. Keep faith with your principles."

She looked directly into his eyes, "Ah believe in you, Micky."

At this, she bridged the small space remaining between them and placed her lips gently on his. He felt an inner glow from the warmth of human tenderness. A warmth which banished the cold contempt he had tholed at Charlie Haggans' funeral. All the hatred and violence in the world of 1915 melted into oblivion in that one light kiss.

She pulled her head back and looked up at him, inviting him to kiss her. His soul lurched.

They held each other tightly and enfolded with an urgency which gave release to the pent up physical attraction which had been building up over the previous weeks.

They broke and cuddled.

For Micky, all the sights and sounds and smells of this wonderful landscape were a sublimation of this beautiful woman in his arms. The world was diminished by her presence. All the globe was reduced to a reflection in her eye. Its every temper broke upon her smile.

"Ah'll be here fur you, Micky McGoldrick, just as long as you want me tae be."

They walked on, pace by pace, with the bike on the outside of the twain and with Micky's free hand arched around Jeanie's waist.

It was Jeanie who broke the silence.

"It's supposed tae be you who does the askin', Micky, but Ah guess tonight it's gonnae huv tae be me. Will you be my beau?"

"Of course Ah will, Jeanie, as long as you don't mind bein' seen steppin' oot wi' a coward."

"Ye're no' a coward in ma eyes, Micky. You stood up for what you believe and that takes real guts. Plus, ye're a really good kisser!"

She laughed as she broke away.

"Ah need tae go noo. Tea's oot an' aw that. Will Ah see ye at the well the morra night?" she asked playfully.

"Aye, if God spares."

"Ah yes, God! Might be best no' tae bring Him intae it fur a wee while yet!" Jeanie laughed again.

She stepped forward and kissed him tenderly on the cheek.

Micky felt like a giant. From the very slouch of despondency, suddenly he was alive again, tasting afresh the very exhilaration of life.

He pedalled through the village like a man possessed, which of course he was. The streets and everyone in it passed by in a blur. He was still fired by the memory of the taste, the touch, the sound and the scent of Jeanie Broon.

And as for God? That would be a problem for another day. A day quite the other side of the very real and immediate problems that Alice Henderson was about to cause them.

★ ★ ★ ★ ★

"See you Ken," Archie Currie lamented, "ye're aboot as useful as a fermer in a U-Boat!"

"Well how um Ah supposed tae know whit the biggest planet in the solar system is?" Ken Butterworth retorted defensively. "Wait a minute! Ah dae so Ah dae! It's the sun! There ye ur."

It was quiz night in Pigs' Square.

From the Tuesday of the traditional Cattle Show week until the last Tuesday in September (22 weeks minus the Paisley Fair fortnight) two teams met each week for a battle of wits – or, as Raymond Henderson put it somewhat more accurately, a battle of half-wits.

Each team batted (asked questions) and bowled (answered questions) for ten weeks alternately.

One team was captained by Archie Currie and the other by Raymond Henderson. Each quiz night a specific topic was chosen by the bowlers upon which all the questions must be based. Three wrong answers and you were out.

This had been his third question and his third consecutive wrong answer, having previously professed a belief that there were 42 planets in the solar system (he later confessed that this had been "a bit of a guess") and that the earth had two moons ("a full moon an' the other wan…").

Last week's early finisher on the topic of English monarchs had been Eddie Miller in Raymond's team who, when asked why William the First was known as 'the Conqueror'? gushed, "Ah, that wid be because he wis the English champion at conkers!" Which king lost his head in 1649? "Wis it no' King Alfred the Lionheart." And then, worst of all: Who was the English King at the time of the battle of Culloden? "Robert the Bruce"!

That said, Ronnie Leech's response to the question 'Which gender was Queen Elizabeth the First?' had to be heard to be believed!

Unfortunately for Archie's team tonight, Raymond Patterson had a genuinely encyclopaedic knowledge of astronomy, the designated topic. His questions ranged from the relatively easy to the downright impossible. As a result he had bowled his opponents' team out for a miserly score of three runs.

The scores were added up over the weeks with the team which had acquired the most 'runs' by the end of September being treated to a barrel of ale in the Traveller's Rest, courtesy of the losers.

Going into the second week in September, 1915, the score was Raymond's Team (The Devils) 97 and Archie's Team (The Irrepressibles) 36.

In the course of this latest drubbing, Raymond had asked Gregor Nesbit to tell him who published *De Revolutionibus Orbium Coelestium* in 1543. It turns out that Gregor wasn't well-versed in Copernican Heliocentrism. Still at least his answer, "Isaac Newton", was an educated guess, which was more than could be said for either "Robert the Bruce" or Ronnie Leech's attempt to avoid looking stupid: "Don't know."

After the game, Gregor wanted to know more about what the book had been about.

"In it, Copernicus proved that the earth moves round the sun and not the other way about," Raymond explained.

"You know," said Eddie Miller, "Ah've often wondered aboot that."

"What? Whether it does or not?" Raymond asked.

"Aye. Ah mean, the sun moves across the earth frae east tae west, dis it no'?"

"Eh, no," Raymond replied.

"Well why then dae they say that the sun rises in the east an' sets in the west if it disnae actually move at aw?" Ken Butterworth asked.

"It's just a sayin' frae the days when everywan assumed that tae be the case. It's no' a scientific fact."

"But if Ah can see it happening' every day an' every night, is that no' a fact?" Ken protested.

"Plus, both Calvin an' Martin Luther said that the sun travels roon the earth. They said it's in the Bible," Eddie Miller argued.

"Oh, the Battle of Gibeon theory," said Raymond dismissively. "You know men, Ah'm beginnin' tae wonder whit century we're in the night."

"Well, if you're so smart," challenged Eddie, "prove it disnae. Show me how at five o'clock the morra mornin' Ah'm gonnae see the sun in the east, but then at nine o' clock the morra night Ah'm gonnae see it in the west an' yet it's apposed tae no' huv moved in aw that time."

"Eddie, ur you serious?" gasped Raymond.

"Look," continued Eddie, who was now on a roll, "people go through their entire lives believing things simply because they've been told that they're true. They never question it. Or even worse, they accept it even though it runs contrary to their own senses and reason simply because they've heard it frae sumbudy in authority, like a teacher or a doctor or a Pope. Aye, Ah'm serious."

"OK," said Raymond, about to take up the challenge. "First of all, Ah cannae prove tae you that the earth goes roon the sun. Neither o' us hus the equipment or the mathematical skills tae enable me tae dae that. But will you settle fur me bein' able tae show ye that it's possible tae view an object from two different angles without the object having moved an inch?"

"Ah'd like tae see that as well," Johnny Byrne piped up.

"So wid Ah," echoed Bertie Boyle.

Todd MacDuff shook his head in despair. "You know Raymond, next these eejits will be tryin' tae tell you that the earth's flat. Whit dae you think, Archie?"

"Ah cannae believe this," Archie replied as eight of Milltown's finest stepped forward to take part in the demonstration.

"Right lads, staun in a circle facin' the gas lamp. You're noo the planets roon the sun. Noo slowly, very slowly, turn tae yer right an' keep turnin' till ye're back facin' the gas lamp again. No, Ken, the other way. Now keep repeatin' it slowly until youse aw get used tae it."

"Raymond, Ye'll make them aw dizzy an' they're confused enough," laughed Todd. Peck, peck, peckity peck.

"If ye stick yer airms oot frae yer sides it stoaps ye getting' dizzy," Ronnie Leech claimed, proceeding to demonstrate.

Within seconds they were all doing it.

Raymond was beginning to see the funny side of all of this and decided to play on it.

"Well men, as I say, you're aw planets roon the sun, but in space planets travel roon the sun at an angle. So come on everywan, tilt yer bodies as you go roon."

Archie Currie was doubled up at the sight. Todd MacDuff was peck, peck, pecking like a chicken on steroids.

"Noo everwan, when the gas lamp disappears from your view Ah want youse aw tae shout, 'Whaur did ye go?' an' the second it reappears within the edge o' yer vision shout, 'Aw there ye ur!'

Incredibly, this bunch of amateur astronomy sceptics did exactly what Raymond had asked without question. Nor, it seemed, without the slightest insight as to how they might be viewed by unsuspecting passers-by.

Which is exactly what Mrs McDonald, the minister's wife, and her two friends were at that moment, as they made their way back home from a Bible discussion group.

The sight of these spread-eagled, angular men spinning round a gas lamp shouting, "Whaur did ye go?" and "Aw there ye ur!" did not go unnoticed.

Worse, one of Mrs McDonald's fellow Bible students was Victoria Harrison, whose husband Andy at that precise moment was doing a passable impression of Saturn with a drink taken.

"What in God's name…?" started Mrs McDonald.

"Andy, whit the fuck ur ye daein'…?!" screamed Victoria who, immediately on realising what she had just blurted out right in front of the minister's wife, started making profuse, if rather flustered, apologies.

"It's quite alright," admonished Mrs McDonald, "I was thinking precisely the same thing myself."

Victoria's outburst had been a "Weel done Cutty Sark..." moment for the men who came to an abrupt stop and for the first time realised what stupid gypes they had been, leaving everyone feeling sheepish and hugely embarrassed.

"Raymond was just..." Andy started to explain before being drawn up short by the sight of the empty space where Raymond had been standing before sneaking off into the night round about their twelfth orbit.

Archie Currie was kneeling on the ground convulsed with laughter and way beyond explanation.

Margaret McArthur looked on disapprovingly as if she had just taken a vinegar mouthwash.

"Men, do you not realise there's a war on?" she asked censoriously, as if perhaps this was a fact of some pertinence which may have escaped their notice.

Heads hung low in abject humiliation.

"Ah'm sorry, Mrs McDonald, so Ah um. It was Corpenicus' fault."

"Who's Corpenicus? Which one is he?" asked the minister's wife, looking round the group for a sense of ownership.

"Oh, he's no' here noo. He's the man that moved the earth an' stopped the sun," Ken offered by a way of reasonable explanation.

"No, Ken," Margaret intervened haughtily, "it wasn't Corpenicus who stopped the sun, it was Joshua at the battle of Gibeon to prevent the enemies of the Hebrews sneaking away in the night."

"Whose side was Corpenicus on?" Mrs McDonald asked naively.

"The Devils," Ken Butterworth replied.

★ ★ ★ ★ ★

Jeanie Broon was on her break outside on the stair. It was a beautiful summer's day. She imagined faces in the clouds and, in her mind's eye, formed the outline of an old woman among the trees lining the ridge on the braes overlooking the mill.

Along came the 10.42 train to Kilmarnock, charging past in a rush of fire, smoke and soot.

The heads and upper torsos, which always seemed to Jeanie to be disconnected from the lower part of their bodies, whisked by in a line.

"People in trains always seem so important," thought Jeanie. "They always appear to be going somewhere far more interesting than wherever you happen to be."

She wondered if she would ever go on a long, important train journey. She was 20 years old and had never been out of the Levern valley, save for the odd shopping treat to Paisley or Glasgow. There had never been any need.

Her thoughts turned to Micky. What would the future bring with him? This was the carefree end of their relationship. It was all about having fun together and looking forward to seeing each other again. No real ties or complications. In about two months it will either peter out or enter into a deeper meaningful phase. What did she want to happen? It would be nice to think that it might become a bit more serious, although that's when the trouble might start over her not being a Catholic. If it really came down to it, much further down the line, she could always become one she imagined. She wondered what might be involved.

"Never mind being a good Catholic, Ah'm no' even a good Protestant," she laughed to herself.

Jeanie had never been what you might call Bible greedy. She kind of believed in God, but only because she couldn't imagine life to have come into being without Him. It wasn't something to which she gave any real thought. Maybe when she was older and had other responsibilities, like children, she would give it more serious consideration. But for now she was relaxed about going out

149

with a Catholic, and Micky seemed relaxed about going out with her. In fact, now that she thought about it, Micky never talked about religion – unless you count Socialism as a religion. That was when she switched off – when Micky started to rant about the need for a workers' revolution. She couldn't imagine that either.

The door burst open. Four angry women breenged out.

"Right, Sharon, you make sure naebody gets past that door," ordered Alice Henderson.

Jeanie spun round to be confronted by a glower of faces.

Alice moved forward. "Just afore we start, Jeanie, Ah owe ye this."

With that she slapped Jeanie across the face.

Instinctively, Jeanie reached out to grab Alice by the hair only to feel a knee in the spine and her arms being pulled back and pinned by big Sadie McKelvie and Sandra Watt.

"Right, bitch-face," Alice resumed. "now that we're equal on that score, let's talk. Or rather, Ah'm gonnae talk an' you're gonnae listen…"

"Aye, that'll be…aagh!…" Jeanie was stopped from continuing by Sadie, who pulled her head back forcibly by the hair and kept it there so that Jeanie was forced to look upward and sideways at Alice's menacing frame.

"We've heard that you an' Micky McGoldrick ur makin' eyes at each other. What kind of low-life scum ur ye Jeanie Broon tae be goin' oot wi' a coward when yer ain brother…yer ain fuckin' brother…was killed fightin' the Germans?

"McGoldrick's a white feathered fenian bastard an' you ur gonnae gie' him up right noo or ye'll answer tae us.

"Normally Ah'd say that youse deserve each other – an youse dae – but right noo cowards an' traitors ur aff the menu tae Milltown girls, even tae wan as trashy as you.

"Dae ye unnerstaun?"

Jeanie tried to reply, but Sandra Watt had her hand placed over her mouth.

150

Alice leant forward mockingly trying to 'hear' what Jeanie was saying.

"Whit's that? Naw you don't? Well maybe this'll help you."

She stepped back from Jeanie and landed a full-bloodied punch on her nose, causing it to bleed and Jeanie to wince in pain.

"We're no' finished wi' thon cowardly excuse o' a man yet – in fact we're just startin', an' it wid be better fur you if you wurnae in the way the next time he hus tae deal wi' us.

"Right girls, come on. We've goat diesel fumes tae sniff!" Alice mocked.

Sadie flung Alice to the ground as she stomped back with the rest of the gang.

Jeanie's carefree days with Micky were over. He now represented something more than just the first flings of a romance. He represented her right to live the life of her choice in the face of intimidation and violence.

Even if their relationship had to go well beyond its sell-by date, Jeanie was determined that she would never give him up while she was under the shadow of threats.

She hoped that Micky would see it the same way.

★ ★ ★ ★ ★

Father Dannfald sat in his room in the chapel house. At the side of his bed were two letters: one from his mother, via Switzerland, telling him the news about Erich, the other from Bishop John telling him that he was being transferred to the Catholic retreat house at Carfin in the morning.

They broke his heart; they nearly broke his faith.

Erich was seventeen years Father Dannfald's junior. He was the youngest in a family of fourteen. A high-spirited adventurer, he was in love with life. A student of philosophy at the University of Freiburg, Erich was already marked for a glittering career in academia.

Then came the war.

Despite Albert's remonstrations, Erich was in no doubt which course of action he should take. Like almost every German of the time, Erich believed that the Fatherland was fighting for its life against the scheming, enveloping super powers of England, France and Russia.

He joined up in the first wave.

Details of his death were scant. Merely that he was killed at Auber's Ridge on the 10th of May, 1915.

Albert's prayers seemed inadequate to really touch the enormity of the tragedy.

"Gott mit uns" had read the motto on Erich's helmet. Erich had always been there for God. Why hadn't God been there for him? His faith had not protected him.

"There are things that are part of the mystery that only God can understand," Albert's father used to say when faced with something painfully incomprehensible.

That answer sufficed when he was a child, even as an adult. But now this war reduced such a response to the realms of a lame excuse, which seemed to mock the very question.

"My God, My God, why have you forsaken me?" cried Father Dannfald.

He listened in his heart for an answer. God wasn't in.

And now this:

*Dear Father Albert*

*First of all, allow me to express my condolences for the great loss of your brother. Be consoled that he is with God now and free from the wickedness of this life. I shall remember him in my prayers.*

*I appreciate that you felt compelled to refer to your brother's death as a focus for your anti-war sermon on Sunday. Nevertheless I am deeply disappointed that you chose to talk about the war at all, especially as I had thought that we had an understanding regarding this matter.*

*Regretfully, therefore, I am obliged to inform you that I can no longer give you licence to use your position as an ordained priest within the Roman*

Catholic Church to preach against His Majesty's Forces overseas.

Indeed, I no longer have a choice as I have been informed by the authorities that, unless I can guarantee them that you will cease forthwith to be a threat to public support for the war effort in France and elsewhere, you will be detained indefinitely as an undesirable alien under the Defence of the Realm Act.

Consequently, a motor vehicle will call at St Thomas' church, Milltown, on Friday morning at 9.00 a.m. to collect you and your belongings, in order to escort you to Carfin Retreat House, where you will remain until further notice.

On no account shall you officiate at mass between receipt of this letter and your uplift on Friday.

A separate letter has been sent to Father O'Keefe, who will become acting parish priest on an interim basis, informing him of the situation.

A new curate, Father O'Shea, will be sent to St Thomas' to assist Father O'Keefe in his duties.

I am genuinely sorry for the situation which has come to pass. I hope you appreciate how little choice I have in the matter given recent developments.

In wishing you God's full grace during your time at Carfin, I should also like to thank you and to pay tribute to your sterling work in God's name at St Thomas', Milltown, both as curate and as parish priest, over the last sixteen years.

I know how hard you worked in the service of Our Lord amongst His flock there and I know how much you will be missed.

Time and other commitments prevent me from raising these matters with you in person. However, please be assured that I intend to pay a visit to Carfin at the earliest opportunity, when we might be able to talk through these and other issues over a cup of tea.

Your brother in Christ
Bishop John

Father O'Keefe had been embarrassed at this turn of affairs. He didn't know what to say except, "We are all in God's hands now."

He had taken himself off to visit the sick that night, grateful for the opportunity not to be confronted by Father Dannfald's crushed spirit.

As he dwelt in despair upon a life that appeared to be unravelling at the very seams, Father Dannfald heard the sound of knocking at the door.

It was Mrs Brophy's night off and, with Father O'Keefe out, it fell to him to be the doorman.

On opening the door he saw a tall, skinny young man in his twenties, cap pulled down over his face. At first sight it wasn't someone he recognised.

Nor when the stranger moved under the light and stepped brusquely towards him, punching him twice in the chest.

"German bastard!" cursed the young man as he kicked Father Dannfald on the ground, before running off with Father Dannfald's blood dripping from his knife.

# CHAPTER TEN

## *Back to Front*

The Irish boat train from Glasgow to Stranraer was numbingly tedious: cramped, no heating and slow, stopping at every station in between, some without places. It tested the human spirit's capacity for patience and endurance beyond measure.

But it did give you time to think. Thankfully, Alan was no longer interrupting Archie's thoughts since striking up a conversation with an elderly Irish couple in the compartment.

He couldn't believe how stupid he'd been. That whole pantomime of Aggie McMillan's, putting on an apple-tasting competition just for him. He now knew for certain that it had been exclusively for his benefit.

After he had left the fair he had been troubled by something Aggie had said, without being able to recall what it was. Then it came back to him: "Someone who *obviously* likes apples." It was that word "obviously" which had a particular register, pregnant with meaning.

A word which betrayed certainty, prior knowledge.

And he knew exactly where and when this prior knowledge had been gained. He thought back to the time when he watched her that afternoon at the crime scene, sifting around the area like a dog sniffing out a buried bone. She had picked up the remains of his discarded apple from which he had taken but one bite. He saw her put it in a poke, obviously with the intention of taking it home. At the time he didn't think much of it other than that she was either wasting her time on trivialities or that she was desperately hungry.

But now he wasn't so sure.

There must be a connection between that apple and the apples he was duped into biting at the fair. Could they leave a particular impression which might identify him. Like fingerprints, but of the mouth? Biteprints?

The more he had thought about it the more certain he had become that, not only was Aggie on to him, she had now managed to collect evidence which could incriminate him. Evidence which would at least place him in the vicinity at the time of Harry's death, contrary to his statement to the police. They had interviewed him after learning that he had threatened to "kill that poofy bastard." Not that the police were too concerned or rigorous in their questioning. They even suggested to Archie that he didn't mean it literally and that it had just been a figure of speech to express his anger and disgust which, they said, they fully understood.

No, they had already decided that it had been suicide and were just going through the motions.

The case had been closed, but this could open it again.

Then there was the button. By the time he had returned home Archie had noticed that another of his buttons was missing, along with the one he had lost in his struggle with Harry. This had definitely been removed between Aggie handling his jacket and the few hours which had since elapsed.

Coincidence? Possibly, but he couldn't afford to take the chance.

That first button must be lying somewhere round the gorge. Could Aggie's twitching eye have discovered that too? Was that the other thing that she had put in her stupid wee poke? Was she looking for a match? Well she had one now.

Which is what set Archie off looking for a match of his own – of the combustible variety that is.

He knew that Aggie was slow of limb. It took quite an effort for her just to get on her feet and another age for her to set her frame in motion. A slow, ponderous, laborious motion. If she were to be unsuspectingly overtaken by a fire in a confined area the chances are that she wouldn't survive it.

So Archie resolved to set fire to her house.

Everything had gone well. Aggie always had the windows to her ground floor back bedroom open. Being so obese she had difficulty breathing at night and needed the fresh air to circulate around the room.

Archie first lit an oil rag which he then used to set fire to the curtains. Within no time the room was ablaze.

Of course, he forgot about Maureen. She had smelled the smoke first and had managed to alert her mother, and the upstairs neighbours, just in time to get her out before she was overtaken by the fumes.

It had not been a moment too soon.

Apparently she had vomited out on the pavement for twenty minutes, nearly passing out altogether. But she survived, coughing and spluttering, only to emerge with a look in her eye which registered the cold steel determination of a mother defending her brood.

Archie knew that the stakes had been raised dramatically.

If the scam at the fair had been her reaction to his stunt with the knife on the bed, he must expect that there would be even more to follow after this. He would take care of it when he returned from the front. But he also had to be careful. He couldn't afford another botched job.

And now there was Breezy to worry about as well...

"...Aye, us yins ur jist awa' tae gie haunners tae the King an' tae dae oor michty maist fur oor wee bit hill an' glen," Alan was just explaining to two terminally confused passengers from Coleraine.

★ ★ ★ ★ ★

## Authuille, the Somme, Northern France. April 1916

Wully Boyle received letters from home every three or four days and a parcel every week.

Letters were usually of the mundane variety and were always written by Wully's mum, Wully's dad being practically illiterate on account of never having been to school. They would recount visits from Wully's gran, or how the price of food and rents were rising because of the war profiteers, or how Aunt Mary was now working in a munitions factory.

They would always end up in his mum's house style of:

*May God and the Blessed Virgin Mary keep you safe and close to their hearts.*

*Dad, Mum and all the family.*

*xxx*

Today's news, however, had a bit of spice in it which he knew the Milltown lads, especially those from Milltown Victoria Football Club, would enjoy.

"Hey lads," Wully announced, "listen to this! You remember Micky McGoldrick, of course."

"Aye, we remember that cowardly bastard," said Fergus Smith. "Ah hope he's deid. Tell me he's deid."

"Well he's been courtin' Jeanie Broon an' it's been causin' quite a stir in the village."

"It's awright fur him," Peter Black spat bitterly.

"Ma mammy's written: '*Some of the Suffragettes (your Daddy calls them suffering gets!) who work in the mill have been virtually laying siege to Micky's home every night with a huge sign saying: A Coward Lives Here.*' "

A huge cheer went up from the Milltown lads.

" '*Whenever Micky comes out of his house or is going back in they chant, "You're no' a man unless you jine the men"* '. "

"Absolutely right," some of the men shouted in unison.

" '*They've already given him a white feather. Micky just ignores them, but his parents went to the police and asked them to do something about it. They just said that it was the girls' right to protest.*

" '*I think it's terrible. You know I never wanted you to go to the war,*

*Wully, and it sickens me to think that they would have treated you like that if you had stayed at home.*

" '*Anyway, not content with that, they got their fellow workers in the mill to refuse to work with Jeanie Broon, because they say she's going out with a coward. To them it's made worse by the fact that her brother was killed at the front last year. A lot of them couldn't stomach that, so Jeanie lost her job.*' "

"She can come over and polish ma gun onytime," laughed Peter Black.

Wully continued. " '*You may remember that Micky worked in Arthur Lea cemetery. Well he lost that job as well.*' "

Another huge roar went up from the men.

" '*The excuse was that they were overstaffed since a lot of the men that are dying now are being buried where they fall in France or Flanders, but I think it was because the foreman had a son at the front and he resented Micky's anti-war stance.*' "

So there ye are boys, McGoldrick's had his come-uppance," said Wully, putting his letter away.

"That Jeanie Broon, is she no' the good-lookin' lassie that wis gaun oot wi' thon homosexual bloke that killed himsel'? You know, what's his name…? Aye, Harry Burchill," asked Tommy Finnegan.

"So how come he wis gaun oot wi' her if he wis wan o' them?" asked Fergus Smith.

"Ah've heard that some blokes can be attracted tae baith," Ian Martin said.

"Whit dae ye think, Lachie?" teased Fergus. "Can a bloke be attracted tae a lassie an' her brother?"

Lachie sat in the corner of the trench. Always on the periphery of the conversation, he had hardly opened his mouth since the regiment disembarked at Le Havre in November, 1915.

When shells flew over the trench he cowered into the mud and quivered. At night he could be heard whimpering for his "mammy".

Lachie had to take two fingers out of his mouth to say that he didn't know.

"Well then, Lachie, could you?" Fergus persisted.

"For God's sake don't say that you don't know this time, Lachie," Wully Boyle cautioned, sensing that Lachie was too confused to stop incriminating himself.

Lachie said nothing, put his fingers back into his mouth and turned instead to face the wall of mud.

"How did they know that it wis suicide an' no' murder wi' thon poofter onyway?" Tommy McLean queried.

" 'Cos we're aw at the front," Menzies Campbell quipped flippantly.

"Apparently they found a letter that he hud written to his parents," Wully said.

"Ah used tae sit beside him in school, as well," lamented Peter Black with great distaste.

"Never mind, Peter, it's no' contagious," Ian Martin pointed out.

"Aye, but…"

"Whit, ye're no' worried that he fancied ye, ur ye?"

"Well ye never know…!"

"Look, Peter, just because he wis a uranian disnae mean he hud nae taste. You're far too ugly fur onywan tae fancy," Menzies laughed.

"Noo that he's no' haudin' doon a job – an' wi' conscription due tae come in soon – dis that no' mean that Micky McGoldrick wull need tae come tae the front efter aw?" Chris Slaven asked.

"If he disnae it should be classed as desertion," asserted Peter Black. "It's no' fair that the only wans that can be prosecuted fur desertion in the face o' the enemy ur the wans that at least hud the guts tae come oot an' face him in the first place."

"Absolutely right, Your Ugliness," Fergus agreed. "They should face the prospect of bein' shot at dawn, the same as every soldier at the front if they disobey a command."

"Wouldn't ye just love tae be in that firin' squad," Peter enthused, while lining up the sights and pulling the trigger of an imaginary rifle.

"Better still, Your Ugliness," rejoined Fergus, "we should use them as fodder."

"Aye, a brilliant idea," acknowledged Tommy Finnegan. "The Red Indians used tae make their pale-face prisoners ride tied tae a horse, which would then be stampeded in front of a charge straight at the cavalry's guns."

"Red Indians didnae take prisoners, did they?" questioned Wully Boyle.

"Well, they don't back in Milltown, that's for sure," Menzies Campbell quipped again.

"Poofs and cowards, eh? Makes ye almost gled tae be oot o' Milltown an' here at the front instead," Peter Black said wistfully.

"Mammy!" Lachie pined.

★ ★ ★ ★ ★

Lieutenant Begg of the 17th Highland Light Infantry was a popular battalion commander. He spoke the common man's as well as the King's English and could inject a tinge of *esprit de corps* into his interactions with his men, even when he was issuing orders or giving reprimands.

He was brave as well and was considered to be a commander who would willingly risk his life for his men.

Just as importantly, however, he was prudent with his own soldiers' lives. He was not regarded, as were some of his fellow offtcers, to be a man on a personal mission towards meteoric promotion on the back of piles of HLI corpses.

So when he asked for volunteers for a raiding party, many soldiers felt confident enough in his leadership to step forward.

Among the 45 selected were Tommy Doncaster, Menzies Campbell and Danny Harkins – erstwhile members of Milltown Victoria Football Club. For weeks they had been practising at Bouzincourt, where the enemy's fortifications had been duplicated, before going down to Dernancourt behind Albert to complete their training. The raid itself was scheduled for April 2<sup>nd</sup>, 1916.

Zero hour was 2.54 a.m. Men stood pensively waiting, hands and faces blackened. "Not that you need it, Danny," joked Menzies.

Tommy Doncaster reminded them of the time at their fateful meeting back at the football club when he admitted that he was scared at the prospect of joining up.

"Well, noo it's come to this, Ah'm absolutely terrified."

"The only reason Herr Fritz ower there isnae as afraid as you ur," Menzies reassured him, "is because he disnae know whit's coming and you dae – and that's tae your advantage. How are you feeling Danny?"

"Fuck, fuck, fuck. Fuck, fuck, fuck. Fuck, fuck, fuckitty fuck."

"Whit's that aw aboot, Danny," an amused but puzzled Tommy asked.

"Ah've just promised God that Ah'll stoap swearin' if He lets me come back frae this, so Ah'm gettin' ma quota in noo."

"That's hardly a good deal fur God," Tommy laughed.

"Well the way Ah look at it, Tommy, is that there'll be many more raids much more dangerous than this wan, so Ah'll save the biggies for then. If Ah get beyond stoppin' drinkin' then Ah'll know Ah'm fucked, because Ah'll huv nothin' left tae gie up efter that."

The order came, "Right lads, we're going over."

In a silent, contemplative shuffle they climbed the ladders on the parapet. There was an air of quiet determination, spiced with the smell of fear.

Once over, they followed the route marked out by guide tape, which had been laid out at great personal risk by Lieutenant MacRobert and Corporal Chapman earlier that night.

Danny looked to his left and to his right. He could clearly see the extremities of both wings of the raid. He looked up at the sky. The clouds which had been hiding the moon appeared to be breaking.

Danny's job was to enter the trench, causing havoc: bombing, destroying, clearing dugouts, wrecking machine guns, barricading communication trenches, killing Germans and handing prisoners back to escorts.

As they crept from one shell hole to the next towards the German lines, the clouds cleared completely to proclaim the glory of a fully illuminated moonlight night.

Danny was now in the shell hole nearest the enemy lines. The Germans' sophisticated listening devices had picked up the rustle of men. A machine gun opened up, spraying a drizzle of bullets from left to right.

Several men were hit. Danny could hear their moaning. Lieutenant Begg wisely decided to abort the mission and gave the signal to retreat.

As they tried to withdraw, their position was revealed by a German Very light.

Now the firing was in earnest and well directed.

As Danny was about to hurl out of the shell hole he felt his back shudder and crumple with an almighty shock, traumatised by a bullet fired from the German trench. He fell back into the hole, staring helplessly into the moonlit sky.

Several German soldiers sprang from their trench into the shell holes where the British wounded lay. A young boy, no more than 19, jumped in beside Danny. Danny looked on in terror as the boy rushed towards him, his bayonet raised. He was as frightened as Danny. He slashed at first in blind panic, marking Danny's face, and limbs, before driving a fatal plunge into Danny's rib cage.

Screaming in German, the boy retracted his bayonet, lifted it again to deliver the coup de grace and fell to the ground stone dead, killed instantly by a single bullet fired from a Lee Enfield rifle which splattered his brains across Danny.

He collapsed at Danny's feet. The shock was still in his dead eyes as he stared accusingly at Danny, moments before Death sucked the spirit out of the young British soldier's body.

Danny never swore again.

★ ★ ★ ★ ★

Lieutenant Begg's quarters at the front were scarcely better than the men under him, save for the provision of a table large enough to accommodate full scale maps.

It was one of these he was surveying when there was a shuffle of men outside from which privates Wright, Black and Smith emerged.

"Begging your attention, sir," said Dennis Wright deferentially.

"At ease men. What can I do for you?"

"Well, sir, all three of us play for a football team back home in Milltown, just outside Glasgow. The whole team, apart from one who is no longer a member, joined up together to come out here."

"A buddie's battalion?"

"Yes, sir, something like that. Anyway, during the aborted raid last night our right back, Private Harkins, was killed out in No Man's Land."

"Ah yes, Private Harkins. He was a really brave soldier lads, and do you know what made him truly brave?"

"Sir?"

"He was intelligent enough to be scared and had the imagination to foresee potentially horrific outcomes. He could never get rid of those images and yet he never flinched. Never spread the fear. Contained it within himself and got on with the job. I'll be writing to his parents to tell them that too."

"Well, sir, our boys in the team – and I mean all of us – would like to be part of the raid when it is rescheduled. We know we've got a lot to catch up with in terms of the training and the tactics, but we're willing to knuckle down and do what it takes to get ready in time. We want to do this for Danny and to get those bastards back."

"If it's any consolation, gentlemen, I can tell you that one of our boys shot dead the German soldier who killed Private Harkins, so at least we're even there."

"Begging your pardon, sir, but Private Harkins was worth the whole German army and then some," Fergus Smith interjected.

"Of course, of course," mumbled a discomfited Lieutenant. "Do you have this one for all and all for one attitude on the pitch too?"

"Absolutely, sir. Won three cups last year."

"Really? Who was your centre forward?"

"He's the bas...sorry, the ex-player who refused to join up," said Dennis.

"I sense that you're still angry about that."

"Sir," exclaimed Peter Black, where was he when young Danny was lying out there in No Man's Land having the life bayoneted out of him trying to protect that coward's home and family? He was lyin' in his stinkin' bed. Won't ever speak to him or about him again, sir."

"Well then, gentlemen, to business. We lost a few men the other night who need to be replaced. I am sure that we can accommodate an extra...?"

"Seven, sir. Privates Doncaster and Campbell are already in the raiding party and Danny and the man of whom we no longer speak are, of course, no longer with us."

"Just one thing though. This raid is obviously a personal matter for you now. That can be dangerous. It can colour your judgement. It makes you apt to take unwarranted risks and leads you to make mistakes, which can result in lives being lost – and not just your own. Can you guarantee me, on behalf of all of your men, that you will follow orders to the letter and not get involved in a personal crusade? I lost a really good man in your friend the other night. I'm looking at three good men in front of me now. I don't want to lose any more."

"We are professional soldiers now, sir," Dennis Wright avowed, "and that's what we will continue to be before, during and after this raid. You have my word."

"Excellent, Private. Right then, if you and your friends will join me and the rest of the party at Bouzincourt at seven tomorrow morning, we'll take you through your paces."

"Sir!" The three Privates shouted in unison, while saluting, clicking their heels and standing stiffly to attention.

"Dismissed, gentlemen."

As they left, Lieutenant Begg returned to his maps.

"Bloody fools," he said. "Bloody, magnificent fools!"

★ ★ ★ ★ ★

## MONTREUIL-SUR-MERE (HEADQUARTERS OF GENERAL HAIG, BRITISH COMMANDER IN CHIEF) LATE MAY, 1916.

"Good morning, Campbell. Is the Chief in?"

"Certainly, sir. Come right through. He's waiting for you."

"What kind of mood is he in this morning, Campbell?"

"He is in very good spirits, sir, and is keeping his silence merrily."

Campbell knocked on the oak panelled door leading to Haig's office.

"Come in!" roared the gruff, tired voice on the other side.

"General Rawlinson to see you, Commander," announced the Adjutant, introducing the Commander of Fourth Corps.

"Ah, come in Rawly. Good to see you. Are you well?"

"Indeed, General. I hear that you were in Paris yesterday."

"Yes, I was attending an athletics meeting of First Corps."

"Was it a success?"

"Splendid. Absolutely splendid, old boy. A fine body of men. I said to them, I said: 'Men, you have run well today. I hope you run as well in the presence of the enemy.' That seemed to go down well."

"I've seen them in the field, sir. They do."

"Anyway, Rawly, General Joffre, our good old French Commander-in-chief, was here the other day with General Castelnau."

"How were they, sir?"

"Both quite exhausted, I think. They're worn out with all this Verdun business."

"Ah yes, sir. They're taking a bit of a hammering there, I believe."

"The Germans have sucked them into a killing field, knowing that the French will fight to their last peasant as a matter of pride, when the sensible thing to do would be to abandon the salient."

"The Germans are losing plenty of men there too, and that's important, sir."

"Yes. They thought that it would be a picnic. General Falkenhayn told them that they would just be able to walk across to Verdun and take it after their artillery had destroyed the French defences."

"Some picnic!"

"Now the French are very keen that we should relieve the pressure on them there by launching a major offensive on the Somme."

"When does he expect our offensive to commence, sir?"

"That's the thing, Rawly. He asked me when I thought our forces would be ready to attack. I told him that we would be ready by the fifteenth of August."

"What did he say to that?"

"Nearly had a heart attack. Got very excited and started to shout, 'By the fifteenth of August the French army won't exist!' Castelnau had to calm him down. They are indeed very difficult allies to deal with."

"Is it really that bad at Verdun?"

"It would appear so, Rawly. I'm afraid that we're going to have to bring the whole project forward to July the first."

"Very good, sir. What is the length of the front to be attacked?"

"Twenty miles."

"And what would our first day objectives be, sir?"

"To reach, take and hold their front-line and then travel

onwards to reach, take and hold their support line."

"Sir, might I offer some words of caution on aspiring to those ambitions?"

"Certainly, Rawly. The floor is yours."

"Well, sir, firstly, for an assault of this nature to have any chance of success we are going to require a penetration of eight men per metre. A twenty mile front will reduce that level by half.

"Secondly, the German support line is four thousand metres plus behind the German front-line. Our guns won't be able to reach those lines to degrade their defences enough for our attacking force to have any chance of overwhelming them, as they rush headlong into the range of German guns over open ground.

"Thirdly, our troops are raw and inexperienced, having not long arrived in France after some very basic training. Over that length of ground they are very liable to become disorganised and be ripe for scattering by an organised counter attack.

"And, finally, if we divert firepower to the support line away from their front-line we might fall between two stools and fail to take even our first objective because the German guns there are likely to still be active.

"I should like to suggest, with respect, sir, that we limit our objectives to a twenty thousand yard front, focused on their front-line only.

"We have enough howitzers to concentrate firepower on their defences over, say, a four or five day period, which is more likely to destroy the German guns, the German barbed wire and the German morale."

"Thank you for your words of counsel. However, you must remember, Rawly, the French sustained a million casualties in the first four months of this war and they've been bleeding profusely ever since.

"We must show our commitment to their cause by attacking on a wide front with enough men and guns to make a breakthrough."

"Is a breakthrough technically possible, sir? The defences at the

Somme are even more formidable than at Loos, and we failed to make a breakthrough there. And they are building a third line behind their support line. I've seen it myself from the air and it's almost completed.

"The most we can hope for, I fear, is to bite and hold, killing as many German soldiers in the process as we can. We just don't have the resources to achieve more."

"I feel compelled to disagree, General. We will need to wear our enemy down, depleting his manpower, his resources and his morale. And then we must break through at his weakest point."

"Even at the cost of a bloodbath?"

"Yes, of course there will be a bloodbath. This is war. We must expect casualties on a huge scale. We are attacking the most fortified war zone that the world has ever seen. Massive casualties are inevitable."

"The object must still be, surely sir, to kill more Germans in any engagement than they kill of us. Otherwise we must eventually lose this war."

"This is a war of positions as well as of men. We must tease out that breakthrough which will allow our cavalry to exploit the situation and turn a victory into a rout."

"Sir, do you believe that horses belong on the same battlefield as barbed wire and machine guns?"

"As you know, Rawly, it was I who successfully campaigned in 1911 for the lance to be brought back into commission in the British army. Of course there is a place for the cavalry."

"I accept, sir, that the area around the Somme is capital country in which to undertake an offensive. The observation is excellent and with plenty of guns and ammunition we ought to be able to avoid the heavy losses which the infantry have suffered on previous occasions, but only if we shorten the front and narrow our objectives."

"Rawly, we are committed to this extended offensive. In fact, rather than a four or five day bombardment, it should be reduced

169

to an intense two or three hour bombardment on the target area to reduce the enemy to a state of fear and alarm before our men go over the top. Any longer gives the enemy time to work out our intentions and to reposition his resources accordingly."

"We won't be able to increase the intensity. We've got the shells. We just don't have the extra guns with which to fire them."

"Nevertheless, Rawly, we can disrupt and overwhelm the enemy here on the Somme in nineteen-sixteen. This battle marks our place in history. It will be the defining moment of the war and one which will ensure our ultimate victory. After this our names will be on the podium of great generals whose wisdom and boldness broke through the ignoble stalemate of trench warfare."

"Sir!"

# CHAPTER ELEVEN

## *See Mince*

It took almost a year for Aggie McMillan to be restored to her throne.

Almost a year of living with her sister, Sally Brooks, who was married to Jack, a hard of hearing unemployed labourer – or, as Aggie put it, "A professional nose picker." Jack's only two passions in life, apart from cranial digging, were horse racing and Rangers Football Club.

If Aggie knew nothing about something it was football. She actually thought at one point that the Rangers "Wore big hats and rode horses around Texas."

However, Jack, to whom a fanatic was just a supporter who didn't care enough, did his best to educate her on the subject.

Firstly, there were his favourite players. There was that Geordie Law, a 'right back'.

"Was there a wrong back?" Aggie wondered.

Then there was wee Alex Bennett who played 'inside Wright', whoever he was, and scored 'goals', whatever they were.

Jack's knowledge of the club, it seemed to Aggie, was truly encyclopaedic.

"Ah can go right back tae Moses McNeil who played on the wing," he declared, as if it was a qualification for a job. "Moses wis wan o' the four founders o' Rangers, Aggie, but he wis the wan who gie'd oor club its name efter a team he read aboot in a rugby magazine."

"So did this Moses chappie play right back and oan the wing?" enquired a baffled Aggie.

"Naw, naw, naw wummin', he wis a forward no' a defender an' he played up front oot oan the wing."

"So why did you say he wis a right back?"

"When did Ah say that?"

"You said you can go right back tae Moses McNeil," Aggie replied.

"Naw, Ah meant right back in time tae 1872, when the club wis still nuthin'."

"So wis he cried Moses because he led the team oot o' the wilderness?"

"Rangers huv never been in the wilderness, Aggie," Jack stated as an article of faith. "Naw, he wis cried Moses 'cos, funny enough, that wis his name. Anyway Aggie, why did you say that you thought the Rangers wur bigots?"

"Ah didnae say Ah thought they wur bigots, Jack. Ah said Ah thought they wore big hats!"


It took Aggie a while, possibly as long as four minutes, to become ensconced by the window in her new home.

It was a bit tricky hanging out a window sill at the top of a tall tenement, especially with her fear of heights.

At length, she found a wooden chair which, with a couple of pillows placed on the seat, gave her just enough elevation to sit bosom-breasted by the open window with her head propped out over her two bloated arms.

She quickly clued in to the dynamics of the street.

Across the way at the four in the block, were two like-spirited "windae hingers": Chrissy Dunne and, on the adjacent side, Sadie Dunbar. Their eyes never left the road below, but they talked to each other as if they were sitting face to face, like two footballers who had played with each other so long that they knew exactly where each was on the pitch without so much as a sideways glance.

A typical conversation might be as follows:

"Chrissy?"

"Aye, Sadie."

"See me."

"Aye, Sadie." (Without looking round!)

"See ma man."

"Aye, Sadie."

"See mince."

"Aye, Sadie."

"He fuckin' hates it."

They were also, like Aggie, very hard to impress.

"She wis talkin' aboot her weddin' an' aw that shite…" was Chrissy's explanation for finding a chance conversation in the street with her niece somewhat boring.

Breezy Breeks would not have found it any easier to tease a penny or a kind word from these two "windae hingers" than it had been to find favour with Aggie. Aggie, of course, fitted in just fine and was disappointed when eventually she had to move on, but at least her house was now ready, rescued from the ashes.

Besides, she had other things on her mind.

The police had found the butt of a cigarette in Aggie's bedroom. When she admitted that she regularly smoked in bed they immediately jumped to the conclusion that she must have left a still-smouldering cigarette on the bed or by the fabrics.

Case closed again.

"Fag end ma erse," Aggie thought bitterly, "An' nae butts aboot it…" This had been "attempted murder by a psychopath who didnae care whether he torched the wean an' hauf the street."

She knew that the only thing that would stop him now would be the distance between them or a German bullet.

He would come again to kill her and next time she might not be so lucky.

"Evidence" that he murdered Harry and was trying to murder her, was no evidence that any jury could even consider. The apples had already turned to mush. And the button, even if it could be proven to have been his, could have been lost there any time in the 2-3 years of the life of the jacket.

It was two years ago since Aggie had taken that reckless, blind guess with Maggie McKinnon that Britain was at war. She was about to play an even wilder and more desperate card now with Alan Johnston, except this time the stakes would be much higher. Get this wrong and she might be lookin' for her own Moses McNeil to lead her out of her own particular wilderness.

★ ★ ★ ★ ★

"Many of you will already know, my dear brethren, that I sometimes dabble in crime. That is to say that the little free time that I am allowed away from my ministry and my commitments as a husband and a father is often to be spent pouring over the details of murders whose perpetrators remained unidentified.

"Indeed, I have an almost morbid fascination for unsolved murders. Whether they date from way back in the distant past, such as the Princes in the Tower when the child-King Edward the sixth and his brother Richard the Duke of York went conveniently missing, almost certainly put to death either at the hand of, or on the orders of the usurper King, Richard the Third; or whether it dates from more recent times such as the Jack the Ripper case, which continues to confound the best brains of the London Constabulary.

"But it is another murder much, much further back in time than any of the aforementioned with which I am principally preoccupied today.

"It was the murder of a man of humble origins. The son of a carpenter. Born in a stable. A man who believed in peace. A man who preached loving your neighbour as yourself. A man who counselled turning the other cheek in the face of provocation.

"This man, Jesus of Galilee, was falsely found to be guilty of blasphemy, a crime punishable by death under Hebrew law.

"His trial, presided over by the High Priest Caiaphas, was conducted in accordance with the regulations governing due process.

"Caiaphas, we know, became so enraged by reports that this humble man claimed to be the Son of God that, in keeping with custom, he tore his garment asunder and sentenced Jesus to death.

"So, was Caiaphas responsible for the murder of Jesus Christ?

"Well, this judgement had to be ratified by the ruling power in Palestine: Rome.

"Despite finding no offence in Jesus, the Roman Prefect in Judea, one Pontius Pilate, decided to wash his hands of the affair and hand Jesus over to the baying crowd to have done with as they willed.

"So, was Pontius Pilate responsible for the murder of Jesus Christ?

"As you know, Jesus Christ, our Redeemer and Son of God, was taken up to the hill of Golgotha and crucified there on Good Friday, only to rise again from the dead on Easter Sunday. The Temple that was his body had been destroyed and rebuilt again three days later as had been prophesised.

"So the question I would ask you today, my good people, on this Easter Sunday morning, in the year of Our Lord, 1916, is this: Who murdered Jesus Christ?

"Was it the men who hammered the nails into the hands and feet of Our Lord into the cross? Was it the man who thrust a crown of thorns onto His sacred head? Was it the soldier who pierced his side with a spear? Was it Caiaphas and the Jews? Was it Pontius Pilate and the Romans?

"Let's look at the evidence. What does Holy Scripture tell us?

"The Scriptures tell us that the Son of God did not die in an attempt to subvert Hebrew law, or to challenge the supremacy of the Roman Empire. He died, we are told, for our sins. For your sins and my sins.

"Each of our sins, therefore, is a nail in those hands and feet. Each of our sins is a thorn on His head. Each of our sins forms part of the tip of that spear in His side. Each of our sins is the judgement of Caiaphas or the washing of Pilate's hands.

"Although no one here was born when these events took place, nevertheless, Our Lord, Jesus Christ, died for the sins we were yet to commit.

"So, when you want to look into the face of deicide, my dear brothers and sisters, look no further than into your mirror and contemplate the great sacrifice Jesus Christ made for your salvation on that cross on the hill of Golgotha.

"And, with that in mind, we should all resolve to sin no more. No more nails. No more spears. No more crown of thorns.

"On Friday last, God was dead. Three days later on this Easter Sunday He is with us again.

"He is risen.

"He is risen in our hearts and minds. He is risen at the breakfast table. He is risen with our boys on the Western Front. He is risen in all our hopes and aspirations and daily endeavours. He is risen in this church.

"He is risen.

"Yet his death is not a mystery. It is not an unsolved murder. He died for our sins – and then forgave us.

"A happy and blessed Easter to you all. May the victory that Christ has gained be yours in abundance.

"Now let us sing, 'Our Lord Christ Hath Risen'."

Mrs Spooner woke up with a start as the first chords of the great organ introduced the hymn's refrain.

★ ★ ★ ★ ★

"...And another thing! Why dae you go on and on and on aboot the Royal Family? Whit herm huv they ever done tae you?"

"Well fur a start they're parasitical..."

"Shite! They work their arses aff all ower the wurrld for this country. Next...?"

"Ah don't even know whit they're fur..."

"They're aw we've goat, Micky. They're the thing that unites this country and gies us aw a common identity, nae matter yer accent or yer class or yer religion."

"They don't respect ma religion."

"They represent religious freedom and religious tolerance, no' like your church wi' its inquisitions. They represent freedom *to* worship and freedom *from* worship for every person in this land."

Jeanie didn't know where these points were coming from, but she found herself agreeing with herself in a way which was strangely powerful in an argument which had nothing to do with the Royal Family and everything to do with her relationship with Micky.

They were indeed past their sell by date.

Micky fell silent. He knew he was losing – losing Jeanie that is.

The last year had been, as a future queen Elizabeth, the first of Scotland, would one day say, their "annus horribilis."

Both had lost their jobs. They had come under vicious hate campaigns and vitriolic personal abuse in the street, both separately and together.

Jeanie's parents had been understanding. They had both accepted Micky. Her father did say to her at an early stage, before their relationship had developed into anything serious, "You know Jeanie, maybe ye should baith think o' marryin' wan o' yer ain. There's enough problems in the wurrld withoot addin' tae them afore ye even start oot." And then said no more.

They respected Micky's stance on a war which they also viewed as an evil force which had devoured one of their own children.

Micky's mother was upset to begin with that her son was going out with a girl who was not of the faith. It had just been a matter of getting used to the idea. As she came to know Jeanie she found herself really liking her.

"Ach sure, she's a wee angel," she said to herself, "and Ah'm sure God makes wee Protestant angels as well."

Micky's dad left all such matters, indeed anything which required communication with the real world, to Micky's mother. A taciturn, uncommunicative Irishman who was never comfortable talking to women, he became the quiet, sullen figure by the fire who only came to life when he was spitting in it.

To begin with, and for quite a long time, the external pressure pressed them closer and closer together into a warm, secure place which kept the hostile world at bay, but lately Jeanie had been asking herself if this defiance in the face of the mob was the only reason she continued to go out with Micky. Not that they did go out that much. Back then, when you had nothing, then nothing was what you had.

Micky had casual work periodically on building sites, but most of his earnings were handed straight over to his mother.

Jeanie had applied for a job down at Cowden House, one of the mill owner's stately homes set in a beautiful orchard with tennis courts and fabulous walks. It had been turned into a house caring for recuperating British and Belgian soldiers from the front.

"You know, Micky," said Jeanie breaking the awkward silence, "Ah've been determined this past year that Alice Henderson and her band o' thugs wurrnae gonnae rule ma life. They wur never gonnae force me tae dae onythin' against ma will. But actually, they've been daein' that fur some time noo."

"How? We're still thegither ur we no'?"

"Aye, Micky, we ur. That's the point."

"Ah don't think Ah'm gonnae like this," Micky responded, sensing what was to come.

"Ah think that aw oor fightin' an' arguin' ower the last few months husnae jist been aboot huvin' nae jobs or nae money or naewhere tae go or bein' subjected tae abuse in the street if we did go onywhere – it's been aboot us."

"Aye, but aw that's been a big part o' it."

"Well maybe if none o' that hud happened in the first place, who knows."

"So, whit ur ye tryin' tae tell me?

"Micky, where did the fun and the laughter and the frisson o' that early passion go? Physically we've jist been gaun through the motions recently. Literally. There's no excitement, just routine fumblin'. Ah mean, last week when we hud sex doon the glen Ah wis daein' it frae memory!"

"Does that no' happen tae every relationship sooner or later...?"

"Ah'm far too young tae wahnt tae live oot the rest o' ma life feelin' bored an' trapped. Ah think we should split, Micky."

The words were a sledgehammer blow. Micky was staring into the abyss. Increasingly over the last year his personality had become a subset of Jeanie's. His confidence, his social life, all revolved around her. She had become the stronger, more dominant one in the relationship. She was the one who looked the world straight in the eye every day. He had become increasingly morose, lethargic and withdrawn. In those early days Jeanie seemed to value his every word. She had made him feel strong, important and clever. Now she finished his sentences for him in exasperation at his garrulous drift before dismissing his points in mid-air.

Where once his soul had lurched in her presence, now it crumbled.

She was right, of course. They had reached the end, but an end which she was ready to accept before he was.

"Let's try for a bit longer an' see if it works oot," Micky pleaded pathetically.

"You know, Micky, in this life Time is a wan way street: nae pausin', nae hesitatin', nae gaun back. We should've split three months ago, an' if it hudnae been fur they mad witches, Micky, Ah assure ye we wid huv. Whit is the point o' wastin' any mair o' oor lives on each other when we both know we've ran oor course?"

"Is there somewan else?"

"Not yet, Micky, but there will be, fur baith o' us. We're still young. Onywey, it'll be a lot easier fur you tae find a new woman than it'll be fur me tae find a new man wance the final tally comes in fur this war. Still, Ah'll take ma chances."

"Ah just thought that wance we hud sex that wan day we'd marry."

179

"Well, Ah canny say that Ah ever looked at it that way, which is why Ah wis so particular aboot ma dates. Ah suppose if Ah'd goat pregnant it might huv been different…"

"Ah canny stand the thought o' somewan else bein' wi' ye… touchin' ye…!"

"Micky McGoldrick, you never owned ma body any mair than Ah owned yours. Is there no' somethin' in your Socialist creed aboot that, or huv ye no' read that page yet? Oor futures will take their own different courses wi' somewan new in baith o' oor lives."

"You sound as if ye're already lookin' forward tae it…!"

"You're right, Micky, Ah um. This chat hus been good fur me. Ah feel that a weight Ah didnae even know existed hus been lifted right aff ma shoulders.

"Ah'm lookin' forward tae the future again – stertin' wi' this job interview the morra."

★ ★ ★ ★ ★

## The Chapel House, St Thomas', Milltown. May 2nd, 1916

Father Stephen O'Shea, an Irishman from Cork, had arrived in St Thomas' the day after Father O'Keefe saved Father Dannfald's life. Father John had returned from visiting the sick that night just in time to stem the flow of blood pouring from the parish priest's wounds. Father Dannfald was taken to the local hospital in Paisley where his recuperation was secured.

Father O'Keefe may have saved Father Dannfald's life, but not his life within St Thomas' parish as he was duly moved on to Carfin upon his discharge.

The last year between Father O'Keefe and Father O'Shea had been fraught, largely on account of: one, Father O'Shea's support for militant Irish nationalism; two, Father O'Shea's attachment to bottles of whisky; three, Father O'Shea's long-winded speeches dominated by the 'I' word.

180

Not that Father O'Keefe was the very epitome of perfection either.

"So tell me, Father John O'Keefe, what kind of an Irishman is it that ye are anyway?" Father O'Shea asked provocatively.

"Well now, Father Stephen, before I answer you that, answer me this: What's wrong wit' bein' an Irish Catholic?"

"Is that a real question ye're expectin' me to answer? What's wrong wit' it? Sure there's nuttin' wrong wit' it, Father, as well ye know. What kind o' question is that to be askin' an honest man?!"

"Oh, there's nuttin' wrong wit' it! Is that right? Well, Father, I'm afraid that I'm goin' to have to enlighten you on that point. Ye see the man that professes to be an Irish Catholic is puttin' bein' Irish before bein' Catholic. So maybe the question to be asked around this hearth is not what kind o' an Irishman I am, Father, but what kind o' Catholic it is that ye are yerself."

"Irish Catholic, Catholic Irish, what difference does it make? What difference did it make to the fifteen unarmed civilians that had the strange misfortune to be bayoneted in their Dublin homes last week by English troops. Were they asked, 'Wid yez be Irish Catholics or Catholic Irish' afore the British soldiers in North King street brutally murdered them! Ye're tryin' to use words where yer heart won't follow, so ye are."

"That was an awful deed, it's true, as was the killin' o' eleven o' their fellow soldiers that provoked it."

"Ye know, Father John, I can just about take the hypocrisy o' the British. They're born into it. It's what they are. It's what drives them to believe that they're superior to the people that they are subjugatin'. But I can't accept, especially comin' from an Irishman such as yerself, that bravely resistin' the overwhelmin' forces o' occupation is the same t'ing as murderin' innocent, unarmed people in their beds in front o' their families.

"After all, isn't this country supposed to be at war in defence o' a small Catholic country in the face o' aggression by a bigger bully? Or is that just a lot o' English horse-manure propaganda?"

"Don't get me wrong, drunk or sober, Father Stephen, I don't support English colonialism any more than you do, and I accept that English rule in Ireland is wrong. But even apart from the morality issue in the killin' o' yer fellow man – English, Irish or Martian – what was the point o' this risin'? It was never goin' to win. The German guns that were meant to arm it were scuttled in the sea. The orders to assemble were hopelessly confused, with most would-be local heroes wakin' up last Monday mornin' to find that they had missed it. And the people weren't for it as we saw wit' the demonstrations by the people of Dublin against those who took part.

"But what makes this futile attempt even more ridiculous is that it was for sometin' that's already been gained. The Home Rule Bill's already been passed and comes into effect after the war's over. We've been waitin' a hundred an' sixteen years for home rule. What's another year or two more?"

"Father John, have ye been livin' in this heathen country for so long ye wouldn't recognise yer own nose supposin' ye met it in the mirror wan mornin' sittin' right in the middle o' yer face? England won't let Ireland go free just like that. Sure they let the Ulstermen land twenty-five thousand guns an' three million rounds o' ammunition openly at Larne. Fifty-seven out o' the seventy British officers at the Curragh threatened to resign their posts rather than put down Ulster resistance to the Bill and the prime minister has already stated that he would never ask them to do that anyway. The King has threatened to dismiss Asquith and to refuse to give Royal assent to the Bill and the Conservative Party has given its official backing to membership of the paramilitary Ulster Volunteer Force to fight against the Nationalists.

"What chance have we? We can't use Parliament. We can't use the law. We must fight for our country and our religion – or, if you prefer, for our religion an' our country."

"I don't need to fight for sometin' that can't be taken from me and no man can take away my faith or my nationality. I'll fight oppression with peace."

"Would that be the same kind o' peace that Francis Skiffington was tryin' to exercise when he bravely went out into the streets o' Dublin in an effort to persuade people not to loot bombed shops? The same man who who was picked up by the British army, taken to Portobello barracks and summarily executed that very same night without so much as a trial? Is it English Peace ye'd be talkin' about, Father?"

"No, Father Stephen, I'm talkin' about God's peace. The kind of peace our good brother Father Dannfald sacrificed his place in this church for.

"Do you really need to take another glass o' that whisky, Father? Haven't ye had enough fer one night?"

"Ah, ye see, Father John, it's all about that provocation ye were citin' five minutes ago. Yer lilly-white, weak-kneed apologetic excuse fer bein an Irishman is drivin' me to drink so it is."

"I know, Father John, that ye were sent here to Scotland by yer superiors because they were worried about yer associations wit' some questionable people back home. But I would ask ye to recognise that the pavements o' Milltown will be riven wit' suspicion an' distrust in the light o' what's goin' on back in Ireland – especially if these executions go ahead."

"Aye, they're goin' to shoot Pearse, McDonagh and Clarke in the mornin' an' that's the pity o' it. There's English peace fer ye: the peace o' the graveyard. 'They create a desert an' call it peace' as Agricola once said after the Romans he was leadin' annihilated the Picts here in Scotland."

"Please, Father, for the love o' God, don't be addin' yer twopence worth to all this. It'll only start trouble."

"*Start* trouble! Father, where do you keep that head o' yours in the mornin'? Up yer arse? The trouble's already started here!"

"What do you mean?"

"Father John, there's a good Scotsman in this very village who is more of an Irishman than you'll ever be – as ye'll shortly find out."

★ ★ ★ ★ ★

The Bottom Shop was packed. The air was crackling with tension on this the fifth day of executions in Dublin. The barman was worried that the feelings would spill over into violence.

The tall, lanky man standing next to the toilets started it.

"So those Irish Nationalists ur fightin' oan the German side noo ur they?"

"They've rounded up ower three thoosan' o' the bastards," announced the fat man playing darts by himself. "Shoot the lot o' them."

"Another week, another war," lamented Droopy.

"They didnae even huv the guts tae take us oan in peace time. They hud tae wait until they knew oor boys wid be ower in France fightin' a real army," Lanky added.

"Wur the Irish too soft fur yez?" asked a Glasgow Irish voice, contemptuously. "Tell that tae yer Sherwood Foresters who were decimated at Mount Stewart Street by just a handfu' o' Irish Volunteers."

"And, for by, despite aw yer big guns an' aw yer big army, ye only managed tae recapture wan o' the places bein' held by the rebels afore Pearse ordered them to surrender," said his wee aggressive side kick.

"The Sherwood Foresters wur just weans who hud only been recruited intae the army weeks ago. They didnae even know how their guns worked. Maist o' them thought they hud landed in France when they disembarked in Dublin," a loud voice said.

"Well, maist o' them wull never see France noo," commented Droopy dryly.

"The thing is," a placatory voice ventured, "there's loads o' Irish Nationalists fightin' in France for Britain. Half o' the Irish Volunteers, including the brother o' their leader John Redmond, got behind the war effort and went tae join up for the Western Front as part o' the Sixteenth Irish Division."

"Maybe so, but their friends back in Ireland are shootin' at everythin' that moves wearin' a British uniform," the fat man continued.

"Dae ye think maybe they object tae yez occupyin' their country," another Glasgow Irish voice, dripping with sarcasm, postulated.

"Ireland's part o' Britain," retorted the fat man defensively, "just like we ur, an' the Welsh an' – who's the other wan? – oh aye, the English. It's no' a foreign country. It's no' Spain or Jersey."

"Just because you lot o' spineless cretins wur bought an' sold fur English gold," the biggest of the Glasgow Irish proclaimed with all the arrogance of ignorance, "don't expect the Irish tae kneel doon beside yez an' kiss the butcher's apron."

It was around about then that the first tumbler came flying through the air. It missed the big Glasgow Irishman and hit Lucky who had been minding his own business up to that point.

The tumbler's intended target must have had a real affinity with Lucky, because he picked up the red-haired freckled man next to him and flung him, complete with his pint, back in the direction from which the projectile had come.

"Right lads, pack it in noo," ordered the barman weakly, "or Ah'll call fur the polis."

By this time, Milltown's answer to John L. Sullivan was holding two of the barman's valued customers in headlocks and was running with them towards the dominoes table.

Lanky and the fat man grabbed him from behind while Hoppy hit him with a chair.

Frustrated at being halted in his tracks, the big fenian lashed out with a kick which sent the dominoes table flying through the air, completely ruining the game between Muscles and Berky (short for berserk).

The first person Muscles hit was Lanky on account of the fact that he "never liked the bastard onywey," followed by Glasgow Irish who was sent flying out through the swing doors of the pub and into the street with both men still in tow under his arms.

"Oh hello, Sammy," said Mrs McGuire to the head under the left oxter, "I nearly didn't recognise you there!"

The left oxter just managed to croak a response before it found that his head was barging back through the swing doors, attached to the Glasgow Irishman who was by now singing "The Mountains of Mourne" in full gusto.

Meanwhile, the barman was attempting to restore good order by hitting for six anyone who came within reach of his cricket bat, which he kept under the bar lest cricket should ever become a popular pub game.

Undeterred, Slinky had managed to slip past his off stump to steal a bottle of Bell's Whisky in the mayhem.

In the corner, a man wearing a collar and tie stood petrified and was left shouting hysterically, "What's happening? What's happening?" as if he had quite innocently found himself in the middle of a game in which the rules hadn't been properly explained.

By this time, Lanky had partially recovered and hit Berky as Muscles was just too big to take on. Berky took exception to this affront and promptly broke a bottle over Lanky's head.

Now there was blood everywhere to add a bit of colour to the occasion. Behind the bar the gantry looked as if it had exploded, so peppered had it become by flying shrapnel.

A dog wandered in to see what all the fuss was about and pissed on Lucky's leg while it was there. Lucky aimed a kick at it, forgetting that his standing foot was still standing in Neuve Chapelle and fell on his arse.

The fight ended by spilling out into the street with everyone hitting no one in particular for no particular reason and in no particular order.

The pub, of course, was wrecked, many heads were cracked, some teeth travelled south, the customers retreated to The Traveller's Rest next door where they bought each other drink and Lucky was propped back up in his seat.

Meanwhile, 190 miles to the south-west, across the Irish sea, James Connolly was being propped up on his seat in Dublin Castle in front of a firing squad.

★ ★ ★ ★ ★

The sun was shining brightly on Milltown on the day of Jeanie's interview. Gay colours expressed the day's delight and she was at one with it. She was dressed, if not to the nine's, at least to the eight and a halves which her purse allowed.

There was a really easy, confident spring in her step. She was young. She was clever. She was free and the future belonged to her.

She arrived a full hour before the interview. Not to sit nervously outside the interview room, but rather to find inspiration in the verdant, therapeutic walks in the gardens around the estate.

Roses were in full bloom. Pink and deep hydrangeas speckled the borders. There was a steep, rocky cliff topped with trees on the south side which gave a sense of grandeur.

The house itself was splendidly grand in the Edwardian sense of that word. It had huge expansive bay windows providing an open vista over the lawns and out across the hedgerows to the trees lining the driveway creating a quite stunning arboraceous effect.

Its strong winter doors were pulled back revealing a door inside the porch which boasted a beautiful stained glass heraldic painting of the Orr family crest.

Beautifully manicured hedges partitioned the area around the home and fashioned avenues alongside the paths and the flower beds

It was here that she met George, standing alone, retching and vomiting.

"Are you all right?" Jeanie asked lamely.

"Yes, thanks. Don't take any notice of me," replied the man politely in what Jeanie took to be a refined accent. "I'm like this every day. I'm used to it."

"What's the matter with you?" Jeanie asked, wondering whether she was overstepping the mark.

"Gas," he rasped. "It's affected my lungs. Probably will do for the rest of my life."

"When did it happen?"

"The nineteenth of December, last year in Belgium. The Germans used a new gas which I've been told combined chlorine and phosgene. The thing is, I felt alright then. We all did. It was the next day that sixty-nine men died and over a thousand of us took seriously unwell. I've heard that we've since developed a PH gas helmet which combats it, but there was nothing like that back then."

He started retching again. Jeanie instinctively put her arms around him, cuddling the pain and indignity of war itself.

He dropped to his knees and punched his chest mea culpa style. It seemed to Jeanie that he would never breathe again. He stared up at her agonisingly, stranded and drowning. He appeared to be pleading to Jeanie for an end to the trauma.

She looked on, confronted by her sense of inadequacy.

At length the airways cleared sufficiently and the prolonged retching petered out.

"I'm really, really sorry," she said as if perhaps she had done something to cause it.

"You won't feel sorry for me, Miss," he said, "once you see the poor buggers in there. At least I've got my limbs and my sight and my mind."

"Where in Belgium did this happen?"

"A place called Wieltje."

"Where's that?"

"Near a town spelled Y-P-R-E-S which we called Wipers. Have you heard of it?"

"Yes. My brother was killed there at a place called Kruseik Ridge."

"Kruseik Ridge? Was he with the Second Royal Scots Fusiliers?"

"Yes. He was killed there last April."

"I was with the Third Royal Irish Fusiliers. After we arrived we heard about Kruseik Ridge and the stand the Scots made there. Your brother died with heroes, Miss. You must be very proud of him."

"I'd rather be less proud and still have him with us."

"Still, God praise his name and give him peace. I'm George by the way. George Armstrong. I'm from Hollywood."

"Hollywood? Where they make the films?"

"No, Hollywood, County Down, just outside Belfast."

"Pleased to meet you, George. I'm Jean Brown. Or at least that's my Sunday name. Folks around here call me Jeanie Broon."

"Pleased to meet you, Jean," he rasped again, followed by another bout of painful retching.

"By the way," he said after his convulsions ceased temporarily, "are you from Milltown?"

"Born and bred, all my life."

"Do you know two blokes called Alan Johnston and Archie Ferguson?"

"Archie and Alan? Yes, of course I know them. I grew up with them. Went to the same school. How do you know them?"

"They joined us for a short while last April before being transferred to another battalion. Came from over here to do it. Mind you, lots of Scots did for some reason. Alan was a good chap, but Archie, he was a bit crazy."

"What makes you say that?"

"Well, I didn't think so at first. He seemed quiet in a serious, repressed sort of way. Until we went into battle.

"One day we had overrun some German trenches. Archie and I were on mopping up duties to ensure that Germans didn't come out of their dugouts and fire into the backs of our troops. Anyway, these five young German lads surfaced from their hole in the ground. The oldest couldn't have been much more than twenty one. There was absolutely no doubt that they were surrendering. Hands firmly crossed behind their heads, guns dropped on the ground. No question about it.

"So Archie went up to this young soldier and starts screaming into his face, drowning him in spittle, "You killed my brother, you…" Well you can imagine it, Miss Brown. "You killed my brother…!"

"He kept shouting it over and over again. We all stood back. This was personal between Archie and the German. It wasn't our place to interfere.

"The boy was petrified. His eyes held a terror I didn't think existed this side of Hell.

"Archie then forced him on to his knees and… I'll try not to be too graphic, Miss…bayoneted him right through the side of his head in a…how will I describe it?…lustful manner, if that makes sense. He really seemed to take great pleasure out of it. An unnatural pleasure.

"Back in our trenches, I said to Archie, 'How did you know it was that soldier who killed your brother?'

" 'I don't,' he said. 'In fact I know it definitely wasn't him.'

" 'How can you be certain of that?' I asked.

"He turned, looked at me coldly and said, 'I don't have a brother.' "

Jeanie got the job.

# CHAPTER TWELVE

## *A Most Satisfactory Lunch*

### Raiding Party, 22nd April, 1916 South-west of Thiepval, Northern France

The British artillery was merciless. For twenty minutes there was an arch of shrieking as shells landed on the German lines. The dirt was churned and hurled skywards, carrying with it fragments of metal and dismembered flesh. The Germans in the targeted trenches were obliged to remain in their dugout or to press flat against the parapet.

The sound was hellish – screaming and roaring drowning out a man's thoughts and leaving him disorientated.

It seemed impossible that anything in the German trenches could survive the hail of steel, incendiary and splinter.

Far less that, at that same precise moment, a group of determined men would be crawling through the mud, with murderous intent, behind the barrage towards the German trenches.

Menzies Campbell was to the forefront. Faces and hands blackened, he dragged himself through the mud on his belly, tasting the earth with every pull. On one forward stroke his hand grazed the forehead of a dead British soldier, possibly killed in the earlier raid of the 2nd of April.

In his head Menzies was singing. It was his way of taking his mind off the horrors to come.

"It's a long way to tickle Mary…It's a long way to…Holy fuck! That was close…!"

A shell from his own lines fell a bit short to his right, blasting a huge crater in the ground.

"…to go…But someday I'll tickle Mary…!" He paused. He was within 30 metres of the German lines. In between shell bursts he could hear them talking. Although he couldn't speak German, to his ear their guttural speech sounded eerily Scottish.

Back inside his head: "…From her head down to her toes…"

The barrage should be stopping anytime now and he would be one of the first to drop into the trench like a quiet assassin ready to strike at the heart of anything that moved.

"…Farewell Milltown main street…" An image of the kirk at the cross entered his mind.

The air whistled in a shrill scream as the final shells of the barrage landed in the trenches.

"…Goodbye old Pigs' Square…" – and there, brought to mind, was Todd MacDuff pecking his way forward to the Germans, disappearing into the shell smoke to give old Jerry a good telling-to.

"…It's a long, long way to tickle Mary…Wee gumsy Mary…wi' nae hair!"

The barrage stopped. Menzies and 49 of his blackened comrades were now about ten metres away from the lip of the trench.

All around him mudslide figures were rising like chocolate soldiers, moving silently towards the Germans.

They all knew their specific tasks and had prepared meticulously under Lieutenant Begg.

However, training was just that – training. No one was meeting your advance with live ammunition and with the intention of literally stopping you dead in your tracks. For most of the Milltown Victoria team this was their first piece of action. For the rest it was only their second.

Menzies had told himself that this was Danny's revenge. The fire it had raised in his belly upon its contemplation back in the days leading up to this raid seemed cold bravado now on the verge of the act itself.

He dropped into the trench straight into the arms of three German soldiers positioned to meet any assault. He was immediately pinned by the throat and thrust against the wall of the parapet, while at the same time a bayonet ripped into his left leg. A rifle butt crumpled him in two. His gun was knocked out of his hand.

All this happened in the space of a split second. Menzies braced himself to be killed. Shots rang out. Two of the Germans fell dead. The third dived to the ground, pulling Menzies down over him as cover. The German's strong hands were killing Menzies in a silent throttle.

Meanwhile, the British were flooding through the trench. Grenades were being flung into the dugouts as the German soldiers retaliated with gunfire of their own.

Menzies was passing out and beyond, when suddenly he felt his neck loosen and air fill his lungs. Fraser Smith was standing over them pointing his gun at the German soldier's head. The German, upon releasing Menzies, was in the act of surrendering. "Kamerad…kamerad…" he pleaded, his hands raised above him.

Menzies looked down. His left leg had virtually been sliced off. Blood was spreading out across his body and over the ground.

Fraser was confused. He had to attend to Menzies *and* deliver his prisoner. The German, sensing an opportunity, lunged at Fraser with a dagger which appeared from nowhere. Fraser stumbled causing the dagger to miss. He wasn't confused anymore and immediately shot his prisoner at point blank range, killing him instantly.

There was havoc all along the trench.

13 prisoners were escorted back to the British lines. Dozens more Germans had been killed. Machine gun emplacements had been destroyed.

The carnage was over within twenty minutes.

Every one of the raiders returned with only Menzies Campbell sustaining a serious injury.

Lieutenant Begg had been slightly injured, but it had been his spirit and his planning which had carried the day. For his efforts he was awarded the Military Cross.

Meanwhile, as the field surgeon amputated Menzies' right leg he was treated to the Milltown version of '*It's A Long Way To Tipperary*'.

★ ★ ★ ★ ★

## Thiepval, July 1st, 1916

"Will ye no' fight fur me, Lachie?" Maureen's plaintive voice was ringing in his head. "Will ye no' fight fur me?"

Well now the moment to fight had come. Here at Thiepval on the Somme, the 17th Highland Light Infantry faced the Liepzig Redoubt.

The previous night of the 30th June, Lachie had arrived with the rest of his platoon via 'Oban Avenue' – the 'Up' communication trench towards the front, just to the right of the village of Authuille. No one could pronounce the French of it, but to the casual observer it looked sufficiently like a drunk man's bad spelling of Arthur Lea and so it duly acquired that name from the lads of the Levern Valley.

Lachie had been walking on automatic pilot. His insides were screaming at him to turn and run, or to at least stop walking towards the German guns, but still his legs moved involuntarily towards the enemy lines.

Not that the previous weeks had been without incident. There was the unsuccessful, followed by the successful, raid on the German trench, of course. He didn't take any part in it, but he lay there listening to the lads from the Milltown Victoria team relating it in detail as if it had been a hard fought football match during which, unfortunately, Menzies Campbell had to be carried from the field of play due to an injury he had accidentally sustained in a 50-50 tackle.

He listened in horror to Fraser Smith's account of how he shot the German who was in the very act of killing Menzies with his bare hands. He shuddered at the thought of being the soldier in Fraser's position. He imagined that he would have wet himself and burst into tears.

Then, on 'X night' (two nights before 'Z night' and the attack itself) their brother battalion, the 16th Highland Light infantry, had sent over a platoon to check the condition of the German lines.

Unfortunately, they were caught in crossfire and had to remain in a wood until the following day. They crept back the next morning bearing 13 casualties and minus the lieutenant in command who had been killed along with two of his fellow officers.

On the next night, the 16th again were indulging in a game of football when a German 5.9 inch shell landed right between the goalposts, killing one man and injuring another.

Lachie witnessed none of these things, but just listening to such events related through the hubris of men trying to pretend that they were eagerly anticipating the next encounter made him tremble uncontrollably.

Zero hour was to be at 07.30 on July 1st: the Battle of the Somme.

The final barrage opened up at 06.35.

It seemed to Lachie that the very air itself was firing at the enemy. Their commanding officer had told them that, even before they went over the top, the German lines – their guns, their barbed wire, their dugouts, their soldiers – would, for all intents and purposes, be entirely obliterated by the most intense, sustained bombardment that the world had ever seen. They would merely have to stroll over to take possession of what was left of the German trenches where they would find any German still alive desperately trying to surrender.

Not that the taking of prisoners was actively encouraged. "Remember," General Rawlinson had said in dispatches, "that you will share your rations with your prisoners."

"Aye, that'll be right!" bellowed Fergus Smith. "The second Ah get their bacca' aff them they're gettin' a bullet between the eyes."

The rest of the lads laughed.

Lachie didn't.

Lachie couldn't imagine a worse sound than the noise of the barrage. He was wrong. He just lacked the imagination. The sound of uncompromising silence after the guns stopped, which seemed to sneer, "Now it's your turn!" amplified his fear greatly.

The whistle sounded. Lachie joined the grim procession of men climbing the ladders over the top of the parapet.

Lachie wasn't really occupying his body anymore. His limbs segued into a nightmare.

Beneath him was Chic Slaven, face drained, determinedly pensive. Behind him was Dennis Wright, goalkeeper and team coach, setting his own example of fortitude and fearlessness, even though he must have been as scared as everyone else.

One last pull and Lachie was over and into the jaws of hell.

Men were walking to his left and to his right in a thick throng.

Then the "obliterated" German guns opened up. Bullets sprayed across and through them. British uniforms fell like skittles. Miraculously, Lachie was unhurt. However he looked straight ahead and saw Harry Miller's dead face staring blankly at him. It looked unblemished save for a red Hindu-like mark just above his eyes.

Fergus Smith knelt to his left. Blood was gushing from his mouth, chest, neck and groin like a punctured water-melon. He would be dead in a few minutes.

Dennis Wright lunged into a shell hole. His steadfastness had broken. He was shaking with fear and gripped his rifle tightly as if he was a child clinging to his teddy. Impelled crazily by the obligation of duty and sacrifice, he jumped out of the hole and ran for all of five yards before being riddled in an enfilade of machine gunfire. He was dead as he fell.

Lachie was transfixed in the midst of it all. His baby eyes could not behold all that it surveyed. His mouth lay open, paralysed by fear. Highlanders carpeted this part of No Man's Land. Men were screaming in agony. Many more made no sound at all.

Lachie turned back towards his own lines, absent-mindedly dropping his rifle as he did so. Angry voices were shouting at him to pick up his weapon and fight. For one it was the last act of his life, being cut down in a hail of bullets at the height of his remonstration.

Lachie descended the ladder of the parapet into the relative safety of the 12 foot deep trench.

At 09.00, an hour and a half after going over the top and with over 400 soldiers from the 17th Highland Light Infantry lying dead on the battlefield, Lachie was arrested in the corner of his trench, curled in foetal position and taking his fingers out of his mouth just long enough to say, "Will ye no' fight fer me Lachie? Will ye no' fight fer me?"

★ ★ ★ ★ ★

## Ancre, The Somme. 27th June, 1916

Alan Johnston loved receiving and sending letters.

Not that many of his letters ever reached home. Or, at least, reached home without being heavily redacted by his superiors.

Despite repeated instructions not to write back with any pertinent details of the war which might be useful to the enemy, his letters invariably included information regarding where they were, who was alongside them, how many casualties they had sustained in their last engagement, the morale of the men and just about everything a curious officer in German Intelligence might wish to know.

His latest epistle was no different.

*The Somme*
*Northern France*
*27/07/1916*


*Dear Mum and Dad*

   *Well, here we are at the river Ancre in Northern France in an area known as the Somme. It looks like a big fight is brewing. Our guns have been blasting away at the Germans for three days and three nights now. You've never heard anything like the sound of this barrage. I'm glad these shells are all going right over my head – a bit like your jokes, dad and, like them, they're not funny either.*

   *I'm in a section of the line known as a salient. I think that's a bit that juts out from the main line – a bit like a peninsula. Anyway, it's known as the 'William Redan'. These Ulstermen like the sound of the word 'William' after their beloved King Billy.*

   *There is another section of the line known as the Mary Redan. Some of the lads are less keen on the sound of that because they think it might be a reference to the Catholic Mary Queen of Scots or, even worse, the Virgin Mary.*

   *Most of them were reassured when they found out that it's probably called after our good King George's wife or maybe after the Protestant Queen Mary who apparently was the wife of King Billy himself.*

   *While this Division is very Protestant, given that they came from Edward Carson's Ulster Volunteer Force, I was surprised to learn that there are in fact some Catholics in it. Apparently there's even a couple of brothers from the staunchly republican Falls Road in Belfast here, although I've never met them myself.*

   *It's an education in Protestant history being part of this bunch! Not that I care, but I'm happy enough for them to confuse me with somebody who does.*

   *We are facing a section of the German line known as the Schwaben Redoubt. The Germans like their redoubts and no doubts about it. Someone told me that the 16th and 17th Highland Light Infantry are facing the Liepzig Redoubt just a few miles along the front on the other side of Thiepval. I wonder how the Milltown lads are getting on there.*

More than the guns and the Germans, the lads are depressed by the weather, the mud, the rats and the lice.

Our uniforms are deloused every once in a while, but within days they are loupin' from head to foot again.

Mud is everywhere, especially after heavy rain. (It's raining now!) You sink in it – some men and even horses drown in it. You lie in it. It's your bed and your blanket. It's like another set of clothes. You live with the taste of it in your mouth.

At night, it's not uncommon to wake up to find a rat nibbling at your toes. We often organise 'raiding parties' to trap and kill them.

However many of them we kill, even more of their family turn up to seek their revenge. A bit like the Germans, actually.

When I say rats, don't imagine those small rodents back home. These things are as big as cats, so bloated have they become from eating the corpses in No Man's Land.

But in addition to the weather, the guns, mud, lice and rats, Archie and I have another problem – the Ulster accent.

Honestly, it's taken me months to catch even the gist of what they're talking about.

For the first two weeks I thought people were calling me "Bitchy" to my face. I couldn't understand it as everyone who said it to me made it sound so pleasant and personable. They even said it with a warm smile on their face.

Turns out they were saying " 'Bout ye" which is an Ulsterman's greeting. His way of saying "How are you doing?" or "How's about you?"

I also got into a weird conversation with a bear of a man called George from Rosslea in County Fermanagh.

I was making a pot of tea (well actually it was in a can) when he says to me, he says: "Is that tay wet?"

So me, I think for some reason that he's asking me a question about the river Tay back in Scotland and I says to him, says I, "Well, I've never seen it myself, but I imagine it is given that it's a river and all."

Thinking I'm trying to make a fool of him – and him as strong as a horse and almost twice as smart – he kicks the can up in the air and shouts, "Well it's not now, you Scottish b★ ★ ★ ★ ★ d!"

*Archie, being Archie, lunged at him only to find this farmer's hands gripping his throat and choking him so hard that Archie started to turn purple. It took half the Division to drag him off.*

*Apparently, he had only been asking me if the tea was ready!*

*But the word that really baffled me was their use of the word 'brave'.*

*Now I'm all for people being brave out here. You'd need to be to face all the horrors that this war flings at you.*

*But a 'brave cup of tea?!' 'A brave day?!' Everything and everyone is brave out here with these Ulstermen – even if you happen to be shaking in the 'brave pair of boots' they are in the process of admiring.*

*Anyway, apparently it means 'good' or 'fine' in Ulsterspeak, but rarely just 'brave'!*

*Mind you, a lot of the words they use are the same as back home. I've heard 'jook', 'weans', 'skelf' and 'scunner' to name but a few.*

*Someone told me that the Ulster dialect is known as Ulster Scots and is a carry over from the Protestant Planters who were settled in Ulster from Scotland in the 16th and 17th centuries.*

*Archie and I were always late for everything!*

*By the way, quite a few of the lads here worked on the Titanic when it was being built in Harland and Wolff shipyards. (Whose smart idea was it to build the Titanic in the city that gave us the Belfast sink!)*

*Anyway it's time to go and do my "fadeegz" – Ulster Scots for fatigues!*

*Hope everything is good with you all back home.*

*Give my regards to granny.*

*All my love*

*Alan*

*xxx*

Just then there was a sudden rush as the men crushed forward and round a soldier with a basket. A basket full of letters and parcels. Letters from places like Antrim and Armagh, Bushmills and Ballycastle, Magherafelt and…Milltown, from Harry Burchill to Alan Johnston.

★ ★ ★ ★ ★

Chic Slaven was never great at identifying different categories of birds. Corbies and magpies (of which there seemed to be an inordinate amount in these parts), owls, chickens and pigeons and that was about his lot.

Certainly the bird he was staring at overhead right now was none of these, although he knew that they were common round here, having seen them before.

He could barely move his head since coming to. His body felt perfectly still and way beyond his summoning. From the periphery of his vision he could see the outline of his bayonet stuck in the ground beside him.

The authorities had decided that men were to be buried where they fell and that no one was to be brought back. The practice was to stick the bayonet of anyone who appeared to be dead in the ground beside them to identify them for future burial.

German snipers were aware of this tradition and kept a close eye on the bundle lying next to a bayonet glinting in the sun, ready to despatch any 'corpse' who showed signs of a resurrection.

Chic wasn't in any pain. That was the problem. He couldn't feel a thing. He had no sense of his limbs. His heart was beating fast and his breathing was fitful.

"Is there anybody there?" Chic cried out. "Is there anybody there? I'm Chic Slaven from Milltown. Is there anybody there?"

"Aye, Chic. Ah'm here," rasped Peter Black lying behind him.

"Ah cannae see ye. Is that you, Peter?"

"Aye, Chic. Ah thought ye were deid. Don't move. There's a sniper just at the crest o' the hill ower there. Stay absolutely still till nightfall and we'll try tae sneak back tae oor trench. Where are ye injured?"

"Ah don't know, Peter. Ah cannae feel anything. Ah can hardly move ma heid tae check an' see if Ah'm missin' onythin'. Can you see me, Peter? Dae Ah look awright?"

"Ye're fine as far as Ah can see, Chic, but Ah don't wahnt tae lift ma heid tae take a right look at ye in case Ah get it blown aff."

"Whit happened tae ye, Peter?"

"Same thing that happened tae you an' maist o' oor battalion: machine gunfire has virtually wiped us oot."

"Who else has been hit, Peter?"

"Aboot two minutes ago Tommy Doncaster got spliced open wi' shrapnel. He's lyin' ower there in bits. Afore that Ah saw Harry Miller and Fergus Smith go doon almost immediately, twenty yards tae oor right. Tommy Finnegan an' Ian Martin charged on right up tae the German wire. Ah don't know whit happened tae them efter that."

"Whit aboot Wully Boyle?"

"Don't know, Chic. Ah didnae see him."

"And Lachie?"

"He flung his rifle doon an' turned back tae oor trenches."

"Poor bastard. He should never huv been here."

A sliver of shrapnel from the same shell that killed Tommy Doncaster had twisted through the air and sliced Peter open in his side, which now looked like a carcass slung on a butcher's hook. He was losing blood profusely.

"Chic…Chic…Oh, Mother…" he whimpered as he drifted off.

"Ah hope they can get us aff this battlefield, Peter, an' back tae Blighty an' frae there back tae Milltown. Ah'll meet ye in the Bottom Shop, so Ah wull Peter, fur a hauf an' a hauf pint efter we're both better.

"Hopefully we'll get back tae playin' the fitba again. Looks like we're gonnae huv tae find a whole new team mair or less. We'll need tae build it aw back up frae scratch.

"Will ye still be oor captain, Peter? Peter…? Peter…?!"

The silence gripped Chic's heart.

Instinctively he used his neck muscles in an attempt to raise and turn his head towards the place from where Peter's voice had come, somewhere from behind and to his left.

"Peter, ur ye…?"

Corporal Lars Dreschler of the 3rd Prussian Unit saw the shape beside the bayonet shudder from the impact of the bullet he had just fired. A top marksman, he had become used to shooting human beings. Not that he now consciously considered them as such. He was used to thinking of them merely as targets.

The German optical industry was the world leader in its field and the German sniper was the most feared soldier on the battlefield as a result.

Before Chic Slaven had followed Peter Black's last breath underneath the flight of the Garganay, Lars had already spotted and was lining up his next 'target'.

★ ★ ★ ★ ★

Alan was by now adept at identifying who the letter was from, even before he opened it. If it was cursive it was from his mother. If it was block capitals it was from one of his three sisters: huge, Betty; tiny, Heather; sloping to the right, Kirsty. If it was like a dog's dinner it was from his brother Andrew.

His gran used to send letters to him as well, but since she couldn't write it would have been dictated to any of the above, apart from Andrew of course.

His dad would say what little he had to say through letters sent by his mum. His sentiments were always delivered in the third person: "Your dad says he hopes you give those Jerries what for"; or "Your dad says to tell you that there was a big fight in the Bottom Shop recently over the trouble in Ireland."

But this? This was different. It was like baby print.

What made it stand out was the smear of blood traced underneath the address.

Still, there was so much blood around, Alan thought to himself, it's probably been handled at some point by a soldier who's just attended to a wounded comrade.

That was until he opened the letter.

*Milltown*

*18th June, 1916*

*Hi Alan*

*Thought I'd surprise you with a letter from someone you thought you'd never hear from again.*

*I know that we didn't part on the very best of terms, what with you leaving me hanging around all night.*

*In fairness, I know that it was Archie and not you who got me roped into that situation and that it's him I should really blame.*

*Still, you were there and I always felt that you should have tried a little bit harder to stop him, even if it had been to no avail.*

*Well now you know I know and that I forgive you.*

*One last thing though, don't you think you should talk to our old friend Sergeant Shaw at Milltown police station and tell him all about this before I do. It would sound a lot better coming directly from you and would go a long way to helping restore your good name in the community.*

*I hope that this letter finds you safe and well, although I know that you are in a very dangerous place right now – being so close to Archie and all.*

*Best wishes from an old friend,*

*Harry Burchill RIP*

The great guns were yelling through the air, followed by massive explosions.

It was difficult to think, to take it all in.

Next to him was a group of soldiers playing cards boisterously. In a rare lull in the shelling one of them looked towards Alan and shouted, "Hey, Jock, say 'girl'."

"Girl," Alan repeated in a subdued, distracted manner.

"Now say 'world'," the squaddie persisted.

"World," Alan voiced mechanically.

At that the group started singing as if on cue, "If you were the only GURRL in the WURRLD and I were the only boy…" followed by mocking, if friendly, laughter.

After a cursory smile, Alan turned back to the accusatory letter in front of him.

The rain was falling incessantly. His heart was pounding and his palms were sticky – and not from the fear of the front.

Who was this from? What was he trying to do?

Alan's thoughts went back to that night. A night he had until now largely successfully repressed from revisiting.

"You wait here!" Archie had barked. "Ah'll be back shortly. Ah've goat some business tae attend tae."

Almost an hour later, he came back with a body slumped over his shoulder. Harry Burchill's body. He appeared to be unconscious.

"Right," Archie said, gesturing with his head to the knot of the rope swing, "unfurl that rope."

Alan did as he was commanded.

Archie tightened the rope around Harry's neck.

"Archie whit the fuck ur ye daein'?" Alan cried in disbelief.

"Ah'm gien' this uranian whit he deserves."

Alan looked more closely at Harry and realised that he was already dead.

"Archie, ye cannae dae this!"

"Who says? You?!"

Alan said nothing, cowed into silence.

"Right, Alan, help me drag his body doon the banking as far as the rope'll stretch."

Alan cried like a baby, but took an end to ease the body down the slope.

When they got to about twenty feet from the ground Archie said, "Right noo, sling him oot!"

As Harry's lifeless body swung over the gorge, Archie looked on with a sense of satisfaction and said, "He'll never boast tae anywan again that he kissed me, the lyin', poofy bastard."

Alan was terrified of the scene and of Archie in equal measure.

"OK, Alan, here's the plan. For the next two or three weeks we'll act normal and pretend tae be as shocked as everywan else.

"Then we'll go tae Belfast and sign up wi' the Ulster 36th Division that's being set up there and go aff tae France or wherever they're sent. We'll be seen as heroes gaun aff tae war as well as bein' right oot o' the way o' the investigation."

Alan's spirit shrank from the the angry, bulging eyes of this maniac.

"And another thing," Archie continued, "if ye ever tell another livin' soul aboot whit ye've seen here this night, Ah'll track ye doon, so Ah wull, and torture ye until ye beg me tae kill ye. Unnerstaun?"

Alan understood.

The aftermath had been a matter of course. From the earliest stage everyone had accepted that this had been a suicide: the police, the family, the community.

No suspicion had ever been raised that it had been anything but.

Until now.

★ ★ ★ ★ ★

## Thiepval, 4th July, 1916

Roll call for the 17th Highland Light Infantry was a depressing affair.

Of those who had boldly proclaimed their presence three days before, 22 officers and 447 other ranks were no longer there to answer their names. Of the Milltown contingent, there was only one left in active service: Wully Boyle.

Most of the rest lay dead or wounded out in the battlefield. It was thought that Tommy Finnegan and Ian Martin had been taken prisoner, but there was no confirmation of that.

Lachie McMillan, of course, was facing his own particular hell.

Wully was angry, as were a lot of his fellow comrades in arms. It seemed to them that this profligate waste of soldiers' lives, and with it any chance of success, had been casually sacrificed by incompetent generals.

Word had come down the line which seemed to indicate that almost the entire offensive had been a disaster.

"Ah heard that we've suffered at least twenty thousand casualties on the first day alone," said one old timer, who would soon prove to have been wildly optimistic when set against the actual figure of 57,000.

★ ★ ★ ★ ★

**General Haig's Diary, 1ˢᵗ July, 1916**

"Reports up to 8.00 a.m. most satisfactory."

★ ★ ★ ★ ★

"And fur whit?! We've hardly gained any ground at aw'," growled another bitterly.

"Ah blame the generals," spat Tony Clarke from Maryhill.

"How? We did the fightin'," replied Bud Neill from the Garngad.

"Aye, but we did it straight intae the mooth o' the German artillery, machine guns and infantry fire that hudnae been taken oot afore we went ower the top. We did it in the teeth o' barbed wire that hudnae been cut. We did it across open ground wi' nae cover or smokescreen and abandoned by oor ain barrage. We did it efter gien' the Germans ten minutes notice that we were oan oor wey when we blew up thon Hawthorn Redoubt – plenty o' time tae man his defences. An' we did it 'supported' by artillery that coudnae hit a barn door in its own back gairden. An' even if it did the barn door would probably still be there 'cos hauf the fuses in the shells don't even fuckin' work."

"Ah think you should be runnin' this war, Tony, an' no' those duffers Haig, Gough an' Rawlinson," proposed Alex Cross from Bishopton.

"We never stood a fuckin' chance," continued Tony. "Ah'll gie the Germans this though: they hud exactly the right men an' equipment in exactly the right place at exactly the right time. They stuck their arses right oot o' the way until we exposed oorsels an' became vulnerable tae their fire. They didnae flinch durin' oor kiddy-oan bombardment. They didnae panic. An' then they just goat oan wi' the job o' massacrin' us."

"Apparently we didnae even get tae the startin' point at times," a sapper from Bridgeton said. "Ah heard that a lot o' soldiers over at La Boiselle were killed by German machine guns afore they even reached their ain front-line."

★ ★ ★ ★ ★

### General Haig's Diary, 2nd July, 1916

"A day of downs and ups...total casualties are estimated at 40,000. This cannot be considered too severe in view of the numbers involved and the length of front attacked."

★ ★ ★ ★ ★

"Dae ye think the Generals gie a toss aboot us?" asked Wully Boyle rhetorically. "We're just tiny statistics on their big board back at the office. They don't care aboot us, or oor folks back hame an' aw the grief this is causin'."

"An whit's it aw fur in the first place?" lamented Tommy McPherson, savagely. "It wis never aboot thon Duke whit's his name that goat shot in Sarabravo or wherever the fuck it wis."

"Or fur fuckin' Belgium..." added Tommy Clarke.

"And definitely no' fur fuckin' France..." Wully continued. "It's aw aboot the generals' ego."

★ ★ ★ ★ ★

**General Haig's Diary, 2nd July, 1916**

"I also visited two casualty clearing stations at Montigny…They were very pleased at my visit."

★ ★ ★ ★ ★

"It's aw aboot money," Tommy Clarke interjected. "The rich capitalists on every side tryin' tae secure their positions, as the gents in the city say."

"Aye," Gordon Butterworth from Scotstoun piped up, "Ah've heard the greedy landlords an' war profiteers in Partick an' Govan ur puttin' their rents right up because o' the influx o' people in the engineerin' an' munition works. Apparently the wummin there huv organised a rent strike an' ur beatin' up any bailiff who turns up tae evict onywan. Their leader is a wummin caw'd Mrs Barbour and the rest o' the wummin ur cawin' themsels Mrs Barbour's Army."

"Maybe they should send her an' her monstrous regiment o' wummin ower here tae win this war fur us," Wully Boyle suggested, partly in jest.

★ ★ ★ ★ ★

**General Haig's Diary, 6th July, 1916**

"Lunch went off most satisfactorily."

# CHAPTER THIRTEEN

# Song of the Beggarman

## Father O'Shea's Confessional, St Thomas', Milltown

"Bless me Father for I have sinned. It has been eight days since my last confession. I have committed the sin of hatred, Father."

"Really, my son? Tell me, which part of God's creation would you have been hatin' now?"

"The English, Father."

"And why would you be hatin' the English?"

"Because of their evil deeds in Ireland."

"How much do you hate the English for their evil deeds in Ireland?"

"Enough to join in the struggle for Ireland's freedom."

"Even if it means breakin' the law?"

"It's law without justice, Father. Their 'law' is just another way of keeping the Irish down and oppressed."

"What name do I know you by my son?"

"Micky, Father. We've talked before."

"What did we talk about before?"

"We talked about me giving sanctuary to some Volunteers."

"Did we now? And what have you decided?"

"I can hide three members on a long-term basis, for as long as is needed, and another one or two on a short-term basis, say up to a week or so."

"When would you be able to shelter our brave Volunteers?"

"Anytime, Father. Tonight if you want."

"Alright, Micky. May God bless you for your good work on behalf of the poor downtrodden people of Ireland.

"Your timing is God sent. Three men straight from Dublin are due to visit me tonight at quarter past nine here in the parish house. I don't want them hangin' around too long arousin' Father O'Keefe's suspicions."

"Were they part o' the Rising?"

"They were, surely. They killed a wheen o' those Foresters in Mount Street before escaping. So I would be grateful if you could be standin' across the street around half past, waitin' to escort them to your house of refuge. Would ye be able to do that for me, now?"

"Of course I'll escort them to a place of safety, Father, but you need to come out now."

"No, Micky, I'm sorry, I can't come out. I've still got confessions to take. I won't be able to come out for another hour. Anyway, it's best that we don't meet face to face here."

"I'm sorry, Father, but your confessions *are* over and when you step outside the door at the end of your corridor you will find five armed policemen waiting to take you into custody."

"What the…!"

"Don't resist now, Father, or you'll be shot where you stand, chapel or no chapel. Right now there are two guns pointing at you through this grill from myself and my colleague here."

"Micky…"

"My name isn't Micky, Father…Oh and by the way, don't worry about your guests tonight. They're already tucked up safe and snug in a Glasgow jail."

"Did Father O'Keefe put yez up to this?"

"He knows nothing about it yet, but he soon will. No, Father, we've been trailing you for the last six months, long before you even left Ireland to come here."

"Ye're just British scum, the lot o' yez!"

"Oh come on now, Father, don't be like that. After all you've not even given us our absolution yet!"

★ ★ ★ ★ ★

For the first month, Jeanie was nauseated by the sights and smells confronting her at Cowden House.

At first she recoiled from changing dressings on stumps, which were no more than bleeding, raw lumps of meat.

She became accustomed to the physical traumas, however, far quicker than to the mental ones.

She didn't understand shell shock and how it affected the human psyche, but she was familiar enough with its symptoms: the lack of coordination, the involuntary muscle spasms, the involuntary verbal spasms, the extreme, frightened responses, the constant terror in the eyes.

Her futile attempts to provide comfort seemed to have very little connection with the men's suffering and needs.

At least with the amputees the needs were visible and tangible. You knew how you were expected to respond and to what you were responding. Indeed the patients were often able to play a role in the process.

With those who had been emotionally and psychologically damaged, however, the needs – and therefore the care – were less immediately obvious. In any event, most of the nursing staff were totally unqualified, merely providing the most basic levels of support with very little understanding of clinical procedures, far less therapies.

The range of needs was vast.

Like Calum, who's complex patterns of social behaviour had been destroyed and who had lost all sense of inhibition. Calum had been reduced to openly attempting to masturbate whenever a pretty young nurse came into view.

Or Derek, who thought that every man in a white coat was the Kaiser coming to kill him.

Many of these patients, it seemed to Jeanie, were not receiving treatment designed to provide long term rehabilitation so much as trying to hide them away out of the public view lest they frighten children or, heaven forfend, offend middle-class sensibilities.

Meanwhile, in the midst of all this mayhem, was George from Hollywood.

George had both his faculties and his facilities. He was a handsome man in his late twenties, articulate and softly spoken.

He had been a music teacher before the war in a state secondary school in the Upper Newtonards Road in Belfast.

In a peak of passion and drama, he married his sweetheart from his schooldays the week before he went to the front. He hadn't seen her since, but six months into the enforced separation he received a brutal letter telling him that he couldn't expect her to sit through the war and sacrifice her needs as a young woman. Consequently she was resolved to seek out the pleasures of other young men, their marital status notwithstanding.

That was over a year ago. He had heard nothing from or of her since.

Jeanie enjoyed talking to George. She became blasé about his retching and simply waited for it to stop before continuing the conversation from precisely the point of interruption.

His Irish accent was gentle and easily understood.

For Jeanie there was something almost intoxicatingly exotic about George. It wasn't so much that he was older than most of the men she had met, or that he was from another country. It was more because of the world of intellect, knowledge and art which he inhabited. She was his novitiate and he her guru.

He loved poetry and had committed to memory numerous poems by Shelley, Byron, Coleridge and Keats.

But his favourite was the Ayrshire farmer poet, Robert Burns.

She loved to hear his soft Irish lilt glide over the lines of a poem Burns had written to his wife, Jean Armour, and blushed when he recited the lines, "O Jeanie fair, I lo'e thee dear/ O canst thou think tae fancy me." She found herself fantasising that George was a Romantic poet and she the object of his desire.

He was a religious man. The Bible was his touchstone and he had been a lay preacher in the Church of Ireland. That said, he was also tolerant and reserved a tiny part of his belief system for the possibility that it was all nonsense.

He also played the grand piano in Cowden House. As well as classical pieces from Bach, Beethoven, Mozart and Chopin he could also turn his ear to the popular songs of the day.

He told Jeanie that his favourite memory of the front was when he was in a trench just fifty yards from the German lines. The soldiers on both sides had adopted a live and let live philosophy which ensured that there was very little action along that stretch.

As he said, 80 per cent of the time he was bored stiff, 19 per cent of the time he was frozen stiff and only 1 per cent of the time was he scared stiff.

Anyway, the Germans had acquired a piano, probably looted from a nearby farm, when suddenly the keys struck up from across No Man's Land. The German accompanist was soon taking requests from both sides!

George had been tempted to go over for a shot, but was too scared – not of the Germans, but of his own side who would probably have prosecuted him for desertion. Instead of getting a shot he was more likely to have been shot.

What had started out for Jeanie as obvious attraction based on tender affection had quickly become more tumultous.

When she was with him she felt happy and excited. When she was away from him her feelings ranged from being distracted to being afflicted with a raging yearning.

Micky had tried to get back with her on two occasions, but her feelings for him had completely frozen over. She rejected his advances coldly, some would say cruelly.

Of course, any relationship between staff and patients in Cowden House was completely frowned upon. She would have to resign her post if anything ever came to light. The recrimination would have been all the more scathing since, technically, George was still a married man.

All of which was completely academic given that she had no idea whether he had any special feelings for her or not. Once or twice she had let her fingers linger over his hand as she passed him his food, but without being able to detect any obvious reaction.

His conversations, though captivating as far as Jeanie was concerned, were guarded in the sense that they never betrayed emotion.

Jeanie knew that she wanted him more, much more, than any man she had ever known. Her feelings for him were so complete and overwhelming. She truly loved him and she felt herself recklessly driven to let him know it.

George was confused. He was married in the eyes of God to a woman who, for all he knew, could be working overtime at that very moment in a harem in Marrakesh. He no longer felt married, nor ready to remarry. Yet this woman had strayed into his life. He could sense an attraction between them, although his natural reserve kept it at bay.

Until he received the letter placed underneath his pillow.

*Dearest George*

*The past three weeks have been the most thrilling and the most troubled of my life.*

*Meeting you has been so wonderful. Each day I am with you is truly magical. I think I have fallen in love with you.*

*I've tried to tell you, but I've never been able to overcome the fear of rejection.*

*However, paper has more courage than flesh and it is to paper that I now commit my thoughts and feelings.*

*I want to be with you after you leave Cowden House. I want to be with you for the rest of my life.*

*I hope that you can find a way of giving me a sign that you feel the same way.*

*Goodnight my dearest love.*

*Jeanie*

*xx*

He put the letter down. While part of him was shocked, part of him wasn't. While part of him was terrified, part of him was exhilarated. His life was about to take a very dramatic turn, but would it leave him still in control of events?

His preoccupation was distracted by the uproar in the corner. Miss Hodge, a young nursing assistant, had now entered the room and Calum was in the act of displaying his appreciation.

"If only life were that simple," George thought to himself.

★ ★ ★ ★ ★

Annie Black was in a delightful mood.

Her husband was making a wee fortune in overtime at Weir's Engineering in Cathcart, which was working round the clock to help supply the war effort.

The children still kicking round her feet were being packed off for the day to their Aunt Elizabeth's, who had promised to take them all on a picnic with her own family.

She couldn't have picked a better day for it. Milltown was bathed in glorious sunshine.

And her mother was due to pay her a visit this afternoon, and that meant a special cake from Baird's the bakers.

Her main task for the day was to wash the windows inside and out. Perversely this was a job she enjoyed. When she was in as light-hearted a mood as this her voice sang along with her heart as she lost herself in the rhythm of the wipe.

The children were all lined up and ready to go. Ian, 11, was a bit sullen. He regarded himself as too big to be going on a picnic with his sister and his younger brothers. Plus, he knew that he would be expected to be responsible for Hamish, 9, Victoria, 8, and Eddie, 6.

His was unlikely to be a happy, carefree experience.

"Now, Ian, you look after the picnic box. Make sure that everyone gets their share."

"Ah hate daein' this, Mammy. Can Ah no' just stay?"

"Naw ye cannae, Ian. The children need you to take them safely up to your Aunt Elizabeth's and to make sure that they behave themselves when they're on the picnic. Anyway, it's a lovely day, you'll enjoy yourself."

"Aye, so Ah wull!" growled Ian gruffly as he trooped off with stooped shoulders and a gaggle of animated younger siblings trailing behind.

Annie took a pot to her sink, which was her pride and joy.

Born in 1876, having water literally on tap was still one of the wonders of the world to Annie. She was in her teens before water in Milltown was piped directly into the homes. Prior to that you had to take a can or a tub to one of the 36 wells in the village and pump and carry as best as you could. Confidence in these though had drained quicker than hope in hell when a team from Glasgow University discovered traces of cholera in a good many of them, especially the busiest ones at Milltown cross.

Once filled, the pot was placed on the open hearth and heated to between tepid and hot.

Given that the weather was so gorgeous now, which could change with the next passing cloud, Annie decided to wash the outside windows first. She lived on the ground floor and with the aid of a step ladder she could easily reach all corners of the windows. The soap was worked to a lather and the cloth prepared.

She had just started towards the ladder when Agnes Brophy went by.

"Fine day the day, Annie, is it no'?" Agnes said cheerily.

"Aye, it is that, Agnes. Where ur ye aff tae?"

"Well tae tell ye the truth, Annie, Ah'm away tae the Parish tae see if Ah can get shoes fur Jamie and Sadie fur school."

"Why no', Agnes. Everywan else is daein' it."

"The children hate the Parish shoes 'cos they punch three holes in them so that ye cannae pawn them, but then everywan knows where they came frae."

"Better that than bare feet, eh, Agnes?"

"Exactly. That's whit Ah'm aye tellin' the weans. Anyway, Annie, Ah'll head on. Ah'll see ye later."

" 'Bye, Agnes."

Annie rose to the challenge and climbed the ladder to face the first window. Once there, she entered her own wee world and before long she was singing a popular ditty of the time called, 'Somewhere in France Dear Mother'.

After la-la-la-ing the words to the first verse, she launched with confidence and gusto into the chorus, which she knew by heart

*Somewhere in France Dear Mother*
*Somewhere that I can't tell,*
*In the midst of the fray,*
*I'm writing to say*
*That I'm still alive and well.*
*There are some fine boys here from Tipperary*
*Somewhere in France with me,*
*So cheer up dear,*
*the next time you hear*
*I'll be somewhere in Germany.*

Annie stopped to admire her work. Once washed, she would dry them off with rolled newspaper. Everything had a second if not a third use in the days before the throwaway society.

However, this would require some elbow power.

She was off again, picking up from the middle of the chorus

*There are some fine boys here from Tipperary*
*Somewhere in France with me*
*So cheer up dear,*
*The next time you hear*
*I'll be…*

"Mrs Black?"

Annie looked down at the telegram in the postman's hand.

★ ★ ★ ★ ★

The men stood at Pigs' Square almost in a trance. Each back was slightly turned against each other. No one spoke.

The streets had an eerie silence. The signs of communal grief were everywhere.

The everyday minutiae of life seemed to be cast in mourning: the mill horn, the Angelus bells, the clink of milk bottles on the doorstep – all seemed steeped in bowed respect, each carrying a different solemn tone. Even the clothes on the washing lines appeared to be at half-mast.

The news had come through about Peter Black. That was followed the next day with the news about Harry Miller and Dennis Wright. Then Chic Slaven. Then Tommy McLean. Then Fergus Smith.

Of Lachie McMillan, Wully Boyle, Tommy Finnegan, Ian Martin and Alex McKinnon nothing was known; everything was feared.

Todd MacDuff used the authority of his seniority to speak for all: "When these young men were roused tae the flag wi' the promise that those who jined thegither would fight thegither, they forgot tae add that they would also die thegither."

Mr O'Neil welcomed his class in silence. They wordlessly filed into the room.

The Reverend McDonald stepped out of his kirk into the graveyard that lay outside like a Tragic Symphony in stone, within which was contained the tears and mourning of generations of the Milltown dead.

The last respects for these new dead would be sunk in the mud of the Somme. No mothers' tears would be shed upon their coffins.

It didn't seem that the war had been lost so much that, at this price, it wasn't worth winning.

Everyone knew just what to say: nothing.

No one talked about 'heroes' or about 'dying for your country' or about 'our glorious dead'. Feelings were much too raw and brutalised to cover over this orgiastic orchestration of dead youth with such a plastic veneer of respectability. That would be for a much later date.

Bertie Boyle looked across the room at Theresa, lying on the floor. Her face, now desiccated, had cried so much that it seemed like a ravine landscape, whose channels once hosted great torrents, now reduced to gorges of dry river beds.

For Mrs Black and Mrs Wright and all those other mothers, the waiting was over. Their misery was complete. For Theresa Boyle the image of impending death crept closer to the core of her heart with an unbearable anguish.

Aggie McMillan looked down towards the McKinnon's tree. The Union flag there seemed drooped rather than draped. She had never contemplated that her son would be killed in action just because he happened to be wearing a uniform in a wee game of soldiers. Over by Christmas, wasn't that what they said? Her pity for the other mothers was mixed with the guilt of knowing that she was mostly relieved that it was their sons and not hers who had been taken.

Mrs Slaven sat frozen with shock next to Chic's favourite toy gun from his boyhood. In those days he used to be a cowboy, or a confederate or in the Seventh Cavalry or a Redcoat fighting for Kitchener at Khartoum and he would be killed ten times before lunch and ten times after lunch, but he was still there to tuck up into bed at night.

Her heart was hollow. She didn't have the emotional capacity just yet to know what to think about it. She couldn't feel for the grief and pain of others, so overwhelmed were her senses and emotions at her own great loss.

Father O'Keefe started to prepare his sermon for Sunday. He wrote, 'My Dear People…' Half an hour later they remained the only words to trouble the page as they stared back at him vacantly in some sort of silent rebuke.

His thoughts were numb, his spirit dry.

To the rest of the world the grief on display in this small village might be seen as a microcosm of the whole tragedy ranging across this European civil war, but for Father O'Keefe and all the other souls in this tomb of sadness, Grief Central was Milltown Cross.

Micky McGoldrick took to the hills for a walk by himself, drowning in troubled contemplation. He once knew these lads like brothers. He had grown up with them, played with them, shared their triumphs and their failures on the football field.

He tried to tell himself that it wasn't the case that he should have been there; they should have been here. "They didn't sacrifice their young lives *for* their country; their young lives were sacrificed *by* their country," he told himself bitterly.

But his heart was breaking along with everyone else.

Menzies Campbell lay in his hospital bed as his dad told him the grim news.

"Ah should huv been there to die with them" he cried out, in defiance of a deep sense of relief that he hadn't been.

Sleekit Tam stood alone on the edge of men at Pigs' Square, mouth dry, unable to spit.

Night arrived over the broken bodies on the Somme an hour before sunset in Milltown. But for the whole of that day and for the many that followed the shades were already closed in the minds and hearts of everyone in that small village.

★ ★ ★ ★ ★

"Chrissy?"

"Aye, Sadie."

"See me?"

"Aye, Sadie."

"See this war?"

"Aye, Sadie."

"Ah think we should stoap it."

"Dae ye think so, Sadie? Whit fur?"

"We're losin' mair than we can hope tae gain. It's costin' too much in young men's lives."

221

"Well we cannae let the Kaiser win noo efter aw we've been through."

"Whit we've been through we've been through, Chrissy. We cannae change that. But whit we can dae is tae avoid mair lives bein' lost. Ma man…"

"Your man the mince hater?"

"Aye ma man the mince hater, they're gettin' so desperate he could be called up so he could. So could yours, Chrissy. Ah wahnt it tae stoap afore we reach that point."

"Sadie?"

"Aye, Chrissy?"

"See ma man?"

"Aye, Chrissy."

"See mince."

"Aye, Chrissy."

"He fuckin' loves it, but that's no' the point. The point is, see this war?"

"Aye, Chrissy."

"He really fuckin' hates it. He widnae go tae France supposed ye shoved a stick o' dynamite up his arse and tried tae blow him aw the wey there."

"But he'll no' huv the choice when this conscription thing comes in."

"Depends. Ah heard aboot a boy caw'd Lafferty frae Arthur Lea who cut aff his right index finger so that he widnae be able tae fire his gun."

"Ma man's ambidiversified. He could shoot wi' either haun'."

"How wid the authorites know that?"

"Anyway, he picks his nose wi' that finger. He's mair attached tae it than it is tae him. Naw, he'd mair likely take tae the hills till it's ower."

"Whit wid ye dae if he's no' bringin' in a wage?"

"Ah suppose Ah'd just need tae find a job."

"Aye, but Sadie they don't gie oot jobs fur windae hingers like us. Windae cleaners aye, maybe. So whit wid ye dae?"

"Ah'd like tae work in Baird's."

"Sadie, you know an' Ah know that ye'd eat yer body weight in cakes in there. Ye widnae be able tae get yer heid oot o' that windae efter a week at thon counter. Anyway, Ah heard that they're strugglin' tae get ingredients fur their cakes wi' aw these shortages 'cos o' they fuckin' U-Boats sinkin' oor merchant ships. They might huv tae close doon soon."

"Ah suppose, then, Ah could work in wan o' they munition factories or jist get a job doon the mill."

"Sadie, when wis the last time you hud a proper job?"

"Well, Ah've been far too busy runnin' a hoose an' bringin' up weans an' lookin' efter ma man the mince lover tae actually haud doon a job that ye'd actually get peyed fur."

"Anyway, Chrissy, see me."

"Aye, Sadie."

"See ma niece, Karen."

"Aye, Sadie."

"Well here she comes tae talk aw her shite aboot her weddin'. Ah'm away. When she chaps ma door gonnae tell her Ah've gaun oot fur the day. Ah cannae staun people that ur happy when Ah'm lookin' fur a moan."

"Aye, Sadie."

★ ★ ★ ★ ★

Mark was the newest kid in the street to find his independence. Just over four years old and the third son of Frank and Jenny Hannigan, he had all the makings of a tearaway, Aggie thought as she surveyed him from her seat in the sky.

A wee snottery nosed kid with bags of attitude and a tennis ball.

He was playing at flinging the ball from cupped hands straight above him. He would then stand underneath it in the hope that it would come down and hit his head. After five clumsy failed attempts the ball eventually landed square on his napper before bouncing harmlessly down the road.

"Weel done, wee Mark!" cried Aggie to the accompaniment of her own clapping.

Mark looked straight up at Aggie and, with real disdain in his voice, said, "Ma daddy says that you're a nosey bastard."

With that he picked up his tennis ball and went about his business manfully.

Momentarily stunned, Aggie broke into a broad smile. "Your daddy's no' wrong," she admitted to herself.

The rest of the morning was routine and boring apart from when Dorothy Slaven went by.

"Bring them hame right noo, Aggie. Ah've lost ma son. Ah don't wahnt others tae lose theirs."

"You know, Dorothy, Ah cannae even remember how aw this started."

"Ah just hope they don't forget tae stoap it someday," said Dorothy scathingly and walked on.

Aggie was just about to pop her head back into the shell of her house when she saw a familiar figure grace the top end of the street.

Tall, balding, boils on his head, tramps clothes. It could only be Breezy Breeks. On his previous visit to the street he had stopped every 50 yards or so to sing outside each cluster of houses before engaging them in his sales pitch. This time, however, he was striding on purposefully, as if he were late for an appointment.

Until, that is, he reached Aggie's house. He looked up at her as if he was on a stage and she was in the Royal Box at the King's Theatre. Without introduction he launched into a hugely popular music hall classic from the 1890s called 'After the Ball is Over'.

It was a song Aggie knew and liked. This time she found herself involved in Breezy's performance and eagerly awaited for the first verse to end so that she could join in the chorus.

Soon they were singing sweetly together.

*After the ball is over*

*After the break of morn,*
*After the dancers leaving*
*After the stars are gone.*
*Many a heart is aching*
*If you could read them all,*
*Many the hopes that have vanished*
*After the ball.*

The next two verses went on to describe how the old bachelor in the song had squandered and rejected his one true love in his youth after seeing her kiss another man at a ball. It was only many years later, after his sweetheart had died, that the man he saw her kissing turned up again only to reveal himself as her brother.

However, Breezy didn't sing those verses. Instead he placed a single finger to his lips hushing Aggie to silence before repeating the chorus, this time with slightly different words.

*After the <u>fall</u> is over*
*After neck breaks that morn,*
*After two chancers leaving*
*After the stars are gone,*
*Many a heart is aching*
*If you could read them all,*
*The two chancers now have vanished*
*After the <u>fall.</u>*

For emphasis he repeated it.

For the second time that morning Aggie was stunned.

Breezy placed a sheet of paper on top of Aggie's hedge and said, "This is for you, missus."

He then walked out of the street just as purposefully as he had entered it.

Aggie clambered down as fast as her frame would allow and rescued the note.

When she managed to drag herself back inside her house, she opened it feverishly.

As well as the changed words of the erroneous chorus there was a message written in block capitals which read:

'I KNOW WHAT HAPPENED. I WAS THERE. I SAW IT. I KNOW YOU ARE IN DANGER. CONTACT ME.'

Aggie slumped in her chair. Was this from an ally or an enemy? Was she receiving support here or was she being set up?

She knew that she had no choice. She had to take the risk.

★ ★ ★ ★ ★

Life had not been good for Micky McGoldrick of late. Over the past two years he had lost his job, a girl he really cared for and some erstwhile, if estranged, good friends.

Now he was being faced with the loss of his freedom.

Along with his mother, father and every other citizen between the ages of 15 – 65, Micky was obliged to sign the National Register. "The last time ye hud tae dae this," commented Archie Currie caustically, "Herod wis in power!"

He had also been subjected to a harassing, if not overtly threatening, letter from an over-zealous recruiting officer, which read:

*Dear Mr McGoldrick*

*Unless you have some good and genuine reason for not enlisting, which I am agreeable to investigate, I advise you to offer to join the Army before you are made to. This is an entirely private and friendly piece of advice. Compulsion may not be so far off as you think. I am only waiting the word to call every man of eligible age, and as you see, I have you on my list.*

*It is possible that you may be one of those to whom this does not apply… but if you are, I can tell you that I have good reason to believe that you will be mightily sorry in the end if you wait until you are fetched…*

The abuse from Alice and co. had subsided since Jeanie finished with him. He had heard that the rest of the women had decided to end their 'recruitment drive' after the news from the Somme had filtered through to Milltown.

Nevertheless, the mood nationally was hardening against the 'conshies, malingerers and cowards' from families who had paid the ultimate sacrifice.

Micky was part of the anti-conscription movement. While perfectly legal, they were treated by the authorities virtually as a proscribed organisation, with Glasgow Corporation refusing to hire out public buildings to any group promoting an anti-conscription message.

Their meetings were regularly infiltrated and wrecked by serving soldiers and their families.

To reinforce what was known as The Derby Act, after Lord Derby who was in charge of recruitment, canvassers were sent round the doors of every single, young male in order to try and attest them on the doorstep for future enlistment.

While Micky had been placed on the 'unstarred list' – not employed as a vital worker in a reserved industry – he refused to be attested.

The men at the door made some derisory comments as they left frustrated in their efforts. "Don't worry son, they'll be bringin' in conscription soon for cowards like you. We just wanted tae save yer time!"

On 15th November, 1915, the noose was further tightened as an official notice under cover of the Royal Arms appeared in the Glasgow Herald:

*Enlist before 30th November. If you do not the Prime Minister has pledged himself and his government that compulsory means will be taken...*

Micky was exactly the kind of young man firmly in the sights of the conscriptionists: fit, unmarried, unskilled and no children.

Furthermore, Prime Minister Asquith had promised the nation that no married man would be enlisted until all unattested single young men had been 'dealt with.'

Micky was in no doubt what that meant.

Nor was he in any doubt what his reaction would be.

Then, on January 15th 1916, the first committed test of Micky's resolve was passed by Parliament in the form of its first Military

Service Bill, which allowed for the compulsory conscription of unmarried men and widowers between the ages of 18 and 41, with few exceptions, none of which applied to Micky.

Micky was one of over a million young unmarried men who had so far not stepped forward for service. Of those, 651,160 were unstarred so, Micky thought, hopefully it would take a couple of wars before they would catch up with him.

By this time, John Maclean, the inspirational left wing street agitator from the Shawlands district of Glasgow, had been arrested, convicted and sent to Peterhead prison for his attempts to undermine the war effort. Glasgow Council lost no time in sacking 'the dominie frae the Shaws' from his position as a teacher in the city.

On the 25th May, 1916, a second Military Service Bill received its royal assent which extended conscription to all unstarred men, single and married, between the ages of 18 and 41.

When the letter came it merely instructed Micky to attend Maryhill barracks for attestation and conscription into His Majesty's Forces at 10.30 a.m. on July, 23rd, 1916.

His mother wept; his father spat.

He contemplated running away. However, he decided that such an act would be a betrayal of his principles and he decided to make a public stand instead.

His opportunity to resist the persuasions of the Crown came on 23rd August, 1916, when they came for him.

Their attempts at bullying only strengthened his resolve.

Micky was committed to the custody of Peterhead prison for at least the duration of the war, or until he agreed to serve his country at the front.

As he walked from the court benches to serve his sentence, it all seemed very unreal to Micky.

He was about to find out just how real, now that he had been 'fetched'.

# CHAPTER FOURTEEN

## *Candles at Dawn*

### Albert, The Somme, 4<sup>th</sup> July, 1916

The trial was set for 10.30 a.m.

The president was Colonel J.P. McEwan DSO RA, officer commanding in the Fourth Division.

He was assisted in his court by a further five commissioned officers from various regiments on the front.

The prosecutor was Robert Sharpe and the defence counsel was Thomas Hughes.

Contrary to court martial procedures, no preliminary sitting took place before the trial itself. Lachie had been with his counsel for a mere 45 minutes on the day of the hearing.

Lachie pleaded not guilty to all four charges and the trial was underway.

The prosecution's first witness was Private Thomas Aitken from Lachie's own battalion.

"Private Aitken, tell us about your experiences on the morning of the first of July during our assault on Thiepval."

"It was grim. We all went over the top and headed straight for the enemy lines. The German guns and barbed wire were still intact. They opened up on us. Men were falling down on every side, but we kept going until it was obvious that there was no point and we were ordered to retreat with the order, 'Every man for himself'."

"Did Private McMillan retreat with you at that point?"

"No, sir. He had already retreated. He had gone back to the trench of his own accord shortly after the fighting started."

"Did you actually see Private McMillan retreat in the face of the enemy and at the point of your advance?"

"Yes, sir. We all shouted at him to pick up his gun and come with us."

"What did he say to that?"

"He didn't say anything, sir. He just ignored us and walked on as if he was in a trance."

"You said that you told Private McMillan to pick up his gun. How did it come to be on the ground?"

"He dropped it there, sir."

"By accident? As a result of combat?"

"Neither, sir. He dropped it deliberately. He just simply let it fall out of his hand and walked on."

"In which direction was he walking?"

"Away from the enemy lines and back to our trench."

"Thank you, Private Aitken. No further questions."

"A further four soldiers who had been on the battlefield with Lachie testified much the same as Private Aitken.

The two soldiers who arrested Lachie testified that they had found him without his gun and curled up in a corner of the trench as the fighting was continuing.

Lachie's counsel chose not to cross examine and advised him not to say anything on his own account.

Given that Lachie's defence had intimated that they were not going to challenge the witness statements, and sensing that it might be better for the court not to be confronted with Lachie's juvenile demeanour, the prosecutor elected not to call Lachie to the stand and entered into summation instead. The prosecutor addressed the court.

"Gentlemen, on the morning of the first of July, 1916, at Thiepval, the 17th Battalion of the Highland Light Infantry went into battle against the enemy and fought bravely in the face of German guns and shells that rained down on them. Over 400 men of the battalion were killed and many more were wounded.

"But one man who did not fight bravely was the accused, Private Lachie McMillan, who refused to advance, refused to carry arms, refused to fight and retreated back down the trench from whence he had come while the fighting continued. He took a coward's way out of avoiding injury or death and left his comrades still in arms to their fate.

"He has betrayed his fellow soldiers, his King and his country in the hour of their greatest need and must be found guilty of all four charges under the strictures laid out in the Manual of Military Law.

"The sentence to be imposed is for the court to decide, but guilty must be the verdict."

He sat down with all the assurance and self-belief of a man who had done his job, while Lachie sat limply, staring into space and wondering what 'strictures' meant.

The court was then addressed by the counsel for the defence.

"Gentlemen, we do not dispute that the accounts of the soldiers called to the witness stand here today are correct in their detail.

"However, Private McMillan was in the grip of shock at the time in question. He was paralysed with a fear which made it impossible for him to function as an active, fighting soldier.

"I have only this morning met Private McMillan, but even talking with him for a short while you realise that he is of very low intelligence. He would be easily confused in a situation with which he was unfamiliar and in which his friends and comrades were being killed all round him. It is extremely debatable whether Private McMillan should ever have passed the enlistment procedures that allowed him to join up for the Western Front in the first place. However, I trust that you will not be of a mind to send a man to his death for being congenitally stupid.

"He is also very young and inexperienced and that too should be taken into account, especially when set against the appalling conditions which prevailed at the time.

"Private McMillan tells me that he is unable to remember a

231

single moment of what happened on the battlefield on the fateful morning. The trauma of it has caused him to block out all memory of it, which is why you did not hear him speak in his own defence during the trial.

"To that extent, I would contend that he was not responsible for his actions and cannot be deemed to have demonstrated – as the Manual of Military Law requires – the *intent* to disobey orders, or the *intent* to desert, or the *intent* to take a coward's retreat in the face of the enemy, as he was emotionally and psychologically traumatised to an extent that rendered him unable to respond to what was happening around him at the time.

"Indeed, he was no different from a soldier on the same battlefield who was unable to further prosecute his own part in the war because he had been disabled by enemy bullets or shrapnel. It was the effects of this battle which destroyed his capacity to fight or respond appropriately, even if the source of his disengagement was less obvious than the demonstrable physical violence which afflicted his fallen or wounded comrades

"As Private McMillan cannot be held responsible for his behaviour on the morning of July first, I plead with the court for this young man's life and ask it to view him, in all humanity, as a hapless victim of this war and to pass a verdict of not guilty."

The court retired for consideration.

The blue court martial form, section E parts 10 and 11, recorded the verdict.

"The court finds that Private McMillan, of the 17th Battalion of the Highland Light Infantry, is guilty of the first charge and all further three alternative charges."

The court reopened the following day to consider the aspects of his character and previous conduct.

The Acting Adjutant of the Regiment was called and duly presented details of the prisoner's character and service:

*Private McMillan has not been convicted of any prior offence. He is not under sentence. The present age of the prisoner is twenty years of age. He is*

*in possession of no military decoration or military award subject to the forfeit of the court.*

The Defence Counsel once again declined to cross examine.

The Court sentenced Lachie to death but recommended mercy on the grounds that he was very young and had no experience of active operations of this nature and that he was of feeble mind and character and would be extremely susceptible to becoming disorientated in the heat of battle.

His file was released for the perusal of the army's most senior member of staff, in whose hands Lachie's fate now lay.

★ ★ ★ ★ ★

The 36th Ulster Division were on the move again after their astonishingly brave but ultimately futile assault on the Schwaben Redoubt on July 1st.

The Ulstermen had faced the German guns and artillery on the Somme with a missionary zeal and fanatical bravery. However, despite some gains at a cost of over 5,000 casualties, they were unable to hold on against German counter attacks and had to fall back.

Many good men lay with their chests riddled or their faces blown away as they sacrificed themselves in the face of German guns.

In the fog of war, however, big George from Rosslea lay dead in the mud, shot in the back by friendly fire.

On the corridor of the train to Flanders, their next posting, Alan pulled out his letter.

"Look, Archie, Ah goat this. Somebody's oan tae us."

Archie looked sternly at the letter with distaste before accepting it. As he read, his face became crimson with rage.

"The bitch…! The fuckin' bitch…Ah'll fuckin' kill her…!"

"Bitch…! Who…? Is this frae a wummin…?!!"

Archie looked Alan coldly in the eye. Alan squirmed.

"Whit ur ye gaun tae dae noo?" Archie asked accusingly.

"Me? Nothin. Sure if we just sit tight nothin'll happen. It'll aw blaw ower an' we'll be awright."

"Of course it'll no' be awright. That mad wummin wullnae stoap until we're baith danglin' frae a hangman's noose. We'll need tae kill her."

"Kill who? Archie, fur fuck's sake gaunnae tell me who ye're talkin' aboot!"

"Aggie McMillan, that's who."

"Aggie…the village gossip? She sent this letter? How does she know onythin' aboot this?"

"How does she know onythin' aboot onythin', but she always does! She's goat an instinct that leads her tae things like this…an' Ah confirmed it fur her by tryin' tae scare her aff wi' thon knife Ah left oan her bed an' by settin' her hoose oan fire."

"You burnt her hoose! Archie there wis a ten year old wee lassie in that hoose. You could huv killed her!"

"So whit? If you wur lined up outside in front o' a firin' squad an' they said we can shoot you or we can shoot the wean you wid say shoot the wean."

"Naw Ah widnae, Archie…"

"Aye ye fuckin' wid. It's easy tae say ye widnae when it's no' actually happenin', but if ye wur lookin' doon the barrel o' eight rifles aw aimed at yer heart ye wid say kill the wean, no' me. Onybody wid an' Ah'm nae different. If Ah huv tae use her tae make sure that nosey interferin' bastard gets aff ma case then that's whit Ah'll huvtae dae."

"Archie, this hus gaun far enough. Ye cannae go aroon killin' wee lassies tae cover up whit you…whit we've done. Ah'll no' allow it."

Archie stopped, menacingly.

He looked closely at Alan and saw a man on the brink of crumbling. He saw for the first time that Alan was capable of turning himself in and incriminating both of them.

"Really…whit ur *you* gonnae dae?!!"

"Ah don't know, but Ah'm no gonnae allow ye tae kill a wean tae cover up whit Ah've done. If ye dae Ah'll go tae the polis masel, so Ah wull, an' pit us baith behind bars."

Archie quietened into a silent brood. He stared hard into Alan's quivering face. Alan was looking away. He couldn't meet with Archie's eyes fixed upon him with such cruel intent. Archie knew then that Alan was nearing breaking point. He knew that he had become a liability. Archie was losing his hold over Alan and when that happened anything could happen.

"Awright, Alan. Ah'll no touch the lassie, so Ah wullnae."

"Promise?"

"Promise," Archie lied.

★ ★ ★ ★ ★

Lachie was detained in a small hut just behind the lines and just in front of the wall where men were executed. There was an armed guard constantly on duty outside the door. The latrine was a bucket which Archie was expected to fill, empty and clean himself.

His only companion was a pack of cards. The only game Lachie knew was Snap. Difficult to play on your own, admittedly, but Lachie managed it and was elated when he 'won'.

He had understood very little of the court case despite his defence team going to great lengths to explain it to him.

He also understood very little of his predicament.

Mr Hughes had seemed like a very nice man. He kept saying sorry to Lachie as if he had done something bad to him.

Just after dinner a Church of Scotland chaplain came to visit Lachie.

"Hello, Lachie. How are you? My name's Reverend Patterson, Derek Patterson. I'm from a town about twenty-five miles outside Milltown called Saltcoats. Have you ever been there, Lachie?"

"Naw, Ah huvnae, Mister Patterson. Is it nice?"

"Och aye, it's nice alright. It's just by the sea looking across at Ailsa Craig, if you know where that is."

"Naw, Ah've never heard o' that either."

"Anyway, Lachie, how are you feeling?"

"Aye, Ah'm fine, Mister Patterson. Ah'm just bored in this cramped wee hut aw by masel. Dae ye fancy a game o' Snap?"

Lachie lifted the first card up as if he was ready to throw it.

"Perhaps later, Lachie, but first I'd like to have a chat with you."

"Whit aboot?"

"Lachie, do you know that you've been sentenced to death?"

"Aye, but they'll no' dae it wull they? They'll just fling me oot o' the army an' let me go hame wi' a bad word aboot me tae ma mammy."

"Lachie, I'm afraid they might."

"Whit, let me go hame? Why should you be afraid o' that?"

"No, Lachie, I'm afraid they might shoot you."

"But Ah didnae dae onythin'!"

"Lachie, in war they shoot you for not doing your duty."

"Ach well, by the time they get roon tae it it'll be years away an' the war'll be ower an' we'll aw be back hame by then"

"Lachie, you don't understand. Your case has already gone to General Haig's office. If he agrees with the sentence you could be shot in the morning."

For the first time a look of recognition came over Lachie's face. "Who'll shoot me?"

"Soldiers from your own battalion, selected by your commanding officer."

"They widnae dae that tae me. They're ma freens. They came here tae shoot bad Germans, no' their ain freens."

"Lachie, if they refuse to shoot you they could be shot themselves."

"Does ma Mammy know they're gonnae shoot me. She should be here. She wid stoap them."

"The only person who can stop this now, Lachie, is General Haig. We must pray to God that the good General grants you clemency."

"Whit's clemency?"

"Mercy, Lachie. If he shows you mercy he will stop them from shooting you out of pity for you. Will you pray with me, Lachie?"

"Ah don't know ony prayers, Mister Patterson. Ah don't even go tae the kirk."

"Do you believe in Our Lord Jesus Christ, Lachie, our Saviour and Redeemer?"

"Ma mammy says that she read the Bible wance an' she just thought tae hersel', 'Thon's a load o' shite!' "

"Lachie, you must believe. Only Jesus can save you, if not in this life then the next."

"Whit dae Ah say tae Jesus, Mister Patterson?"

"Hold my hand, Lachie, and we'll pray together. I'll just say what's in my heart. When I pause you say 'Amen'."

"Amen."

"No, Lachie, we haven't started yet.

"O Lord, look upon your poor beloved son, Lachie McMillan, of Milltown, who now kneels before you begging your devine forgiveness for all the sins he has committed in this life by deed, word or omission...Lachie?"

"Whit?"

"Say 'Amen', Lachie."

"Amen."

"Find it in your heart, Lord Jesus, to guide our good General Haig to grant mercy to Lachie McMillan from Milltown...Lachie?"

"Amen. Whit did he say?"

"Who?"

"Jesus. The wee man ye wur talkin' tae."

"He speaks to us in our heart, Lachie. Through the Holy Spirit."

"Ah cannae hear onythin'."

"You need to be quiet, Lachie, and listen to your soul. It is there that God speaks tae us. He is speaking through your turmoil and anguish and is preparing your salvation."

"So, Ah'm saved then?"

"No, Lachie, I can't say that…"

Just then the door opened and an officer from the 17th Battalion of the Highland Light Infantry, Lieutenant Gordon McGregor, entered.

He addressed Lachie.

"Private Lachie McMillan of the 17th Battalion of the Highland Light Infantry, I am authorised to tell you that the sentence of the court held on the fourth of July, 1916, at Albert on behalf of His Majesty King George the Fifth, will be promulgated at dawn tomorrow. You will be executed by firing squad at six a.m. precisely.

"May God have mercy on your soul."

With that he clicked his heels, turned smartly and left.

Lachie looked stunned and scared. He still wasn't exactly sure just what he had been told, but he was almost certain that the news was bad. Very bad.

The chaplain explained that General Haig had decided to carry out the sentence of the court in full and ignore its recommendation for mercy.

"But Ah thought you said that Jesus wid save me, Mister Patterson?"

"Jesus will be waiting to save you for Heaven, Lachie."

"That's nae fuckin' use tae me. Ah need Him here noo… where's ma Mammy? Wait till she hears aboot this…Mammy… Mammy…!"

Lachie crumpled the card still in his hand. It was the Ace of Spades.

★ ★ ★ ★ ★

Wully Boyle's battalion, or what remained of it, was now on rest leave at Bouzincourt.

Sitting alone in a local estaminet, coffee in one hand, cigarette in the other, Wully's thoughts drifted back and forward over the events of the last few weeks.

He thought of Fraser Smith and Dennis Wright and Peter Black. They had seemed to Wully like giants. Invincible. Yet there they were, snuffed out like candles at dawn.

It seemed unreal.

Chic Slaven – a man you could talk to about anything. Full of sympathy, humour and insight. He was like a professional counsellor: he could give advice when it was called for and just listen when it wasn't. Dead.

Wully shuddered at the gap their extinguished lives created. So many lives lost in the mud of the Somme. How many great scientists or writers or musicians or doctors or teachers or world leaders would be left behind in that mud? How many would now never be born?

Wully had joined up in a fit of patriotic zeal. His father had stood proudly by him. Was he right?

Wully took the thought out with him as he left the estaminet and headed back to his battalion. He was coming more and more to view war as a crime against humanity – by humanity. Yet surely this sacrifice was for something worth dying for? 'The war to end all wars,' they had said.

"Naw it isnae," Wully said wryly to himself.

Of course his mother had pleaded with him not to go. Was she right? What about Micky McGoldrick? Was he right? Wully reflected that if everyone who had joined up from all sides had just stayed in their beds, this senseless, evil slaughter would have been avoided.

"They tricked us," thought Wully bitterly. "The politicians and the generals and the press and the old unfulfilled men standing on street corners who wanted to live their adventure boy fantasies through their children. It was lies and deceit."

He thought of back home and of the girls handing out white feathers to confused young men who were either too scared in their minds or too troubled in their souls to commit themselves to this great conflict. How naïve those girls seemed now.

When Wully had gone down to the mill to join the enlisting parade that was marching from Irvine on the Ayrshire coast to Maryhill Barracks in Glasgow, he had proudly strutted past the cheering onlookers and accepted the kisses of pretty girls who wouldn't have looked at him twice outwith this great fall-in.

He felt proud. He felt important. He felt like a man. His country needed him and he would not let it down.

What did he know back then? What do they know back there now? Have they any idea of the daily terrors and gross indignities that replaced their romantic notions of being at war?

If he made it to go back home would they call him a hero? He didn't feel like a hero, hoping that the bullets would miss him and hit his mates. He didn't feel like a hero, still being alive when almost everyone else from Milltown was dead or maimed or taken prisoner.

Then there were the Lachies of this world. Poor Lachie. A child trapped in a man's body or a man's body trapped in a child's mind, he didn't know which.

In a sane, civilised world Lachie wouldn't have come within a country mile of being given a gun to point at strangers, but such was the system's appetite for fresh young meat for their mincing machine that he was packed up and sent off with everyone else.

Lachie had lain down his arms, unable to cope. Lachie couldn't cope with peace-time never mind war.

He thought of his 'dance' with Lachie, when Lachie lifted him round the dance hall, much to everyone's amusement.

He thought of Archie Ferguson's cruel treatment of Lachie and how he had set out to humiliate and belittle this burbling baby.

Such were his thoughts on returning to camp where he was told that his Commanding Officer, Lieutenant Jeffreys, had selected Wully to be part of the firing squad which would execute Private Lachie McMillan at six the following morning.

★ ★ ★ ★ ★

The chaplain stayed with Lachie all night.

Lachie's mind was totally befuddled.

"Whit ur they gaun tae dae tae me?" he kept asking, as if the answer must surely in time change to something more favourable if he asked it often enough.

At one point he just sat in the corner, rocking backwards and forwards with his thumb in his mouth repeating, "Will ye no' fight fur me, Lachie? Will ye no' fight fur me?"

"Are your mother and father still alive, Lachie?" the Reverend Patterson asked.

"Ma Mammy's still alive, but ma daddy died six years ago wi' consumpshun."

"Well, just think o' yer daddy, Lachie. You'll be meeting him tomorrow in Heaven."

"Whit ur they gonnae dae tae me?"

"You're going to Heaven, Lachie. They'll put you to sleep and when you wake up you'll be with your daddy in Heaven. Are you not feeling tired?"

"Naw."

"Is there anything you want me to pass on to your Mother or your wee sister, Maureen?"

"Aye, Mister Patterson. Can ye tell them that Ah love them so Ah dae. And can ye tell Maureen that Ah'm sorry Ah didnae fight fur her. If they gave me another chance Ah wid. Dae ye think they'll gie me another chance, Mister Patterson?"

"No, Lachie. Your place in Heaven is booked and ready. They're waiting for you."

"Whit ur they gaun tae dae tae me again?"

"They're going to put you to sleep, Lachie, and when you wake up you'll be with Jesus and your daddy in Heaven."

"Will it be sore, Mister Patterson? Ah don't like pain. It makes me cry."

"It will be too quick to be sore, Lachie. One minute you'll be in this world with all its wickedness and evil, and the next you'll be with God and all His glory in Heaven. There will be beautiful music there and everyone will be happy."

"Mister Patterson, why did ma Mammy say, 'Ah read the Bible wance an' Ah just said tae masel, Thon's a load o' shite?'"

"Some people aren't always ready to hear God's word, Lachie, but I'm sure God will talk to your Mother soon."

"Will Ah meet ma Mammy again?"

"Some day you'll both share God's grace in Heaven."

"Huv you been tae Heaven, Mister Patterson?"

"No, Lachie, you have to die before you can be reborn in Heaven."

"Ah'm Ah gonnae die then?"

Just at that the door opened and a doctor came in with half a bottle of brandy.

"Excuse me, chaplain, but I'm sure you won't mind if I just give this brandy to Lachie, for medicinal purposes."

"Not at all, doctor. I can't see that it will do him any harm at this stage."

The chaplain turned to Lachie, who was still pondering this reference to having to die to get to the place he was about to visit, and said, "Lachie, would you like a brandy? It will help you to go to sleep."

Bizarrely, the doctor gave Lachie a medical: blood pressure, heartbeat, checking of the eyes. He even made him say 'Ah' as he looked down his throat.

"His blood pressure's through the roof," the doctor whispered to the chaplain.

"No wonder," the chaplain sighed.

"I'll be back in about an hour to see if the 'medicine's' working."

Lachie took a glass of brandy and drunk it like water.

"Mister Patterson, Ah don't wahnt tae go to Heaven."

"Everybody wants to go to Heaven, Lachie. You're very lucky to be going there."

"Ah just wahnt tae stay here – Ah mean in Milltown – wi' ma

Mammy an' wee Maureen. Don't let them send me tae Heaven, Mister Patterson. Don't let them. Mammy, don't let them…" Lachie started shaking and sobbing.

"God loves you, Lachie."

"Naw he disnae. Naebody loves me except ma Mammy an' Maureen. Tell them tae just let me go hame, Mister Patterson…Ah just wahnt tae go hame…why can Ah no' just go hame?"

★ ★ ★ ★ ★

Meanwhile, Wully Boyle was confronting his Commanding Officer, Lieutenant Jeffries.

"I can't believe that you're asking me to do this. I know this man. I grew up with him. I'm from the same village. Have I to go back to Milltown and tell his Mother that I shot her son? You cannae dae this tae me!"

"Well, actually, I can and I will. Is there anyone out there who would volunteer to swap with you? It's a horrible job for whoever does it. This is war and in war we are all asked to do things which are abhorrent to us. You'll just have to get on with it like everyone else.

"Anyway, nobody will know that you shot Private McMillan because you won't know yourself. Only two out of the eight guns have live ammunition and no one knows, or will ever know, whose that is."

"Ah don't know if Ah can dae it."

"Private Boyle, be in no doubt that if you disobey an order of this magnitude and extend that poor man's suffering by as much as one iota of a second, you may find yourself in front of a firing squad as well."

"But…!"

"You are dismissed, Private Boyle!"

"No, sir, not yet. Not before I tell you that you're a callous, jumped up wee bastard and that your rotten army is about tae kill

243

a wean wi' a mental age o' nine. You should be fuckin' ashamed o' yersels. Sir!"

"Thank you for the character reference Private Boyle and for your compliments to His Majesty's Forces overseas. We will deal with this outburst later, after the execution I think and not before, as I perceive your plan to have been. Kindly remove yourself from my sight, Private."

"Sir!"

★ ★ ★ ★ ★

The brandy was all but finished when the doctor returned. Lachie was tearful, talking to himself all the while.

"Ah don't wahnt tae go tae Heaven…gie me another chance tae fight…Ah don't wahnt tae go tae Heaven…Ah don't wahnt tae huvtae die…"

"Right!" said the doctor, "I thought it might come to this."

He went up to Lachie and from his bag produced a syringe which he straightaway injected into Lachie's arm.

Lachie looked on in astonishment, then in shock. Then he fell asleep.

"That'll keep him sleeping till the time comes. I'll inject him with something to rouse him later."

"He is a very troubled soul," said the chaplain. "He's very childlike. We shouldn't be shooting people like him."

"We need to shoot people like him *pour encourager les autres.*"

"Where did you read that in your Hippocratic oath – or did I just mispronounce that?"

"Don't take your spiritual anguish out on me, Reverend. I'm just doing my job the same as you. His fate isn't in my hands; his care is up until the moment of his death.

"I'll see you again in a couple of hours."

★ ★ ★ ★ ★

The eight members of the firing squad were led to Lachie's last post by Sergeant Jones.

"Right men, you have been asked to undertake the most difficult and most unpleasant task a soldier can be asked to do, namely to shoot one of his own men. We have played no part in this man's plight. Others put him here, principally himself no doubt. We are merely doing what every soldier has to do; we are just following orders.

"But remember, your chances of getting through this war alive depend on every other soldier doing just that. When that is not done sometimes, in the interests of us all, it is necessary to take extreme measures to restore discipline.

"Above all else today, we must carry out our task professionally and humanely.

"The prisoner will be brought out of the hut already wearing a blindfold, I am told. He will be escorted to the post in front of the wall and tied there. The doctor will pin a white ribbon on his chest denoting where his heart is. Aim at that.

"When the prisoner exits the hut we will be standing four to each side of him in silence. When he reaches the post we will move together smartly to form a continuous line.

"Once the doctor pins the ribbon on the prisoner's chest I will give the command 'Ready', at which command you will cock your weapons. Three seconds after that I will give the command 'Aim' and five seconds after that I will order you to fire. You will then shoot the prisoner.

"It is vital that we do not prolong the prisoner's agony and that we despatch him cleanly, efficiently and quickly.

"After you have discharged your rifles, the doctor will give him a medical examination to confirm that he is dead. If he is still alive I shall execute him with my small arm.

"Any questions?"

The men stared ahead, drawn and grimly silent.

★ ★ ★ ★ ★

"It's time to bring him round," the doctor said.

He reinjected Lachie, who immediately revived.

"Is this Heaven?" he asked, bemused.

"Not yet," the chaplain answered. "You're just going to Heaven now."

"Ah don't feel well," Lachie complained. "Ah need tae see a doctor. Ah feel dizzy."

The door opened. Lieutenant Jeffries, accompanied by three soldiers and a group of witnesses stood on the threshold.

Two soldiers entered brusquely and took hold of Lachie, tying his arms behind his back as they did so.

The third soldier put a blindfold over Lachie's eyes.

"Whit's happening? Ah cannae see! Whit ur ye daein' tae me?"

The soldiers silently led Lachie out of the hut.

The Reverend Patterson started praying: "From the depths I have cried out to you O Lord. Lord hear my voice. Let your ears be attentive to the voice of my supplication…"

A sobbing Lachie passed the silent soldiers on either side and was placed quivering at the post.

The firing squad immediately moved together facing the prisoner.

As he was being tied to the post, Lachie started screaming; "Mammy, Ah didnae wahnt tae be a sodger…Mammy tell them tae leave me alane… Tell them Mammy…"

The doctor pinned the white ribbon to Lachie's chest and nodded to the Sergeant.

Dark patches began to form down Lachie's trouser leg.

A rifle came flying through the air in the direction of Lieutenant Jeffries.

Wully Boyle took one step out of the line and stood to attention, both his arms straight down by his sides, his stoney face staring impassively ahead.

The stunned Sergeant regained his composure quickly and shouted, "Ready…Aim…..Fire!"

The volley resounded. Lachie fell to the ground, wounded by a single bullet to his shoulder.

He fell to the ground screaming in pain.

Sergeant Jones rushed over to the spot where Lachie was writhing in shock, drawing in large gulps of air. He unfastened his holster, removed his gun.

Lachie lifted his head towards the Sergeant. His big, round watery eyes pleaded, like a seal helplessly waiting to be culled.

The Captain knelt down on one knee alongside the fallen soldier. He looked into Lachie's eyes with a rheumy gentle cradling, while slowly – almost tenderly – raising the gun towards his head. "Mam…" Private McMillan wailed as Captain Jones drew his life to a close.

An agitated Lieutenant Jeffries ran to retrieve Wully Boyle's rifle. He opened its gun cartridge and yelled, "It's live! It's fuckin' live!" Turning to face Wully, he screamed, "You bastard! You let him die in agony!"

He moved to strike Wully with the butt of the rifle. Sergeant Jones intervened just in time.

He turned to the soldiers who had led Lachie out to be executed and shouted, "Arrest this bastard. Now!"

Wully was bundled past Lachie's twitching corpse, slumped heavily at the bottom of the post.

# CHAPTER FIFTEEN

## *Betrayed by a Kiss*

Micky's notion of being granted political prisoner status was quickly disabused at Peterhead (pronounced Peterheed) prison in the north-east of Scotland.

He was told to strip naked and don a prisoner's uniform, which resembled striped pyjamas made out of very thin cotton.

He refused.

He was instantly beaten by the wardens and left battered, bruised and naked on the stone floor of a holding area beside the prison uniform.

His own clothes were collected in a bundle and carted off for incineration. The room was cold, damp and smelly and had no heating, lighting or furniture.

Micky shivered uncontrollably in the dark. He eventually gave in out of desperation, putting on the uniform in a vain bid to ward off the biting cold.

He curled into a corner and huddled into himself.

He tried to find solace in sleep, but as he started to drift off he was roused in alarm by screeching and scuttling.

The rats had arrived.

Outside the room, Micky could hear angry shouts, the barking of orders, screaming threats, dull thuds and yelps of pain.

Micky was in hell.

Some hours into his ordeal the door crashed open and two wardens entered, accompanied by a doctor.

"Ah see you've seen sense, ya cowardly, conschie bastard," the senior warden said.

"Pity", said the other one, "Ah wis lookin' forward tae gien' him another hidin'."

"Ye'll get yer chance again, Norrie. We all will," the bloated senior warden laughed pointedly.

"Right noo," he continued, "Ah've brought Doctor Simpson tae ye tae gie ye a check ower. Doctor, if you will…"

After making him say "Ah" and looking down his throat, Doctor Simpson checked Micky's pulse, chest and heart.

He twiddled with Micky's nose, causing him to cry out in pain.

"Nose is broken," the doctor announced.

"Well whit can he expect if he will hit his heid aff stane walls, eh, doctor?"

"Quite," the doctor replied wearily.

The doctor made some clumsy attempts to "straighten" Micky's nose, with little regard for the obvious pain it was inflicting on the patient. He ordered an ice pack for Micky to hold against it.

Meanwhile, the wardens marched Micky off to his zero-star accommodation to meet his roommates – Geordie, a poacher; Billy, a thief; Arthur, who had been convicted of sedition at an anti-war rally in Aberdeen after repeating John Maclean's line, "If you want to fight a Hun, go and fight the King of England."

Big Tam, the senior warden masquerading as an estate agent, gave Micky a guided tour. "That exquisite, flea-ridden tap bunk's yours. That bucket full o' shite, pish and vomit is your communal luxury latrine. You get the chance to slop it oot wance a day – if we remember to let you that is. Take your turn.

"Reveille is at 5.00 a.m., a healthy breakfast of bread and water follows fifteen minutes later. Ye'll be working in the quarry by six and ye'll be back by six at night. Dinner a la slops is at six-thirty in the evening. Lights oot is when it gets dark. We dinnae huv lamps in the cells here.

"Basic rule: dae whit yer tellt, when yer tellt or ye'll get a slap. If ye gie cheek or any shit tae a warden we'll beat that shit oot o' ye. Whit youse dae tae each other short o' murder – 'cos we cannae be arsed wi' the paperwork – is up tae you. Ah couldnae gie a fuck."

With that he left.

Micky turned round to face his new cellmates. They were beaten men. Their eyes dulled with pleading; their hands palmed to parry; their knees primed to bend, to kneel, to beg; their spirits cowed and fearful.

Billy spoke first. "Welcome to the Peterheid Savoy, Scotland's prison of no hope."

Micky looked past Billy towards Arthur who was as gaunt and frail a man as he had ever seen in his life. Not surprising really, given the beatings and force-feeding to which he had been subjected.

Micky was looking at a picture of himself come six months time.

★ ★ ★ ★ ★

Jeanie knew that George was behind the hedge before she saw him. His retching told her that.

Her stomach tightened. How would he react to her letter?

Technically, she could be sacked for gross misconduct should its contents ever come to light.

She stood waiting for George to compose himself, glad of the enforced delay. At length she took a small step for man from behind the hedge to meet him.

"Hello, George," she said, attempting unsuccessfully to sound confident and in control.

"Hello, Jean," George replied, without, it seemed to Jeanie, betraying any sign of emotion or overt recognition of the special circumstances surrounding this potentially fateful meeting.

Jeanie couldn't bear the suspense any longer. It was time to get right to the point.

"Did you read my letter?"

"Yes," George replied flatly.

"And...?"

"You're taking a big risk writing to a patient like that."

"You're no' just any patient, George. The risk o' losing you and never seeing you again far outweighs any other risk. Anyway, Ah'm no' here tae discuss risk, Ah'm here tae discuss us. Is there an 'us'?"

"In what sense?"

Jeanie could feel frustration flood through her veins.

"George, you know Ah love you, Ah've told you that, but Ah cannae stand this evasion. You've faced German guns and German gas. Surely you can face a wee lassie frae Milltown telling you that she loves you and wants tae be with you for the rest of her life!"

"Jean, you know I'm married…?"

"Aye, tae a trollop who abandoned you for other men while you faced death on the battlefield fightin' for her country. Whit kind o' a wife – whit kind o' a marriage is that?"

George bit his lip. For two years now, his life had lacked the tenderness and compassion of female companionship. Instead it had been full of brutality and fear. What was so wrong with accepting this opportunity to embrace kindness and comfort? He put his arms out and she rushed into them

The smell of her hair was almost intoxicating and he found himself kissing her affectionately on the head.

One moment later, as Jeanie turned her eyes upwards to meet his, they were locked in a passionate kiss which seemed to seal their commitment to one another.

They broke away and held on to each other tightly. They both needed this moment.

George broke into another bout of retching. Jeanie stepped back to give him his space and his dignity.

Just then she heard her name being called from the steps of the house. A batch of Belgian soldiers had arrived and Jeanie was needed.

She pressed George's hand as he was coming out of his choking and said, "I love you, George. We'll meet later."

George pressed her hand in return and looked fondly at her as she disappeared with a lightness of foot and heart back to her duties.

Moments later, however, his ardour had cooled and he began to feel differently.

"Oh drat," he thought, "what have I done?"

★ ★ ★ ★ ★

Conscription had been bad for business in the Bottom Shop. One by one they had been called up, leaving only the old and the infirm to chew the fat by its bar.

Hoppy and Lucky had formed a solid partnership and were now the mainstay of proceedings during opening hours.

"Wimmen!" spat Hoppy contemptuously.

"Whit aboot them?" asked Lucky.

"Efter this war they'll be takin' ower."

"How?"

"Well look at them noo, Lucky. They're daein' men's jobs in the fields…in the factories…in the docks…in munitions…"

"Aye, an' they're daein' it well."

"This war hus done mair fur votes fur wimmen than fifty years o' Suffragettes and Suffragists…"

"…an Suffrathats an' Suffrathis! Aye, Hoppy, efter the war's ower they'll get the vote awright. Nae doubts aboot it!"

"But there is wan thing they're no' daein' that the men ur."

"Whit's that then?"

"They're no' killin' or dyin'. If they cannae fight fur their country they shouldnae be able tae vote fur it."

"Well, Hoppy, they ur on the front-line as nurses an' run the same risks as the men. Ah mean look at thon English nurse Edith Cavell, executed by the Germans fur helpin' wounded soldiers tae get back tae England."

"How low can the Germans get…executing wimmen!"

"Mind you, the French huv just executed Mata Hari fur bein' a German spy. Do you know that she wis married tae a Dutchman named McLeod. His family came frae Skye."

"Mata Hari McLeod? No quite as exotic is it!"

"Anyway, if getting' a vote is dependent upon yer ability tae fight an' die fur yer country, does that no' rule you oot, Hoppy?"

"Ah'd be willin' tae fight and die fur ma country, Lucky. Just put the King's uniform oan ma back an' haun me a Lee Enfield rifle an' Ah'd dae ma duty, so Ah wid."

"So wid a lot o' wimmen, Hoppy. Ah mean if Ah wis a German an' Ah hud tae choose between fightin' wan o' us or Aggie McMillan, Ah know which wan Ah widnae choose an' she's no' in this bar!"

"Aye, poor Aggie. Whit a tragedy, losin' her son like that."

"Lachie should never huv been sent tae the front. He should huv been kept here tae peel tatties an' hing oot the wahshin'"

"Tae be killed in the war is bad enough, Lucky, but tae be executed fur cowardice an' desertion in the face o' the enemy…"

"Aye, his family will huv tae live wi' that, but if ye ask me we should huv executed the morons who sent a simpleton into that war in the first place."

"How's Aggie taken it?"

"Dunno, Hoppy. Ah've seen her aboot the street recently, but her whole demeanour hus changed. She seems distracted from the world aroon her, as if she's set on a mission."

"Huv ye heard the rumours, Lucky?"

"Aboot whit?"

"Aboot Aggie an' Breezy Breeks?"

"Naw, whit aboot them?"

"Apparently Breezy's coortin' Aggie."

"Naw, surely no'!"

"They've been seen a lot wi' each other recently. Quite engrossed in each other's company, Ah've heard."

"Well she's certainly no' efter his money, that's fur sure."

"Aye, an he's certainly no' efter her looks. Ah'm no' sayin' she's ugly, but the tide widnae take her oot!"

★ ★ ★ ★ ★

Aggie was shocked when she saw how Breezy was living. His home was literally a hole in the ground, dug like a grave with a sheet of tarpaulin laid on the bottom and a corrugated tin sheet for a 'roof'.

Her enquiries had led her to this spot in Kirkton Wood, on the top of a slope overlooking the gorge where Harry Burchill had been found.

It was a mild night. The tin roof had been shoved over to one side and Breezy was lying on his back, cigarette hanging loosely from the side of his mouth, his eyes staring wildly up into the starry night.

Aggie came upon him and looked down over his prostrate body, stupefied.

Breezy made no move, no flicker of emotion or recognition crossed his face.

After an unnatural silence he said in a mechanical, matter of fact tone, "I knew you'd come."

Breezy stirred and climbed out the 'steps' dug into the side of his 'house'.

"You live like this?" uttered Aggie in an incredulous tone.

"Yes. Not much I know. Still it's better than the conditions of the trenches in France and Belgium. At least no one here is trying to shoot, bomb or gas me."

"You know why I'm here?"

"Of course I do. You want to know what I know. It's what you do after all."

"What do you know?"

"I know that Archie Ferguson killed Harry Burchill, then brought his corpse here and swung it over the gorge to make it look like suicide."

"You know...how do you know?"

"Because I saw it. I was here in the forest collecting wood to build a fire. I heard voices. It was Archie and Harry. It sounded like

254

Archie was trying to seduce Harry. I then saw Archie lean forward and kiss Harry, who responded. During the kiss Archie placed his hands around Harry's throat. There was a brief struggle, then Harry went limp. Archie had broken his neck.

It was all over in a matter of a few minutes."

"…and what did you do?"

"Nothing, which is why I am still alive. I see lots of things I shouldn't see in my itinerant life. I found out long ago that the best thing is to see no evil and to hear no evil, even if you did and can't forget it."

"Was Alan Johnston involved?"

"In the cover up, but not the murder. From what I could hear Archie had ordered Alan to wait for him by the gorge without telling him what he was about to do. Alan was shocked when Archie returned with Harry's dead body. He didn't want anything to do with suspending the body over there, but Archie made him do it in the way that Archie makes people do things."

"Why didn't you tell the police?"

"Two reasons – Archie and the police. Archie is capable of murdering me just as easily as he murdered Harry. The police are capable of blaming the whole thing on me if they knew I was there. Either way I was going to come out of it smelling even worse than I do now. And it wasn't going to bring Harry back."

"So why tell me now?"

"Because you need help and you're not dead – yet!"

"*I* need help?"

"Yes *you* need help. That was a stupid attempt to flush Archie out at the Cattle Show. All you did was to make yourself a target without being able to prove anything to anyone beyond yourself. And then of course he was watching you when you came to the wood to play amateur detective."

"Watching me!"

"Yes. Archie set up camp overlooking the gorge from the other side to see who might be taking an interest in the scene of the crime.

Apart from some grieving friends and relatives, you were the only person to show up out of 'professional' curiosity.

I was watching him watching you. He couldn't make any more sense of what you were doing than I could until your little stunt at the best apple in show contest made it all too obvious."

"What are you going to do now, Breezy?"

"I will go to the police and tell them what I saw if you can persuade Alan Johnston to go first. Then at least there will be corroboration and Archie will hang. If that happens you're safe, I'm safe and the community will be a whole lot safer. The trouble is Alan might get a prison sentence for his troubles, although my testimony should save him from the gallows.

He might not go for it, but it's our only chance.

The name's Mark, Mark Manson by the way."

Aggie looked closely at Breezy for the first time. He had a distinguished face and a noble bearing that, in her mind, denoted good breeding. He also sounded educated. This was a man with an interesting past which she would have to get to the bottom of one day. Just not today.

She told Breezy about her letter to Alan which would possibly precipitate the very course of action Breezy was advocating.

He just shook his head.

"Alan will take this straight to Archie. He'll know immediately that it's from you, just as surely as if you had signed the bottom of it in your own blood, and that will just make him more determined than ever to add you to his list of victims."

"Where's a German sniper when you need him?" Aggie thought that night in bed.

The night before that telegram and the worst day of her life.

★ ★ ★ ★ ★

During her lunch hour, Jeanie sat by the burn in Milltown glen and wept. Her breasts were tender and swollen. She suffered from nausea, headaches and lower back pain and had a strange craving to eat coal. And now she had missed two periods.

She was pregnant. Not to George, to Micky.

Since her clinch with George they had only managed to secure the odd moment of restrained passion, which had left her feeling cheated and abandoned afterwards.

Now she felt lonely and confused. Micky was going to be the baby's father, but she was emotionally committed to another man. Micky was so far out of her life it was almost as if he had never been in it in the first place.

She knew that George would always be between her and Micky. She needed George.

She had tried to urge George to go further in their few entanglements, hoping that if they made love she might be able to convince George and herself that it was his. George's puritanical mindset, however, put a massive brake on things from going that far.

She knew of a backstreet doctor from Glasgow who helped women in her predicament.

The thought of getting rid of her baby, though, was repulsive to her. If there was anyone in this world more vulnerable than her right now it was the child living within her.

She had heard stories of unmarried mothers being committed to institutions while their babies were removed from their care and given to married couples. She was determined that wasn't going to happen, but she didn't know where or to whom to turn.

Her mind flitted back to Micky. She was sure that he would agree to marry her and that they could live a normal life with their child in the village. She didn't love him, never had, but he was a kind person who would be good to both of them. If there had never been a George then perhaps she could have made some sort of fist of it.

Still, even if she was prepared to accept a life without passion, excitement or love, getting in contact with Micky would be a trifle difficult right now given that he was currently indisposed at the King's pleasure in a penitentiary in Peterhead.

Then again, she could always confront George with the situation in the hope that he might accept the baby as if it had been his own and agree to marry her, before taking her away from all the petty scandal that would forever trail her around Milltown.

Jeanie knew she might be indulging in wishful thinking, bordering on fantasy. But that was her preferred option and she resolved to take the risk.

She stood up a mere 50 yards from where the baby had been conceived and made her way back to Cowden House.

When she arrived, George was sitting on his own by the lawn reading the Glasgow Herald.

"George, can we go somewhere private. Ah need tae speak tae you urgently."

"Of course, Jean. What's wrong?"

"George, Ah want you to know that Ah love you and that you are the only man Ah've ever loved. Ah'll never love anyone more than Ah love you…"

"Why do I sense a 'but' coming?"

"There's no but, but…"

"But…?"

"But… Ah huv hud other boyfriends…"

"Hopefully not Archie Ferguson."

"No, not Archie, although Ah did fancy him once."

"I'd say you were lucky to have avoided that one."

"Anyway, George, just before you there was a young man, Micky McGoldrick, who Ah hud been stepping out with for over a year."

"Micky McGoldrick? Sounds like a Taig."

"A whit?"

"A Taig. It's a term of bitter endearment Ulster Protestants have for Irish Catholics."

"Well, Micky is a Catholic and his father came frae a small village in Ulster called Rasharkin."

"There are a lot of Taigs in Rasharkin right enough. Was he a good man?"

"Yes, George, he wis a good man. He wis a very kind man. Ah didnae fall out o' love with him because Ah never loved him in the first place, but Ah did find him attractive at one point."

"Jean, why are you telling me this? Or, at least, why is it urgent that you tell me this now?"

"George," Jeanie gulped, "Ah'm pregnant."

George could not have been more stunned if Jeanie had just announced that there had been a minor oversight regarding her birth lines and that she was actually a boy called Rupert.

The roar of silence drowned out their thoughts.

George took a step backwards. His face exploded in fury and contempt.

"To who…? To this Taig…?"

"Yes, tae Micky McGoldrick. Ah'm gaunnae huv his baby."

Jeanie moved forward to take hold of his hand, but George brushed her aside angrily.

"It was before Ah knew you, George," Jeanie pleaded. "Ah didnae mean tae get pregnant."

"You didn't mean to get pregnant! Shouldn't you have kept your knickers on and your legs closed then?"

"George, don't be angry with me…please…"

"I'm not angry with you. I'm disgusted with you. Don't ever touch me or look at me that way again…!"

"George…forgive me!" Jeanie gasped as she watched her life dissolve in front of her.

"Oh, don't worry about me forgiving you. You'd better hope and pray that the Lord Jesus Christ, your Saviour and Redeemer, forgives you."

"George…!" Jeanie pleaded desperately.

"Goodbye, Miss Brown. What we never had is now over. I leave you to Micky McGoldrick and that fenian bastard growing inside of you."

With that, he turned his back and walked away, leaving Jeanie on her knees sobbing.

★ ★ ★ ★ ★

Later she would say that she had known all along that there was something wrong.

She had been restless for weeks, if not months.

Alex McKinnon never wrote, unlike other men at the front.

Oh, she knew, of course, that he was useless with a pen. Give the man a hammer or a spanner or a spade and he could make you a world out of a hatbox, but a pen in Alex's hand was as incongruous as a ballerina in a rugby scrum.

There were little signs which troubled her at the time and which were to haunt her later.

Firstly, there was the missing shoe. Alex meticulously kept his shoes in a small cupboard under the staircase, rudely polished, ready for church on Sunday. Months ago now, the left one went inexplicably missing and was never found.

Then there were his gloves, ruined after Maggie accidentally knocked a tin of red paint all over them.

And finally, there was the mirror in the bedroom – Alex's mirror which he used to examine his face each morning pre and post shave. It fell without warning, explanation or permission and smashed to pieces on the floor.

The signs were telling me," she would moan. "The hoose knew afore Ah did!"

It was hard for Maggie to have to listen to extracts of letters sent from sons, boyfriends or husbands, read with flushed enthusiasm by their recipients at the Steamie.

"Never mind, Maggie," others would console, "if there wis onythin' wrang ye wid hear right quick. Good news keeps its ain counsel; bad news spreads like manure ower a rhubarb patch."

Still, she was peppered with an uncomfortable dread, which had intensified of late.

The day started like any other. Up at 5.30 a.m. Cold ablutions by the wash hand basin. Dressed. A modest breakfast. Tidy up both rooms and make the bed.

She looked out of the window. It promised to be a fine day. Not a cloud in the sky.

It would be a lovely walk down the mill brae to the Turning Shop where she worked making bobbins for the thread.

She laughed anew at a joke Frances McGlinchey had told the women yesterday about a minister, a sermon, a cheeky wee rascal and a twopenny pie.

She looked down at herself. All appeared to be in order. She prided herself on her trim figure and luxurious locks. She could still turn heads.

"Aye, Alex McKinnon," she chuckled, "ye're a lucky man tae huv me as yer wife, so ye ur."

At that, she heard a series of bumps at the door. An unusual sound. Someone, or something, was trying to attract the attention of the occupants, while for some reason disdaining to use the knocker.

She paused and listened intently. Yes, there it was again. Most definitely someone was hitting the door.

Was it a child? Was it an animal? Surely it couldn't be another war vagrant begging for money at this time of the morning?

Maggie opened the door gingerly.

Standing there was a grotesque stranger in shreds of army uniform. A man supported by two crutches under two stumps of arms. Standing on his right leg with his left one starting above where a knee used to be, he looked at Maggie from a horrifically disfigured face. His right eye focused while the left eye stared downwards eerily through an empty socket.

The mouth – twisted, swollen and semi-paralysed – toothlessly opened and Alex's voice rasped, "Hello, Maggie, Ah'm hame."

## CHAPTER SIXTEEN

# *On the Conformity of Maps*

Alan stood on sentry duty looking across at the German trenches less than 100 yards the other side of the barbed wire. At the slightest hint of movement in No Man's Land a Very Light was sent up illuminating the whole area.

So far there had been three false alarms. At least it kept everyone on their toes and prevented Alan from falling asleep, the penalty for which could be execution by firing squad.

While one part of Alan's mind was focused on what might be afoot out there in front of the Germans, another part of his mind had wandered back to Milltown and to Aggie McMillan and to the risk she posed to both Archie and himself. Not to mention the risk that Archie posed to Aggie and to little Maureen.

Things had become so complicated. He couldn't see any other way than that they were destined to become even more complicated still.

He didn't like Aggie McMillan – never had. Nevertheless he recognised that she was a force of nature not to be trifled with, anymore than was Archie, upon whose promise not to touch Maureen he knew he couldn't rely.

" 'Bout ye?" asked Corporal Sammy Brown. Alan and he had formed a close bond over the previous months and Alan had found he could talk to him about most things. But could he talk to him about this?

"Hi, Sammy," Alan replied. "Ah wis away there."

"Anywhere nice?"

"Just back home."

"Is there a wee Scottish girl back there you'd be missing now, Alan?"

"No, but there's one or two that it's almost worth bein' here just to be missed by them."

"Popular man then, eh?"

"Aye, but for the wrong reasons."

"What reason would that be?"

"Ach, ye don't wahnt tae know."

"Jock, you're right, I probably didn't want to know. With me being starved frozen out here and all, I was hoping to sneak off back to a warm fire rather than stand here and listen to all your Scottish drivel. But that was before you said that I wouldn't want to know and now I couldn't think of going anywhere until I get to know what it is that I don't want to know, if you know what I mean!"

So Alan started to tell him, after extracting the usual promises to be sworn by everything that was holy – in a Presbyterian sort of way, of course – never to tell anyone.

He had just given the background to Harry Burchill and his crush on Archie, with the part being reached where Archie had left Alan in Kirkton Wood to go and meet Harry, when suddenly Alan was aware of a presence by his side. It was Archie. Alan stumbled to a stop. Sammy blanched, took a step backwards and excused himself, resuming his quest to seek out a blazing fire.

"Wis Ah interruptin' somethin'?" Archie asked accusingly.

"Eh, naw. Ah wis just tellin' Sammy aboot how we used tae go huntin' fur rabbits in Kirkton Wood."

"Aye, those were the days," Archie said almost wistfully.

"Dae ye miss them, Archie?"

"Well, if Ah remember rightly oor last excursion in Kirkton Wood ended up wi' us catchin' mair than a rabbit!"

"Don't talk aboot that," Alan pleaded.

"Naw, Ah suppose it's best if naebody talks aboot that," Archie said threateningly, sending a chill right through Alan.

"Mind you, we've got Aggie McMillan tae worry aboot. Whit should we dae aboot her, Alan?"

"Absolutely nothin', Archie. Ah mean, ye cannae even be sure that she wis the wan that sent the letter."

"Naw, in the same way ye cannae be sure that they Germans ower there actually wahnt tae kill us," Archie sneered.

"How dae ye know that it wisnae sent by somebody else that might even huv actually seen us dae it?"

"Because Ah know there wis!"

"Wis…whit wis?…Ah mean how?…Ah mean why?…Fuck Ah don't know whit Ah mean!"

"Breezy Breeks saw us dae it. He lives in a hole in the ground up in Kirkton Wood. Ah didnae know that till later. When Ah discovered that was where he lived Ah made a point o' seekin' him oot just tae say hello tae him. Wan look at his face tellt me everythin' Ah needed to know. His eyes held a terror for me an' Ah knew he hud seen us.

"At least he's very obligingly dug his ain grave, which will save me daein' it when Ah get roon tae killin' him."

"Maybe he sent the letter."

"Naw, he's too petrified. He's too scared o' the police and he's far too scared o' me."

"Archie, this is aw gettin' very, very messy."

"Tell ye whit then, Alan, why don't we just walk in tae the police station when we get back hame, tell Sergeant Shaw whit we've done an' just wait till they get roon tae hangin' us fur it?"

"Between Aggie and Breezy an' whoever sent this letter, if it wisnae wan o' them in the first place, somebody's bound tae talk an' then the cat'll be well and truly oot o' the bag."

"No' if Ah kill them first."

Archie stomped off back to the dugout leaving Alan to shiver – and not from the cold.

★ ★ ★ ★ ★

Wully Boyle occupied the same jail in which Lachie McMillan had been incarcerated before his execution.

On the wooden chair, exactly where he had left them, lay the cards with which Lachie had been playing Snap.

Wully had been charged with refusing to comply with an order, attempting to assault an officer and with discarding his weapon. He could be shot three times over.

He didn't regret his actions, but that didn't prevent him from being terrified of the repurcussions.

Every time he closed his eyes he was haunted by the vision of Lachie's dead body lying twitching in the yard, like a stray dog that had just been put down. Would that be him in a few days?

The war didn't make sense to Wully anymore. It was a masque of madness and death, which looked as if it could go on until an entire generation of European male youth had been virtually wiped out.

He wanted to live, but not to kill. He wanted his freedom, but not to continue with his part in this European genocide.

He wanted to go home, just as Lachie had wanted to go home. He wanted to swim in the Snypes dam just above Milltown. He wanted to stand alongside his father at Pigs' Square and tell the men there what he had seen here: the bravery, the stupidity, the tenderness, the cruelty.

He wanted to find warmth and security in the arms of a sweetheart. He wanted to hug his mum and tell her that he loved her and that she had been right along.

He wanted to climb the hills above Milltown on a clear summer's day and look over Glasgow, or across to the Pentland hills 50 miles to the east, or up towards Ben Lomond at the foot of the Highlands, or out to the west towards Ailsa Craig nestling 75 miles out in the Clyde Estuary marking the milestone to Ireland.

He wanted to earn money and have choices as to how to spend it. He wanted children and grandchildren. He wanted a future in peace and prosperity.

But most of all he didn't want to die tied to a post in front of a firing squad.

* * * * *

Lieutenant Jeffries stood to attention in front of his Commanding Officer, Major Ronald Lambie.

"So, Lieutenant," the Major began, "how did you select your men to take part in the firing squad that executed Private McMillan?"

"Well, sir, it was as random as choosing the first men whose names came into my head. There was no prejudice involved. It was just a job that had to be done. I gave no more thought to the personnel involved than I would have given to selecting a party to trap, corner and kill rats in the trenches."

"I trust that Private McMillan's life meant a bit more to you than a cornered rat, Lieutenant."

"No, sir, I didn't mean…"

"So you just plucked the names out of the air and there we were and that was that, yes?"

"Exactly, sir."

"I see. Now, Private Boyle, who is currently under arrest, were you aware that he came from the same village as the condemned man and had, in fact, grown up with him?"

"Not until he told me, sir."

"He told you?"

"Yes, sir. He came asking to be excused from his duty, sir, as he was a friend of Private McMillan's and, as you say, had come from the same village."

"What was your response to Private Boyle's request?"

"I refused it, sir."

"Really? On what grounds?"

"On the grounds that it was a job that had to be done which everyone would find distasteful whether they had known the prisoner or not, and that it was his duty to carry out his orders, however unpleasant they might be."

"Sterling stuff, Lieutenant! But tell me, would it have been possible to have found another soldier to take his place in the squad, one to whom Private McMillan was a stranger?"

"Yes, sir, it would have been possible."

"Did you consider the effect on the morale of your men when they found out that they could be asked to execute their own childhood friends?"

"I considered the effect on the morale and discipline of the men if they thought that all they needed to do to get out of an unpleasant task was to come up with some pretext or other by which they might be excused."

"While it was unfortunate that the issue ever arose in the first place, Lieutenant, could you not have agreed to his request with the proviso that he would be included in the next firing squad to be formed from your battalion?"

"Didn't think of that, sir."

"Well now that it has been placed before you as an option which may well have been considered, do you agree that it would have been a better way forward?"

"I'm not sure, sir."

"Why not?"

"Private Boyle's attitude was an issue in itself, sir. He was belligerent and abusive. I was reluctant to accommodate his request and to reward his bad behaviour."

"A huge price to pay for an attitude is it not? Although Lieutenant, I would point out that Private Boyle's military service record has been exemplary until this unfortunate incident."

"It wasn't this time though, sir, and you have to think of the condemned man whose agony he prolonged."

"Ah, the condemned man! Yes, Lieutenant, it would have been a great consolation to Private McMillan, had he insisted at the last moment not to wear a blindfold, to have seen a well-kent face in the firing squad aiming a rifle directly at his heart.

"You have brothers in the regiment, I believe."

"Yes, sir, three brothers."

"If you were ordered to be part of a firing squad that was due to execute one of your brothers would you merely accept the order as given without question?"

"No, sir, probably not."

"Would you ask to be excused the onerous duty on the grounds that the order was unreasonable?"

"Yes, sir. I suppose so, sir."

"Yes sir – and that is what should have happened here. The same rule as to what might or might not be considered to be reasonable should have applied and you should have accommodated Private Boyle's request.

"What followed at the execution, therefore, I deem to have been at least as much your responsibility as Private Boyle's.

"He will receive an official censure for his part in the affair and returned to his duties.

"Meanwhile, I shall recommend that you are demoted to the rank of Corporal for your insensitivity which threatened to undermine the morale of the soldiers under your command."

"Sir…?"

"Dismissed, Corporal!"

★ ★ ★ ★ ★

The door of Wully Boyle's prison hut was barged open vigorously and Major Lambie entered, bristling with authority.

His demeanour was relaxed and the corners of his mouth appeared to be attempting to conceal a faint smile.

"Private Boyle," the Major boomed censoriously, "You are a fool and fools in war are dangerous, which is why I am releasing you now to inflict your foolishness upon the Imperial German Army.

"I have to tell you, however, in all candour, that your military record will henceforth be tainted with the charge of 'ungentlemanly conduct towards your superiors.'

"You will need to live with that for the rest of what I hope will be a very long life!"

Wully didn't quite know whether to laugh or cry, so he did neither but instead merely looked stunned – and foolish.

★ ★ ★ ★ ★

## Sandringham, December, 1917

"Now, Prime Minister," King George the Fifth said, looking up from his stamp collection at Lloyd George, "tell me, what is your considered estimation of the conduct of the war in 1917 and your predictions for its progress throughout 1918?"

"If Your Majesty will permit me, I think that this year has been dominated by the dissolute failure of the Nivelle offensive – which has led to large scale mutiny within the French army – the entry into the war of the United States on the side of the Allies, and the withdrawal from the war of Russia.

"On the battlefront we have had some success with the Canadians at Vimy Ridge, but have managed to sacrifice hundreds of thousands of souls at Passchendaele for a few miles of indefensible mud and have failed to make any meaningful progress anywhere along the line from Belgium to Switzerland.

"Nineteen eighteen will undoubtedly see a big push from Germany as they bring troops freed from the Eastern Front to bolster their forces in the west in an attempt to win the war before the Americans arrive in sufficient numbers to tip the balance in favour of the Allies."

"Hmm. Not an entirely positive or optimistic report, Prime Minister. How do you explain the impasse we appear to have been in throughout the year just ending?"

"I believe, Your Majesty, that General Haig must take a large proportion of responsibility for the losses and failures."

"General Haig? I was under the impression that he is

considered to be quite brilliant in his field?"

"Forgive me, Your Majesty, I would agree only in so far as to say that he is brilliant right up to the top of his army boots!"

"You are not a great supporter of General Haig, I take it?"

"I believe his ambitions are thwarted by delusions which can be truly myopic."

"Such as?"

"Such as exaggerating the achievements of small advances against French farms and hamlets, while ignoring the massive scale of casualties required to bring it about.

"Such as continued faith on the effectiveness of cavalry on a front bristling with heavy artillery, machine guns and barbed wire.

"Such as employing a bull-headed approach to battling against the strongest sections of the German lines without ever acknowledging that a clear breakthrough is neither achievable nor sustainable, resulting in the senseless slaughter of brave young men.

"Such as lumbering armies of men and countless heavy artillery pieces within sight and sound of the enemy for months on end before firing a single shot, thereby giving the Germans plenty of time to organise their defences against us.

"Such as…"

"That'll do Prime Minister, no need to go on and on."

"Forgive me, Your Majesty."

"His wife, Doris, was a lady-in-waiting to my mother, Queen Alexandria, you know."

"Yes, Your Majesty, I am aware that there are personal connections between yourself and the Haig family."

"Lovely woman, Doris. Very loyal to Bertie and to Mum."

"I would never seek to question General Haig's loyalty – especially to himself!"

"You sound, Prime Minister, as if you've a personal dislike of General Haig."

"I struggle to respect him either as a man or as a professional soldier, Your Majesty."

"Well, out with it man! What is your opinion of him?"

"In summary, sir, I think that he is slow of mind, an underhanded intriguer and backstabber, a man who blames others for his failures and a man who claims their successes. He is a planomaniac, quite incapable of flexibility or accepting counsel which might run contrary to his own ill-founded opinions. He has rejected evidence based on maps on the basis of, and I quote, 'Maps should conform to plans and not plans to maps'!"

"Why don't you remove him then if you have such a low opinion of his worth?"

"It would result in a running battle with the media and the establishment which could have a very injurious effect on the day to day prosecution of the war."

"Not if you could find an able replacement."

"That's the difficulty, Your Majesty. Anyone who might be of a more independent mind, with real vision and imagination, has already been buried under the welter of mediocrity with which Haig surrounds himself.

"Which is one of the reasons I have pushed for a system of joint command with the French under the authority of General Foch."

"Ah, yes, Haig hates surrendering our sovereignty to the French. I must say I'm a bit uncomfortable about that myself."

"If we want a totally coordinated response against Germany, Your Majesty, we must have a coherent vision, coherent planning and clear and unambiguous execution."

"You're beginning to sound like a bit of a planomaniac yourself, Prime Minister.

"At any rate, handing over to the French? Sometimes I think we're fighting on the wrong side!"

★ ★ ★ ★ ★

It all started off as a joke.

"What did you do in civilian life, Tommy?" asked the German

clerical officer in Gutersloh prison of war camp.

Tommy Finnegan had gone over the top on that first day of the Somme with high hopes.

He had rushed forward towards the German lines and headlong into the machine gunfire.

At first one or two comrades fell. Then a handful. Then, it seemed, by the dozen.

By the time he and Ian Martin had reached the uncut barbed wire there was no one left to fall. And, by then, even Ian had been wounded in the thigh and the shoulder by strafing bullets.

Time to surrender.

Surrendering on a battlefield when the blood was up could be a very dangerous task. Both sides had heard horror stories of how the other lot had treated prisoners or those trying to surrender.

Often soldiers were killed out of hand, dismissing their attempts to lay down arms. Often they were killed on their way to a field prison by escorts who just couldn't be bothered with the hassle of the journey.

Sometimes they were even murdered in the field prison itself by soldiers who had just returned from the front, enraged at having just left their friends dead on the battlefield.

Tommy and Ian had been lucky.

Ian had been taken to a military hospital in Lille where he was to receive treatment for his wounds before being sent to Coburg prisoner of war camp, while Tommy had been taken directly from his field prison to this camp in Westphalia.

"Eh?" Tommy stirred.

"What did you do in civilian life?" the German officer repeated.

"Oh me? Ah wis a Professor of English at Glasgow Patter University," Tommy replied flippantly.

"How do you spell 'Patter', Tommy?" asked the business-like German bureaucrat.

"As in 'pitter' but with an 'a' instead of an 'i'," Tommy replied helpfully.

"An 'a' instead of an 'i', the secretary confirmed ponderously to himself, while writing it down meticulously. "Good, I think you may be useful to us."

"So, Professor Tommy, my English good is not. Help you can please?"

Tommy looked down at Erich Bachmeister, a dapper tailor from Nuremburg who had aspirations of going to live and work in England after the war.

"Oh aye, sure," Tommy replied, rubbing his thumb and his middle finger together as he did so to indicate that some remuneration would be expected.

"Fifty pfennigs enough good is not?" asked Erich, "For one whore?"

"Fifty pfennigs is enough good for one hour," Tommy agreed. As an introduction to the matter on hand, the Prof. firstly explained that the King's English was only spoken by a very few toffs and not by the ordinary people in the streets, homes or workplaces of Britain.

"The King's English," Tommy further elaborated, was "a lot of keech," and that if he wanted to get ahead in ordinary everyday life in Britain then he would have to learn to speak and understand it's most widely spoken and valued version: Glaswegian!

Erich became an enthusiastic learner of the "people's English!"

At the first session, Tommy introduced him to the present tense conjugation of the verb 'to be'. By the end of the lesson, Erich had absorbed it in full, replete with Milltown accent:

*Ah um/ You ur/ He, She, It is/ We ur/ Youse ur/ They ur.*

Tommy also introduced Erich during this session to a limited vocabulary, providing him all the while with a Tommy's guide to a complete misunderstanding of their true meanings, viz:

*Bawheid – 'A hugely intelligent person'*
*Scunner – 'A person noted for his great wisdom'*
*Boggin – 'Scrupulously clean'*
*Sleekit – 'Honourable'*

By the end of the lesson both Professor Tommy and his avid student took a great deal of pleasure, albeit for widely different reasons, in Erich being able to construct and deliver sentences like:

*Ah um a bawheid.*

*Ludendorff is a scunner.*

*Germany is boggin.*

*The bawheid Kaiser is a boggin sleekit wee scunner.*

For the second session, Erich brought with him his tall friend Karl Zimmermann, a bricklayer from Hamburg who, it was planned, would accompany Erich on his trip to Britain.

It became immediately obvious that Erich had made Karl literally conversant with the content of the first session when, on entering, he extended his hand towards the Prof. and said in a broad Milltown accent, "Ah um sleekit. You ur a bawheid scunner."

Tommy took it as a compliment.

Tommy announced that he would distinguish between them on the basis of their height and that henceforth Erich would be known as 'Mocket' – 'Little', and Karl as 'Mingin' – 'Large'.

Mocket and Mingin' were delighted at this honour and felt as if they had just been inducted into a secret society.

Before continuing, the Prof. made each of them introduce themselves by their new titles.

"Ah um Mocket," announced Erich proudly.

"And Ah um Mingin'," a bloated Karl pronounced.

"Aye, so youse ur," confirmed the Prof. as he divested them of 50 pfennigs each.

★ ★ ★ ★ ★

The battle of Cambrai has gone down in history as the first battle in which the tank played a significant role.

For the British it proved to be a battle where they managed to enlist what had hitherto been a most elusive partner in this war – the element of surprise.

They were further aided by greater sophistication in the use of a creeping barrage.

For the rest of the battle it was like all the rest: Grand Old Duke of York tactics capturing useless land which couldn't be defended against determined counter attack; attacks which extended themselves far too far and far too quickly; narrow country roads churned into mud which became blocked every time a vehicle broke down on it; single-track railway inadequate for the job of moving people and munitions from A to B on a large scale.

And, above all, astronomical losses for little effective gain.

For the 36th (Ulster) Division, their role was clear: attack, overwhelm, secure.

If only it were that easy.

The combination of their continuous relentless attacks over many months, combined with the unforgiving rigours of General Winter, had reduced many of the men to dissipated empty shells, living on the last of their nerves masked behind vacant grins.

Alan tholed; Archie thrived.

Their brigade was now being moved up to attack a section of the Hindenburg line. After travelling from Lechelle and stopping in Havrincourt Wood for dinner they proceeded to their front-line trench between Beauchamp and Villers-Plouich.

The sight which greeted them there was grim. Corpses were lined along the banks of the trench, touching each other as if the end had visited them all simultaneously during some kind of trench version of Auld Lang Syne.

Their target loomed above them – the great Bois de Bourdon – Bourdon Wood.

Fighting was up close and personal. The Germans had the advantage of being able to throw their stick bombs further than the British could throw their Mills bombs.

They were also, as always, better entrenched, positioning their machine guns expertly to rain down on the attacking force.

To the military minded, it appeared as if it could not be approached, never mind taken, without due artillery preparation and tanks.

On this section of line there had been no artillery preparation; there were no tanks.

Still when the order came to go over the top, over the top was where you went.

The Hindenburg line – also known as Der Siegfriedstellung – was truly formidable in its positioning on the landscape, in its engineering, in its military hardware and in its human software.

Running towards it with a silly wee rifle was as futile as attacking a tank with a bunch of flowers.

The result was more or less the same.

At any rate, Archie and Alan were eventually to find themselves cowering in a shell hole, which they were forced to share with a dead German who was lying flat on his back, arms outstretched and eyes wide open towards the heavens. Next to him lay his fallen rifle with fixed bayonet.

"This is fuckin' hopeless Archie. We cannae move."

"We'll just huv tae wait here till it gets dark an' then we'll try an' sneak back."

"If Ah don't move till then Ah'm gonnae freeze tae death," Alan bemoaned bitterly.

"We cannae huv that then, Alan," said Archie as he drove the dead German's bayonet into Alan's stomach, twisting it up inside him all the while.

Alan's screams were drowned out by the sound of gunfire all around.

Alan fell back against the bank of mud, staring in shock at Archie who, with masterful nonchalance, was lighting up a cigarette he had found on the German corpse.

"Archie…Archie…" Alan groaned.

"Ye'll be deid in aboot five minutes, Alan. So deid ye wullnae be able tae tell onywan aboot oor escapades in Kirkton Wood."

Blood was pouring out of Alan's mouth. He was becoming catatonic.

"Ye wur killed by this German bastard here. Don't worry, Alan, Ah'll get him back fur ye."

At this Archie shot the corpse between the eyes and stuck his bayonet into the German's stomach, which had already been sliced open by shrapnel.

"See Alan, that's us even. The bastard got what he deserved."

"Archie…don't touch the wee lassie…please, Archie…"

"Ach, Alan, yer just a big softie. Ah don't make up the rules o' life, Alan. Nature's aw aboot survival. If Ah huv tae kill that wee lassie just tae survive then that's whit Ah'm gonnae huv tae dae. Ye can see that, Alan, can ye no'? Naw of course ye cannae see that 'cos ye're deid already."

Alan had indeed joined the ranks of the Glorious Dead, 1914-1918.

After finishing his smoke, Archie drove the German's bayonet into his own thigh. He then crawled back, slinking from one shell hole to another until he reached his lines. He took with him a story in which he was the hero.

"He just came from nowhere, sir, leaping into our trench, screaming in German and lunging at Alan. He bayoneted poor Alan before we could move."

"What did you do then, Private Ferguson," asked the adjutant.

"In his rush to get to Alan he had barged into me, knocking my gun out of my hand. Before I could recover it and take aim he had turned his attention to me and had stuck his bayonet into my left leg. As he raised his bayonet again to finish me off I managed to retrieve my rifle and get a shot off which went right through his brain. I was so angry at what he did to Alan I went into a frenzy and bayoneted him several times, even though he must have been dead by that point."

"Well done, Private Ferguson. You'll be mentioned in dispatches for this. I'll see that there's a medal in this for you."

"…and one for Alan too, sir?"

"We'll see son. I know he was your friend, but you're the real hero of this action."

"Just like Mrs Collins' cat," thought Archie.

The medical orderlies took Archie back to the field dressing station.

Two days later he got the news he had been waiting for: he was going back to a hospital in Blighty and from there to Milltown – and to Aggie McMillan.

# CHAPTER SEVENTEEN

## *True to the End*

For the past six months, Aggie and Breezy had been in each other's company constantly.

In the early days the sole preoccupation of their conversation had been that of Archie Ferguson and his murder of Harry Burchill.

As time passed, however, a tenderness grew between them and awakened feelings within their breasts which had been frozen for a long, long time. At length, they spoke to each other of matters deeply personal.

Aggie told Breezy about the untimely death of her husband, John, to tuberculosis eight years earlier.

Their lives, she told him, had been largely bereft of passion and romance. They were more like adjacent working farms – joined together for breeding and rearing, even if the product was relatively sparse given that it had delivered a mere two offspring set against the six or seven which was at that time commonplace.

She shared with Breezy the enormous guilt she felt at persuading Lachie to join up in the early days of the war. Like almost everyone else she had been unable to imagine that it would turn out the way it did.

Her heart broke in pieces when she received the telegram telling her of Lachie's death. She was quick to appreciate the distinction between the circumstances being described as having been 'Shot' as opposed to having been 'Killed in Action'.

Breezy had been there for her to pick up those pieces and she loved him for it.

As Aggie had suspected Breezy was a man with a past. He had qualified as a medical doctor from the University of Glasgow in

1891 and had practised in the Springburn area of the city for slightly over a decade.

In 1895, he married his childhood sweetheart, Jacqueline Clark, who fell pregnant two years later. Jacqueline and her son both died during childbirth. Breezy had shut the reality of his loss completely out of his mind for several years as if it had never happened.

Until, in 1902, that mind broke.

The first overwhelming indication of this came when he diagnosed pregnancy in a 37- year-old man with stomach cramps.

This was followed by him stopping complete strangers in the street to announce, "I'm a doctor you know."

Eventually, he was jailed for three months after shoplifting with menace when he threatened to split a grocer's infinitives, before trying to sprint away with a one hundredweight bag of coal.

He came out of prison to no job, no family, no friends, no support whatsoever.

In time his mind healed and he discovered that he could sing for his supper, which was all he wanted or needed out of life.

His wanderings brought him to Milltown, which offered him the privacy and seclusion of the countryside close to a village where he could earn a few coppers a day to purchase his meagre provisions – especially now that he had given up shoplifting!

Aggie was the only person who understood or appreciated him.

He also understood that underneath the dirty pinny and those layers of fat was a clever woman with a strong mind and a stout heart.

Their conversations grew more familiar, spiced with gentle, warm mockery.

He called her his Lady MacMuck, she called him Sir Claptrap.

"Where would Lady MacMuck care to dine today?" he might say.

"If it would please Sir Claptrap, a piece and jam presented in the scullery would greatly satisfy my culinary requirements."

"Would the aforesaid bread conserve be prepared by the good Lady's own fair hand, pray tell?"

"Alas kind Sir Claptrap, 'tis the cook's night off, so 'twill be incumbent upon me to do the Order of the Spreading myself."

"And will Lady MacMuck be partaking the pleasure of good wholesome butter with her delicacy?"

"Indeed sir, thickly lathered if you please. And where will Sir Claptrap be dining tonight, might one enquire?"

"At the club, as usual."

"Would that be the same club that's been lying beside the oak tree in Kirkton Wood these past few years?"

"The very one and a very fine cudgel it is too!"

"And what, in good taste, may be presented to Sir Claptrap for his evening victuals?"

"A fine turnip provided by Farmer White's field and washed down with sparkling water from the stream which traverses Kirkton Wood."

"'Tis little wonder there is a fine stench to thy breath, my dear Sir Claptrap."

"Only to be matched by the pungent whiff of aromatic odour emanating from under her Lady's arms."

And so they went on with such 'pleasantries' until, inevitably, the conversation returned once again to the demise of Harry Burchill and the ever present threat of Archie Ferguson.

They had heard the news that Alan Johnston had been killed and that Archie had been wounded.

Would, they thought, it had been the other way round.

It effectively put an end to any plan of Breezy reporting his sighting to the police. Without Alan's corroboration he would merely be setting himself up as a target and a suspect. And worse, Archie was almost ready to be released from the hospital and would be arriving back in Milltown within the month.

Breezy and Aggie decided to take Maureen and to move to Barrow-in-Furness where Aggie had a brother who worked for Vickers.

A week before they were due to leave, Archie Ferguson stepped off the train at Milltown High.

★ ★ ★ ★ ★

Jeanie Broon's world was in a mess.

There were no outward signs of her condition to the rest of the world, but there soon would be. The only person in whom she had confided had utterly rejected her. She was alone and friendless.

On her way to work she saw Alice Henderson. There was a tacit agreement between them that they would pass by each other coldly, without any form of acknowledgement, like two goldfish in a bowl.

Jeanie could imagine, however, Alice's reaction when she eventually heard of her predicament: joy unconfined.

Jeanie walked into the splendid grounds around Cowden House. She was still ultra-sensitive to the sight or sound or, indeed, to any sign of George's presence.

There was no one in the lanes and pathways. "Probably a bit cold outdoors today," Jeanie told herself.

She clocked in and set about making her way to the staff quarters where she would change into her uniform. As she passed George's ward her heart sank. There was no sign of him or of his things. The photograph of his mother which permanently adorned his bedside cabinet was gone. The bedding had all been removed.

A sickening feeling arose in her stomach that had nothing to do with her being pregnant.

In the midst of her confused state she heard the terse tones of the matron, Mrs Langshaw, call her name.

"Miss Brown, I should like a word with you in my office, now."

Mrs Langshaw always spoke formally to subordinate members of staff and patients alike, but it seemed to Jeanie that this command was infected with a special tone of disdain which bordered disgust.

With trepidation, Jeanie followed the diminutive high-heeled 'camp commandant' into her office.

Instinctively, Jeanie sat down on the wooden-backed chair, the door side of Mrs Langshaw's desk.

"I don't recall giving you permission to sit there, young lady," Mrs Langshaw spat.

"Would you prefer that I stood, mam?" Jeanie asked timidly.

"I insist that you stand, Miss Brown," Mrs Langshaw said haughtily from her raised seat behind the desk.

"Perhaps I could begin by showing you these letters, the first of which I trust you are already familiar."

Mrs Langshaw handed Jeanie the love letter she had left under George's pillow, plus another letter from George to Mrs Langshaw describing how Jeanie had behaved inappropriately towards him and informing her that Jeanie was pregnant with another man's child.

She started to cry.

Mrs Langshaw continued unmoved in the same vein.

"The first letter sent to Mr Armstrong, is that written in your hand?"

Jeanie was unable to answer through her tears.

"Unless you choose to contradict the blindingly obvious, I intend to take that as an answer in the affirmative.

"Now *Miss* Brown, is it true that you are pregnant?"

Mrs Langshaw paused for a split second before screaming at the top of her voice, "Well is it?!"

Jeanie just managed to whimper, "Yes Miss…I…"

"You filthy slut! To think we allowed a dirty whore to sully the presence of these brave young men! You will remove yourself from these premises immediately, Miss Brown, and never return. Any wages due to you will be sent through the post. Do you understand?"

Jeanie recovered enough composure to ask, "Where's George… I mean Mr Armstrong?"

"Nowhere you will ever find him. He left last night, but not before issuing specific instructions that no forwarding address be passed to yourself. Mr Armstrong is a man of quality and worth and a man of God who is far too good for the likes of you. Now get out of my sight and leave these premises immediately, Miss Brown."

Her walk back down the corridor and out the front door was a lonely one, with every back it seemed turned against her.

Now the word was out she was obliged to tell her parents and Micky's parents – and, of course, Micky.

Worse of all, she still loved George and felt that somehow she had let him down.

As she turned to take one last look through her tears at Cowden House, she noticed, for the first time, the Orr family motto which was inscribed in stone above the door.

It read, 'True till the End."

★ ★ ★ ★ ★

Todd MacDuff, born sometime in 1850 (the exact date was never established as it took his dad four months to register the birth, by which time the precise day was but a vague memory), was something of an institution in Milltown. He *was*, in fact, Mr Milltown.

He grew up at the height of the railway expansion across Britain and during his lifetime witnessed not one but two railway stations arrive in the village: Milltown Low, to be followed by Milltown High.

He had lived through many wars, though never one like this one.

As a young boy he remembered his dad reading extracts from the paper about the siege of Sebastopol during the Crimean War.

As a teenager his newspapers were filled with news about Vicksburg and Gettysburg.

Like everyone else at the time, he could remember exactly where he was and what he was doing when he heard that Abraham Lincoln had been assassinated and when Custer's 7th Cavalry had been annihilated by Geronimo.

He had felt anger and frustration at the fall of Khartoum to the Dervishes and joy at its recapture ten years later.

He read extracts from the newspapers to his grandchildren about the siege of Mafeking during the Boer War and felt embarrassed at Britain's pathetic showing against the farmer-soldier Boers of South Africa.

Locally, the Milltown Parish area, which had then incorporated Arthur Lea, had expanded rapidly, from 2,330 in 1791, the year before the mill opened, to over 8,000 and rising 40 years later.

A whole section of the town called the Mill Houses had since grown up in the village to accommodate the influx of workers from Greater Glasgow, Ireland and the North of England.

In 1801 there had been but one Catholic in the village. Due to Irish immigration, that had grown to a number warranting the building of a Roman Catholic church in the main street in 1862 when Todd was 12.

Every day of Todd's working life had been spent in the mill. In the 1880's Todd saw another three mills being added to the complex. One of these, number four mill, was redesigned as a five storey building when the owners discovered that a rival company had built a four storey mill.

As a gaffer he had mixed feelings when the women went on strike in 1910. However, he secretly agreed with them and was inwardly pleased when they took on the big bosses and won.

He had seen, too, the great changes being brought about by the 1878 Education Act in Scotland, which had made schooling compulsory for the vast majority of Scottish children.

He had rejoiced in the innovations which had enabled fresh water to be piped directly into homes in the late 1880s.

But by and by life trickled on much the same as it had always done these past hundred years.

Until now.

This war had changed everything. The industrial scale of the slaughter was truly appalling and beyond comprehension. It threatened the lifeblood of an entire generation. Of an entire continent. It had brutalised society The whole purpose of the community seemed to be to rear children to prepare them for human sacrifice in France or Flanders.

He had found himself looking at young boys and wishing that time could be suspended so that they might never reach fighting age.

The news early in 1918 had not been good for the Allies. The German spring offensive had crashed through their lines and had broken the deadlock of trench warfare. Times were reminiscent of the first few months of the war (how far away that seemed now) when Moltke's army was racing across open fields towards Paris.

In spite of himself, Todd permitted himself the hope that this might be the end. By now the only outcome really worth wishing for was an end to the killing and the dying, however it came about.

Pigs' Square, like the Bottom Shop, had been denuded of its main characters. Archie Currie, Ken Butterworth, Raymond Patterson, Eddie Miller, Johnny Byrne, Gregor Nisbet and even Sleekit Tam were all now in uniform, after conscription age for married men was raised to 41 in May 1916. Only Eddie showed an initial reluctance, but this had been put to one side when the Parish informed him that if he didn't join up he wouldn't be considered for further Poor Law allowance.

Of the usual suspects only Bertie Boyle remained, and that only because he failed the medical due to bronchial problems.

It was Bertie now who had arrived to join Todd at the Square.

"Mornin' big man."

"Mornin', Bertie. Bitter the day, is it no'?"

"Aye, bring tears tae yer eyes so it wid."

"Whit's the news the day frae the front?"

"The Germans huv us oan the run. The 5th Division goat wiped oot. They've broken right through oor lines."

"Is this the end, dae ye think?"

"Depends. In 1914, the rush fur the Germans wis tae get the job finished afore the Russians entered the theatre of war. Noo the rush is tae dae the business afore the Yanks turn up in strength."

"They faltered first time roon. Maybe they'll falter again," said Todd.

"And then this war'll go on and on an' fuckin'on. Mair lives lost."

"It cannae go on much longer, Bertie, we're runnin'oot o' men. Ah've heard that the government is plannin' tae stert callin' up essential male workers o' a certain age."

"We'll know its gey close tae the end when they start callin' you up, Todd."

"How's Wully?"

"Aye he's fine, Ah hope. He never writes, so every day withoot a telegram's a bonus. Just keep prayin' fur him. That's aw ye can dae."

"How's the wife?"

"Same as usual. A nervous wreck wi' aw that's goin' on. Mind you she wis ecstatic when Ah failed the medical fur the front."

"How did you feel aboot that yersel, Bertie?"

"Guilty Ah suppose, especially wi' haein' a boy riskin' his life fightin' fur his country.

"But tae tell ye the truth, Todd, Ah felt relieved so Ah did."

"Quite right, Bertie. That's only natural. Ye've nothin' tae feel ashamed aboot. It's no' as if ye wurnae prepared tae go. Ye wid huv gone if ye'd been sent. They didnae wahnt ye, so that's aw there is tae it."

"Onywey, Todd, tae change the subject, can you tell me this fur by – who's the oldest livin' Milltown man?"

"Well it's no' me if that's whit yer thinkin'!"

"Aye, Ah know you're still a young thing, Todd. Wid it be Andrew Wyper?"

"Andrew is in his seventies right enough, but Chris McNaught is a good five years older at least."

"Whit age is Chris?"

"Oh Chris must be aboot seventy-seven or seventy-eight."

"Whit aboot Shuggie Logue?"

"Aye, of course, Shuggie must be at least eighty."

"Imagine that! Born in the Eighteen Thirties. Shuggie's dad might huv fought Napoleon. So Shuggie's the oldest then?"

"Wait a minute! Whit aboot Sammy McGinley? Is he still alive?"

"Aye, Ah forgot aboot him. Mind you ye never see him oot these days."

"Probably because the man must be ninety-three or ninety-four if he's a day. He wis a good few years older than ma faither who wid be eight-eight if he wis still alive."

"Ninety-four! Yer kiddin' me on! That's almost Biblical. That means he must huv been born roon aboot 1824, before Victoria wis on the throne.

That officially makes him ancient."

"Aye, Sammy must be the oldest livin' Milltown man. There's old Fraser McCarthur. Let's ask him."

"Fraser!" Bertie shouted across the street, "come here a meenit wull ye?"

It took Fraser a lot more than a minute just to shuffle his feet across the street to the Square.

"Fraser, Bertie and I wur just wonderin' who the oldest livin' Milltown man might be and the best name we can come up wi' is Sammy McGinley, who we think is ninety-four. Can you think o' anywan who might be older than that?"

"Naw, Ah cannae, but Ah can tell youse that Sammy McGinley isnae the oldest livin' Milltown man."

"Whit dae ye mean?" asked a perplexed Bertie Boyle. "If you cannae think o' anywan that's older than ninety-four and Sammy McGinley is ninety-four, then surely Sammy must be the oldest livin' Milltown man, or am Ah just getting dited?"

"Ye're forgettin, ur ye no lads, that Sammy didnae come tae Miltown till he wis three. Sammy wis born in Govan."

"Aye, right enough!" they both chimed in unison.

"Right, ya cowardly bastard! Up ye get!"

Five guards burst into Micky's cell to drag him out of his bed. It was half past three in the morning and the temperature was minus six.

He was scraped along the floor, being punched, kicked and verbally abused as he went.

After being dumped in a holding area, he was unceremoniously made to strip naked. Awaiting him there were buckets filled with freezing cold water which were flung over him by mocking guards.

The shock nearly stopped his heart.

He fell onto the stone floor and, pleading, slivered across to one of the guards only to be met with a tackety boot full force in his face.

The comments were as vicious as the blows. The size of his penis, his "puny" muscles. He was a "scumbag", a "traitor", a "poof", a "mammy's boy" and a "fenian bastard".

Twenty minutes later he was dragged back and deposited on the floor of his cell with threats to expect more of the same at any time of the day or night.

His cell mates 'slept' through it grimly, heads turned fixedly towards the wall.

Later that day, Micky demanded a meeting with the governor of the prison. This was refused.

Micky then put in writing his demand to voice his complaints directly to the governor, failing which he would go on hunger strike.

His answer came in the form of his letter ripped into pieces and mixed in with his food.

His hunger strike began.

Day after day, Micky was ordered to the canteen. Day after day, food was put on his plate and placed in front of him. Day after day, Micky refused to touch it.

After two weeks, Micky was taken from his cell to a basement somewhere in the building.

In the room was what seemed to Micky like a dentist's chair, four guards, two doctors, a man that Micky assumed was the governor and a boiled egg.

"Now, McGoldrick," the senior man began, "you have a choice. Either you come off this silly hunger strike now by eating that egg or we will have no choice but to force-feed you – and, believe me, that will not be a pleasant experience."

"Are you the governor?" Micky asked.

"Are you questioning me?" the senior guard replied indignantly.

"McIntosh," he said quietly to a guard behind him.

At that the guard stepped forward and bent Micky over with a crushing punch to the solar plexus.

"Now, let's start again shall we?" the senior guard continued. "Never mind who I am. All you need to know is that I am your superior in every way, you piece of toley shit, and you will do as I command. So, what's it to be, the egg or the chair?"

Micky, still winded and in incredible pain, managed to blurt out that he would remain on hunger strike until his complaints had been heard and dealt with.

"I see. Well if you think that we're going to allow you to become a martyr for your cowardly cause while the real heroes are dying in France for your country you've another think coming. Guards!"

Micky was pinned into a chair which was then tilted backwards. One of the doctors produced a two foot nasal tube with a funnel at one end and a glass junction in the middle to allow a view of the food as it passed along. The doctor inserted the tube up Micky's left nostril and started to push it down about 20 inches.

The pain was intense. Micky's eardrums felt as if they were exploding and there were bursting surges of excruciating pressure in his throat and in his chest.

The second doctor poured a pint of milk and egg down the funnel end. Micky started to scream. A hand came across his mouth, blocking the passage of air. He felt he could no longer breathe and he started to panic. His whole body was being held rigid. He had no control of his movements, voluntary or otherwise.

The physical and mental terror of it all was horrific. He didn't know how much more he could take.

At length, all was reversed and Micky was returned to his cell.

"They can make it a lot worse fur ye," said a kindly guard. "Gie it up son, ye're no' gaunnae win."

For the first time, Micky contemplated suicide. What had he to live for? Physically, mentally and emotionally he was deteriorating badly. He didn't know if he had the resources to stand up to the system anymore. As the guard said, he wasn't going to win.

Unless he cheated them through his own death.

The door opened and a guard entered. "Whose been a dirty bastard, then?" he mocked as he flung a letter in Micky's face.

Two minutes later Micky knew that he had something to live for. He knew that he was now so strong that the system could never defeat him.

Jeanie, pregnant with his child, was coming to see him.

★ ★ ★ ★ ★

Six months into the project and Mocket and Mingin' had come on by leaps and bounds.

By the end of that second session, they were familiar with and could use the simple past tense of the verb 'to be', viz: *Ah wis/ you wur/ He, She, It wis/ We wur/ Youse wur/They wur.*

This was followed by the negative versions of the present and simple tenses of the same verb, viz: *Ah umnae – Ah wisnae/ You urnae –You wurnae/ He, She, It isnae – He, She, It wisnae/ We urnae – We wurnae/ Youse urnae – Youse wurnae/ They urnae –They wurnae.*

Mocket and Mingin' ate it all up.

By the tenth session, they were using auxiliary verbs like *Gonnae (Would you)/ Gonnae no (Please refrain from)/ Huftae (It is imperative)/*

*Koodnae (Unable to)/ Shoodnae (Oughnt to)/ Didnae (Didn't – usually a lie!)*

And by the fifteenth session, they were using demonstrative adjectives and pronouns like *Zis (This)/Rat (that)/Zat (Is that)* as well as the omnipresent possessive pronouns *Ma and Oor.*

Their vocabulary, meanwhile, had exploded exponentially, albeit with wholly different meanings attached to them from what one might have considered to be Standard Glaswegian.

The Prof. had also introduced them to Glaswegian colloquial phrases such as:

*"Yer erse is oot the windae" /"Zatno diabolic!" / "Yer heid's full o' mince"/ "No a snawbaw's chance in hell",* replete with wholly positive and wholly corrupt meanings

They were also introduced to inconsequential sentence endings like, *"by the way"* and *"there ye are",* as well as the ubiquitous glottal stop, *"but".*

Finally, they were told that what we would regard as expletives were linguistic markers of courtesy and respect in deference to your superiors.

Not, mind you, that the Prof. prepared his lessons in any way. "We'll just see where fillin' their heids full o' rubbish takes us the night," was his teaching and learning strategy.

And so it came to pass that the social committee for the British prisoners in Gutersloh was arranging a concert to raise spirits and boost morale. The Prof. came up with the idea of writing a short script for Mocket and Mingin to perform on stage "to demonstrate their new found language skills and to provide a touch of camaraderie across the great divide of the war."

Aye, right!

Mocket and Mingin', however, were delighted at the prospect and practised their lines to perfection.

The concert also caught the attention and interest of the camp commandant, who happened to be entertaining Colonel Fassbinder, Adjutant to none other than General Hindenburg himself.

Unfortunately, Colonel Fassbinder had been a Maritime Engineer before the war and had spent many years working in John Brown's shipyards on the Upper Clyde. Consequently, he was fluent in Glaswegian.

Mocket: "Hi everywan. He's Mingin' so he is but."

Mingin: "And he's Mocket by the way."

M & M: "An thegither we're Mocket and Mingin'."

Mi: "So Mocket, whit dae ye think o' oor Kaiser?"

Mo: "His heid's full o' mince, the wee fucking scunner. Dae ye think he'll win this war fur us, Mingin'?"

Mi: "Dae Ah look like a dafty? His erse is oot the windae. No' a snawbaw's chance in hell."

Mo: "Ah agree. The Kaiser's a fucking bawheid by the way but…"

The howls of laughter coming from the audience left Mocket and Mingin' disconcerted, especially when they saw Colonel Fassbinder jump onto the stage with a face like Big Bertha in full ballistic action and they realised that in some way they had offended the Kaiser, the sacred memory of Frederick the Great and Ludwig van Beethoven all in one go.

'Ra gemme' ( The current project), as they say in Glasgow, 'Wis a bogie' ( Had taken a terminal turn for the worse.)

Later that night, Mocket and Mingin' were on their way to spearhead an attack on the Western Front while the Prof. was sentenced to six weeks solitary confinement for defrauding soldiers of the Reich and for ridiculing the Fatherland.

Zatno diabolic?

\* \* \* \* \*

Maureen was at school. Aggie was off her perch. It was Wednesday afternoon, time for Aggie's weekly shopping excursion.

The street was quiet. Hardly a mouse stirred. Unless you count Archie Ferguson emerging from the grass bank at the back of the houses on his way to break in to Aggie's home.

Not that he had to be a professional house breaker to do so given that, as usual, Aggie had left her back door wide open. Archie walked straight in.

Aggie's house was nothing if not absolutely filthy. Dirty dishes, pots and pans littered not just the scullery but also the living room, along with half-eaten meals and discarded pieces.

The bedrooms were a study in mess. Not a single square inch remained uncluttered.

Aggie's room alone played host to a bike, a sledge and a toboggan – or 'taboogie' as it was called in Milltown – as well as bags of client's laundry awaiting her attention.

Towels demonstrating Aggie's menstruation adorned her bed.

This was a veritable tip of the lowest order.

Not that Archie was the slightest bit interested in the appearance or hygienic standards of Aggie's domain.

What he *was* interested in came easily to hand: a very sharp and sturdy carving knife and a dress.

Just before sneaking out the back with his swag, he heard Aggie approach the front door. For a moment it crossed his mind that he should wait for her to come in and slay her on the spot. He hesitated, however, on the grounds that what he had in mind was altogether neater. So neat that it was almost elegant.

Then again, this way he gets to kill her himself. Right here... right now...

★ ★ ★ ★ ★

The pupils in Miss Lochery's class sat in rows. Those sitting at the front closest to the teacher were the ones from the 'better' homes. The ones whose fathers had jobs or, even better still, owned their own business.

Foremost of them all was Martin McLeod, whose father owned the Traveller's Rest. He sat right at the front, 'closer my God to thee', and was the one entrusted with the teacher's special tasks and messages: the 'teacher's pet'.

At the back, the very back, sat Bridget Martin. Bridget was an unfortunate soul. Her father, Ian, was 'missing, presumed dead', at the Somme. Her mother, Frances, struggled to make ends meet. Her entitlement to her husband's military pay and separation allowance had been stopped the second Ian had been presumed dead, forcing her and her family to endure the harsh indignities of poverty.

Bridget was sitting quietly doing her work. Not that the work was particularly stimulating or challenging or even educational. Copying from a book was a means by which Miss Lochery ensured that her class was quiet and did not disturb her unduly.

As the teacher paraded her authority up and down the rows of desks, Bridget put her hand up.

"Martin?" Miss Lochery acknowledged.

"Yes, Miss?" Martin McLeod responded in anticipation.

"No, not you Martin. I meant Martin up the back."

"Gonnae geeza ruler?"

"I beg your pardon!"

"Gonnae geeza ruler?" Bridget repeated innocently.

"How dare you bring your gutter language into my classroom, Martin."

Even Miss Lochery was bored by the class routines that morning. She now had a victim to hold to scorn. An opportunity, once again, to reinforce her superiority over the working-class ignorance of the village. It was time to perform.

"I gather, young lady – if I may use that term loosely, very loosely – that you wish to borrow a ruler. Am I correct in that assumption?"

Bridget stared hard ahead, uncomprehending.

"You want a ruler, do you not?"

"Aye, Miss."

"I miss? Who do you miss, Martin?" the ungrammatical Miss Lochery asked obtusely.

"Nothing, Miss."

"I see. You didn't mean 'I miss' at all, did you, Martin, as in 'I miss my father'. You meant 'Yes, Miss,' did you not?"

"Aye, Miss."

"'Yes, Miss…?' 'I miss…?' Which is it?"

"Miss, 'Yes Miss', Miss."

"Right, let's see if we can pull you up from the dregs from which you come and teach you how to make a polite request of your teacher using the King's English – even if it is hardly spoken elsewhere in Milltown, and certainly not in the Martin household obviously.

"Repeat after me, Martin: Please, Miss…"

"Please, Miss…"

"…may I…"

"…may I…"

"Please, Miss, may I…"

"Please, Miss, may I…"

"…borrow…"

"…borrow…"

"…a ruler…"

"…a ruler…"

"…borrow a ruler…"

"…borrow a ruler…"

"Please Miss, may I borrow a ruler?"

"Please Miss, may I borrow a ruler?"

"Again, Martin."

"Please Miss, may I borrow a ruler?"

"Right, Martin, let's start again from the beginning, shall we? Put your hand up and ask me your question now in proper English."

"Please, Miss, may I borrow a ruler?"

"Of course you may…" Miss Lochery crowed while delivering the ruler to Bridget's desk in an arc de triomphe over her head.

Miss Lochery felt good, very good, about herself. She had

reinforced the system, the class system, at the very heart of the British Empire, and she was heartened by her position in it.

She started to walk on in magisterial fashion, Lord and Lady over all she surveyed, until frozen to the spot by the wee gravely voice behind her which rasped, "Gonnae geeza rubber an aw?"

★ ★ ★ ★ ★

As soon as Aggie stepped over the threshold she knew. She sensed a presence. Someone was or had been here. She tried to summon up as much courage as she could to try and make her voice sound calm and in control.

"Who's there?" she shouted.

Nothing.

She paused and listened intently for the slightest rustle or movement.

Again, nothing.

She slipped out of the front door and tiptoed round the back to the cellar where she kept a small hatchet used to split wood and coal.

It was then she saw them.

On the wet bank leading down towards the back of her house were the four inverted v's with the breach on the left side of the pattern on the third row down. Footprints she had seen and drawn all those years ago.

It was Archie's. Archie had been here. Archie *is* here!

Somewhere in there, Archie was waiting to kill her. Aggie's mind was working overtime. Her blood was up. This man had tried to burn her and her daughter to death. He was now in her house, threatening her and her family again. This was her turn. Her chance. Right here…right now…

She took the hatchet, entered by the back door and moved stealthily through the house, careful not to disturb any of the mess lest it alerted Archie.

She stopped again. She listened again. This time she was certain that she heard movement.

There it was again. It was coming from the hall. It was now in the living room. It was heading straight for the scullery where Aggie stood petrified.

Aggie visualised Archie and roughly imagined where his head would be when he appeared round the door.

She knew that she would only get one chance. She had to strike with all her power, giving him not a second to respond to the blow.

The door creaked open. Aggie's axe was poised. As the door widened and the footsteps entered the scullery Aggie brought the axe down with a terrible force and a screech of "Bastard!" stopping a fraction of an inch from Maureen's face.

Ten minutes later and Aggie, Maureen and bag were travelling across Milltown to her sister's for refuge.

Tomorrow she would alert Breezy to the fact that Archie was here.

★ ★ ★ ★ ★

Not that she ever did, for that night Breezy woke up dead.

Archie was upon him as he slept. It was like jumping into a trench and onto an unsuspecting German sentry.

Before Breezy could open his eyes, Archie had taken Aggie McMillan's knife and slit his throat, digging deeply in towards his spine and through and across in jagged movements to ensure that his wind pipe was severed.

Breezy stared into Archie's eyes, unable to scream.

Archie stood up to view his victim as if Breezy was a spectator sport. He liked this bit. It gave him time to appreciate his work and to watch it come to fruition. It also gave him the opportunity to apply that last wee bit of humiliation and mental cruelty.

"Ah know ye saw me kill Harry Burchill, Breezy, and when Ah heard that ye wur teamin' up wi' thon bitch, Aggie McMillan, Ah knew Ah jist hud tae kill you as well. Ye can see that can ye no? Aw, there ye go again! Ye cannae see that either 'cos you're deid as well. That wis quick Breezy, Ah'll gie ye that."

Archie looked down at Breezy's corpse, drained of all colour. He bent down and picked up Aggie's dress which he smeared with Breezy's blood'

He then walked over to the oak tree and picked up the shovel he had brought for the purpose of filling in Breezy's grave.

Soon it was all over.

"Right," a satisfied Archie grunted, "now time to inform the polis o' this dastardly deed."

He took a pre-written letter from his pocket and read it smugly to himself.

*Aggie McMillan confessed to me that she killt the tramp known as Breezy Breeks by cutting his throat with a sharp kitchen knife as he slept in his hole in the ground in Kirkton Wood.*

*She tellt me she did it becoz he had killt Harry Burchill in that same wood years ago becoz Harry was trying to force Breezy to have sex with him. She said she couldn't stand the thought of him getting away with it as he had already managed to convince everyone that Harry committed suicide.*

*I don't want to give you my name becoz I'm scared but I just thought you should know.*

On his way to drop the letter through the letter box at the police station, Archie once again broke in to Aggie's empty house and returned the stolen items to their rightful owner.

The next day Breezy's body was dug up and Aggie McMillan found herself incarcerated in Milltown jail.

# CHAPTER EIGHTEEN

## *Wet Kippers and the Honey Trap*

Jeanie sat at the table in the cold, empty room waiting for Micky to appear. She was nervous. The whole atmosphere of the prison was ugly and intimidating. It felt like a rabid dog about to be let off its leash.

Her letter had told Micky that she was pregnant with his child and suggested that they meet up to talk.

But now she was here she wasn't sure what she should say. What would he expect from her? He might, of course, refuse to accept that the baby was his and reject her completely, just as George had done.

What was she hoping for? A father for her baby? Probably. The respectability and security of a family framed in an arranged marriage? Possibly. Someone to love and to care for her? Hardly.

She couldn't offer love to Micky. She would never be able to offer that. But Micky was her best option. Micky was her only option.

In time she might forget George, although the sign above the door at Cowden House seemed to her to be an omen. She would always be true to George till the end.

The door opened and Micky came in handcuffed to a grim-faced guard.

He sat down opposite Jeanie at the table, still attached to his enforcer. Jeanie was shocked by his appearance. Three months of beatings, force-feeding, abuse and ridicule had reduced him to a walking shadow. His eyes, though, retained something of the old sparkle – a combination of defiance to his captors and excited anticipation at seeing Jeanie again.

"Hello, Jeanie. It's great to see you again."

"Micky, you look terrible…"

"Well this isn't exactly a holiday camp. How are you?"

"Is that 'you' singular or 'you' plural?"

"How are both of you?"

"Ah'm fine, Micky. Ah'm beginnin' tae feel oor child move inside me. It's an amazing experience so it is."

"When is he expected?"

"How do you know it's a boy?"

"Ah dreamt of him last night. It's a boy."

"Don't be daft, Micky, you cannae tell onythin' frae a dream. Let's just wait an' see when it drops by sometime next November."

"Ah'll love the wean anyway, be she a boy or be he a girl."

Jeanie laughed involuntarily, but instantly stifled it under the fiercely disapproving gaze of the guard.

"Jeanie, can Ah get tae the point, because Ah don't huv much time and Ah know that this gorilla will want tae take me away fur ma daily beatings at any minute…"

"The prisoner will refrain from talking about any aspect of prison life in accordance with his agreement," warned the guard.

Jeanie was startled by the degree of violence in the guard's tone.

"Well, Ah know that this is hardly the most romantic setting – an' Ah cannae even get doon oan ma knees tae dae this – but will you marry me Jeanie and make sure that oor child grows up surrounded by the love o' its mum and dad?"

Jeanie looked down to the floor, twisted her fingers together nervously round each other and mumbled something into her chest.

"What was that, Jeanie?" asked Micky.

Jeanie looked up at him, tears streaming down her cheeks and said, "Yes".

Micky stretched his fingers out across the table searching for Jeanie's hand.

"The visitor will not touch the prisoner," the guard growled.

"See, Jeanie, these guys huv nae sense o' occasion…"

"This meeting is now over!" the guard announced. "It is time to return the prisoner to his cell."

"He knows ma name is Micky, Jeanie, just like oor son's will be. He just cannae bring himsel' tae use it. He's much more comfortable shoutin' abuse at me in between punches…"

The guard dragged Micky violently from his seat and hauled him towards the door

Micky turned to Jeanie and shouted, "Write to me, Jeanie. Take good care o' Micky."

Jeanie looked on, tears streaming down her face. Not out of joy at Micky's proposal, nor even out of pity for Micky and the way he was being treated, but because she already knew what the baby's name would be if it was a boy – and it wouldn't be Micky.

★ ★ ★ ★ ★

When Sergeant Shaw and his men came for her she was sleeping on her sister Sally's floor, even though it was eleven-thirty in the morning and Maureen had slept in for school.

Two policemen marched her down the street to the local police station where she would answer questions in relation to 'something that had happened', or what we today would call 'an incident'.

Maureen was crying, Sally was screaming, Jack was picking his nose.

After an hour spent in some sort of waiting room, Sergeant Shaw and Constable Gebbie came in to interview her.

"Now, we can dispense with the need to ask you your name or where you live or any of that stuff, because we already know you and you know us. Just for the records, though, can you tell us your date of birth?"

"Ah'm led to believe it was the fifteenth of October, Eighteen Seventy-Nine."

"So that makes you thirty-eight, yes?"

"Yes, something like that."

"When was the last time you met Breezy Breeks?"

"You mean Doctor Mark Manson?"

"Do I?"

"Yes, he was given the name Breezy Breeks as a nickname by the children around here, but Mark Manson is his real name and he is a practising doctor."

"Very clever… You see, Constable Gebbie, I told you she wouldn't be easy to break!"

"Ah'm tellin' ye, it is his name an' he is a practisin' doctor!" Aggie reiterated indignantly.

"There's just one wee detail that doesn't exactly quite match up with that description, even if we accept your fantastic claim that Breezy was a doctor of medical science."

"What's that then?"

"You said 'is'."

"Well obviously he isnae a practisin' doctor noo, but he used tae be."

"Yes, but you said his name 'is' Mark Manson.

"Aye, *is*. His name *is* Mark Manson."

"A funny way to describe a dead man is it no'?"

"Deid…? Who's deid…?!"

"Awright, Aggie, we'll play it your way…for now.

"Now tell me, Aggie, when was the last time you saw this Doctor Mark Manson, dead or alive?"

"Yesterday mornin'. Who's deid? Tell me, who's deid?" Aggie started screaming.

"Just answer our questions, Aggie. We're not here to answer yours.

"You knew each other well?"

"Aye, very well, but…"

"Were you courtin'?"

"Ah suppose ye could say that. Sergeant, please tell me, whit's aw this aboot?"

"I'm surprised you don't know, considering you were almost certainly the last person to see Doctor Manson. Or, rather, I should say, the last person to see Doctor Manson alive."

Aggie stopped and stared. The full impact of what he was saying had now hit her like a wet kipper slapped round her ears. Her face became impassive, showing no emotion, save for a faint dribble of tears trickling down her cheeks. She was like a miraculous statue of the weeping Virgin.

The Sergeant handed her a handkerchief.

"No use crying now, Aggie. What's done's done. We all have to take responsibility for our actions. Now, to continue, how was Doctor Manson when you left him yesterday morning?"

"Fine." Her voice was cracking. The terseness of her language betrayed the shock she was now in.

"Fine? Are you sure?"

"Fine."

"Was he alive?"

"Yes."

"Aggie, we'll need to stop pussy-footing around with this. We received a letter from an anonymous source last night telling us that Breezy Breeks had been murdered by you down in Kirkton Wood. It told us precisely where we would find the body.

When we looked we found him there as described, dead as described with his throat cut as described."

"Ah didnae dae it…Poor, poor Breezy…" Aggie started to wail.

"Ah, but it gets better, Aggie, because when we searched your house looking for you, guess what we found? The blood-crusted knife used to kill Breezy and your clothes stained with his blood.

"And then when we went to Maureen's school to see if she could tell us where you were, we find that you had decided to take Maureen out of school altogether within the next couple of days with the intention of taking her away to England.

"Then we find you and Maureen hiding out in your sister's

house with a bag packed and ready for the off. Suspicious or just coincidence? What do you think?"

"Ah didnae dae it…"

"Come on, Aggie… Look we've got the letter, we've got the knife, we've got your clothes, we've got the head teacher's statement, we've got the dead body, we've got your packed bag and we've got you. If you just admit your guilt, say that you were defending yourself, tell the judge that you're sorry and you'll never kill Breezy again, then he might take pity on you and just give you time in prison. A long time admittedly, but at least he'll let you live. If you keep up this "Ah didnae dae it" in the face of all this evidence he'll hang you for sure."

"Ah didnae dae it…Ah didnae dae it…"

"OK Aggie, you didnae dae it, but maybe you've forgotten a minor detail like slitting Breezy's throat in his sleep, so I'm going to charge you with his murder in any case and we'll take it from there.

"Ah didnae dae it…Ah didnae dae it…Ah'm tellin' youse Ah didnae…"

★ ★ ★ ★ ★

Mrs Ferguson opened the door to two men in army uniform. Had it been a month before she would have panicked, fearing the worse. Since Archie, however, was at that very moment in his own bed in the room behind her, her countenance was altogether more relaxed and welcoming.

"Good morning, gentlemen. What can I do for you?"

"Excuse us, Mam, but is this the house of Private Archie Ferguson of the First Irish Rifles?"

"It certainly is, I'm very proud to say."

"So you should be, mam, so you should be. Would it be possible for us to have a word with him on a matter which would be to his advantage?"

"Certainly, gentlemen. If you would just like to come in I'll get him for you,"

"Thank you, mam."

"Archie," Mrs Ferguson screamed, "there's two soldiers here wanting to speak to you about a matter which would be to your advantage."

Archie came out of his bedroom encrusted in sleep, wearing nothing but his pyjama trousers.

"Ah, Private Ferguson, it's a great pleasure to actually meet you face to face. This is Corporal Broadfoot and I am Captain Arkwright of the Military Police."

Archie startled.

"Relax, Private," the Captain reassured him. "For once our visit is to impart good news. It is our great pleasure to inform you that you have been awarded the Bar to Distinguished Conduct Medal by the military authorities for bravery shown in the face of the enemy at Bourdon Wood."

"Oh, Archie, this is wonderful!" cried an overjoyed Mrs Ferguson.

"Aye, that's where ma mate goat killed."

"I'm sorry to hear that, Private," the Captain said, "but we're sure that he would have been very proud of your actions to avenge him."

"Well, Ah managed tae kill the German that killed him while he wis tryin' tae kill me."

"Wonderful," added Corporal Broadfoot, "it's a privilege to be standing in the same company as a brave hero such as yourself, Private Ferguson. "

"Anyway," continued the Captain, "the top brass want to present you with your medal back in France along with other war heroes. You are to be decorated by none other than our Commander-in-Chief, General Haig himself, at his headquarters in Montreuil in Northern France.

"You will be relieved to hear, Mrs Ferguson, that Montreuil is many miles behind the front, well out of harm's way."

"Especially now that Jerry's sprinting back towards Berlin as fast as his boots will carry him," Captain Arkwright chirped.

"That's fantastic news, Archie. I'm so proud of you."

"Thank you, Major," Archie said politely. "When is the presentation, sir?"

"A week from now," said Corporal Broadfoot. "You will be provided with a brand new spick and span uniform when you arrive back in France next Tuesday. The ceremony will take place on the Thursday following. You are required to present yourself at Maryhill Barracks by three o'clock next Saturday afternoon for onward transportation."

"Gentlemen, you have really made my day. Will you stay for a cup of tea?"

"We would love to, mam," apologised the Captain, "but we are due back at the barracks ourselves within the hour. However – Private Ferguson, Mrs Ferguson – it has been a pleasure to have met you both. You are a credit to the British army and your country, Private Ferguson. We salute you."

At this, both soldiers clicked their heels together and saluted Archie.

"Ah wis just daein' ma duty, sir."

"And doing it with distinction," Corporal Broadfoot added.

The two soldiers left with Mrs Ferguson's thanks ringing in their ears.

She closed the door behind her and returned to her son.

"Ah know ye're heartbroken at losin' yer wee pal, Archie," said his mother as she enfolded him in her arms. "He wis a great wee fella an' Ah'll miss him tae, so Ah wull. So many Milltown men huv been killed or maimed, but your heroic stand gies us aw a sense that we're staunin' up tae the Hun.

I'm so, so, so prood o' ye son."

"Ach Ma, it wis nothin'. Ah only did whit anywan wid huv done."

"Ah don't know aboot that, Archie. Ah only know that you did dae it an' you're ma hero.

"This is the proodest moment o' ma life, Archie. A moment Ah'll never forget."

Archie didn't so much as flinch.

★ ★ ★ ★ ★

"Chrissy."

"Aye, Sadie."

"See me?"

"Aye, Sadie."

"See God?"

"Aye, Sadie."

"Ah cannae."

"Cannae see God?"

"Naw, Chrissy, Ah cannae feel God either. Whit if there's nae God?"

"Nae God, Sadie? How wid we aw be here if there wis nae God? Somebody must have made it aw possible."

"Whit fur?"

"Whit fur? How does there huv tae be a fur?"

"Well it's gaun tae an awfy lot o' trouble tae make aw o' us an' aw they trees an' aw they burds an' aw they fishes in the sea if there isnae a fur!"

"Well He went tae aw o' thon trouble because if He didnae He widnae be God wid He? Ah mean, He'd jist be the ruler o' His ain disposition."

"So he went tae aw that trouble just so that He could be worshipped by His ain creations?"

"Aye, we're supposed tae love Him in this world so that we can be wi' Him in the next."

"And if we don't?"

"That's whit Hell's fur."

"So Hell's goat a fur as well?"

"Aye. It's tae keep aw they evil bastards an' aw they non-believers who refuse tae worship God."

308

"Who made evil onyway?"

"That'd be the devil, Ah suppose. Efter aw, it could hardly be God."

"An' who made the devil?"

"Naebody. He just ae wis."

"So if God just ae wis an' the devil just ae wis can we no' hae been just ae wis as weel?"

"Naw, Sadie, we cannae make oorsels."

"Well, Chrissy, Ah'm pretty sure ma mammy and daddy made me an' Ah've goat a fair idea how they went aboot it."

"Aye, but who made sex in the first place?"

"God?"

"Maybe, but maybe no'."

"Who else could huv made it. Is there a God o' sex?"

"Maybe the devil."

"The devil, Chrissy?"

"Aye, Sadie, think aboot it. How many folks ur rottin' in hell right noo because o' aw the impure thoughts and actions they hud when they wur in this life. It's a honey trap fur the devil, Sadie."

"Chrissy."

"Aye, Sadie."

"See me?"

"Aye, Sadie."

"See impure thoughts."

"Aye, Sadie."

"Ah huv them."

"Whit, ye mean dirty thoughts."

"Aye, Chrissy. Especially since ma man the mince hater wis taken fur the front."

"Whit kind o' impure thoughts, Sadie?"

"You know…"

"Ye mean like kissin' somewan?"

"Aye, an mair fur by."

"Wi onybody in particular?"

"Naw, that's the funny thing, Chrissy: in ma impure thoughts he never hus a face."

"You know why that is, Sadie?"

"Naw Chrissy, why is that then?"

"Because it's the devil temptin' ye, Sadie."

"So if Ah could see his face it wid be the face o' the devil?"

"Aye, Sadie, it wid be. But he cannae show ye his face fur if he did ye wid be repulsed."

"Chrissy, never mind his fucking face. You mean that thon broad shoulders and rippling muscles and thon…whotsit thing… that's the devil?"

"Aye, Sadie, that's who it is."

"Chrissy?"

"Aye, Sadie."

"See me?"

"Aye, Sadie."

"See Hell?"

"Aye, Sadie."

"Ah wahnt tae go there when Ah die!"

★ ★ ★ ★ ★

Aggie stood motionless and in silence as the judge donned the black cap and sentenced her to death.

The words seemed to reverberate all over and around her, devoid of structure, coherence and meaning. Her fate, her life, seemed to drift off into the very air itself to no purpose.

"Taken from here to a place of execution…hanged by the neck until you are dead…may God have mercy on your soul…"

From the moment of her arrest to this moment of sentencing the meaning of her life had been reduced to the inexorable outcome of due process. She had long been resigned to the inevitability of it all.

Her only defence had been her denial.

310

How did the murder weapon come to be found in her house? She didn't know (although she did!).

How did the bloodstained dress come to be in her house? She didn't know (although she did!).

How could she explain the fact that she had arranged to run away with her daughter Maureen just days after the murder of Breezy? Her assertion that Breezy was due to come with them (supported by her sister) was met with incredulity and dismissed as a ploy to disguise the real nature of the moonlighting.

The only testimony that came close to being powerfully in her favour was that of the coroner who maintained that it would have taken someone a lot stronger and agile than Aggie to have inflicted the wounds found on Breezy. This, however, was dismissed as a technicality, especially when the prosecutor put it to him that someone filled with adrenalin, aided in this case by the force of gravity and meeting no resistance from a man who was asleep, might be able to perform feats of strength which would otherwise be beyond them. The coroner's expression of doubt on these points was heard by almost everyone on the jury as a doubt against his own testimony rather than doubting if these were factors in the case of Aggie.

The jury took just under an hour to decide. Guilty. Unanimous.

The judge vilified Aggie as, "An unnatural murderess" who had planned her horrific deed meticulously and with aforethought. "She was," he determined "an abomination to her fair sex" and "truly evil."

"In another age," he suggested, she would have been taken from his judgement there and then, "handed over to a baying crowd and burned at the stake as a witch."

She would be detained in Duke Street women's prison in Glasgow until the 4th November, 1918, when she would be escorted to the gallows forecourt below and subjected to judicial execution.

Did she have any last words? Well, yes she did.

"The court hus made its decision an' Ah huv tae accept it. However, Ah repeat, Ah didnae dae it. Ah didnae murder the man Ah hud grown tae love.

311

"Ah huv been framed by the real killer, who is still at large, roamin' free tae kill again. An' kill again he will, of that Ah'm sure, unless he is stopped.

"Ah just hope tae God that he hus exhausted his appetite fur killin' ma family an' will leave wee Maureen alane.

"Maureen an' Mark ur ma biggest regrets in all o' this sorry business, apart frae no' bringin' Mark's murderer tae justice.

"I beg the court tae make sure that she is looked efter an' cared fur when Ah'm gone."

She was led from the dock to the dungeon below and then delivered to her cell overlooking her eventual place of execution.

From that point on, as a condemned prisoner, she was treated to almost cowed deference by both fellow prisoners and staff. She was the object of morbid curiosity. It was as if she was already tainted with the after-life and it would not bode well to get too close to her or to treat her with disrespect lest you got a whiff of it coming in your direction.

The days drifted by, tick-tocking away the rest of her life. Her only escape was through the portals of her own memory or imagination. Her dreams were dark, cold and sinister. She was always alone and caught out in the howl of a timeless slipstream, buffeted by its random violence.

Maureen, Sally and Jack visited every night. Soon there was nothing left to say. Every night Maureen arrived and left in tears. Every night Aggie wept.

She had no prayers to supplicate on her own behalf. She had no secular word for 'miracle' to wish for. Hope never visited.

With about a week to go to her last appointment, her cell door opened and she was ushered through to the visitor's room to await a mystery caller.

★ ★ ★ ★ ★

Major Wishart sat dumbfounded across from Corporal Brown of the First Irish Rifles. He had just listened to the Corporal's most

312

fantastic story claiming that, far from being a hero, Private Ferguson had actually murdered his colleague, Private Johnston, with the bayonet of an already dead German soldier.

Just as incredible was the allegation that Private Ferguson committed this heinous crime in order to stop Private Johnston from talking about a murder he had committed back in Scotland, before joining up with the Division.

"So, let's go back over this again, Corporal, just to make sure that I haven't dreamed all of this up over the last ten minutes. You maintain that the German soldier was already dead?"

"Yes, sir, killed by shrapnel from a Mills bomb flung towards him when we went over the top and attacked their lines."

"You actually saw this with your own eyes?"

"Yes sir, I ran past him moments after he had been hit. He must have been dying then. When I passed him on my way back he was lying dead and alone in the shell hole where he had fallen. His rifle with fixed bayonet was lying beside him."

"Are you sure that we're talking about the same soldier, Corporal?"

"How many dead Germans were found in that shell hole, sir?"

"One."

"Well unless the dead German I saw got up and ran back to his lines to be replaced with another dead German soldier, I would suggest that it was the same one."

"But Private Johnston was definitely killed by a German bayonet. There's no doubt about that!"

"I'm not doubting that, sir. All I am suggesting is that it wasn't plunged into him by a dead German, but rather by a live Scotsman."

"What makes you so sure?"

"Private Johnston confided in me that he was scared of Private Ferguson and the level of criminal violence of which he was capable. He tried to tell me a story one night about when Private Ferguson killed a man back in Scotland, but he was interrupted by Private Ferguson who was clearly suspicious. However, he managed to tell me the full story two nights later.

"I believe that Private Ferguson knew that Private Johnston could no longer be trusted to keep the secret they shared and that is why he killed him, tragically justifying Private Johnston's deep fear of him."

"That's just conjecture around an unverified story, Corporal."

"Except that Private Ferguson's story of how he came by his wound, and how this German and his friend ended up dead, is a fabrication. Why would he want to lie unless he had something to cover up?

"The only part of his story that is true is that Private Johnston was alive when he went into that shell hole and was dead when he came out, struck down by a German bayonet. But it wasn't the already dead German that killed him, that's for sure."

"Thank you for your unsolicited testimony, Corporal Brown. From you I would seek your assurance that you will speak to absolutely no one about this. Meanwhile to you I would give you my assurance that this whole matter will be investigated thoroughly and dealt with as appropriate."

"Thank you sir."

★ ★ ★ ★ ★

*Publishing House*
*Collins Publishing Group*
*Cathedral Street*
*Glasgow*
*11/10/1918*

*Dear Reverend McDonald*

*Thank you for submitting the outline of your book, "They Got Away With Murder", as well as supplying samples of your writing on the subject.*

*Ordinarily, the public at large have a great fascination for the macabre. That they should be introduced to the dark side by a practising minister of the Church of Scotland certainly adds a twist of spice to the topic.*

*That said, our country has now been at war for four grim and gruelling years. A war which has touched almost every family in this land. Consequently, we are unsure as to the public appetite for the gory and the harrowing.*

*Certainly, the earliest we would be prepared to consider publication of material of this nature would be two years following the cessations of hostilities.*

*Assuming that the war ends this year (and at the point of writing that is far from certain) then we may be in a position to consider a publication date of late 1920 at the earliest.*

*However, there are two outstanding issues remaining, over and above the one already mentioned.*

*The first is that all the information that you intend to provide in the book is already in the public domain. While it may indeed be useful to have it in compilation form, directed by your own strong and interesting viewpoint, nevertheless it would be most advantageous if you were to be able to construct fresh and compelling evidence on at least one of your subjects.*

*In terms of promoting your book, it would be doubly helpful if the crime in question were to be contemporaneous and that your account might have an impact on the case itself.*

*Secondly, the largest audience to show an interest in your work, given your position in society, is likely to be from Scotland. It would be a matter of some considerable regret, therefore, if your book did not include a significant case from your native land.*

*Our programme outlining titles for publication in 1920 is scheduled for the end of January 1919. We would welcome, therefore, sight of your book in its entirety by the middle of November 1918 – provided you can attend to the two points raised above by then.*

*Wishing you every success in your endeavours.*

*Yours sincerely*

*Godfrey Collins*

*(Editor-in-Chief)*

Reverend McDonald put down the letter carefully. His mind was troubled. "It almost makes you want to commit a murder so that you can reveal its details in your book," he thought to himself.

That night as he lay tossing and turning in his bed, the thought of Aggie McMillan kept drifting in and out of his thoughts.

He resolved to visit her in Duke Street prison before the week was out in order to offer ministry to her soul…and to tease out some pertinent details for his book!

★ ★ ★ ★ ★

"So, Corporal Brown was right. Private Ferguson did murder that poor young man," Major Wishart lamented in disbelief.

On the day in question, as the British went over the top, an Airco De Havilland DH9 two seater fighter and reconnaissance plane, had taken great risks to fly very low over the battlefield, photographing that section of the Hindenbrug line as it revealed all its gun placements hitherto disguised. It had flown over the area for four hours and taken many damning photographs.

The plates were sent for analyses and interpretation to Flight Sergeant Laws, the Senior Photographic Officer at GHQ, accompanied by a very specific and unusual request from Major Wishart of the First Irish Rifles.

From the professional interpretation of the stills, it was clear that a German soldier had lain dead in the shell hole before the arrival of two British soldiers. However, at the last sweep of aerial photographs there were two dead soldiers in the shell hole, one British and one German, the other British soldier having left to crawl back to his lines.

An examination of the dead German revealed several pieces of lethal shrapnel from a British Mills bomb in his stomach alongside the frenzied bayonet marks that Private Ferguson accounted for.

"When is he due back in France?" Major Wishart enquired.

"Tomorrow," his subaltern replied.

"I think we had better interview him before General Haig decorates him for bravery," Major Wishart said, shaking his head in his hands in disbelief.

CHAPTER NINETEEN

# Signpost to a Lie

The small church at Peterhead prison was as cold and foreboding as the rest of the penal establishment. The Catholic chaplain, Father McPherson, tried to brighten the environment by infusing it with the sensuous theatre with which Catholicism imbues its forms of worship. He brought portable statues of the Madonna and Child, St Theresa and St Joseph. Further flourishes for the faithful were provided by a bunch of flowers, candles, religious cloths and vestments. At the door was placed a bowl of Holy Water.

For Father McPherson, however, it wasn't a Catholic church until the Tabernacle containing the 'Body of Christ' was in place on the altar.

The chaplaincy was bereft of a name as it was a multi–faith building and the various denominations couldn't agree what to call it.

Members of the Free Presbyterian Church were distraught at the very idea of holding their services in a building within whose walls the Roman Catholic mass was celebrated on a regular basis. To them it felt like blasphemy by association.

However, the authorities, in the form of the Prison Board of Governors, would not budge in its arrangements for the accommodation of religious observance.

If truth be told, many of the Church of Scotland members who dominated the Board took some smug satisfaction at the discomfiture of the schismatic "Wee Frees", even if they weren't entirely comfortable themselves with the thought of sharing a building with Catholics.

However, for the next hour the chaplaincy was to be given over to a Roman Catholic wedding: the wedding of Mr Micky McGoldrick and Miss Jean Brown, both of Milltown.

Jeanie had recently 'converted' from the Church of Scotland to Catholicism which, for her, was as much a union of convenience as this marriage with Micky – her being seven months pregnant and all.

Micky had survived all the privations and indignities with which the prison could abuse him. Indeed, after a five minute meeting with the governor, which allowed him in principle to call off his hunger strike, the random beatings had stopped. He was by now largely accepted, however grudgingly, as a genuine prisoner of conscience rather than an outright coward.

Both sets of parents were there. The mothers were united in their sense of horror that their children were getting married in a prison. What would the neighbours think? However the authorities would not accede to the proposal that Micky be released for a few hours to be married in the local RC church.

Micky's best man was Stephen Leckie, a fellow 'conshie' from Banknock.

This was a great day for Micky, marrying the girl he loved and thought he had lost.

Not so for Jeanie. She was desolate at the thought of finally giving up all hope of being with George again. It felt as if she was the one entering a lifelong prison sentence.

On this morning of her wedding she found herself thoroughly resenting Micky for stealing her dreams.

In her head she started to sing Jock O' Hazeldean. In this song a young maiden, who is betrothed to the Laird's son, elopes on her wedding day on the back of a horse 'Ower the border and awa', with her true love, Jock O' Hazeldean, leaving the groom jilted at the altar in the process.

If George would only turn up right now and whisk her 'ower the border and awa' in his arms.

*But aye she let the tears doon fa'*
*For Jock O' Hazeldean.*

Everyone thought that they were tears of joy, not sensing the inner rage against the inner cage in which she was to be imprisoned.

Within half an hour it was over. Jeanie Broon was now Mrs Jean McGoldrick.

Half an hour later Micky was back in his cell, and Jeanie and her small entourage were heading for their train to Glasgow.

Jeanie's father took her aside.

"Jeanie, I know that this hasn't been the best of starts. I'm sure it's not how you imagined your wedding day would be, but it's the days that come after this that are *really* important. I don't know if you married Micky because you love him or because you feel you are obliged to under the circumstances, but first love vanishes, Jeanie, like a rose in winter. Real love is what's left to grow after its first bloom is shed. It's something that settles over time like a mature whisky. Micky is a good man. A bit idealistic for this world maybe, but life will temper his naivety.

"Focus on the good in each other Jeanie and let yourself learn to appreciate and treasure it. Only then will you have a good and fulfilling life together."

He then held his daughter in his arms and said no more.

For Micky's mother, her son's Protestant angel had come home, even if her son hadn't.

\* \* \* \* \*

Aggie felt so tired, apathetic and indifferent towards life that she couldn't even be bothered getting up to greet Reverend McDonald when he entered the room.

"Good morning, Aggie," said the minister as he sat across the table from her. "God has kept His better days for the rest of the week, I hope."

"Whit dae ye wahnt?"

"Well, Aggie, I was hoping that we could have a wee blether…"

"Aboot whit?"

"About you, Aggie… about you…"

"Ah'm no bein' cheeky vicar, but whit's ma life goat tae dae wi' you?"

"I know you weren't a regular churchgoer in our congregation, Aggie, but…"

"Just stop there, Meenister, but Ah don't huv a lot o' time left and Ah sure as fuck don't wahnt tae spend the last wee bit Ah've goat listenin' tae your pious, pontificatin', patronisin', pish. Ah *never* went tae church an' Ah *wisnae* a member o' ony congregation."

"Yes, Aggie, I know that you aren't a strong believer in Our Lord Jesus Christ."

"Christ? Him? Och aye, Ah knew Him personally. Ah just hope he's got a few holy tricks left up his sleeve tae get me oot o' this wee predicament."

"God works in mysterious ways, Aggie."

"Fuck, ye can say that again. That's why Ah'm in here waitin' tae be hanged for somethin' somebody else did. Some fuckin' sense o' humour!"

"You didn't do it?"

"Whit is this at aw'? Ur you here tae try me aw ower again? Naw Ah didnae dae it. Tell that tae yer God an' ask him whit he's gonnae dae aboot it."

"Do you know who did?"

"Aye, of course Ah dae. It wis Archie Ferguson. He killed Harry Burchill afore that. He knew Breezy and me knew, so he killed Breezy and implicated him in Harry's murder and framed me wi' Breezy's murder. Devious bastard, Ah'll gie him that."

"Did you tell this to the authorities?"

"Oh aye, Ah tellt them awright. They just said, 'Thanks fur that Mrs McMillan. We'll ask him aboot it efter he's won the war fur us. In the meantime you wouldnae mind if we hanged ye fur it, wid ye?' "

"You've had a lot of bad luck recently, Aggie."

"Ye're right there. Lost ma son tae the war. Hud ma hoose burned aroon ma erse. Archie did that as well. But at least Ah met Breezy. A kind and lovin' man. Ah'm grateful fur that."

"Did you love him?"

"Aye, Ah did. Ah loved talkin' tae him. Ah loved bein wi' him. Ah loved bein' enfolded in his erms, not that we ever did…you know…but it wis lovely tae be cherished by him."

Aggie's tone had changed. It had become softer. Gentler. It was almost distant and dreamlike. Reverend McDonald bore witness to how much she loved this man. How much she missed this man. How she could never have murdered this man.

"Aggie, have you prepared yourself for the end?"

"In whit way, Vicar?"

"Have you made your peace with God?"

"Naw Ah huvnae because Ah never fell oot wi' Him in the first place, considerin' Ah don't believe in Him. Ye might as well ask me if Ah've made ma peace wi' the tooth fairy. Ah don't believe in Him or his miracles. Mind you, if he can show me a miracle noo, like getting' me oot o' here wi' ma neck still intact, Ah might start believin' in him then."

"Is that a deal, Aggie?"

"Naw, Ah'm just teasin' masel. If there is a God He widnae wahnt tae risk His reputation by takin' on ma case. It's hopeless."

"I could say that I'll pray for you, Aggie – and I will – but I know that probably wouldn't mean too much to you."

"Prayer is just a madman's way o' getting' away wi' talkin' tae himsel', but Ah appreciate the thought, Vicar."

"Well, Aggie, I'll do more than that. Firstly, I know that you have a young daughter. If there's anything you might want me to do for her I will. Secondly, I'll ask the God you don't believe in to guide me in my mission to uncover the truth of this sordid affair in time to save you from the rope."

"Meenister, Ah know ye spend yer life feedin' simple folk's minds wi' far-fetched fantasies, but tae gie a wummin waitin' tae be hanged false hope is kinda takin' it a bit far, dae ye no' think so?"

"We'll see, Aggie, we'll see, but I've got two very powerful things on ma side."

"Aye?"

"I believe in God, Aggie… and I believe in you."

★ ★ ★ ★ ★

Maggie McKinnon stood on the platform waiting for the Glasgow train. Most of the northbound passengers were commuters to Arthur Lea, the south side of Glasgow or the city centre. Maggie was dressed for a day out. She wore her best shoes, hat, coat and gloves and proudly boasted her red crocodile leather handbag slung over her arm. She looked across the rail at the opposite platform where she saw her friend, Daisy Lochhead.

"Whaur ye gaun the day?" Maggie chirped.

"Just up tae Stewarton, Maggie," Daisy replied. "Ah'm workin' up there noo, in a bonnet factory."

The two exchanged pleasantries across the chasm until Daisy's train arrived. Daisy had been Alex's girlfriend before he chucked her for Maggie. There had never been any hard feelings between them and Daisy eventually married Andy Thorpe, whom Maggie had once gone out with.

Maggie thought back to those early days with Alex when they were both teenagers. He was bright, handsome and dependable, all important qualities as far as Maggie was concerned. A man of principle too. You could trust Alex, except for the very odd Friday night when his workmates in the pub became great pot holes on his road to good intentions.

Within three months of stepping out together they were engaged to be married. They tied the knot just over a year later.

Try as they might they were never able to produce offspring, which had been a source of great sadness. That they would now never be able to do. Not since his genitalia had been atomised by that shell on his camp at Authuille before the battle of the Somme.

In the year since returning, Maggie had tried to 'see' the old Alex and recapture her feelings for him. However, she was repulsed by him. She recoiled when he tried to cuddle her with his little, pathetic stumpy arms. She could offer him no physical comforts, nor even allow her eyes to look in his direction for more than a fleeting, disgusted glance.

The sound of Alex dragging his body across the floor made her flesh creep. She even cringed listening to him talk about how he had been making his brew when a whizzbang landed to his left wiping out a group of squaddies, some horses and carts and 75% of him.

Alex woke up four days later in a military hospital. He had forbidden the authorities to make contact with any member of his family. He had resolved to do so himself in his own way and in his own time.

Eventually, he was transferred by night to the Royal Infirmary in Glasgow through one of the underground tunnels which connected the ships in the Broomielaw with all the major hospitals in the city. The genteel populous who had once waved and cheered their heroes off to the war were thus deprived the opportunity of providing a reception for the return of their broken shells.

Still he refused permission for any contact to be made with his family.

He also declined to look in a mirror. In his mind he was still the same young man who had arrived in Coplawhill tram depot that fateful day in September 1914 to sign up with the other fresh-faced recruits, hoping to head off to the adventure that was war.

Maggie knew differently.

Her days had become a routine of gut-wrenching duties. Bathing and bandaging till her stomach lurched. The touch, the sight and the 'gangareneous' smells from Alex's suppurating stump left her gagging. At night in bed she slept as far over the mattress as she possibly could, trying to stop herself listening to her husband's whimpering and to avoid bearing his touch.

She hated herself.

She hated even more the thought that this was now her life. Forever. She couldn't run. She couldn't hide. She couldn't divorce.

She was his wife. For better or worse…

Maurice Stevenson from Dennistoun had been the driver of the 09.05 train from Kilmarnock to Glasgow, which pulled into Milltown at 09.47.

He saw the pretty young lady with the red handbag step forward to the edge of the platform on his approach. She stared up expectantly before beaming him a beautiful smile, mouthing the words "Thank you" and dropping her body like a leaf floating on a sigh onto the track in front of the still moving train.

★ ★ ★ ★ ★

The mood in Milltown and across the country was lightening. The Allies were winning the war.

The great German push in their spring offensive had exhausted itself by June, overreaching its supply lines and running out of steam and direction.

Now the Allies were ready for their big push and, on the 8th of August, 1918, 'Ludendorff's black day', the Germans suffered a massive defeat at Amiens which resulted in them being driven right back to the Hindenburg line itself.

Hindenburg and Ludendorff urged the Kaiser to seek a treaty with the Allies, based on President Wilson's 14 points issued in January of that year.

The arm-wrestle was nearly over and it was Germany's hand that was falling and falling fast.

Lucky, Hoppy and Menzies Campbell were in high spirits in the Bottom Shop.

"We'll be in Berlin by the end of the year," a happy Hoppy said confidently.

"Ah wish Ah wis there tae march intae Germany wi' them," said Menzies wistfully.

"Don't get yer hopes up, lads," warned the barman, "there's still a lot o' killin' and dyin' tae be done yet."

"Aye, but it'll be us that'll be daein the killin' and the Huns that'll be daein' the dyin'," exclaimed Hoppy.

"The barman's right," agreed Menzies, "Lucky and Ah baith know aboot the fightin' qualities o' the German soldier. Noo that we're threatenin' the Fatherland itself he's gonnae be even mair difficult tae beat."

"Aye," agreed Lucky, "but they've shot their bolt. They're exhausted and demoralised. If they could surrender right noo they wid. They're brave but they're beaten."

"Ye know whit Ah'm no' lookin' forward tae," sighed Hoppy.

"Whit wid that be?" asked the barman.

"Huvin' tae listen tae the Yanks tellin' us how they won the war fur us."

"Mair like we won their war fur them," suggested the barman. "They didnae come in tae support us. They declared war on Germany on their own behalf because the Huns were encouraging Mexico tae invade Texas, then they piggy-backed oor war tae win their ain war fur themsels on the cheap."

"How many men huv they goat in the field, onywey?" asked Hoppy.

"Aboot a quarter o' a million, but they're pourin' in fast," said Menzies.

"Aye, and they needed British ships tae bring them ower, and British hats tae wear and French guns tae fire when they goat here," Lucky pointed out.

"Still, Ah'm glad they're fightin' wi' us and no' against us," the barman added.

"They'll be the big boys aroon the peace negotiation table, just wait and see," bemoaned Hoppy. "They'll end up losin' aboot as many men in total as the Allies might lose in a week, but it'll no' stop them comin' in an' dictatin' terms, 'cos that's whit they're like."

"The barman's right, though," agreed Menzies, "the German morale has been crushed by the prospect o' facin' mair an' mair fresh an' enthusiastic American troops. Their entry intae the war will shorten it by months, if not years, and will save countless lives oan baith sides."

"God bless America," said Lucky, raising his glass.

"God bless President Wilson," said Hoppy, raising his.

"God bless General Pershing," said Menzies, joining the trio of drinks.

"God bless Elsie Bierbower," said the barman.

"God bless who?" said the bar in unison.

"Elsie Bierbower, better known to youse, gentlemen, as Elsie Janis, the American Forces sweetheart. Ah've seen her photo on the picture postcards. She's as beautiful as she is brave."

At the thought of his beloved Elsie, he launched into a rendition of one of her hits from the beginning of the war:

*Florrie was a flapper*

*She was dainty, she was dapper...*

And from that moment on, till the moment he died in 1951, the barman was known as Florrie Flapper.

★ ★ ★ ★ ★

At eight pounds, Jeanie's little boy had been a pound for every hour of his delivery.

He looked like Micky. He was going to have red hair and blue eyes, just like his dad.

From the beginning, though, Jeanie fantasised that he shared George's features. To her he was George by proxy.

She whispered to him about his soldier daddy from Hollywood, Northern Ireland, and how he would grow up to be clever, musical and handsome just like him. She promised him that they would go to Ireland to be with him some day.

Her letter to Micky was brutally brief.

*Micky*

*Had an 8 lb boy last Sunday.*

*We're both healthy.*

*Jeanie*

She blamed Micky for being the boy's father instead of George.

She blamed him and dismissed him at the same time.

The Catholic tradition insisted that the baby be baptised as quickly as possible, hypothesising that, should the baby die before being baptised, it may not be allowed to enter the kingdom of Heaven as it still retained the original sin of Adam on its soul which only baptism could remove. Unbaptised babies, therefore, may be condemned to spend eternity in Limbo, being denied the beatific vision.

Father O'Keefe called round to see her.

"Wait till I tell ye, Ah wis just hearin' yer good...did Ah say 'good'?... no, it'd be more like great...no, that hardly does it justice either...yer absolutely fantastic news, Jeanie. Wid ye ever be lettin' me see the wee fella, wid ye, so?"

"Sure, Father, here ye are."

Jeanie pulled back the bottom drawer of the sideboard which sufficed as a cot to reveal a little baby sleeping in swaddling clothes. "Ah now, isn't he a gorgeous wee chappie. Isn't he just a tiny miracle. God's tiny miracle. Your tiny miracle, Jeanie. Sure he has your nose right enough, but wait till Ah tell ye, he looks like the spit o' his father, don't ye t'ink?"

"No, Father."

" 'No, Father' a voice from somewhere is sayin'. Sure wit' his red hair and his blue eyes and that wee dimple on his cheek ye widn't be able to tell which one was Micky and which was...well, Micky."

"His name won't be Micky, Father."

Father O'Keefe went rigid. He looked round slowly at Jeanie. His face fell.

"He won't be called Micky? An' him havin' a father called Micky and a grandfather from Rasharkin called Micky afore that? What kind o' betrayal is this? It's tellin' me somethin' Jeanie and Ah don't like it."

"What does it tell you?"

"Well now, before Ah answer ye that, let *me* tell *you* what it is you are intent on callin' the wee fella instead, will Ah? You're set on callin' this son o' Micky McGoldrick, George. Am Ah right? It's

George you've got planned for this baby."

Jeanie looked away, stunned.

"Jeanie, in God's name tell me Ah'm wrong. Let me be wrong on this, sweet Jaysus!"

Jeanie couldn't answer him or look at him.

Father O'Keefe took her face in his hands and turned her towards him. He looked at her severely.

"Holy Mother of God, Ah am right! You're goin' to call Micky's son after a man you can't have. I heard about your liaison with that Irish soldier in Cowden House, Jeanie. I'd hoped and prayed that you had managed to get over him and settle into married life with Micky. Don't live a lie, Jeanie. Don't for the sake o' the blood o' Christ make your son a signpost to that lie!"

"He will be called George, Father...after the king."

"The King? The King is it? The King ma feckin' arse, Jeanie. You will call that baby Micky or you will find another priest to baptise him."

"Would you risk his immortal soul over a name?"

Father O'Keefe went over to the sink, ran the tap over his hands and sprinkled water over the baby, saying as he did so, "I baptise you Michael in the name of the Father and of the Son and of the Holy Ghost. Amen."

Turning round to Jeanie he said, "There, that's his immortal soul saved. Now you do what you like. His name is Micky now and forever as far as I am concerned."

Jeanie summoned up her courage in both hands, supported by a rising anger, looked Father O'Keefe in the eye and said, "Get oot o' oor house 'now an' forever' you demented papish wizard. A sprinklin' o' cooncil wahter will no' come between me an' callin' my son efter the only man Ah will ever love. His name will be George...but you're right, no'efter the King!"

Father O'Keefe stared at her in disbelief. He shook his head in tired resignation, picked up his cap and left in the disdainful silence of bitter disapproval.

# CHAPTER TWENTY

# *There is a Happy Land*

The bus taking the soldiers to be decorated for their war exploits was waved into the side of the road alongside a military camp in northern France.

Archie hardly noticed. His thoughts were elsewhere. He had heard that Aggie McMillan had been sentenced to death for killing Breezy Breeks.

What a pity, he thought, that public executions had been banned since 1868. He would have loved to have been there at Duke Street prison to have seen the life garrotted out of her.

He wouldn't even be able to indulge his morbid curiosity, as he had been able to do with Harry Burchill, by visiting her grave. The remains of executed prisoners passed to the property of the crown and she would be buried in an unmarked lime grave in the grounds of the prison.

A song came into his mind that his grandfather used to sing to the tune of 'There Is A Happy Land'.

*There is a happy land*
*Doon Duke Street jail,*
*Where aw the prisoners stand*
*Tied tae a nail.*
*Ham and eggs they never see*
*Dirty water for yer tea,*
*There they live in misery*
*God Save the Queen.'*

The thought of Aggie McMillan 'tied tae a nail' and 'drinking dirty water for her tea' amused him.

And now look at him: on his way to be decorated for bravery by the Commander-in-Chief no less.

He was amazed at how easy it was to dupe people. He seemed to have a special talent for it. From his mother, to Mrs Collins, to the police, to the Commander-in-Chief of His Majesty's Forces overseas himself, he was masterful at disguising his thoughts and deeds.

But then, he was a mere amateur compared to the generals in this war who had been decorated many times over for the wholesale slaughter of their own men.

He almost felt in awe of a meritocratic system which recognised the worth of evil in society.

"Private Archie Ferguson of the First Irish Rifles...Is there a Private Ferguson on the bus?" shouted a Sergeant.

Archie looked up, startled, having just come out of a daydream. He put his hand up to identify himself.

"Come with me, son," the Sergeant beckoned. "Bring your things with you."

Archie stepped off the bus which was then allowed to drive on.

"What's the matter, sir?" asked a slightly nervous Private Ferguson.

"There's an officer here that wants to talk to you," said the Sergeant as he escorted Private Ferguson to a tent within the encampment.

"Presenting Private Ferguson of the First Irish Rifles," the Sergeant announced as he retreated to stand guard by the door.

"Ah, Private Ferguson. I wonder if you would be good enough to reacquaint me with the details surrounding the encounter you and Private Johnston had with that German soldier you managed to kill?"

Archie recited his account word for word.

Major Wishart waited patiently until he had finished and then said, "Thank you, Private Ferguson, only I have to tell you that, far from killing the German soldier who had just killed Private Johnston, we have significant evidence that the soldier was already lying dead when you and Private Johnston entered the shell hole and that, in fact, you killed Private Johnston with the dead German soldier's bayonet. What do you say to that allegation?"

"Absolute rubbish, sir. The situation was as I said in my debriefing statement and as I have just repeated to you now."

"Really! I am so relieved. However, let's go through the evidence which we have to the contrary, shall we, and give you the opportunity to unpick it."

Major Wishart painstakingly took Archie through the evidence piece by piece until, at length, Archie flung his hands in the air and said, "OK, I admit it. I did kill him, but only after he tried to kill me with that German's bayonet, forcing me to defend myself. He was jealous of me because a girl he fancied back home was crazy for me."

"I don't suppose you have any idea how desperate you're beginning to sound, Private Ferguson. I have to say that it's bad enough having murdered Private Johnston, but now you are compounding the felony by traducing his name after his death when he is not here to defend himself.

"At any rate we'll hand you over to a military tribunal and let them decide."

Turning to the Sergeant he said, "Take this man into custody. Charges will follow."

Archie was handcuffed and taken to a waiting car.

The tribunal was a formality. Archie admitted his guilt, but entered a special plea of self-defence which was dismissed out of hand.

Private Ferguson was found guilty and sentenced to death by firing squad.

The order approving the execution was signed by the very hand which was to have decorated him – that of General Haig.

★ ★ ★ ★ ★

Micky lay back on his cell bed and stared hard at the ceiling, his mind in turmoil. In his hand he loosely held a letter from Jeanie.

331

*Dear Micky*

*I want to tell you about a decision I arrived at today.*

*Before I do, however, let me explain my motives by way of a story which I heard from an Irish patient in Cowden House.*

*Apparently in Belfast there is a public house which in the last century had a Catholic owner. This Catholic owner had a Protestant wife who was desperate to call the pub The Crown to express her royal affiliations.*

*The Catholic owner, probably an Irish Nationalist, was dead against it for obvious reasons.*

*The issue was causing great arguments within the household until one of them, I don't know who, came up with an imaginative solution.*

*It was suggested that the pub could be called The Crown, but only on the condition that a motif of a crown was placed on the ground at the door on the way in so that people would have to walk over it as they entered.*

*This was agreed, the pub was called The Crown and domestic harmony was restored.*

*Now, Micky, as a married couple from mixed backgrounds, we are also going have to compromise from time to time.*

*I have already compromised by becoming a Catholic and by agreeing to bring our children up in the Catholic faith. No small matter I am sure you will agree.*

*Well, now it's my turn.*

*I intend to register our son under the name of George, after King George the Fifth, who has led us through this war.*

*I know that you will be disappointed that I haven't followed the McGoldrick tradition of naming the first son after the father. I also know how you feel about the royal family and, of course, the war.*

*However, these have been exceptional times for our country, Micky, and I just feel that it would be an act of respect to all those young men who have been killed in the war to call our son after the King who reigned through it all.*

*I hope you will understand and accept my reasons.*

*Your wife*

*Jeanie'*

Micky might have read this letter with more 'understanding' had he not just read a letter from Father O'Keefe on the same subject ten minutes earlier.

★ ★ ★ ★ ★

Archie sat in the hut from which he would eventually emerge to see his last dawn.

He had quickly come to terms with his fate. He consoled himself with the thought that he had come so close to getting away with it.

Not only did he not care about his victims or their families or his own family, he didn't care about himself.

He had seen many, many people die up close. Death, like life, Archie thought, was what you made it. He would enter it openly and without fear. He would face it down.

The door opened and a Corporal entered.

"Visitor to see you, Private Ferguson," said the Corporal.

Archie recognised Reverend McDonald step from behind the Corporal.

"Hello, Archie. Do you mind if I come in for a blether?"

"Suit yersel, Vicar. Suit yersel."

"Do you want me to stay, Reverend?"

"Not at all, Corporal. This will be a quiet, private conversation."

"I'll be just outside if you need me, then."

"Ye're a brave man, Reverend, allowin' yersel tae be caged up alone wi' a convicted murderer."

"Archie, I doubt if you would kill me just for the sake of it. Why would you?"

"Well there's not a lot to stop me now is there? Whit mair can they dae tae me? Onyway we're wastin' time. Of course Ah'm no' gonnae kill ye, but whit ur ye here fur?"

"I'm here to ask you a favour, Archie."

"Don't see how Ah'm obliged tae dae you a favour, Vicar, but go ahead."

"Absolutely not. Of course you're not obliged to do anything. However, back in Glasgow, Aggie McMillan is due to be hanged for the murder of Breezy Breeks."

"Aye, Ah heard. Whit's that goat tae dae wi' me?"

"Archie, she thinks you did it."

"Ah could be tempted tae be mair cynical an' say she *says* she thinks Ah did it, but whit dae you think?"

"I think you probably did it as well."

"Thanks fur that vote o' confidence, Vicar. So whit dae ye wahnt me tae dae?"

"Admit your guilt and save her from the gallows."

"When does she hang?"

"Tomorrow morning at six. Unless you confess. The court knows I'm here and a telegram from me will suspend the sentence being carried out until the 'new evidence' can be assessed. You are her last hope, Archie."

"Well then she's doomed if she's waitin' oan me givin' her a deathbed confession that will save her grubby neck. Let the bitch hang."

"Archie, I noticed that you didn't deny killing Breezy or framing Aggie. Did you?"

"Wow! Someone who could kill Breezy Breeks and get off with it by framing someone else that he also wanted rid of – that person would need to be very, very clever. Don't you think?"

"I agree that it would take a very clever man to engineer all that successfully, but why would you want any harm to come to Aggie?"

"Because the bitch stalked me for years over the Harry Burchill affair. She said Alan an' Ah murdered him an' it turned Alan into a nervous wreck who had tae be killed afore he blabbed. Aggie is the reason Ah'm here an' you wahnt me to save her skin? Not oan yer life! As Ah say, let the bitch hang. Ah just wish Ah wis releasin' the trapdoor."

"Archie, have you no pity for an innocent woman with a young daughter, being sent to the gallows?"

"Pity? Whit is pity, Meenister, except weakness? Whit dae Ah care aboot Aggie McMillan or her daughter? Ah don't unnerstaun the concept o' pity. If you huv somethin' tae dae just get oan an' fuckin' dae it. Never look back. Never say sorry."

"What about your own conscience, Archie? You'll have Aggie's death on your conscience and you'll be meeting your Maker soon."

"Well ma conscience an' Ah will be partin' company soon onyway. An' as fur ma Maker – if he exists – didnae He make me what Ah um? He can take responsibility fur me.

"Besides, a conscience is just a moral straightjacket put in place by people like you. The free spirit is true tae its urges and disnae need tae ask society's permission fur bein' true tae it's nature. Look at the fox in the chicken coop. Does it hesitate in doubt before its murderous attack or become bogged down in guilt afterwards. It kills because it's in its instinct to do so an' because it can."

"But why allow Aggie to die when you could save her life with just a word which can have no possible repercussions for you?"

"Ah think Ah just told ye why, Vicar. Ur ye no' listenin' or dae yer ears no' work when they don't like what they hear? Let me make it even clearer then: when Aggie McMillan is hanged Ah'll huv killed her by proxy. Ah've wahnted tae kill that gossipin' scumbag fur years an Ah'm gonnae dae it – or at least Ah'm gonnae huv it done – at six o'clock the morra mornin'. But don't expect me tae apologise on behalf o' ma conscience any more than Ah'll expect the firin' squad tae apologise tae me afore, durin' or efter they shoot me."

"Archie, Ah'm begging you."

"Why? So ye can feel good aboot yersel? Become the big man o' the moment? You so-called 'good' people make me sick wi' your hypocrisy. You do good because it makes you feel self-important an' smug aboot yersel. You serve yer ain self-interest just like me and then applaud yersel fur bein' good."

"What's wrong wi' bein' good?"

"Good is insipid and fearful. Good is just a weak man's attempt tae beg society's approval. Evil, as you call it, on the other hand, is the exercise and domination o' the will, fearless an' unrepentant.

"Ah um evil in your silly wee book an Ah'm prood o' it. Ah wid love everyone tae know how evil Ah um. Ah don't apologise fur it. Ah embrace it. Fur humans tae huv evolved tae become the dominant species oan the planet we've needed hate an' violence every bit as much as love an' peace. Whit dae ye think this war's aw aboot?"

"This is the war to end all wars, Archie."

"Aye, so it is. Just like the next wan wull be an' the wan efter that. An' don't forget tae add infinitum!"

"Archie, when I walk through that door all hope for Aggie will walk out with me and she will die within eight hours unless you can offer a reprieve by admitting that you killed Breezy Breeks…"

"…and Harry Burchill and a big stupid Irish soldier named George and fuck knows how many Germans. But Ah'm no' gonnae admit tae ony o' them this side o' the hangman's rope stringin' up Aggie McMillan the morra mornin'! As Ah said afore that Ah said afore: let the bitch hang!"

"May God have mercy on your black and damned soul, Archie Ferguson," said the minister in disgust.

"God can go hang as well…oh, Ah forgot – He did! A fat lot o' good 'Good' did God," Archie laughed hollowly at the Reverend McDonald's back as it slouched out the door.

★ ★ ★ ★ ★

Jeanie felt extremely lethargic. She was constantly tired and irritable. She had no motivation to do anything. For most of the day she just sat and stared. Her baby had become her anchor, keeping her from flight.

When George cried, she screamed. She couldn't take his constant demands and shrill reminders that her life wasn't her own any more. She had now entered a phase where her needs were subservient to a bawling piece of blubber.

Her mother took over much of the responsibility for ensuring that the baby was looked after in all of its basic needs.

She worried deeply about her daughter. She often expressed her concerns to Jeanie in a series of negative demands. Why didn't she do this or why didn't she do that?

Till at length at the height of a tirade, Jeanie said, "…And why don't you fuck off!"

It seemed to Jeanie's mother that her daughter's whole personality was changing. Almost as if she was being possessed by an inner demon.

Things came to a head when her mother found Jeanie shaking a screaming George violently while yelling back at him through her tears, "Shut up you little bastard…Fucking shut up!"

Jeanie wasn't capable of looking after her baby. She was hardly capable of looking after herself now. She had stopped washing. Her dirty hair was a constant mess that just hung limply and flatly over her face. The same unwashed clothes remained on her back for weeks on end. She slept through great chunks of the day and could not sleep at night. She often went through the day without eating, hardly noticing.

Of course, back then no one had heard of the term post-natal depression, although that didn't stop women from experiencing it.

One day, when she was out pushing George in his pram, she heard footsteps behind her and a voice calling 'Jeanie'. It was Alice Henderson.

"Oh naw," thought Jeanie. "Ah cannae be daein' wi' huvin' a scene wi' her oot here in the middle o' the street." Still, Alice's demeanour confused Jeanie. She seemed too unsure of herself to appear openly friendly, but she was hardly hostile or even angry.

"Jeanie, Ah just wanted tae congratulate you on yer marriage tae Micky and oan the birth o' yer son. Ah'm sure that when Micky gets oot o' the jile ye'll aw huv a great life thegither.

337

"Ah also wahnted tae apologise tae ye fur gossipin' aboot Harry Burchill and you and fur the way Ah treated you and Micky efter that. Ah've hud a long time tae think aboot it and Ah've come tae realise that Ah wis wrang. In fact Ah wis doonright wicked and nasty.

"Wull ye forgive me, Jeanie? Can we be friends again?"

Jeanie was stunned. For a fleeting moment she wondered whether this was one of Alice's stunts. Was there a crowd round the corner waiting to jump out and laugh her to scorn the moment she reciprocated?

She looked at Alice's face. She saw the tears begin to form.

"Dae ye wahnt tae hold ma wean, Alice?"

Alice emitted a yelp that was a combination of laughing, crying, relief and delight all rolled into one.

"Ah wid love tae hold him, Jeanie. Whit's he called?"

"George…efter the King…"

"Efter the King? Whit does Micky say tae that?"

"Well, Alice, ye know that Ah'm a Catholic noo – well, sort of – an' Ah've agreed tae bring aw oor kids up Catholic. So this wis ma choice. It wis ma turn."

"That's great tae hear that ye can compromise wi' each other. Ye'll need that tae get through life thegither."

"Whit ur ye daein' wi' yersel, Alice? Ur ye still doon the mill?"

"Aye, Ah'm a floor manageress noo. Ah've hud tae eat a lot o' humble pie, Ah can tell ye, tae a lot o' lassies whose boyfriends, in some cases noo husbands, Ah used tae hand oot white feathers tae. Ah feel ashamed o' that noo as well."

"The whole country wis caught up in the madness back then, Alice. It wis a bit different efter the Somme an' we started to get some idea o' whit it wis really like."

"Naw, we hud nae idea," Alice agreed. "Here, let me haud him."

More tears started to run down Alice's cheeks.

"Tae think Jeanie, if you hudnae been so strong Ah might huv split you an' Micky up an' this wee fella might never huv been born."

"Alice, in a perverse sort o' way you were a big part o' Micky an' me stayin' thegither fur as long as we did. It might just as easily huv been the other way roon an' ye widnae be staunin' there wi' George in yer arms the noo if aw that hudnae been gaun oan."

"Everythin' fur a reason, eh."

The next 15 minutes were spent in what we would now call a girlie chat that gave both women a tremendous release from the pent up pressure of their past and, for Jeanie at least, started the process of healing.

They parted after agreeing to meet at least once a week to push George around the town in his pram and share a natter.

That night Jeanie bathed, fixed her hair, changed her clothes and looked at herself in the mirror.

"I am Jeanie McGodrick and I am strong" she confirmed to herself. Jeanie was back.

★ ★ ★ ★ ★

The door of Archie's cell opened. The same Corporal ushered Reverend McDonald back in. The minister's head was stooped, hiding the fact that he had been crying. He was disconsolate. He slumped down on the wooden-back chair opposite Archie.

For a moment or two there was silence between them. Then the minister slowly and deliberately handed a telegram over to Archie.

It had been sent to Reverend McDonald from the court authorities in Glasgow. It read:

MRS AGNES MCMILLAN HANGED TODAY SIX AM STOP PRONOUNCED DEAD SIX EIGHTEEN AM STOP BODY INTERRED UNMARKED PRISON GRAVE STOP

Archie's face lightened in equal measure to Reverend McDonald's darkening furrows.

"It's over," the reverend sobbed.

"That's a piece o' wonderful news Ah'll take tae wi' me happily tae ma grave," whooped Archie.

"How can you say that?" protested the minister. "She was innocent. An innocent woman with a twelve-year-old daughter has just been hanged. How can you possibly rejoice in that?"

"Naw in ma court she wisnae innocent, Vicar. That's whit she gets fur messin' wi' me. Fuck her."

Some further minutes went by with Archie registering his delight at the news and Reverend McDonald sitting silently, ashen-faced in grief-stricken contemplation.

"So whit ur ye sittin' oan fur Meenister? It wis good o' ye tae bring me the news, but…"

"It grieves me to say this, but I've got another favour to ask of you," the minister said, drying his eyes all the while.

"Well, Ah'm Ah no just the popular wan all o' a sudden? Whit can Ah dae fur ye noo, Vicar? Join in a prayer fur Aggie McMillan's soul? Ah don't think so!"

"No, I'd hardly ask you to do that, under the circumstances.

"As it happens, I'm writing a book. It's got nothing to do with religion. It's about unsolved murders. The title of my book will be, 'They Got Away With Murder.'

"You said last night that you would like everyone to know how evil and clever you are after you're dead. Well, here's your opportunity. If you would write me an account of all your murderous exploits and how you set them up and got away with them I'll include them in the book.

"Your story will be told alongside that of the Austin, Texas murders, the axeman murders of New Orleans, The Lizzie Borden murders, The Princes in the Tower and, of course, Jack the Ripper. You will be in very good or, rather, evil company.

"I hate asking you to do this. Hate, that is, in that it demeans me rather than that it inconveniences you. But you do represent a unique opportunity to not only have a chapter on a Scottish murderer, but also to include an exclusive posthumous account from the murderer himself. What do you say?"

"Sure. Now that Aggie McMillan's in the ground Ah'll sing like – well, like Breezy Breeks! However there is wan condition."

"What's that?"

"That Ah get tae hold oan tae this telegram and keep it in ma breast pocket next tae ma hert when Ah'm in front o' the firin' squad."

"A perverse request, but I suppose I can expect no less.

"However, there is one problem. I'm due back in Scotland by Thursday and my publishers in Glasgow are looking for the first draft of the book by the end of the week, so if you could write your account today I'll pick it up at around nine o'clock tonight."

"Ah wis gonnae go tae a gin palace the night wi' a duchess oan ma airm, but Ah'll just put that aff till efter Ah'm deid and stay in and write this instead."

"Have you any idea when your execution is due?"

"Naw, it could be ony time. Ah don't know if they're obliged tae gie me ony notice, so Ah'd better get started writin' in case Ah'm rudely interrupted."

"Right, I'll drop by around nine tonight," the minister said as he slouched out the door.

"Aye, Meenister, you dae that" said a doubly elated Archie.

★ ★ ★ ★ ★

Father O'Keefe's letter was full of remorse.

*St Thomas's RC church*
*Main Street*
*Milltown*
*2nd November, 1916*

> *Micky*
> *I visited Jeanie at her mother's house this morning to see your newly born son.*
>
> *He is a wee cracker, Micky. He is your double. You'll be so proud of him when you lay eyes on him.*

*However, I am afraid that I overstepped the mark as your parish priest by baptising your son with a name contrary to that chosen by his mother.*

*Jeanie has her own reasons for wanting to call your son George and I should have accepted and respected them without question.*

*In an act of impulse, which I deeply regret, I baptised him Michael after his father and his grandfather from Rasharkin.*

*Now the name I've given him has no standing in law, so he can be registered in whatever name Jeanie chooses, but the important thing is that the baptism itself has legitimacy in Heaven in terms of removing original sin should any unforeseen tragedy occur. I hope that you are reassured by that.*

*I'm sorry for my transgression, Micky, and I will personally apologise to Jeanie and offer her the option of a full public baptism in St Thomas' whenever might be convenient, and in whatever Christian name that is acceptable.*

*God Bless you, Micky.*

*I'll keep you all in my prayers.*

*Father John O'Keefe.*

Micky put the two letters together, side by side. He felt saddened that his wife and priest were at loggerheads so early in their marriage and so soon after Jeanie's 'conversion'.

He also felt a bit ashamed that Father O'Keefe clearly felt that he had to stand up for Micky's integrity within his marriage. Especially since Micky already knew about Jeanie's relationship with George from Northern Ireland.

A guard, as it happened in the way that these things often do, had a friend who had a relative from Milltown. He had been kept posted about Jeanie being sacked from Cowden House and all the reasons for it. This had been passed round the prison establishment and used to humiliate Micky.

He felt crushed by the choice of name, but at the same time he consoled himself with the thought that Jeanie was his wife now and that he would have with her what this Irish soldier would never have: time.

He turned round and faced the wall, full of anger and frustration. "George it is after George the fucking fifth." Micky told himself. "God save the fucking King!"

★ ★ ★ ★ ★

Archie enjoyed the process of writing an account of his murders and intrigues. He made sure to accompany the facts with a description of the relish he took from watching his victims die.

"…and by the time Breezy opened his eyes the fatal blow had already been delivered…the look of surprise on Alan's face when I stuck the German's bayonet into his guts made me laugh for ages afterwards…Aggie's house was the biggest coup I've ever seen. I had to make sure that when I planted the bloodied knife and the blood stained dress back in her house, that it didn't look as if they had been tidied away because nothing else had been…in the mayhem of war no one took notice of another soldier falling in the face of enemy fire. This soldier from Rosslea, however, was surely the only soldier on the front to be shot in the back while facing the enemy…"

Finally:

" …I dedicate this true account to Aggie McMillan whose death by execution I engineered this day and in whose death I take enormous pride and pleasure…"

So proud was he that he gloried in the sight of his name adorning the bottom of the script, taking responsibility for all that had been written above:

"…Archie Ferguson
Northern France
November 1918."

Reverend McDonald called at the appointed time with the Corporal, who remained behind him.

"Well, Archie, how did you get on?"

"There it is, Vicar, for your book and for posterity."

The Reverend read it through carefully.

"You've certainly included a lot of detail, Archie."

"Ah enjoyed writin' it. Ah wahnted everywan to know how powerful Ah felt bein' in control o' other people's lives and in manipulatin' everywan."

"Yes, I see that. I also see that you've very obligingly signed it. Very good Archie, very good."

The minister turned with the script towards the soldier standing behind him. "Corporal, as we agreed, would you take this piece of King's evidence into your custody for the moment and give this note to the driver waiting outside to take it to the nearest telegraph office. It is to be sent as a telegram to the Governor of Duke Street Prison and to the Procurator Fiscal of the High Court in Glasgow, but not before I read the contents to the prisoner:

PRIVATE FERGUSON CONFESSED IN SIGNED AFFIDAVIT TO MURDER OF DOCTOR MARK MANSON STOP CANCEL EXECUTION OF MRS MCMILLAN STOP VERIFIED DOCUMENTS BEING SENT BY COURIER STOP

Archie lunged at Reverend McDonald, grasping the vicar round the neck before anyone could move.

The minister, however, instantly extricated himself from this potentially tricky situation by offering Archie a Glasgow kiss, which both flattened him and broke his nose.

"Bastard...bastard...Ah'll fuckin' kill you, ya lyin' bastard..."

"You know, Archie, you're right. Sometimes it doesn't do much good being good! You're also right to say I lied. I did lie. Aggie's execution isn't due until six *tomorrow* morning. Now, thanks to you, it won't ever take place at all. However, by coincidence, there is one that will..."

Major Wishart appeared at the door on cue, brushed past the Corporal and proclaimed:

"Private Ferguson of the First Irish Rifles, I have to inform you that the sentence of the military tribunal held in Bouzincourt on October thirtieth, 1918, of death by firing squad will be promulgated on the morning of the fourth of November, 1918 at six a.m. precisely.

"May God have mercy on your soul."

Archie sat with his hands holding his bowed head and rocking backwards and forwards.

"Just tell Aggie it wis personal," he said in a final act of defiance.

★ ★ ★ ★ ★

Captain Laidlaw of the First Irish Rifles addressed the assembled firing squad.

"This morning men we will be obliged, by order of the military tribunal, to execute Private Ferguson of our own battalion.

"As you have all volunteered to be part of this squad, I assume that, if you didn't know Private Ferguson, you at least knew the victim of his crime, Private Alan Johnston, may God have mercy on his soul.

"I would urge you, men, to put all thoughts of revenge or hatred out of your minds in the course of your sombre duty this morning.

"While this is a judicial execution for which you have been granted immunity under the law, nevertheless, as God-fearing Christian men, you may not have immunity from God's judgement if you kill this man with malice in your hearts.

"I should now like you to take a minute in silence to pray for the soul of Private Alan Johnston and also to pray that God, even now, will find a way to save Private Ferguson's soul from the clutches of the devil…"

Corporal Sammy Brown prayed earnestly for Alan but could not find it in his heart to ask God to temper His judgement of Archie.

He hoped that his gun was one of those loaded with live ammunition.

To his right he heard a soldier whisper his own prayer for Archie: "Fuck the bastard."

The minute over, Captain Laidlaw continued with the usual formal instructions regarding procedures.

As they stood in silence facing the execution post, they heard a noise and a scuffle behind.

Archie, handcuffed and manhandled by four soldiers, was being dragooned to his fate, spitting and swearing all the while.

As he was being tied to the post, Captain Laidlaw offered him a blindfold.

"Stick yer blindfold up yer arse. Ah'll look these fuckers in the eye an' see if they're man enough tae hold ma gaze.

"Come oan. Whit ur yez waitin' fur ya shower o' Irish bastards?!"

The doctor pinned the white cross next to Archie's heart and stood back.

"Ah'll see youse all in hell wan day lads, an' Ah'll pay youse back wan by fucking wan. Ah'll fucking torture the lot o' youse. Especially you, Sammy Broon. Ah know ye went behind ma back. Ah'll be waiting fur ye oan the other side. Just remember that in yer dreams and oan yer fucking death bed!"

"Ready…!" shouted the Captain.

"Aim…"

"Fuck the lot o' youse…!" Archie screamed rabidly.

"Fire…!"

The report of the rifles echoed far into the breaking morning. As its reverberation began to fade, Archie stood still, fixedly staring at Corporal Sammy Brown.

For a moment the world seemed to be captured in a freeze frame.

Suddenly Archie fell to his knees while simultaneously, in one violent convulsion, his spine spasmodically arched, thrusting his head backwards towards his heels.

The doctor moved forward and examined Archie for about 15 seconds.

He turned gravely towards Captain Laidlaw and nodded his head solemnly.

Archie Ferguson was dead.

# CHAPTER TWENTY ONE

## *Aftermath (May, 1919)*

"And what name do you give to this baby?" the reinstated Father Dannfald, supported by a beaming Father O'Keefe, asked the proud couple. Micky looked across at Jeanie and smiled. Jeanie nodded in approval.

"Michael Glen, Father," Micky replied.

The church baptism had been delayed six months until Micky had been released from Peterhead.

George had been diminished by Michael Glen McGoldrik, forsworn by Jeanie.

At that very moment, Aggie's bosoms presented themselves at the window sill, followed by...oh, well, you know the rest.

On the street below, Frank and Jenny Hannigan's boy, Mark, was playing football by himself.

He had just 'scored' another 'goal' for Celtic against the imaginary flailing figure of Rangers' beaten goalkeeper.

"Hey, Mark! Whit's the score? Ur ye winnin'?"

Mark looked up at her with contempt and said, "Ma daddy says, 'Never tell that nosey bastard onythin'!' "

"Well Ah hope Rangers ur thrashin' ye then!" Aggie resounded with a laugh.

The Reverend McDonald had changed tact. After viewing his complete manuscript, the publisher had ultimately rejected his book, *They Got Away with Murder,* on the grounds that the tone was too sensationalist and that the material was not sufficiently well researched or argued. Helpfully, however, they suggested that he might wish to explore his interest in this topic through a work of fiction which would, by and large, bypass these objections.

Reverend McDonald flung his heart and soul into this proposal with gusto, writing a 400 page mystery-murder – well, a mystery at least for those who, on their way to the final exposé had managed to miss the title: *The Butler Did It.*

"Sadie."

"Aye, Chrissy?"

"See me?"

"Aye, Chrissy."

"See Mary Queen of Scots?"

"Aye, Chrissy."

"See marmalade."

"Aye, Chrissy."

"Apparently, she loved it."

"Aye?"

"Aye, Ah wis readin' aw aboot it the other day. Her French maids made it fur her when she wis ill 'cos it's full o' thon vitamin C shite that's apposed tae be good fur ye when ye're aw boaky."

"Aye?"

"Aye, they wid stert tae make it fur her when the cry went oot, 'Marie est malade!' – thon's French fur, 'Mary's no' weel', by the way, but. Anyhow, that's where we're apposed tae huv goat the word 'marmalade', frae: 'Marie est malade'!

"Chrissy."

"Aye, Sadie."

"See me?"

"Aye, Sadie."

"See Mary Queen of Scots?"

"Aye, Sadie."

"See thon story ye've just tellt?"

"Aye, Sadie."

"Ah think somewan's just made that up tae make themsels sound aw clever an' superior."

"But it must be true, Sadie – Ah read it in the *Scottish Daily Spin.*"

"Aye, right. Naw, here's ma theory that Ah've just made up, an' Ah'm guessin' it's goat aboot as much chance o' bein' right as thon drivel aboot 'Marie est hauf mad' or whitever it wis."

"Aye, whit?"

"Well, Chrissy, Ah don't think it came frae her French maids at aw, Ah think it wis frae her Scottish wans."

"Aye? How?"

"How? 'Cos ye see it's weel kent that Mary wis a greedy bitch…!"

"Aye, but…?"

"Aye, well she loved her vitamin C concoctions wi' a passion that she wid kill fur, an' efter she hud flung away the spoon an' licked aw the royal emblems aff her empty plate, wan o' her Scottish maids wid say, 'Mair ma Lady?' And *that's* where we get the word 'marmalade' frae – 'Mair ma Lady?'"

"There ye ur, Chrissy, stick that in yer *Scottish Daily Spin.*"

"See you Sadie…!"


Mr O'Neil, in the minds of the other teachers in the school, was now considered to be seriously weird.

He had come up with a new word which he had dug up from some educational anarchist textbook or other: 'Holistic'. You could hardly hold a conversation with him about the price of bread without the word spewing out, up and over every second sentence.

"The curriculum should be delivered holistically…language should be acquired through holistic immersion… relevance and motivation can only be appreciated within an holistic context…" and so he went on and on, and on and on.

He shocked his colleagues further by announcing that he was not a teacher of sums and spelling – he was a teacher of children.

And, to top it all, he had the cheek to ask them, "If the child cannot learn the way you teach, can you teach the way the child learns?"

They suspected the question was rhetorical, but their answer was always the same: "Why? If it's wheat, it's wheat; if it's chaff, it's chaff!"

Florrie Flapper was true to his principles by giving every returning soldier a free drink.

In an attempt to capitalise on the mood of the times, he devised a new drink which he called an AVC (Allied Victory Cocktail).

It was comprised of Scotch whisky, American bourbon and topped with French champagne.

For one night it was very popular until the pub was wrecked again after a fight broke out over whether it was the Argyll and Sutherland Highlanders or the Highland Light Infantry that had actually won the Great War.

It was never on offer again.

Alice Henderson still worked at the mill but had, in addition, become a 'soldier' in the Salvation Army.

When asked if she thought she would fit in with that organisation, she replied, "The early converts were alcoholics, morphine addicts, prostitutes and other undesirables. I'll fit in fine." And so she did.

Teresa Boyle looked down at Wully, sleeping on the couch. Her heart melted at the sight of her son, fired by pity at the thought of everything he had seen or had to do.

Wully hadn't been able to talk about the horrors of the trenches and Teresa didn't want to know.

All she did know was that he was here, safe in front of her tired eyes. Her joy was undiminished, even by the harrowing thought of those ninety-six brash, belligerent and bewildered boys – boys who had set out from the town for the front, transported by train, boat and silly songs – who would never again see Milltown.

Sleekit Tam was standing at Pigs' Square with only Todd MacDuff to keep him 'company'.

"Todd", Tam said apprehensively.

No response.

"Todd, is it no' aboot time ye let me back in…efter aw it wis seventeen years ago…"

"Naw, Tam, it's no' time the day, it'll no' be time the morra an' it'll no be time ony time efter that!"

"Todd, Ah've been away tae the war fightin' fur ma country. Surely Ah've done my bit as weel as ma time?" Sleekit Tam pleaded.

"Naw, ye huvnae, Tam. Ye cannae. The man that kicks a man when he's doon in a fight – the wey you did tae Andy Seymour in 1902 – will never himsel' get up again in oor eyes."

Alex McKinnon had lost his house after losing his wife and had moved into a poor house in Clyde Street in the centre of Glasgow. He set up a patch at the bottom of Jamaica Street where he could use his deformities to incite charitable donations from the Glasgow populous.

He was competing, of course, with numerous similarly homeless veterans, though few excited so much pity and revulsion in equal measure.

Alex died of pneumonia in a Glasgow back street in 1923, aged thirty-seven.

★ ★ ★ ★ ★

"You'll never see Pigs' Square' again."

Craig Brown's words, when they lay side by side facing the Germans at Kruseik Ridge, were still vivid in Tom Carlton's memory, as they had been all through his captivity.

Now his feet were just about to turn the bend that would bring it to view. His heart was beating fast. This was the moment he had dreamed of. He had just come off the train, still in uniform and with his bag over his shoulder. The orderly release of prisoners between the Allies and The Central Powers had taken an age. Most prisoners resented the delay. Why couldn't they just be allowed to make their own way back the minute the referee whistled for the end of the game? Here he was, only now tasting his freedom at home in May, 1919.

Still, in one sense, his timing was perfect. It would be Cattle Show day on Saturday and everyone would be there. Or, rather, everyone who had been lucky enough to survive would be there.

A lump came into his throat when he thought of having to seek out the families of Craig Broon and Paddy Lynch to give an account of their last moments.

That would be for tomorrow. Today belonged to him and his reception.

As he turned the corner, he could see that Todd had just made some highly significant point that must surely have put an end to all discussion on the matter in hand. His head was peck-peck-pecking away in an orgy of self-satisfied smugness, having just pronounced that wars *were* now a thing of the past; this *had* been the war to end all wars.

Archie Currie was nodding in approval…and there was Eddie Miller, Raymond Patterson and big Tommy Finnegan (or the Prof. as he would be known until the excitement of a match at Wembley between England and Scotland, in May 1967, did what German gas, bombs and bullets failed to do and stopped his heart) as were Ian Martin, Eddie Miller, Gregor Nesbit and Johnny Byrne, who had acquired a greyhound "to chase rabbits".

Sleekit Tam spat on the pavement a perfect map of Italy, slevering on down towards Sicily, and turned his back on the world to once more embrace his anchorite existence.

It was Ken Butterworth who saw him first.

The shout went up, "There's Tom Carlton", followed by a whoop and an eerie silence as if they might have been mistaken.

The return of the soldiers in dribs and drabs like this poignantly underlined the tragedy of those who would never come back. The silence also marked a deep respect for those who had marched away.

Tom's pace quickened. Their faces were coming more clearly into view. His own face brightened and broke into a big, broad smile to meet the warm grins and open arms of Milltown.

He was home.

He had a story to tell…

# *Silence*

## Thiepval, The Somme, August 4, 2012

Silence. The absence of noise. A space to think, to feel, to meet and to get to know yourself.

We paid dearly for it, this silence of the Somme; this silence of the lambs. Their silence spreads a shroud over this once-torn land, like the rebuke of an accusing finger.

It makes us feel the inadequacy of our words. This silence has no appetite for words: no reasons, no pride, no justification, no honour, no victory, no defeat. Just silence.

"We're here because we're here because we're here because we're here,

We're here because we're here because we're here because we're here."

Their songs have now all been sung to death.

Their silence surrendered to this soil, to this air: their blood cooled, their passions reined, their fears quietened.

Leaving us to look on. In silence. No words to summon, no attitude to strike. Left to sense meaning in the silence of eternity.

The cry of, "Tea's up", summoned our little group of World War One tourists back to the bus, where the organisers of Battlefield Tours, Steve and Susan, had prepared hot drinks and nibbles, keeping us warm, comfortable and safe.

Children from another group were playing 'tig' around a bus from Cardiff, cheerily breaking the silence with their carefree spirit.

Whilst, cloaked in silence, the class of 1916 remained cold and indifferent at a molecular level, their own youth having been captured and destroyed forever at the very same moment.

They have been joined now by the rest of the cast of their generation, who have all acquiesced to their own silence: Aggie McMillan, Tom Carlton, Micky McGoldrick, Jeanie Broon, Alice Henderson, Father O'Keefe, Reverend McDonald, Mark Hannigan, Todd MacDuff, Tony O'Neil and all those people back then from all their parishes and village squares all over the world. Their words and passions of both petty and great import have now disappeared into that Great Silence which can neither be kept nor broken.

That night, back at the hotel, we left them to their graves and took up anew the battle among nations, cheering on Britain against Germany, against France, against Russia, against the USA, against the rest of the world, on a day when, on the 98th anniversary of Britain entering the First World War, we brought home six gold medals at the 2012, XXX Olympiad in London. A day when no one was gassed or bombed or bayoneted or shot and we all basked in the glory of celebrating our common differences, in our family of nations. At the bar I watched as two Englishmen, three Frenchmen and a German family laughed together while attempting a MoBot.

Divided they stand.

# Acknowledgements

To:

Eileen Thomson for sharing a personal anecdote with me in 1973, which incubated for 38 years before becoming the initial inspiration for this book.

Bernice Bryant and Janice Todd for their wonderful patience, support, mentoring and professional critical advice.

Daniel Brendan Gillan for his marvellous creative and technical skills in the design of the front and back covers.

Michael McGoldrick for his amazing efforts to help promote the book through his creation and maintenance of a Social Media Plan on Facebook.

Neilston, for enriching my life and for providing me with a wonderful cast of unforgettable characters.

The many family and friends who supported and encouraged me during this project.